CONTESTING FAITH

Steve McNeilly

NATIONAL
LIBRARY
OF AUSTRALIA

A catalogue record for this book is available from the National Library of Australia

DEDICATION

In memory of Wayne Dalton. Your faith was never a contest but your journey is reflected in many ways in these pages.

And to all those who struggle, as I once did, to understand death and what follows. May you find something meaningful in this story.

DISCLAIMER

This novel contains comments about a wide assortment of religions and ideas that some readers may consider objectionable or even false. My aim has been to present these matters in a believable way rather than definitively. Please remember that, in the end, this is a work of fiction.

CONTENTS

CONTENTS Continued

1 - STRANGER IN THE DISTANCE

Monday 23rd February

"Hi Matt. This is my third message. I just wanted to know what the doctor said. Please call. Love you. Sophie."

Matt Sherwin had heard his girlfriend's first messages but he remained motionless on the wicker chair in his sunroom. The direct sunlight on this warm Australian afternoon produced beads of sweat on his forehead but Matt hardly noticed. Three in the afternoon: he should still be at work. Probably should call Greg to say he wouldn't be back in today. He stared blankly at Moggy, his lilac Burmese, curled uncaring on a cushion in front of the window.

First things first. Resting his phone in his lap, he tapped 'Favourites' and then 'Sophie work'. This had terrified him long enough. He lifted the phone to his ear just in time to catch her answer.

"Raymond Hill Dental Clinic, how can I help you?"

"It's me ..."

"Matt! Hi! How'd it go?"

"Umm … It's definitely cancer." A choking silence. A brief moment that threatened to go on forever. "The biopsy results were clear. I've … got cancer."

Sophie swore and then swore again. "No! No! How bad?"

"The doc didn't say much. But it's bad. Very bad. I have to see a cancer specialist urgently." The dryness in his mouth made it difficult to talk. "I've already got an appointment."

"Matt! This can't be happening."

"It is, Soph. Can … can you come over after work?"

"Of course! I'll come now!"

"No, no, don't do that. It's only a couple of hours till you knock off. I'll be OK."

"Oh Matt! I'm so sorry! I don't know what to say."

"You're not the only one. My head is messed up something crazy."

"I … I'll help you. Maybe together we can beat this."

"Yeah, well, Doctor Tan didn't give me much hope. Something about the way he said 'sorry'."

"Well doctors aren't always right."

Matt nodded weakly. "Yeah, I suppose. Uh, listen. I have to go now. See you in a couple of hours?"

"Sure. Sure Matt."

He pressed the 'end call' button and drew a deep breath. The number one most dreaded call was out of the way. Now for number two. Sure, all hell was about to break loose but there could be no other option. He pulled a handkerchief from his pocket and wiped his brow. Tried to settle his racing heartbeat. Swallowed hard as he made the next call.

"Uhh. Hi Mum. How you doing?"

Sophie called back fifteen minutes later. "Did you ring your Mum?"

"Yeah."

"How did she take the news?"

Matt sighed. "She fell apart. Started crying. Couldn't put

4

two words together by the end of the call. She was too upset."

"Yeah, I get that."

After this call, Matt sat for a few minutes, head in his hands. But feeling sorry for himself was not going to help. He jumped up and performed a brief stretching exercise. The body still felt responsive and good. He stopped at the mirror in the hallway and instinctively brushed his straw blonde hair back with both hands. Pointless habit, since most of it instantly flopped back over his forehead. He stared at his face, the angular, stubbly chin, the nose that never quite looked right, the grim curve of his mouth. And the eyes, those dark blue eyes. So familiar and yet so weird. How could your own reflection feel so intensely foreign?

He wandered into the kitchen and grabbed a piece of chicken from the fridge. How could it be cancer? It was only a small area of skin near his underarm that had started to look a bit funny. It wasn't even a full-blown mole. How could such a stupid little thing become a potential death sentence?

The doctor's words swirled in his head. And his bewildered response. "But I'm only thirty-two. I'm only thirty-two. I'm only …"

Sophie had first drawn attention to the spot on New Year's Eve, some eight weeks ago. His confident "it's nothing" mantra now haunted him. Even Donna, Sophie's younger sister, had chimed in with a warning. But life was busy.

"Yeah, yeah. I'll get it checked. Soon." He shook his head in despair at the memory of the words. If only.

Matt's Dad called ten minutes later. Terry worked as a high-level consultant for local government agencies. "Matt! Your Mum just told me the news."

"Yeah, seems I've suddenly got a death sentence."

"It's OK son. We can fight this."

"I'm not so sure, Dad."

"Sure we can. You've just gotta be positive."

"Dad, I know you've always got an answer for everything. But there might not be an answer for this. Looks like I'm going to die."

"Matt! Don't say that!"

"Why not, Dad? You want me to pretend that everything's fine and dandy? Huh? Is that what you want?"

Terry back-pedalled. "No, Matt. I'm not telling you what to think or anything. It's just that, well, you remember Auntie Bev. They told her she was going to die and she lived another twelve years. She fought the damn thing and went on to have some of the best years of her life." He paused.

"Matty?"

"Yeah, yeah, I'm still here."

"Look, I'll make some calls. I know some people. Maybe we can get you in to a top specialist."

"Dad, please! Give me a chance to deal with this. I've got to get my own head around all this before anyone else starts making plans and decisions. Just give me some time, OK?"

Pause. Then: "OK, son. I'm sorry. It's all a bit much to take in. First your cousin, then my old mate Bill, and now this."

"Yeah, Dad, I know."

"I love you, Son."

"Yeah, Dad, I know. Thanks."

Matt had been close with his older sister, Annie, during their childhood but they drifted apart when Annie married an ambitious young businessman named Ivan. Not only had Ivan's business activities taken them interstate, but within six months of their marriage, he casually advised Annie one evening that he had no intention of maintaining any kind of relationship with her family. Nevertheless, Matt was not surprised when Annie called. He knew his mother would have called her immediately on hearing the news.

There was neither pity nor panic in Annie's voice. She simply reassured Matt that she would make every effort to keep in touch. She asked practical questions. "Have you seen an oncologist yet?" "Do you have income protection insurance?" "Will this make you more inclined to get married?"

Annie and Ivan had one daughter, eighteen year old Jennifer. But Annie didn't think Jennifer would be calling any time soon. Preoccupied with her fledgling acting career in Sydney, Jennifer had a bit too much of her Dad's attitude to life and family.

Matt's younger brother, Josh, was more the family man. He and Leslie lived across town in Mona Shores with their three children. Terry called with the news but Josh decided to wait until he could visit. He called his mother instead. As expected, Julie was not handling things well. She wanted answers to questions that Josh couldn't answer. He urged her to be patient and not to panic. The answers would come in due time.

The ocean was calm and gentle, deeply blue. The afternoon sun warmed the back of Matt's neck as he walked over the moist, compacted sand, dodging tangled clumps of kelp and other 'weeds' from the sea. The beach was almost deserted, just an elderly couple walking at measured pace higher up, near the tussocky dunes, and an athletic-looking young man running effortlessly past them.

This was intended to be a moment for thinking about how life was going to change, a time for sorting out the fears and ideas that were racing in his head. A walk on the beach to help bring some calm, some perspective, some sort of handle on what was going on. But, even as he tried to concentrate on thinking, his brain was not responding. It was a dream state, a blur of unexplored emotion. He could hear the screech of some seagulls but they were in a different world, some alien world, whole dimensions away. All he could do was walk along the beach and watch the tranquil swelling of the ocean and the lazy waves breaking on the sand.

When Matt arrived home, Sophie was already there, sharing a coffee with Shaun, a friend of Matt's from his cricketing days, some three years earlier. Sophie's teary eyes lit up when she saw Matt and she ran at him, throwing her arms around his neck.

"Tell me everything. What did the doctor say? Where did they find the cancer?" She pulled back from the embrace, the better to read his face. But Matt closed his eyes momentarily and bit down on his bottom lip. How many times had he looked into those ultra-expressive brown eyes and seen playfulness and giddy, life-intoxicated stubbornness? Now those pretty features were vexed and contorted. Her long auburn hair was unbrushed, messy.

"Well, like I said, it's already in the liver. And my lymph glands."

"But can't they operate? Can't they do something?"

Matt sighed. "Look, I don't understand it all. But the cancer in my liver is secondary. It started with a meta-something under my arm. They might have been able to do something if I picked up on it sooner. But when it gets into the lymph system ..." His voice trailed off.

"It spreads all over?"

"Yeah, that's right. So ... so where do you operate?"

"It's all so unreal," she stammered. "Just the other day you were saying how well you felt."

Matt pulled up a chair at the table and Sophie offered to make him a coffee. "I'm so sorry," she said, pleadingly.

"It's not your fault!"

"Yeah but I should have ... I don't know ... done something."

Matt shook his head grimly. "I should have done something! I should have made an appointment when you first noticed it."

Shaun waited his turn, respecting the situation. But then: "Geez mate! Bit of a kick in the guts!"

"Yeah ..."

Shaun swore, mostly to himself. "Are you going to have chemo?"

"Maybe. I'm seeing a cancer specialist week after next. But that's one of the things I have to think about. If it's not going to cure me, why would I want to put myself through all that?"

"Well, there's always hope ..." offered Sophie.

Shaun chimed in with the old cliché. "You know what they say. As long as there's life, there's still hope."

Matt shook his head in frustration. "They also say that you go through a stage of denial. So how come everyone seems to be in denial except me?"

"Mate, I'm sorry. I didn't mean to upset you. I wish I could say something intelligent but ... I don't know what to say. I can't even imagine what you're going through."

"Just be normal. I don't need you to say anything clever. Don't sweat it. It's OK."

Sophie placed Matt's coffee in front of him on the table. "It's so hard to believe. First your cousin. And now this!"

Matt sighed yet again. "That's not all, either. Did you know old Bill Jenkins? Good friend of my parents since way back when. He collapsed and died yesterday. How's that? I've got two funerals in the first four days after getting told I've got cancer."

Tuesday 24th February

Matt had been with the Little Bird Marketing Agency for eight years but it felt weird to be back at work this time, despite only missing one day. Lauren at the front counter cleared some time for Matt to meet with Greg Sparrow, the company's owner and CEO. Greg asked his secretary to bring two coffees and pointed Matt, not to his desk, but to the black leather lounge chairs in the corner. Matt explained his health situation and briefly reported on the status of the accounts he was managing. Greg assured Matt that he could work as long as he wanted. The firm would assist Matt to work from home if and when he became too weak to come in to the office. But, in return, Matt would promise to hand over his accounts the minute there was any doubt that he could perform at his best. Greg also offered Matt the option of immediate retirement, in case he felt the need to concentrate fully on whatever treatments might be recommended. Or indeed, if he wanted to pursue some long-cherished bucket-list fantasy.

Matt smiled at the thought but said: "No, I'm fine to keep working. At least for the time being."

Thursday 26th February

The first of Matt's two funerals was for his cousin Justin who, at 26, had been killed instantly when he lost control of his car and ploughed into (or more accurately, under) an oncoming semi-trailer. Matt and Justin had never been especially close, Matt being six years older, but they had done some surfing together. That was enough. Matt knew he should be grief-stricken for Justin's life ending so suddenly. But death was circling, threatening. This was a complicated grief.

The high-vaulted old church was dark and musty, despite the colourful brilliance of some stained glass windows above the altar. The low wooden pews were steadily filling with mourners, many of them chattering to each other in hushed tones. Some of the older, more churchy women wore scarves over their hair and shoulders, very formal and religious-looking, while most of the younger women looked like they were out for a night on the town. Some of the men wore suits and ties, while some wore jeans and open shirts. One man wore a bright yellow woollen jumper and Matt wondered if he knew how much he stood out in this sombre company.

All Matt's relatives were there, except for one uncle who was in England. Sophie and Matt sat in the fourth row, a good vantage point to observe Justin's parents and grandparents, his sisters and their boyfriends. One of the sisters was sobbing quite violently. People were comforting each other, arms around shoulders of loved ones. Some were using the last few minutes before the service started to express condolences to Justin's immediate family. Kisses on the cheek, hugs that varied between this-is-what-I'm-supposed-to-do and genuinely profound grief. Painful looks on all the faces.

Matt took it all in. Is this what his funeral would be like? Most of the same people, with all the same expressions and the same awkward silences?

But it was the coffin that most arrested Matt's attention,

elegantly poised at the front of the church on a glistening trolley, draped in the blue and white of Justin's favourite football team, lavishly covered with spectacular flowers, and yet standing strangely alone. His cousin was in that wooden box. Not breathing. Not moving. One day soon, he might be in a similar box. Only he wouldn't know it. He would never see the flowers on his own coffin. Or the mourners at his own funeral. And yet, somehow in his imagination, he was lying awake inside that coffin, surrounded by silk padding, dressed in his best clothes and looking up at the underside of that wooden lid.

Sophie held his hand tightly as the service began. Neither of them knew the first hymn, Abide With Me, but they made a token effort to join in. Church had never been part of Matt's life so this whole scene was utterly foreign. Unsettling. His marketing brain kicked in and, for a minute or two, he found himself wondering how he would design a marketing campaign for the church, for Christians, to bring them into the twenty-first century. If they asked him. But this was clearly an institution that wouldn't be seeking his services anytime soon.

"A fine young man," crooned the greying, middle-aged preacher, when his turn came to comment on Justin's life. "An inspirational young man taken from us far too soon." Matt picked up on one word. Taken. Who or what could have taken Justin? Why? And what did that even mean?

"Life can be so cruel but we hope in Christ to see our beloved Justin again." Matt cringed inwardly. Yes, life could be cruel. He'd been raging against that already. But how could this preacher talk about the cruelty of life and some vain hope for a future reunion all in the same breath? It didn't make sense. If life was so cruel, how could there be a heaven? And if everyone goes to "a better place" when they die, why was everyone in this building so sad?

Matt couldn't remember Justin ever talking about God. And yet, this service was more about God and his alleged love, than it was about Justin. Prayers and affirmations, in old-style English, were offered from a printed program that featured a photo of Justin on the cover. A few friends got up, uncharacteristically dressed in charcoal suits, white shirts and striped ties, to read recollections of Justin from crumpled bits of paper. Things that could never have been said to Justin's face while he was alive now gushed out in rivers of emotion. "We'll miss you, mate! Geez! Why'd you have to die? Love ya, mate! Put in a good word for us with the man upstairs, will ya?"

After the church service, hundreds of people piled into their cars to follow the hearse out to the cemetery. Terry and Julie asked if they could ride with Matt and Sophie. In the privacy of Matt's car, Julie tried to ask a question but her grief overwhelmed her and she struggled even to speak. Terry came to her rescue. From the back seat, he leaned forward to be heard more clearly.

"Son, you know we haven't spoken to anyone outside the immediate family about your diagnosis. We thought perhaps you might want to tell people yourself. But ... well, this is the perfect opportunity. Nearly all your uncles, aunts and cousins are here. Your grandmother is here. What do you want to do? Do you want to tell them your news or would you like us to?"

Julie found her voice. "We just thought it was better telling them face to face. Since they're all here anyway."

"You don't think people would already know?" asked Matt.

"No," said Terry. "We had this conversation with Josh and Leslie. On the phone last night. It's totally up to you."

"I'm surprised no-one already picked up that something was wrong," said Matt. But Sophie shook her head.

"No Matt. This has been an extremely emotional funeral. Your Mum and I were bawling our eyes out all the way through the service but no-one would ever have guessed the real reason why."

"What do you say, Matt."

"Dad, it seems to me that there's enough grief around today. If I say anything, it'll come across like: 'Hey everyone, forget about Justin, spare a thought for me!' It wouldn't be right for me to speak up here at Justin's graveside. But …"

"But what?" pressed Julie.

"But if you guys want to quietly … and discretely … tell people, well that's OK with me."

By the time they arrived at the cemetery, the shady parking spots were all gone. The best Matt could do was to park along the side of the main road, a hundred metres or more away from the graveside. The mid-afternoon sun scorched their backs as they gathered with the crowd of mourners around the ominous hole in the ground. Justin's final resting place, so deep and so permanent. Several of the men had left their suit jackets in their cars and most people were wearing sunglasses. Matt knew that was not just to protect their eyes from the sun.

The fine oak casket sinking slowly into the earth triggered loud wails of grief, followed by dozens of little groups of people hugging, wrapping arms around each other's shoulders and burying faces in the strong chests of grieving men. And so many of these mourners were so young.

Matt watched his parents as they moved around among the mourners. Each time they told someone about his cancer, he would know because they invariably looked at him, suddenly and stunned. Grief on grief. One by one, his relatives made their way to him, to say whatever could be said. Matt was glad to get so many unpleasant conversations out of the way so quickly.

Uncle Gavin, Julie's brother, said something that especially stuck in Matt's brain.

"It's so cruel when young people die. If Justin knew the pain he was going to cause, maybe he wouldn't have been so reckless with his driving."

Six o'clock. Matt and Sophie were sharing a table at the Southern Cross pub with two of Matt's other cousins, Wayne and Geoff. Matt stared into his half-empty glass of beer.

"What happens when you die?" He looked at his drink as though he expected it to answer.

"Nothing," said Geoff with gruff confidence. "You just

13

die."

"What, you just cease to exist?"

"Yeah. Of course. Well, I mean, your body doesn't suddenly disappear but … you know … you cease to exist … as a person."

Matt wasn't convinced. "How can you just cease to exist? I can't get my head around that."

"I don't know," fumbled Geoff. "That's just what I believe. Isn't it obvious? When you're dead, you're just dead. Nothing else happens. Shut the door. Turn out the lights. That's all folks!"

Sophie jumped in. "I read somewhere that, when people die, they go through a long tunnel with a bright light at the end. And then they sorta get judged for everything they did in their life."

"Bad news for Justin if that's the case," offered Wayne. "I reckon it'd take years to judge all the stuff he did!" Everyone laughed but the laughter fizzled quickly.

"I don't think anyone really knows," conceded Wayne after a gloomy few moments of silence.

"I suppose Justin knows by now," offered Sophie but Matt snapped a quick reply.

"Not if Geoff's right! If you don't know anything when you're dead then Justin doesn't know any more than we do. He doesn't exist anymore and he doesn't even know that he ever existed. He's nothing more than a lifeless pile of skin and bones and stuff, lying in a box deep under the ground."

Friday 27th February

The second funeral was for Bill Jenkins, an old friend of Terry and Julie. Julie told Matt she wouldn't expect him to come, that he probably didn't need yet another reminder of death and dying. But Matt was determined. "I guess I've got a vested interest at the moment in seeing how people cope with death," he said. Julie didn't know how to answer that but she was more than usually impressed with her son.

As Matt walked through the austerely decorated foyer

and into the funeral house chapel, he was immediately struck by the contrast between this and the majestic other-worldly strangeness of the church that had hosted Justin's funeral. This was brighter. The flowers on the coffin seemed more colourful somehow. Yet everything was plain and simple. And small. There were seats for, he guessed, about eighty people, whereas the big old church must have seated quite a few hundred.

Sophie couldn't come with him because she had to work. And, as she explained to Matt, she never really knew Bill anyway. Terry & Julie motioned for Matt to join them in the second row from the front but Matt declined with a wave of the hand and took a seat right at the back. From this vantage point, he did a quick head count. Forty-three people. The place wasn't even full, although a few old people were still arriving. Forty-three people. Maybe a few more. Is that what old Bill's life came down to?

Matt noticed some men joking with each other and laughing. That wouldn't have seemed acceptable at the church but it didn't seem out of place here. And then he wondered why no-one was crying. The women in the front row were sitting perfectly still, apparently staring ahead. They might have been crying but Matt couldn't see their faces.

There were no hymns in this service. No singing at all. Two of Bill's favourite Slim Dusty songs (Pub With No Beer and Duncan) played over the public address system while a slideshow chronicled the various people and places of his life. It was oddly entertaining. The photos coming up on the screen stirred some long-forgotten childhood memories for Matt. But there was much he didn't know, like the revelation that Bill had been President of his local Rotary Club back in the sixties. Matt found himself wishing he'd known Bill better. But that was a pointless thought now because Bill was … dead.

One of Bill's friends gave a very irreverent eulogy, swearing copiously and making people laugh with yarns about things Bill had done on fishing trips and in the early stages of his relationship with his first wife. "Bill wouldn't want us to be sad today!" the friend boldly pronounced. "He'd want us to go

15

down the pub and have a few beers, spare a thought now and then for the old bugger but otherwise just get on with life."

This was affirmed by nodding heads and a general murmur of approval. Matt was a little shocked but he could understand the attitude. It was just Aussie culture. Aussie funeral culture.

That night, Matt found it difficult to sleep. Two funerals played out in his thoughts. One highly religious, the other unashamedly *ir*-religious. One confidently asserting an ongoing life in heaven, the other using the same sort of language but condescendingly, an obligatory but ultimately implausible concession to the hope that the person lived on somehow. So many words. So many ideas. None of them bringing any real comfort. Death was still a stranger in the distance, a phantom threat that always claimed someone else, but now it was starting to get personal. What would his funeral be like? What would people say?

The questions churned relentlessly in his head. How am I going to deal with this? How painful is it going to be? Should I be trying to fight it? He tried to smother his thoughts in a pillow.

Arrgh! I wish I could just get to sleep!

2 - BRAVE IN THE WHITE WATER

Monday 2nd March

Sophie's lunch-break was non-negotiable but Matt merely needed to advise Greg when he would be out of the office. And when he would be back. He met Sophie at the South Wood Plaza bakery, where parking was easy and they did those glorious olive and rosemary focaccias.

Sophie asked Matt how he was coping.

"It took me a while to concentrate properly this morning," admitted Matt. "Too much tossing and turning last night. It was pretty hard to focus on my work."

Sophie nodded. "I can understand that."

"Yeah but I was OK after a while. And about a hundred cups of coffee." She smiled. "Oh and I just remembered," Matt continued. "Mum wants me to come over for dinner tonight. Can you come too?"

"Sure, what time?"

"Just come over to my place after work and we'll go

from there."

"OK."

"To be honest, I don't really want to go. They're going to have so many questions that I won't be able to answer. And you can bet Dad will have a million suggestions that I really don't want to hear."

"Mmm."

"But what can I do? They're my parents. I can't leave them out of my life, not now."

Sophie nodded again. "This is their worst nightmare."

Matt grunted. "Their worst nightmare? Ha! What about me?"

Sophie was about to take a bite of her focaccia but she hesitated, then deliberately lowered her food to the table. "Matt! You're the one with the terminal illness. We all know that. But it's not all about you."

Matt was annoyed. "No? It's not? Well I've got news for you. I'm the one staring death in the mirror."

Sophie looked puzzled for a moment. "In the mirror? That doesn't make any sense. But hey, this is what I know. I'm scared too."

"You're scared? Why?"

"Well … I suppose I'm scared for what might happen. And how I'll manage."

Matt's confusion spilled into anger. "Sophie, you can walk away any time you like. You don't have to go through this. If it's a problem for you, then I suggest you walk away now. Forget about me. Save yourself all that pain." The last word came out with a sarcastic sting.

"Matt, I …"

"No, seriously, it's OK. If you're scared, just go!"

Sophie grabbed Matt's hands across the table. "Look at me!" she demanded. With eye contact assured, she accentuated every word. "I'm … not … going … anywhere. What do you think I am? What sort of girl would turn away from her man just when he needed her the most?"

"Well you said you were scared."

"Damn-right I am. So what? You've got cancer. OK, the outlook isn't pretty. But you're not in this on your own. It's going to be hard on all of us. But I will be there for you. Just don't push me away."

Her stern glare softened into a hopeful smile and Matt relaxed. Awed by her passion, stunned by the gentleness of her eyes and the beauty of her devotion, he wondered what he could ever have done to deserve this woman coming into his life.

"Maybe you can stay over tonight?"

"Sure, I could do with some company."

That afternoon, at his work desk, Matt took a call from his doctor's clinic. They had arranged for a meeting with the Palliative Care Unit at the Mona Shores Hospital, also known as City Central Hospital.

"Palliative Care? I thought that was only for people that were almost dead."

"No, no," replied the woman on the other end of the line, the faintest chuckle in her voice. "Palliative care kicks in as soon as a terminal illness is diagnosed. They'll meet with you and talk up front with you about your options. Don't worry. They'll respect your wishes in everything. But it's important that you know what to expect. After the first few meetings, you probably won't need to see them for a while. But they'll keep up to date with your progress and, when the time comes, they'll visit you as often as you need them. They have some wonderful people in the unit. Very professional and very caring."

Matt drew a deep breath. "This is all so sudden for me. I'm not sure I'm ready to talk with people who want to help me die."

"Mr Sherwin, you do understand, don't you, that Dr Tan asked me to make this appointment for you? But if you really want me to, I can cancel the appointment."

"No … no, it's alright. I'll meet with them."

"OK, Mr Sherwin, thanks for that. Is three o'clock

19

Thursday OK with you?"

"Three o'clock Thursday?" Matt glanced at his boss and realised that Greg had picked up enough of the conversation to understand the request. He nodded his approval without hesitation and Matt relayed the confirmation to the doctor's receptionist.

"I'll be there."

On the way home from work, Matt called in on his mechanic. His Toyota was running a bit rough and he realised it was overdue for its regular service. The mechanic booked the car in for the following week but then offered some free advice. "You know, you've clocked up more than 300,000 kilometres in this thing. If I was you, I'd be thinking about trading it in in the next year or two. After that, the repair bills are likely to get worse and worse."

The mechanic noticed the shock on Matt's face and, not knowing why, quickly added: "Something worth thinking about, that's all I'm saying."

"What can we do to help you?" asked Terry. "You know we'll do anything for you." Sophie and Matt were sitting with him at the dining table while Julie, her eyes red and puffy from a week of on-and-off weeping, listened from the kitchen where she was taking a spaghetti casserole from the oven.

Matt sighed. "I know. I appreciate you both very much but I honestly don't know what I need. I suppose the best thing you can do right now is to just be around. Like, maybe this is not the best time for that six month tour around Australia that you've always talked about."

"Point taken," said Terry. "But what happens now? What's your next step?"

Matt stared blankly at his hands interlocked on the table in front of him. "Umm. I told you that I'm seeing an oncologist over in Walkley Gardens, Dr Andrew Barlow. On Wednesday. Then, on Thursday … well, I have an appointment with the local Palliative Care people."

Julie came to the table, bringing the first two plates of spaghetti. "Go on," said Terry.

"Uhh, what else can I say? Dr Tan thinks Dr Barlow will order a heap of tests to try and work out exactly how far the cancer has spread. I suppose after that, he'll want to talk with me about possible treatment options." He paused grimly. "But, Mum and Dad, you must understand, he was very clear that nothing is actually going to cure me. Barring some kind of miracle, this is the year I'm going to die."

Julie accidentally knocked over an empty glass in front of her husband, but caught it before it could fall to the floor.

"It's all so hard to believe," muttered Terry with a shake of his head. "It was only a few years ago I was watching you play cricket. You were so ... so athletic and strong."

"I still feel strong most of the time. It's just these waves of sickness that come and go. And this weird ache in different parts of my body."

"What are they giving you for that?"

"Well, I'm getting some tablets but I forget what they're called. They might help but they might cause side-effects too."

"Don't they know how to control these things? Haven't they treated hundreds of cancer patients before?"

"Sure, Dad. But Dr Tan said it doesn't track the same for everyone. They have to work out the best way to treat each separate case. Things that work for other people might not work for me."

The doorbell rang. Sophie, being least involved in the conversation, quickly volunteered to answer it. Matt's three-year old niece, Shirelle, entered first and sprinted to her grandmother in the kitchen. A quick hug with Julie, then off to greet the others. Her older siblings Ryan and Chelsea followed, smiling at her sing-song exuberance. But Matt's brother Josh and wife Leslie weren't smiling. Apart from Justin's funeral, this was their first visit with Matt since hearing the news.

Another awkward round of hugs, questions and sighs. Matt was grateful for the children. Chelsea, the six-year-old, couldn't wait to show off her new Wiggles slippers. Ryan, the nine-year-old, answered the obligatory enquiry about school with an animated report about a big lizard that someone had brought to his school. The children, at least, were focused on life, not death.

Tuesday 3rd March

Sophie's sister, Donna, was, in her own words, "on fire for God". When she heard about Matt's cancer, she kept her thoughts to herself for as long as the "fire" would allow. Then she turned up one night at Matt's house.

"Oh, hi. Sophie went home five minutes ago."

Donna knew that. She'd been waiting around the corner for hours. "Oh, that's OK. I was wondering if I could talk with you."

He looked at his watch and frowned. "It's gone 10.30 but … I suppose so. Come in. Can I get you something to drink?"

"Sure, but not coffee at this hour. Can you do a hot chocolate?"

Donna took her place on a stool by Matt's kitchen bench while he turned his back to make two hot chocolates. He didn't see her bow her head in brief but urgent prayer.

"I'm so sorry to hear about your sickness."

Matt sighed. "Oh well, that's life, I suppose."

Donna saw that he was already tired of talking about his condition. But she had to press on.

"I want you to know that I've been praying for you."

Matt brought two cups over to the bench and went back for the milk. "Thanks. Can't do any harm, eh?"

"No," she replied with a self-conscious giggle. "Certainly not."

Drinks made, Matt took a seat opposite Donna and waited for whatever was coming. She mustered her courage, assumed her kindest smile, and jumped in.

"Matt, you know I'm a born-again Christian. And, given what's happening with you, and all, well, I'd like to talk with you about Jesus."

Matt cringed but Donna was just getting started. "No

please, hear me out. It's very important."

"Donna I …"

"Please Matt, this is not easy for me but …"

"It's no walk in the park for me either."

"I … I know. I'm sorry. But I want you to know that God loves you."

"Ha! Funny way of showing it."

"Well that's just it. We all have to die someday but Jesus died so you wouldn't have to be cut off from God forever."

"You mean Hell?"

"Well, yeah. I believe that if you die, if anyone dies, without asking Jesus into their heart, they seal their fate for all eternity."

Matt grimaced. "Wow, tough call."

"But it's not all bad news," she gushed. "Jesus died on the cross to pay for your sins. And mine. If you trust in him, and ask him into your life, you can be saved."

A suspicious frown crossed Matt's face. "What, from cancer?"

"No, no, I didn't mean that!" This was not going how Donna would have liked.

"So let me get this straight. You think I'm going to Hell. And you're here to tell me how I can go to Heaven when I die."

Despite herself, Donna couldn't look him in the eye. "It's not just you. We've all sinned. The Bible says so."

Matt pressed his advantage. "But it's more important for me to know this because I've got cancer."

"I'm worried about you," she countered. "Don't you want to go to Heaven when you die?"

"Donna, listen to me! I'm not even sure if I believe in Heaven … or Hell. I don't know what I believe but I'm not inclined to believe in a God who gives people a choice like that." He faked a deep, supposedly God-like voice. "Believe in me and go to Heaven. But if you don't, you'll burn forever in Hell!"

"Matt please …"

23

"Look, I tell you what," said Matt, standing to indicate that the conversation was over. "If and when I decide that I need Jesus in my life, I'll give you a call. OK?"

Donna went home and cried herself to sleep.

Wednesday 4th March

To Matt's surprise, the consultation with Dr Barlow lasted for more than an hour and twenty minutes. The doctor explained what he already knew about Matt's condition and what he still needed to learn. He spoke about cancer in general terms and pressed Matt to ask as many questions as he could. Matt had planned to go back to work, if possible, after the consultation but it was after 4.30 by the time he left the doctor's rooms. Work would have to wait.

Sophie met Matt, as arranged by text message, at the Botanical Gardens car-park. Together, they walked the three kilometre circuit that, in places, afforded magnificent views of the ocean. Maintaining general fitness, Matt explained, would be critical in the coming months.

"So, what else did the doctor say?" asked Sophie, holding Matt's hand a little tighter than usual.

"Well …" Where to start? "He said that the cancer, my cancer, was a bit like the early settlers in Australia."

Matt caught Sophie's puzzled frown for just a second. Then, looking ahead once again as they walked, he tried to elaborate.

"The cancer started in one spot but soon branched out, looking for new places to settle. In my case, there are little outposts in various places through my body. Including my liver."

"Does that mean you might be less resistant to other types of infection?"

Matt tried to remember what the doctor had said. His mind had been racing throughout the consultation and he was aware that he hadn't always been listening properly. "Yeah, I think so. It's all pretty complicated."

They continued to walk, hand in hand, in silence. When

they came to a bench seat near a pond with a small fountain, Sophie suddenly stopped.

"Can we sit for a minute?"

Matt obliged willingly enough. He understood that Sophie needed more information. Normally, in her serious moments, she would burn him with her fiery brown eyes but, this time, her eyes were closed. When they finally opened and she looked at him, Matt saw only a fragile optimism.

"Is there any hope? Anything that can be done?"

Matt attempted a smile. "Umm, Dr Barlow spent a lot of time telling me that there are heaps of different kinds of cancer and heaps of different possible treatments. Some treatments are designed to get rid of the cancer altogether and some are just designed to help the patient live longer and better. Until, well, you know, the inevitable. He said, in my case, a complete cure seems to be out of the question. The type of cancer I have is particularly ..." What was the word the doctor had used? "Particularly ... um ... aggressive. Stage four, level four, or something."

"Did the doctor say how long he thinks you might have?"

"Yeah, I asked him that question. He stressed that you can never be sure but ... but he thinks maybe six months."

Sophie responded with a passionate hug. Then she pulled away enough to look in his eyes.

"Is there a 'but'?"

Matt nodded, less convincingly than he would have liked.

"Only that he thinks I can still enjoy a good life ... for whatever time I have. He said that I'll probably have some pain and other symptoms but they can mostly be controlled. Good nutrition, exercise, plenty of fresh air, and good emotional support. All these things will help, he reckons."

The breeze coming up from the ocean fluttered the edges of Sophie's hair, blazing a golden-red glow in the late afternoon sunlight. "Well at least I can help with that last one," she said.

"Oh, and keeping a positive attitude. Dr Barlow said that a positive attitude is one of the most important things for cancer sufferers." Matt stood, inviting her to continue the walk. "Trouble is, so far, all the news has been bad. He hasn't given me anything to be positive about."

Uncle Gavin phoned as Matt was clearing away after dinner. "Dear, dear Matt. What are you going to do?"

"What do you mean? I don't know yet."

"Well, like, are you setting yourself to fight this thing?"

"Uhh, I'm not really setting myself for anything at the moment. I'm still trying to get my head around it."

"Cancer is God's curse. Horrible, horrible curse."

"Easy, Uncle Gav. Don't make this harder than it has to be."

"Yeah, I'm sorry … but it really is a curse."

"Uncle Gav, you don't even believe in God. How can this be a curse from God?"

"Hmm, good point."

"And if it is some kind of curse, tell me what have I done to deserve it?"

"Sorry Matt. You're absolutely right. Look, I don't have any answers. But I promise I'll do my best to keep in touch."

Thursday 5th March

At work on Thursday morning, Matt fielded more questions. Two co-workers had decorated his desk with hopeful sayings on little white cards. And they had infiltrated his computer so that "Please get well Matt" flashed up when he logged on. But one of the current contracts at Little Bird reminded him of something else Dr Barlow had said. High and Mighty Adventure Tourism featured, among other things, a white water rafting experience. During a staff coffee break, Matt explained the comparison.

"White water rafting is a one-way experience. Once you've started, there's no going back. Sometimes, it will be an incredibly rough journey through the rapids and you might be tempted to wish you were someplace else. But you just have to see it through. All you can do in those times is to try to stay upright and to steer clear of the rocks. Sooner or later, according to Dr Barlow, you'll come through to a place where the water is calm again. The Doc told me that I'm already in the canoe. I'm already in the rapids." Matt tapped nervously on his coffee mug. "Trouble is, no-one ever knows in advance how long or how bad the rapids are going to be."

Julie called Matt when she knew he would be home from work. Sophie answered the call but brought the cordless receiver to Matt in his sunroom.

"Just checking in. What did the Palliative Care people have to say?"

"Not much, Mum. They just explained what sort of things they do. What sort of resources they provide. You know, getting-to-know-you, introductory stuff. I guess it was good to meet some of their people but I don't think I'll be calling on them anytime soon."

Matt thought he could hear the stress and worry in Julie's voice. "It frightens me," she said. "The very words 'palliative care'. Is it all going to be about dying from now on?"

"No, Mum. The people I spoke with insisted that palliative care isn't really about dying at all. It's actually about relieving pain and helping people to be comfortable. It's not such a bad word."

"Oh well, if you say so. I guess we all just have to be brave."

Matt smiled at Sophie as he spoke. "Yes, Mum. Brave in the white water."

3 - MAKE IT A CONTEST

Friday 6th March

Was it an act of rebellion against the cancer or raw stubbornness? Matt chose to walk to work, even though it would take an hour each way. Lauren, the receptionist, noticed his empty parking spot and asked what was wrong with his car. Before the day was out, he would have three separate offers for a lift home. But, despite a general ache in his body, compounded by some digestive discomfort that he blamed on his cheeseburger lunch, he refused all offers.

The world looks different when you walk through it, rather than driving. Matt noticed some oddly cluttered houses, a few shockingly overgrown gardens, and some double-story homes that portrayed a pleasant, unassuming elegance. Different people doing life differently.

And cancer? Matt marvelled at the different reactions his news elicited in different people. Some people could communicate compassion in a confident, easy-going way.

Others stumbled over every word. No-one wanted to seem callous or unresponsive. Several relatives had called to follow up on their brief conversations at Justin's graveside. Most followed the "we're thinking of you/ praying for you" line.

"So the news is out. I've got cancer. But life goes on." That was all he'd written in a social media post at breakfast. He knew it would cut across the normally inane, light-hearted content that dominated his online friendships. But now, walking home, his phone opened a window to dozens of concerned friends and relatives who expressed their solidarity with "OMG", sad faces and exclamation marks.

Was it all going to be about dying from now on? He put his phone back in his pocket and quickened his pace. Twenty minutes more and he should be home.

Sunday 8th March

Matt's life-defining decision snuck up on him the following Sunday. The game on his laptop was boring so he shut the lid and walked over to the living room window. The sky was darkening, indicating the possibility of a late afternoon thunderstorm. Terry and Julie had not long left, along with Sophie and two friends. Now that he was alone, he steeled himself to consider his options. Suicide was not one of them. At least not yet.

He began to rationalise. If he had six months to live, how should he spend that precious time? If it was all destined to end in a painful, humiliating exit from the land of the living, what could be done to make it better? Advice about physical and medical issues was already in place. The Palliative Care nurses were well-resourced and obviously knew their stuff.

So what was the problem? He listed his greatest fears in his mind, starting with the obvious. He would never be able to do the things he thought he would do with his life. The holiday in America, doing the Grand Canyon, Las Vegas, Hollywood and New York. Following an ashes cricket tour in England. Starting his own production company, working on hit movies. Suddenly, there was not enough life left for any of these things.

And Sophie. Ever since they'd been together, he had dreamed of a time when he would be wealthy enough to offer her the life she deserved. Well, so much for that dream. In Uncle Gavin's words, he was now a cursed man. Would the curse rub off on everyone around him?

Saying forever goodbyes to people was another fear. And everyone feeling sorry for him all the time. That was a big one. Maybe he could resolve right now to be Mr Funny Guy. Make everyone laugh. Hide the pain. Tell everyone he was OK.

He shook his head. That would never work. He couldn't sustain that kind of act in the best of times, much less now that he had a terminal illness.

Who else could he ask for advice? There must be people out there who knew about these things. But probably not anyone he knew.

Then again, so what? This was the information age. You could get answers on the internet for any question you could ever think of.

He went back to the table, opened his laptop and started to type 'terminal illness' into the search engine but then reconsidered. Opening 'asksomeone.com' he wrote: "I'm dying. The weeks are slipping away too quickly. I don't know what to do." But that wasn't even a direct question. How could anyone answer that? He deleted it and started again. "What's the best way to approach death?" No, 'approach' didn't sound right. What's the best way to face death? He made the change and entered his request.

But it still wasn't right. A ding on his computer indicated a new e-mail. For just a second, he wondered if they could possibly have answered his question that promptly but, of course, it was just an automatic response acknowledging his question and promising a speedy answer subject to a long-winded disclaimer.

Matt buried his face in his hands. One person's answer, or one web-site's answer, was never really going to help. There had to be a better way.

Then suddenly, there it was. He knew what he had to do.

Monday 9th March

Monday was Labour Day holiday and Julie took the opportunity to invite Matt and Sophie, as well as Josh, Leslie and their children, to a barbecue dinner. Terry spent more than an hour cleaning the barbecue in preparation and setting it up in the covered carport area of their home. So no-one was surprised when he insisted on doing all the cooking himself. Julie ruled the kitchen but Terry ruled the barbecue.

"It seems weird," said Leslie to Matt. "I always imagined palliative care as kicking in when people were, you know, on their last legs."

"Kicking? Last legs?" Matt grinned at the unintended gag.

Leslie groaned but continued regardless. "There's so much I don't know about these things," she admitted. "What does palliative care involve? What local services do we have here in Mona Shores? Does it happen in the hospital, or your home, or both?"

Matt answered the questions to the best of his ability. He tried to remember the slogan from their brochures. "What was that tag line again? Oh, yeah." He emphasised each word. "Striving for optimum holistic outcomes."

"Wow, that's a mouthful," said Sophie.

"Yeah, they obviously didn't consult Little Bird Marketing on that one," laughed Matt.

As Josh and Leslie were leaving with their children, Julie called out: "See you next Monday night, then?"

A quick glance with his wife and Josh called back: "Sure thing, Mum. See you then."

Monday night family meals, for six adults and three children, had officially become a weekly tradition.

Tuesday 10th March

"Yeah, that's perfect," said the young woman behind the video camera. "Lighting's just right, background looking good. I think we're ready to roll."

Francine worked for one of the multi-media companies

that supplied footage to Little Bird. But this was a freebie, negotiated by Greg. It was obviously going to be a long lunch break for Matt but Greg was happy to oblige.

Matt was seated behind his normal desk but it had been moved into the conference room where the lighting was better and there was space for a photographic backdrop. The video would show Matt wearing a cream-coloured shirt and a red tie, behind him to the right a city skyline and, to the left, a freeway going over a bridge. Dark clouds hovered over a red and gold sunset. Francine wondered aloud whether Matt was overplaying the symbolism but he knew what he wanted.

Greg called for Lauren, the receptionist, and she rushed in with a set of large cue cards designed to keep Matt on track. Walter appeared in the doorway, keen to see this. Only Kerry was still working, taking a telephone call in her office.

Matt self-consciously straightened his tie and ran his fingers through his fashionably scruffy almost-blonde hair. "Yeah, I think I'm ready."

"Hello. My name is Matt Sherwin. I'm thirty-two years old, I live in Australia and I'm hoping you can help me. I've recently been diagnosed with terminal cancer. I'm probably well into my last six months of life. So I want to talk with you about dying."

Matt paused thoughtfully, looking down at the top of his empty desk and gently biting his bottom lip, before raising his eyes again to the camera. "See, I don't know what to believe about life and death. I've heard lots of different theories. Some of my friends say there's no such thing as any life after death. But … well … how would they know? If they're right, then how should I live what's left of my life? If they're wrong … well … what exactly is there after we die? Are Heaven and Hell real places? If so, why can't we see them? Are any of the religions right?

"And if there is life after death, I come back to the same question. How should I live what's left of my life?

"If you have any answers to these questions, please take the time to write your comments on the blog page that I'm starting for this purpose. This is not a joke or some kind of a trick. I'm fair dinkum about this. Um, that's Aussie talk for sincere. I'm really sincere about this. I need answers. What should I believe? What should I do?"

He took a deep breath and signalled to Francine that he needed a pause. He looked around the room. Lauren was almost in tears. Walter and Greg were deep in thought. "What do you think?" asked Matt.

"It's good," suggested Francine. "You should get some interesting responses."

"Yeah, it was OK," pondered Greg, "but I think it needs more of a hook. Yeah, you'll get a few responses … but it's hardly going to become a media sensation."

"Well, maybe I don't want to be a media sensation."

"Yeah, fair enough," conceded Greg. "But look at it this way. You can go online with this and you'll get all sorts of fundamentalist crackpots on your case. But I'd have thought you want to tease out responses from the best people, you know, the people who are too busy to bother with obscure no-consequence blogs."

"Well, what are you saying? That I should pretend to kill myself and make out like I'm writing blogs from the other side?" He uttered the last few words with a spooky, twilight-zone voice.

Greg laughed. "No, I guess I don't really know what I'm suggesting. I just thought a wider circulation would get you better results."

"Make it a contest," offered Francine, poking her head out from behind her camera. Four sets of eyes suddenly turned on her so she decided she'd better continue.

"Make it a contest between the various religions," she said. "You know … umm … which religion, or belief system, can give the best answers for someone with a terminal illness? You could work out some sort of points system, say one point for every new and original comment that you find helpful. And keep a running tally on your blog. You might end up with a full-blown contest between atheists and Christians, or

Buddhists and … I don't know … whatever."

Greg liked the idea. He pointed an approving finger at Francine. "That is one highly marketable idea!"

She blushed slightly. "I was just trying to think of ways to make the video stand out."

Greg nodded. "What do you think, Matt?"

"I … um … yeah … seems OK."

"You don't sound too convinced."

"Well, I was just wondering if we might be getting a bit carried away. I mean, this is very personal for me. It's not about which religion is best. It's about how I'm going to live the rest of my life. I don't want to be a clown in a media circus."

That was met with a thoughtful silence. "But, on the other hand, I can see your point Greg. I do want the best possible answers, and this might be, like you say, the best way to tease them out. Would I need to reshoot from the beginning?" he asked Francine.

"No," she replied hastily. "No problem there. Simple bit of editing."

"I'll have to write it up properly. I'm terrible at putting words together on the spur of the moment, especially in front of a camera."

"No worries," said Greg. "Let's do it!"

The mood in the conference room had lifted noticeably. Lauren expressed what the others were feeling. "This is going to be great!" she said. But then, glancing at Matt, she remembered what they were talking about. She started to apologise for being insensitive but Matt cut her off.

"It's OK. I know what you mean. If we do this right, it should bring out some very interesting discussion."

"Can I make one more suggestion?" asked Francine. Matt nodded. "Can I suggest you set a cut-off date? I mean, don't let it drag on too long. The last thing you want is to go downhill physically so that the whole thing just fizzles out to nothing."

"I know what you mean," said Matt. "And besides, if I'm

going to get answers, I need to get them while I still have time to put them into practice."

Greg came over to Matt and placed his arm around Matt's shoulder. "Mate, I really don't know what to expect from all this. I hope you find what you're looking for."

Matt smiled. "Whatever happens from here on, I think the journey is going to be worth it."

4 - THE ROTTENNESS INSIDE

Thursday 12th March

Matt knew all the tricks for promoting a personal video through the various social media but these were just background noise to the real promotion. He wanted coverage on TV news bulletins around the world so his main goal was to attract the interest of the various news agencies that provided 'odd spots' and tips for human interest stories to media networks. The tone of these communications had to be just right: quirky enough to make busy sub-editors take a second look but serious enough to provoke real people in a real world to look him up.

Matt consulted the latest edition of the Australian Media Guide, a huge volume with contact details of journalists and news outlets. He tagged his e-mails with the subject line: "Dying Aussie looking for answers", or, when space permitted: "Dying Aussie launches contest to find the best religion". The e-mails, of course, contained a link to Matt's video, which linked in turn to Matt's blog page. Since people would need to find him easily, he spent a full two hours on search engine rankings for the phrase "Dying Aussie". He found websites that were popular with academics and e-mailed the site managers. He worked out the best way to infiltrate some large online religious communities with the message: "What should I do?" He posted on all the newest and best social media platforms. Finally, he looked up a handful of popular atheistic and anti-religious sites, posting messages to subscribers about his "quest to know the truth about religion, and what happens when you die", and challenging them to provide rational alternatives to the major religions. Surely, there were people out there who would not be able to resist a chance to take a pot-shot at religion.

Most of this advertising was free but Matt decided to place two paid advertisements in print media, one in a weekly Australian magazine called New Spirit that focused on exploring new and imaginative ideas about spirituality, and the other in a popular mainstream newspaper in Melbourne. Both of these ads carried a précis of his video message and directed readers to his blog.

He quickly added a chart as a separate page in his blog. No data as yet, just a disclaimer. *"Points are awarded purely at my discretion. No arguments will be entered into. One point will be awarded to each different religion or philosophy for every posting to my blog that makes a new and genuinely convincing contribution to the discussion. The contest will run until 31st July and, depending on my health, I will conscientiously dedicate myself to the winning religion or philosophy on August 1st."*

When does enough become enough? It was already well past midnight and Matt leaned back in his chair, stretching his arms and resting his eyes, grateful for the chance to feel alive and focused again. It was all so surreal. He now had a new identity, the Dying Aussie. But, just for the moment, death could not have seemed further away.

Friday 13th March

The first blog comment appeared at 7.30 the next morning. But it was far from promising. Someone calling himself Nev wrote:

When you tern into a ghoste, come back and let us no how it all wenr down.

Matt shook his head in disbelief but decided not to delete the comment. Quickly, he tapped out his own reply.

What, you're telling me that people turn into ghosts when they die? What evidence do you have for this? Have you really thought this through?

There was no further correspondence from Nev.

A more serious comment was next.

All religions are basically the same. They all teach that we should love our fellow man. If we do the right thing, our good karma will help us in our next life.

Matt wondered about that. What sort of viewpoint was this? Did all religions now believe in karma? Even Christians? Sure, there had been times when he'd believed, or at least wanted to believe, that all the religions were pretty much the same. But this was too vague. No point could possibly be awarded here. Matt didn't want to stifle the discussion this early but he typed out an angry response.

Are you an idiot? ALL religions the same? Man, there must be HUNDREDS of different religions! There's even some weird religions that worship UFOs and stuff. How can you possibly expect me to believe that ALL religions are the same?

The next day, Matt would read a reply from the same correspondent.

Dude, take it easy! You asked the question, man. I'm just saying what I think. OK, maybe not all the religions are the same. But all the main religions are. When you look into them enough.

Another early respondent simply said:

I feel for you. What a bummer! I'm sending you my best positive vibes. Hope it works out ok for you.

Matt got up to make himself a coffee. By the time he got

back, there were four more entries on his page. And it hadn't even hit any TV or radio bulletins yet.

Ten thirty in the morning, Matt arrived at the radiology department of the City Central Hospital, dressed in track pants and t-shirt. No metal anywhere in his clothing. His keys, wallet and a few coins, were left in his briefcase outside the Magnetic Resonance Imaging room. Julie sat praying in the nearby waiting room, ready to drive Matt home when the procedure was complete. From there, he would get changed and return to work.

The young woman who prepped Matt for the MRI scan only managed to make him more nervous. Lying still on an uncomfortable table moving through a tightly confined tube of radio waves, or whatever they were, hardly sounded like fun. But Matt handled it with ease, simply closing his eyes and concentrating on the Australian rock classics that he had requested from the available music selection. The nurse wasn't impressed with his choice. "Just be careful you don't start tapping your feet or dancing around to the beat." she had warned.

At least he could smile.

Sophie and Matt chose to spend the evening watching action movies, at Sophie's place because her TV was bigger and the picture was sharper.

"Do you want me to move in with you?" asked Sophie, gently stroking Matt's hair. "I could look after you more easily."

Matt shook his head. "Nah. I think I need the privacy. Just for the time being. Please don't get me wrong. It's not like I don't want you around. But it looks like it'll take a fair bit of my spare time just to keep up with all the stuff happening on my blog page. And I kind of need to be alone to process it all."

"I understand," nodded Sophie. "I'm working through a lot of stuff myself. But I'm happy to be a sounding board for you. You know, bounce your ideas off me any time you like."

At that moment, the hero of the action movie blasted a military jeep that was chasing him. The vehicle exploded violently and bodies were thrown about, silhouetted against the mushrooming flames. The hero allowed himself only the briefest moment of celebration before turning his attention to his next challenge. Matt pointed an accusing finger at the TV screen.

"See! Right there! That's one of the things I've been wondering about. We see it all the time in movies. All those guys die like that and we don't even care. Sometimes we even laugh at the way they die. But … well … aren't they supposed to be real people? Wouldn't they have families? How can we just watch people being blown to bits and not feel anything ourselves?"

"Oh Matt, it's just a movie."

"I know it's just a movie. But they make death so cheap. They kill hundreds of people that they don't care about to save one person that they do care about. What sort of message do we get from that?"

Sophie exaggerated a shrug of the shoulders. "Good point … I suppose."

"It's just so hard to get your head around. Every time an Aussie soldier dies in Afghanistan or wherever, we get a full news report on it. Or some lunatic goes on a shooting spree in America and it's all over the news. But there was a car bomb in Iraq last week that killed more than a hundred people, some of them little children. And it didn't rate a mention. Except on the ethnic station."

"Violent death is just accepted as normal in some places," suggested Sophie. "It hits home more when it's Australia or England or the like because we expect people to be safe."

Matt nodded. "And yet, we're obviously not. Take Justin, for instance."

"I don't know, Matt. I can see that it doesn't add up but I don't have any answers."

Matt pressed the mute button on the remote. "Here we

are, me diagnosed with terminal cancer, and all, but there's no guarantee that you won't die before I do."

"Thanks a lot!" she gasped. "What are you trying to say?"

"Oh, don't take that the wrong way. I'm just saying. We really don't know when death is going to come. Maybe I shouldn't be thinking about it so much. Maybe I made a big mistake going online like I have."

Sophie smiled and gently shook her head. "Honey, you're a deep thinker. You can't just ignore the type of questions that are coming up now. You're going to have to find answers." Then she thought of something else. "And even if you don't get the answers you want, your blog is going to be one damn fascinating read."

Sunday 15th March

The first point was awarded under the category 'Atheist'. A blogger calling himself Peter wrote the following:

There is no scientific evidence that any kind of god exists. The 'god' that Christians, Muslims and Jews worship is judgmental and vindictive. They try to make him out to be kind and loving but their scriptures make a mockery of this. Any 'god' that destroys his own creation, with war, violence, diseases like the big C, and then has the nerve to threaten eternal punishment on top of it all, must be either a fool or a raving psychopath. My friend, don't waste your time on any religion. My advice is just to make the best of whatever time you have left in this life.

Matt responded:

OK, well said, Peter. I still don't know if you're right about God not existing, but you make an excellent point. You should have a talk with my girlfriend's sister.

Another correspondent, identifying herself as Mrs Smith, picked up on the same point.

This is a well-established piece of logic. The seventeenth century French philosopher, Pierre Bayle, put it best. 'If God is almighty, then he is able to prevent evil; if God is all-good, then he is willing to prevent evil; but there is evil; therefore, God is either unable or unwilling to prevent evil.' Peter is right. Forget what you might have been told. The 'god' of the Christians, etc, cannot logically exist. Trusting such a god to give you eternal life after you die would be stupid.

Matt thought about adding another point to the Atheist column but, in the end, this was just a variation on the first point. Two consecutive comments referred to a book called 'God Is Not Good'. Again, Matt thought they were making the same point. He also dismissed the comment that the world would be better off without the idea of an omniscient god. That brought nothing positive to the discussion. Another comment read simply: *God is bulls--t!!! And yet another comment said: People who still belive in god are nuts. They need ther heads read. No sane person belives in god these days.*

"Wow!" whispered Matt to no-one in particular. "I had no idea there was so much rage against God out there." He decided to kill two birds with one stone. A call to Grandma Davis would placate his Mum, who kept urging him: "Call your grandmother." But Grandma might be able to shed some light on the hostility against God that he found so surprising.

"So Grandma," he ventured after the discussion about his cancer had run its course. "I wanted to ask you something and I hope you won't be offended."

"What is it Matty?" Odd that she still called him that.

"Umm, I know you used to attend church and that you suddenly stopped. I was wondering if you could tell me why. It strikes me that there's a lot of people out there who are not just …" What was the right word? "… not just disinterested in God. They're … well, they seem to be angry with the very idea of God."

"Oh Matty, I don't really like to talk about those things. Ancient history, you know."

"Yeah, I know. I've never been involved with any church myself. As you well know. And I'm not sure if I believe in God, or whatever. But things have changed for me. I really need to know now."

"Oh Matty," she replied with a deep sigh. "I can understand that. But what happened to me doesn't concern you in any way."

"Grandma, please!"

Finally, she relented. Matt had been four years old when his grandfather died in a car accident. After the funeral, reports had started coming out about bad things Grandpa Davis had done under cover of the church they had attended. There were arguments about how things had been handled. On one hand, Grandma Davis still carried an obvious bitterness over the way her husband's name had been slandered within the church community, but paradoxically, she also condemned the church for the lack of accountability and transparency that had allowed these "bad things" to go on for so long.

Matt thought about this. "So you're telling me that people blame God when things like that happen?"

"Of course. If God can't get things right in his own house, why would you want anything to do with him? I certainly don't. But then I don't initiate conversations like this either, because I don't think it's my place. Other people might not see things the way I do, and that's their right. But as for me, I vowed that I would never again get sucked in to the whole church scene, with all its hypocrisy and judgementalism. And it's nearly thirty years now I've kept that vow."

Sophie tried to cook a shepherd's pie to share with Matt but it didn't taste right. Matt wondered if the meat she used was a little off. The potato mash was lumpy and too salty. It was an easy decision to order in some Chinese.

It had been a warm Sunday afternoon but the forecast was for a late-night storm. Sophie stayed through to the end of a pre-season football match on TV, redeemed herself somewhat with a fluffy mint-chocolate pudding, then drove home from Matt's house just before midnight. Matt was still awake at 1.30 when the lightning started. He sat in his sunroom, lights out, just watching the display.

He thought about his mother's faith in God, the kind that

bubbles along under the surface, always there but mostly out of sight. She would never want to talk about Grandma's aversion to the church. But the question remained: "Should I blame God for the cancer in my body. Am I supposed to be angry?"

A brilliant flash of lightning lit up his back garden for an instant. No, to be honest, he wasn't angry. He didn't understand what was going on, so how could he blame God? He literally didn't know enough to be angry.

This blog, this contest. It had to start with a clean slate. No prejudices, no preconceived ideas. It had to be rational, profoundly honest. It had to be real. Was an answer even possible? It was too early to tell. But, as another sheet of lightning exploded in the distance, Matt knew he should be grateful that Grandma had been so conscientious about keeping her grievances to herself.

Tuesday 17th March

Julie brought her phone to her doctor's appointment and showed her Matt's video. "My husband and I are really worried about our son. I mean, it's bad enough that he's got cancer. But now he's got people writing to him from all over the place. All about death, and religion, and stuff. It's like he's fixated on dying. We just think he should be trying to fight the disease. Or at least that he should be thinking about living, not always talking about dying."

The chubby fortyish doctor with the engaging smile tried to reassure her patient. "It's OK Julie. People handle this sort of situation in all sorts of different ways. I wouldn't worry too much about that."

"Look, I realise that everyone has to deal with news like this in their own way. But I just thought he might need a counsellor or something. I guess I was hoping you could recommend someone."

"Well, I ..."

"He probably won't want to talk with anyone. If his Dad organised something, he'd just be angry. But I think I can get through to him."

"Julie, I understand your concern, but ..."

"Please Maggie! Just a name! Someone you have confidence in."

"Well, what about Matt's own doctor? Can't he talk things over with him?"

"Dr Tan's a fine doctor but he's so matter-of-fact about everything. He doesn't relate well on a personal level. And he's already so busy. I know he won't give Matt the time he needs."

"Oh, I don't think you can write him off so easily."

"What about you? Would you talk with Matt?"

The doctor hesitated. "I don't think so Julie. I'm not good with the sort of questions Matt's asking."

"But that's just it! I don't want you to talk with him about all that religious stuff. Can't you just help him to see that he needs a bit more balance in his life? That he's still got a life to live?"

"No Julie, I can't do that. I'm not a counsellor. And even if I was, I'm not sure I would want to impose someone else's agenda on my client. But I'll tell you what I can do." She scribbled a name and a phone number on a piece of paper. "I'll give you a contact. John Vickers is a good counsellor. But I strongly suggest that you make an appointment for yourself before you try to get Matt to see him."

Matt's earliest responses on his blog page were all antagonistic to religion, and especially Christianity. Matt assumed that these people had found his post on one of the atheistic sites. But after a few days, the comments broadened considerably. One correspondent offered to "send someone around with some literature" if Matt would supply an address. Someone else claimed to represent a prayer group that was praying for Matt every day. A few comments pointed Matt to websites that would, they assured him, answer all his questions. He looked up a few of these sites and spent some forty minutes reading and following related links. One site that seemed to be Christian was actually ranting against the "Satanic deception" in all other churches. Matt couldn't quite understand what they were trying to say but one Bible verse was quoted prominently. "The soul that sinneth, it shall die."

It was after eleven at night but Matt closed his laptop, donned a jacket and headed out for a walk. Although the days were still warm, the evenings were getting cooler and the light breeze played with his hair. Down the street, a service station was closing for the night. An elderly man with stripes on his pants that glowed in the dark was walking two greyhounds. A young couple were kissing and embracing under a streetlight.

Matt was frustrated. So many different opinions. Was he going to have to read a million pages on a thousand obscure websites? He shook his head. No way! How could that be anything but a waste of time? Then again, was he serious about his quest? If reading was going to provide the answers, would he be stupid to ignore all this stuff?

He walked past the young couple and the girl briefly caught his eye from over her boyfriend's shoulder before resuming her long goodnight kiss. Matt knew he didn't want this to be about reading heaps of religious dogma. He didn't need to know what every strange religious cult believed. He wanted people to talk with him, to share their own ideas and thoughts, the down-to-earth, real life stuff. In the late-night Autumn breeze, he decided that it had to be a dialogue. No more links to websites that had "all the answers".

After walking for some ten minutes, Matt's breathing became more laboured. Normally, walking wouldn't be a problem but this body of his was reminding him of the cancer, demanding attention. He stopped at a bus-stop, took a seat, rested his forehead in his hands and tried to breathe normally. But the effort was painful.

Damn! he thought. This is so damned unfair! How can you fight something that you have to carry with you everywhere you go? How can you face a deadly enemy that's already set up camp right there in your own body? A creeping death eating up the only body you'll ever have. How can you live with that?

Matt realised that the battle was not going to be about

making the best of whatever time he had left. It was going to be a daily battle. There would be new challenges, more intense challenges, more frightening challenges, day by day as the disease progressed. The battleground would shift continually, as it already was. He shivered in the cool night breeze and cursed his fate. This was a war he couldn't run away from but it was a war he would eventually lose. The rottenness inside would eventually kill him.

A distant ambulance siren cut for a few seconds over the sound of rustling leaves in the nearby trees. Matt stood slowly and started for home.

5 - SILENCE SHATTERED

Life is an endless cycle, wrote one blog commentator. *It's just the way things are. You've already been part of thousands of lives and you'll eventually hand your essence on to thousands more. People come and go but life goes on. People are dying all the time and others are being born, sometimes as fish, insects or animals, sometimes as gods or spirits. Go peacefully. Show kindness to your fellow creatures. Let go of all desire and accept death as a friend that only takes away what you can never keep. Then you will go quietly into the night and it will go well for you in future lives.*

Matt raised his eyebrows. This was a bit different. But was it worthy of a point? And if so, what religion would get the point? So he wrote back: *What religion are you? And why do you think I should follow your religion?*

The reply came through the next day.

Thursday 19th March

I follow the teachings of the Buddha but it's not really a religion. I think of it more as a pathway. I became a Buddhist when I was sixteen because it was the only way of looking at life that made sense of all the suffering I saw. The teachings I read taught me to accept my place in the universe. We're all just puffs of smoke, you know. We can enjoy good food, good sex, good friendships and so on but we can't make anything last forever. The lotus flower blooms for a season but then it perishes. All of life is like that. But when you understand how things work, you don't fear death.

Someone else picked up on this conversation and wrote the following:

It's all about karma. Whether you do good or do evil, it always catches up with you. It might be in this life or it might be in the next. Judgement isn't personal. It's more like a cosmic principle. You can use up your bad karma and be born into a better life. Or you can use up your good karma and be born into something worse.

Matt discussed this with Sophie over a pizza supper. "Do you believe in karma? And reincarnation?"

Sophie obviously had no idea about such things. "I suppose so … sort of."

"Why?" pressed Matt.

"I don't know," she half laughed. But then she remembered something. "I've heard stories of strange birds appearing at people's homes the night after their husband or wife had died. Like they were coming back in reincarnated form to check on their loved one."

Matt thought about that. "Have you ever heard of someone coming back as a cat or a mouse?"

Sophie almost choked on her pizza. "Uhh, no. I don't think it was ever a cat," she grinned. "Or a mouse."

"Well what about a spider?" He made a creepy gesture with his hands.

She glared at him, a friendly don't-be-so-stupid glare. "No. But what would I know?" Then: "Why are you asking these silly questions?"

Matt shrugged his shoulders and grabbed the last piece of pizza. "Well, some people seem to take the whole reincarnation thing very seriously. There were some blog comments yesterday … and today. One person said I've lived thousands of lives already and I'll probably go on to live thousands more."

"Wow."

Matt wondered if the conversation was getting too ridiculous but Sophie kept it going. "Imagine if you had memories from all those past lives!"

"You'd be a whiz in history," suggested Matt after a moment's reflection.

"You might remember living in a birds' nest or a mouse hole."

"You might remember building the pyramids."

Sophie broke into a funny giggle. "You might have been your own great-grandmother!"

"Ha! And you might have been a flea in your great-great-great grandfather's beard!"

"You might have been a cow that became a hamburger that your great-great-grandfather ate!"

Matt ramped it up even more. "You might see a spider on the wall and think 'Mummy!'"

They both collapsed laughing. Sophie managed a final shot. "If someone asked you where you came from, you'd have to say 'From every-when and every-where."

The next morning, Matt opened his blog and officially awarded one point to Buddhism.

Progress score: Atheism one point, Buddhism one point.

Friday 20th March

Matt's appointment with Dr Tan ran later than expected. Once again he could only manage a quick lunch with Sophie. They met at their favourite bakery and ordered salad rolls with roast pork. Good nutrition? Maybe. And that apricot slice couldn't do any harm, could it? A coffee? If that was bad, it was something he would have to deal with later, when his brain was a bit more settled.

They took their food to a small table on the footpath outside the bakery door. They had almost finished eating when Sophie's sister, Donna, came along. Matt hoped she would keep walking but, when Sophie invited her to join them, what could he say?

Donna had already eaten so she merely pulled a third chair to Matt and Sophie's table.

"Well?" Sophie asked Matt. "What did he say?"

Matt glanced from Sophie to Donna and back again. Should they have this discussion in front of Donna?

"It's OK," insisted Sophie. "Donna's family too."

"Yeah, right," mumbled Matt but his sarcasm sounded harsh and he hastily adjusted his attitude. "Well there were no surprises. I'm basically riddled with little tumours. Um … some of them could be removed surgically but that wouldn't improve my overall prognosis. There are one or two spots that can probably be treated with radiotherapy. I have to have another blood test but, depending on what that shows, Dr Barlow apparently thinks that chemotherapy is worth a shot."

Sophie jumped in, optimistically. "To stop the cancer?"

Matt shook his head impatiently. "No Sophie, not to stop it. Not to cure it. Not to fix anything. Just to slow it down."

It was an uncomfortable moment. Both sisters squirmed at Matt's irritated outburst. He tried to regroup.

"Look, it's OK. I'm going to die. I get it." He tapped his fingers nervously on the little table and tried to ignore the two pairs of sad eyes staring at him. "Look, I don't want to die. You must understand that. I just don't know how to handle this. That's why I've started my Dying Aussie blog. I know I need help with this."

"Blog?" asked Donna. It was the first word she had spoken since joining them.

Matt quickly explained what the blog was all about. Then it was time to get back to work.

Matt resisted the temptation to check the blog page during work hours. Greg had been so understanding that Matt felt obliged to work as well as possible for as long as possible. The work helped to keep things real but it was *sur*-real at the same time. Marketing was all about looking ahead. Weeks, months and years. Often the goal was long-term awareness and market share. He was literally helping to set up a future for people and businesses that he would not be around to see. It didn't bother him all that much; it just felt weird.

Some aspects of marketing accounts were routine. TV campaigns called for a certain type of imagination. Print campaigns required a thorough knowledge of the relevant print media and a different kind of imagination. The work was fun at times but it could still get predictable. Web campaigns were more interesting for Matt but Little Bird clients were often reluctant to venture too far from traditional web pages.

From time to time, Greg would call brainstorming sessions. His uncle, Jim, who worked part-time for Little Bird, always came in for these meetings. Matt enjoyed the flow of creativity that was released and his own ideas often went over well. And now he was getting something of a celebrity status. Lauren had already fielded three calls from radio stations and one from a TV network in the UK.

Some of Matt's clients were obviously unaware of his disease and internet activity. Others were keen to talk about how it was going. Some were extremely uncomfortable. You would have thought cancer could be caught over the telephone. That was upsetting. On the whole, though, work was a big positive. Meeting people, working long mornings and resting when necessary in the afternoons. It was all good. For now.

Discussions on the blog were heating up, diverging into different streams and taking on a life of their own. Matt flirted with the idea of allowing advertising. Perhaps there might be some money in this. But no, it was his personal project. Sponsorship would probably trivialise the whole thing. Maybe even compromise it in some way.

Some Christians appeared, incensed that atheism and

Buddhism had points but Christianity had none. Repeat bloggers started to argue with each other. Some hateful and crude entries had to be quickly deleted, some of them leaving a trail of replies that also had to go. Matt suddenly found himself spending up to two hours every night keeping up with the arguments and throwing in comments as required.

One comment especially got him interested.

What a fantastic conversation you're having! I've been checking it every night. I just love the whole idea. Cancer is such a foul disease. I really admire your courage and your whole way of approaching things. I'm a Christian myself but I understand that there are lots of different ways of looking at things. I hope you find the answers you're looking for.

It was unsigned but Matt wanted to know a name. *Thanks for your thoughts,* he replied. *You sound like a decent person. Can I have a name?*

A few minutes later, a reply came up. *Robert Smith.*

Matt wanted to avoid turning the blog into a chat page but he needed to know. *So Robert, have you been a Christian all your life? If not, how old were you? And what's your take on life after death?*

The reply came through in just over half an hour.

I haven't been a Christian all my life. That happened when I was 12. Long time ago now. So what do I believe? I believe Jesus is the key to eternal life. I definitely don't believe in reincarnation. But I think some Christians jump in too quick and make out like they know everything about everything. What they say doesn't do justice to the love and goodness of God. Some of the comments I've seen on your blog made me feel positively embarrassed to even call myself a Christian. I don't have all the answers, Matt. I don't think anyone does. And I think you're looking for a serious conversation, not a barrage of religious clichés.

Signed Robert S.

Matt quickly scanned several e-mails before finally retiring his computer for the night. Nothing important there. Was Robert Smith just another misguided religious nut? Or was there something deeper there? Either way, Matt found himself hoping he would hear from Robert again.

Monday 23rd March

This Monday night family dinner was special because Annie was flying down from Sydney for a few days. Terry arranged catering from a local chicken takeaway so that Julie could relax and enjoy the occasion. He picked up the food on the way back from the airport. Josh and Leslie were already there with their children when Matt and Sophie arrived but it was a further half an hour before Terry and Annie pulled into the driveway to complete the family gathering.

Annie burst into tears when she saw Matt. "I'm sorry," she spluttered, greeting him with a strong hug. "I was determined I wasn't going to do that."

"That's OK. I'm glad you could come."

"Hey, I have to look after my little brother." She held him tightly for what seemed like an eternity. Matt nodded hello to his Dad over his sister's shoulder and Terry managed a grim "Hello Son."

Annie was an exceptional conversationalist. One by one, she engaged the three children, until each felt especially privileged by her interest. Ryan, the eldest, was fascinated to hear that his cousin Jennifer had recently auditioned for a part in a movie version of a computer game he often played.

Annie quickly perceived that her parents were struggling to rise above what they saw as the doom and gloom of Matt's 'Dying Aussie' persona. She gently guided the dinner conversation with stories of parties she had attended and people she and Jennifer had met. She talked about a little continental food shop that she had discovered in her neighbourhood shopping centre and some of the recipes she'd been experimenting with. Julie and Sophie picked up the pace of the conversation but Terry had little to say, even when Annie mentioned her husband's latest exotic fishing expedition off the north Queensland coast.

After dinner, Josh and Leslie took their weary children

home, promising to be back next Monday night. The five remaining adults retired to the lounge room with coffee and chocolates. Annie surprised everyone with a bold question aimed at Matt and Sophie.

"So when are you guys finally getting married?"

Matt and Sophie both gulped. They consulted each other with a glance and Matt was wordlessly appointed to answer the question. "We haven't really talked about it," he admitted.

"Why not?" pressed Annie. "No point waiting around now."

Julie started to say something but Sophie jumped in. "We're OK as we are. Why would getting married make any difference?"

"Oh, I don't know. For one thing, you could still have a family."

"I don't think I've got that much time," countered Matt.

"Who says?"

Matt threw his hands up in the air. "Annie! I love you and all but you're crazy! I can't have children now!"

"Why not?"

"Well, I'm not going to be around to see them grow up or anything."

"Maybe," conceded Annie with a hint of a smile. "But some people seem to think that leaving a child behind in this world is a good way of making your life count. How do you know? You and Sophie might have a future Prime Minister in your genes."

"Oh, this is ridiculous," groaned Matt. But Annie wasn't finished.

"Have you ever thought that Sophie might love to have a child with you? Maybe to keep your memory alive. Maybe just to keep a part of you in her life after you're gone."

Sophie couldn't let that pass. "Annie! Take it easy! Of course, I'd love to have Matt's baby but I absolutely refuse to put any pressure on him. And this is none of your business."

But Annie was undeterred. "It doesn't have to be about having kids anyway. You love each other, don't you? I would have thought getting married would be one of those unfinished things that you'd want to tie up while things are relatively OK."

Matt was perplexed. He honestly hadn't thought of it in those terms. "What do you think would be different?"

Annie laughed. "Well, as you know, I'm not the world's greatest expert on happy marriages … but there are so many uncertainties. Who knows what's going to happen in the near future? But this is one really positive thing that you can do for each other. It's a chance for Sophie to say 'Hey, I'm there for you. My life will be one with yours, no matter what happens.' And Matt, it's your chance to fully welcome this wonderful young lady into your heart. I think you've been taking her for granted. She wants to love you on a deeper level but you're always holding her at arm's length."

Matt looked enquiringly at Sophie and, slowly, almost apologetically, she nodded. "It's true. I do want to feel closer to you Matt."

"Well, what can I say?"

Annie flashed a cheeky, big-sisterly smile. "Hey, little brother, let me tell you something about women, 'cause you don't seem to know all that much. Women want to feel connected. They want to get inside their man's head and understand what makes him tick."

Terry spoke at last. "Nah, women have their own agenda for their men."

Annie noticed her mother's indignation at that but pressed on with a grin. "Women want commitment. You've been with Sophie for … how long now?"

"Almost three years," answered Sophie, rather too quickly for Matt's liking.

"See! What are you waiting for? Can you imagine someone better for you than Sophie?"

Matt smiled and shook his head. "No. No I can't."

Annie turned solemnly to Sophie. "Do you want to marry my little brother?"

"Yes!" she enthused. "Oh yes!"

Now it was Matt's turn to face his sister's probing glare. "Well? What are you going to do about it?"

"I don't know," stammered Matt. "I ... wasn't expecting this conversation."

"It's not complicated," said Annie. "You just get down on one knee and say: 'Sophie, will you marry me?'"

Matt laughed. This was outrageous. "What? Right now?"

"Good a time as any."

"But I don't have a ring!"

Annie slipped her engagement ring from her finger and handed it to him. "Here. You can borrow mine."

Matt's mouth dropped open in shock but the three women were thoroughly enjoying this. Sophie's initial annoyance had all but disappeared. This was a fascinating turn of events. She gave Matt a look that said: "Come on, are you game?"

"But shouldn't this be a private moment? You know, just the two of us in some romantic setting?"

"I don't care," said Sophie.

Matt had one more excuse. "Look, it's not that I don't see what you're saying. But I'm in the middle of sorting out my faith. What if I decide I'm going to be an atheist, or a Hindu or something? Won't that affect how a wedding would work out?"

Annie thought for a moment. "Tell you what. Why don't you get a quick registry office wedding? Then, when you get your religion sorted out, you can have a more official ceremony."

"Good idea," chirped Julie, sensing that a longed-for wedding was materialising in front of her eyes.

Sophie grinned. "I'm okay with that."

Matt looked to his Dad for some help but none was forthcoming. He was on his own. He sighed self-consciously, almost vanquished. "Does it have to be right here? Right now?"

Annie had that covered too. "Why not? I don't think Sophie will mind."

When Matt closed his eyes for an extended moment, it looked as though he was searching for another excuse. But he was actually focusing, catching his breath, shutting out the randomness of the circumstances. Finally, he knelt before Sophie, looked deep into her wondering eyes, and whispered: "Sophie Gardner, I want you to know that I love you very deeply. I can't offer you a long and happy future but I would be very, very honoured if you would consent to marry me." Surprised at the ensuing silence, he said it again. "Will you marry me?"

This time, the silence shattered. Three women yelled "Yes!" at the same time. Sophie threw her arms around Matt's neck and kissed him over and over. "Yes, yes! Oh Matt! I love you so much!"

6 - WHERE THE BODY WAS

Tuesday 24th March

In what was rapidly becoming an established daily routine, Matt arrived home from work, made himself a decaf and took his laptop through to the sunroom for a pre-dinner session on his blog. This left the evening free for Sophie, or the whole family on Monday nights. He could check whenever he liked, of course, but the pre-dinner time slot seemed to work well.

He noticed that several comments were coming through that misunderstood the purpose of the contest. People wanted to prove that their religion was the truest and best. Some comments could have been described as detailed studies in comparative religion. They were interesting enough but Matt's criteria were clear, at least to him. Which religion or life-philosophy could best help him prepare for death? That was what he wanted to know.

A few correspondents wanted to share their own stories

of religion and faith. Others parroted out a potpourri of clichés. You must find your own path. The truth is within you. And, of course: You must be born again.

"Sorry peeps," said Matt to no-one in particular. "None of that is helping me."

You should become a Jehovah's Witness, wrote one blogger. *Jehovah God promises resurrection to an eternal Paradise on Earth for all those who follow the true religion. We are the only truly worldwide, organised witnesses to God's truth. We are the only ones who obey God's commandments as they were meant to be obeyed. In every nation on earth, we are always going door to door with the good news. We are the only Church that accepts the full truth of the Bible without corruption. Some people think of God as three in one, a trinity. Not only is that mathematically impossible but the Bible never even mentions it. Other people think God sends unbelievers to an eternal hell. But that's not true either. Those who don't believe in Jehovah simply die but Matt, you still have a chance to follow the one true doctrine that will lead to eternal life through Jesus Christ.*

Matt had some previous experience of Jehovah's Witnesses and he judged them to be sincere. But their dogmatic attitude worried him. He thought about allocating a point because, after all, it was a genuinely new contribution to the discussion. It offered a unique view of life after death and certainly attempted to prove its point. Matt tapped thoughtfully on the sides of his laptop. No, it just wasn't convincing enough. Everyone he had ever spoken with about the JW's, as far as he could remember, wrote them off annoying fanatics. They claimed to be the one true religion, but they would say that, wouldn't they? He typed out a response.

Thinking about giving a point to the Jehovah's Witnesses. But I need some more info. Can anyone explain the doctrine of the trinity? I'm not sure if it has anything to do with life after death, or which religion is most true, but if the trinity is crap, I think I can eliminate a lot of other things. If it's true, I can rule out the JWs.

When Matt returned to his blog the next evening, he found several comments that linked to other websites and these were deleted without hesitation. One comment identified the trinity as *"God the Father, Jesus Christ and Mary, the Mother of God."* Something about that didn't seem right but Matt left it up. Another comment simply said: *"There is no God but Allah and Muhammed is his prophet."*

After the usual rubbish was discarded, Matt identified seven genuine comments about the trinity. Two were obviously from Jehovah's Witnesses, one saying that the trinity doctrine didn't come in until the fourth century, and the other quoting someone called Arius who apparently preached convincingly against the idea of a trinity around 325 AD, got in trouble from the Church hierarchy and then got exonerated. It was all a bit mystifying for Matt.

Another comment quoted Bible verses where Jesus said that his Father God was greater than he was. Matt wasn't sure how this proved that the trinity wasn't true. Maybe the Father, Son and Holy Spirit were supposed to be perfectly equal in the trinity doctrine. If so, then fair enough, there seemed to be a problem.

One obviously Christian comment likened the trinity to water, steam and ice. Despite the obvious differences, they were all still $H2O$. Ironically, another comment used the same illustration to prove that the trinity wasn't real.

$H2O$ occurs as ice, water or steam in different settings and this is how God works. Sometimes he appears as God the father, sometimes he appears as the Spirit and two thousand years ago he appeared as Jesus the Son of God. One God, different manifestations.

It was all so confusing but one comment stood out as a credible explanation.

It's true that the doctrine of the Trinity wasn't carefully formulated by the earliest Christians. They just accepted Jesus as God without trying to explain it. And the Holy Spirit was actively working in and through them as they went around preaching the Gospel. They experienced God as Trinity and simply accepted it as a mystery of faith.

They baptised people in the name of the Father, and the Son, and the Holy Spirit. All three were credited with creation, with writing the Bible and with salvation. Sometimes Christians prayed to the Father, other times to Jesus and other times to the Holy Spirit. They believed it because they lived it, not because they understood it.

Josh W.

And finally, there was a comment from Robert Smith.

Ahh, my friend, you're getting into some deep theological stuff now. But hey, it's not really that difficult. Have you ever seen a husband and wife that have grown so close over the years that they seem to think as one? Well I think God is a bit like that, only much more so. God is three persons so perfectly united in love, purpose and understanding that you can really think of them as One.

Or look at it this way. You might have a thought, then speak it out, then act on it, and all three are really one and the same thing. Thought, word, action. I hope you can see what I mean.

And just one more thing that I find helpful to think about. We all have a body, a soul (mind) and a spirit. So, in a way, we're all little trinities!

Robert S.

"Wow," said Matt to his laptop screen. "Give me something relevant to the discussion about life after death and Christianity might get its first point."

Thursday 26th March

Thursday morning, Matt woke with his alarm but, when he visited the toilet, a wave of nausea struck him. He crawled back into bed, reasoning that, if he lay still for long enough, he might be able to control the problem. Instead, he drifted back to sleep, a restless semi-conscious sleep that magnified and distorted his thoughts. No-one was there to hear his groaning but it continued intermittently until after eleven. When he finally saw the clock on his dresser, he groaned again. No anger or frustration this time, just awareness of physical misery that somehow had to be endured. He managed a call to Greg, and dragged his doona out to the lounge room, where he planned to sleep in front of the TV. He tried to eat some toast but it stuck in his throat like dry cardboard. His coffee tasted like mud. He called his doctor's clinic, making an appointment for 4pm, the best time available. Then he sent a text to Sophie. "Doc appt 4 today. Don't think I can drive. Can u help? I'm at home."

The next twenty minutes were something of a blur. Matt roused enough to see a talk show on TV. A doctor was talking about out-of-body-experiences. At least this was interesting. The doctor described a typical experience based on hundreds of personal interviews with near death survivors. Some of the common elements in these stories were the sensation of flying rapidly through a long dark tunnel, a bright light at the end of the tunnel, a rapid-fire montage of memories from different times of life, encounters with deceased relatives, a dazzling, pure, awesome but loving presence, and a sensation of being called to account.

The talk show hostess mentioned a cousin of hers who had a similar experience. "But there was no long, dark tunnel. Just a sensation of being out of the body, looking down at the operating table."

The doctor nodded and explained that few people experienced all of the classic components.

"Well, what do you think this proves?" asked the hostess. Matt turned the volume up a notch. That was the exact question he wanted to ask.

"There are two main theories," answered the doctor. "One is that it proves there is life after death. Christians believe that the presence and sense of being judged line up perfectly with what the Bible teaches. But other religions say the same thing, so I really can't make a definitive call on that one."

"And the other theory?"

"The other theory basically says that there's something in

the chemistry or physiology of the brain that triggers a kind of hallucination when it senses that a permanent shut-down is imminent."

"I've seen movies where space robots do something like that," offered the hostess. "When they're about to be destroyed, they send out an emergency message or signal … or something … with instructions about how to retrieve their information and hopefully rebuild them."

The doctor smiled. "Well, I don't know if it's the same sort of thing. But you might be on the right track."

The hostess then invited another guest to join the conversation, a philosophy professor from a local university, who pulled no punches about what he believed.

"When your brain stops working in death, all thinking has to cease. And if all thinking ceases, there can be no consciousness. So I conclude there can be no conscious life after death."

When the hostess asked her audience for questions, a young Chinese woman in the front row had a question for the professor.

"Please Sir, if you need to concentrate on some particular problem, say for instance, your computer isn't working properly, are you able to get your brain focused on finding a solution to the problem?"

The professor could not see the point of the question. "Well, of course. I think I'm quite good at solving logical problems."

The young woman boldly launched a follow-up question. "So you can effectively tell your brain to shut out other distractions so it can concentrate on solving the problem?"

"Well, yes," he admitted, now more suspicious than impatient. "What are you getting at?"

"Well, Sir, I submit that, if you can give instructions to your brain, then there is something about you that operates independently of your brain. If you can tell your brain what to think, you are obviously not your brain. So, Sir, how can you be sure that the part of you that operates outside of, and apart

64

from, your brain, doesn't go on after the brain ceases to function?"

A few members of the audience clapped enthusiastically and their clapping erupted into cheering when the stunned professor floundered for an answer. "I … I …"

The hostess jumped in. "Interesting question. Let's see if we can come up with any answers after this commercial break."

Forgetting for a while how sick he was feeling, Matt grabbed his laptop and typed a new question on his blog.

Who are we really? Who or what am I? Am I just a brain or am I something more?

Later that day, some smart aleck posted a reply. *My girlfriend is a brain. I'm not. Not sure about you!*

Later that afternoon, Uncle Gavin called.

"Heard you got engaged," he said sharply.

"Yep!"

"Well, Matt, I was just wondering. Do you think that's wise?"

"What? Getting engaged?"

"Well I assume you're planning a short engagement, with the cancer and all. No, I meant, is it wise for you to get married?"

"Uncle Gav, just what are you trying to say?"

"Oh nothing. I suppose … But yeah, I'm worried for you guys. Wouldn't things be simpler just as they already are?"

"Sophie wants to get married."

"Of course she does. But what if that wedding ring makes her think she has the right to make all the decisions? What if, with all the best intentions in the world, she ends up taking control of your life?" Pause. Matt wanted to object but the words didn't come. "Arr, what am I saying? You're a smart lad. I shouldn't have said anything. Don't know what I was thinking."

"That's OK, Uncle Gav. Look, I have to go. Talk to you later."

"OK, Matt. Bye for now."

Terry called that night but Matt was in no mood for talking. Sophie took the call and explained that Matt was lying half asleep on the couch. "Please put him on," pleaded Terry. But Matt just groaned: "Tell him I'll call him back tomorrow."

"Sophie, please. Let me speak with Matt."

Reluctantly, and without a word, she handed the cordless phone to Matt. His annoyance gave way to resignation and he answered: "Hi Dad."

"Hi son. Sounds like you're having a pretty rough day."

"Yeah, you could say that. What can I do for you?"

Terry hesitated. "Uhh, no, it's not like that. I … Um … well, I was up all night last night doing some research on the internet."

"Dad, please …"

"No Son, please hear me out!"

Matt rolled his eyes in frustration. "Do I have to?"

"Oh come on Matt," begged Terry. "Every time I try to talk with you, you give me the brush-off. It seems like you want to die. Have you even looked up any sites about alternative cures for cancer?"

"Dad, I'm following the advice of a cancer specialist. What more can I do?"

"Well I think there's some credible research out there that contradicts almost all the common medical wisdom about treating cancer."

"Oh, come on Dad! What are you trying to tell me? That there's some magic potion out there that'll make all my tumours shrivel up and disappear?"

"Well, not exactly …"

"Look, Dad, everyone knows that they're spending millions of dollars every year trying to find a cure for cancer. When they do find a cure, don't you think it'll be all over the news in a heartbeat? If they already found the cure, don't you think my cancer specialist would know about it?"

"Uhh … I'm not so sure."

"What do you mean?

"Well, I don't think it's quite as simple as that. I'm not sure there'll ever be one cure. Cancer is not just one disease. The answer for some kinds might turn out to be a combination of factors, you know, proper nutrition and … I don't know … meditation … other stuff."

"Are you for real?"

"Yes. There are studies on terminal cancer patients who were cured by alternative therapies, cutting out red meat from their diet, eating apricot kernels … having coffee enemas … There must be thousands of articles on the internet about these sort of things."

"Dad. Just because something's on the internet doesn't mean it's true."

"No, but these people can't get their research published any other way. Well, that's not quite true. They publish their own books and newsletters. But it's not mainstream medicine so they don't get any funding. And they don't get any publicity through the big medical journals. Doctors don't hear about their successes."

Matt laughed scornfully. "I didn't know you were so into conspiracy theories."

"OK, but tell me this. What treatment is Dr Barlow recommending for you?"

"He's not really recommending anything at this stage. He still hasn't ruled out a liver transplant but otherwise I'll probably start a course of chemo. Just to give me a bit more quality time."

"He doesn't think this will significantly prolong your life?"

"No, not really."

"Matt, listen to me. Our medical system in Australia is meant to be right up there with the best in the world. Our success rate for curing cancer is good for early detection. But don't you think they should at least be open to alternative therapies?"

"I thought they were. Dr Barlow mentioned all sorts of options. He said some of his patients try acupuncture or aromatherapy or … well, I can't remember everything he said. But I know he said he hasn't personally seen any cures from those sort of things."

"OK, Matt, but you only get one chance at this. And we don't want to lose you. Not if there were things that we didn't even try."

Matt sighed. "Look, Dad, I appreciate that. But you said yourself that there's thousands of articles to read. I guess … well, I've still got a life to live. I've got this blog thing taking up most of my spare time as it is. How am I ever going to find time to plough through all this stuff? And even if I did, how am I supposed to sort out the truth from the rubbish?"

"I'll do that for you," answered Terry, faster than even he expected. "I'll sort through all the information I can find and give you a few simple recommendations. Then you can discuss them with Dr Tan or Dr Barlow, whoever. Would you at least do that?"

Matt sighed again. "OK. I'm very sceptical but I can do that." He caught Sophie's eye and spoke it out for her benefit. "I'll think about your suggestion and, if my doctors are OK with them, I might give them a try." He paused. "Thanks, Dad."

Friday 27th March

It was Easter, Good Friday in fact. Day off for almost everyone. Matt drove to Sophie's and found her still in bed. He woke her with a kiss but, rather than getting up, she merely invited him to join her. She didn't have to ask twice. Sex had been a comfortable aspect of their relationship almost from the beginning.

Later in the morning, they watched some TV together. Nothing exciting. A telethon for a children's hospital and a choice of old religious movies from the 1950s.

The school that Josh and Leslie's oldest two children attended was having a sports day to mark the beginning of term holidays. The cricket season was over and the football season was about to begin in earnest once more, so the school had arranged for some footy skills workshops, both for boys and girls. They also provided coaching opportunities for basketball, hockey and tennis. The whole thing was put together as a family day, complete with a barbecue (fish and prawns for those whose religious sensibilities prevented them from eating red meat on Good Friday.)

Matt and Sophie arrived in time to watch young Chelsea trying to kick a football. At just six years of age, her main difficulty was timing the swing of her foot with the dropping of the ball. Over and over again, the ball would hit the ground before her foot reached the spot where the ball was supposed to be. Josh and Leslie watched as Matt went to her and gently showed her how to time the backswing of her foot with the release of the ball. She giggled happily when she finally connected, even though the ball only dribbled a metre or so away.

Sophie took the cue and, after lunch, took the chance to play some tennis with Ryan, the nine-year old. Matt wandered around the school grounds, taking it all in. Chelsea could go on to be a star in women's football but he wouldn't be around to see it. Yet another aspect of this curse called cancer. How would his nieces and nephew turn out? He would never know. Before they were much older than they were now, he would be gone forever, buried deep in the ground.

Religious holidays had never meant much to Matt. Perhaps it was only the family thing that made them important for most people. Easter Sunday, just two days away, was supposed to be all about Jesus overcoming death. Matt wondered if that would feature in the blog conversation.

Sunday 29th March (Easter Sunday)

Sophie asked Matt to close his eyes while she went to retrieve something from her car. He'd been sitting in his sunroom reading a book about Aussie rock band AC/DC but he dutifully closed his eyes until instructed to open them again. When Sophie returned, she was carrying the biggest chocolate bunny Matt had ever seen.

"Happy Easter," she said with a grin. "This should keep you going for a while."

Matt nodded and stroked his chin, feigning serious thoughtfulness. "Yeah, I'd say five minutes at least. Thank you."

Matt's gift to Sophie was much less extravagant but she accepted the basket of chocolate eggs with grace. Matt wondered aloud about the connection between chocolate and Easter. Sophie went out to the kitchen and returned with two standard cups of coffee, which she carefully placed on the little table beside Matt's chair. Then she gave him a kiss and nestled herself on his lap.

"I really hope I get to share at least one Easter with you as husband and wife," she said quietly. "More than one, actually. I hope we get to share lots of Easters. And Christmases. And birthdays." Her eyes, wide with sadness, contradicted the hope in her words. "I don't want to lose you."

The only Easter greetings Matt found when he went to his computer were in his e-mail. But he was correct in guessing that the occasion might produce something in the blog for Christianity. After reading several brief, unimpressive comments, he came across one from Robert Smith.

OK Matt, you know I'm a Christian. So here's why I believe in life after death. Jesus died on Good Friday but he was resurrected on Easter Sunday. Now he lives forever. And because he did this, we also have confidence that eternal life is real. The four gospels all tell different aspects of this, just like you would expect from eye-witnesses. One said there was one angel at the tomb, another said there were two. One said Mary Magdalene was there, another said that Peter and John went there. But they absolutely agree that the tomb was empty. The body of Jesus simply wasn't there.

The enemies of the early Christians said that the disciples stole the body away. But how? It was guarded by Roman soldiers. And even if they did steal the body, how could they all keep up their story under pain of death? All the disciples except one were martyred for their belief in Jesus but they never wavered in their testimony that they knew Jesus to be alive.

I love the fact that Christianity is based on historical events, ie, the death and resurrection of Jesus. So far as I know, it's the only major religion like that. The other major religions are all based on ideas and theories. Christianity stands or falls on a few key historical facts. And, believe me, it stands! Jesus, the one who rose from the dead, is the key to life after death.

And Matt, one more thing. The absolute clincher for me is that I have a relationship with Jesus. I know that he's alive because I meet with him every day in my prayer time.

Robert S.

The next day, someone calling herself Suspicious Sue (Matt loved the name) would write that the disciples all had hallucinations and that the Jewish authorities had simply moved the body to a different tomb. But Robert would have a ready answer for that.

Oh right! So tell me, if the authorities knew where the body of Jesus was, how come they didn't just go and bring it out? We know they wanted to stop the Christians preaching that Jesus rose from the dead, and it would have been so easy. IF they knew where the body was!

Robert S.

Matt wasn't sure about the link between the resurrection of Jesus and eternal life for anyone else, but he had to admit that Robert's original point was well made.

Progress score: Atheism, Buddhism, Christianity – one point each.

71

7 - GETTING WEIRD

Monday 30th March

The Tuesday after Easter was Julie's birthday but she was more than happy to celebrate with her family at the regular Monday night dinner. To make the occasion a bit special for Julie, Leslie hosted and prepared all the food. Julie gratefully received the cards and gifts from her family but Matt's birthday was coming up and that, in her mind, easily took priority. "This one has to be special," she said, more than once. When Matt asked "why?" adding that thirty-three wasn't normally a special birthday, she merely glared at him.

"Don't be flippant with me, young man. You know exactly why this one is important. It may be the last time we get to celebrate with you on your birthday." She didn't actually say the words. Her look said it all.

Sophie jumped in. "I'll help you Julie. I've got some ideas."

"There's not much time," said Leslie, "but we can do it.

Let's get started!"

Wednesday 1st April

A cable TV network based in New York picked up on the growing internet buzz and called to arrange an interview with Matt. Greg understood and allowed Matt the necessary time off. The network's Australian contact arrived with a single cameraman at Matt's home at 10.30 in the morning and spent twenty minutes setting up and working out the angles. They took some footage of Matt working at his computer and some where he was just looking out a window. (When Matt saw the footage later that week, he was amazed, and amused, that they also showed a clip of boats going under the Sydney Harbour Bridge as part of their introduction. Apparently, for Americans, everything in Australia was close to Sydney.)

The freelance reporter worded Matt up on the questions he was planning to ask. Then it was time.

"What are you hoping to achieve with your blog and video?"

"Well, it's like this. I'm going to die soon and I didn't know how to live what time I have left. My friends didn't have any real answers so I thought this blog might help."

"Has it helped you so far? Have you had many comments?"

"Yeah, I've had hundreds of good, sincere comments, from all sorts of people."

"And … has it helped at all?"

"Oh well, it's all been a bit bewildering. And overwhelming. Lots of interesting ideas to sort through. In the end I just have to work out what makes the most sense for me."

"You're dealing with some of the great philosophical and religious questions of all time. Do you really expect that you can work out which religions are right and which ones are wrong? After all these centuries, do you really think that you can be the one to find the answers?"

"I don't know. I'm not trying to change the world."

"Do you think that whichever religion wins your little

competition will get more followers?"

That question was not on the list. The reporter was beginning to mock the whole thing. Matt answered thoughtfully.

"No, I don't think my blog is ever going to get that big!" He laughed. "It's not really about proving anything or solving anything. I can't judge what other people believe. All I can do is to work out what seems right to me. And that's a big enough challenge! I'll gladly leave the broader issues to people smarter than me!"

That night, after a home-cooked meal and a TV movie at Sophie's, Matt came home and checked the blog. One comment attracted his attention.

There are answers, my friend. You are an eternal being. Whether it happens soon or in fifty years, you will pass on to another body. But that is not your real concern. You can live better in the meantime. I therefore recommend Scientology because it has technologies that can help you achieve genuine spiritual awareness. Scientology is the only religion that lets you find your own way to emotional and mental health.

Signed Tim.

It was late and Matt needed to turn in for the night. The Scientologist comment raised more questions than it answered. Matt tried to mentally review things he had heard about Scientology over the years. It was mostly a little scary. Mind control, weird secret meetings, running legal battles in the US about whether they were entitled to tax concessions for religious organisations.

He typed a simple question below this latest comment.

Any comments? Is Scientology something I should try?

By the next evening, he had received several responses. The blog conversation was branching out and it was getting hard to keep track of all the lines of comment. Tim's simple recommendation was reinforced by some and viciously attacked by others.

It's helped me a lot, wrote Jerry. *I've been taking some courses and auditing sessions. That's where a trained counsellor asks questions and listens. I'm learning a whole new way of looking at the world and I've even picked up on some incidents from a previous life. I wholeheartedly agree with Tim. There's a church in Melbourne. Is that close to where you live?*

Someone called Mia trotted out a host of "reasons" for Matt to choose Scientology.

Scientology is the only religion that's truly modern and scientific. Ron Hubbard's book on Dianetics has been a bestseller for more than sixty years. Millions of people have proved that it works. It makes you a better person. The more you progress in Scientology, the more your thoughts become clear. That's why so many members are so incredibly famous and successful in their chosen fields. They use these things called e-meters to access the reactive mind. No other religion has awesome technology like this.

Also, Scientology members always look for ways to help other people because they understand life and human reactions. The Church teaches us that loving the world around us is part of surviving well. The starting point is to see that you're an eternal thetan looking out through the eyes of your body. You can use your mind for either good or bad.

A reader named Richard wrote a blunt reply to that.

Scientology is a dangerous cult!!! Don't even give it a second thought!!! It shouldn't be called a religion because it's really a psychological theory. None of its claims have ever been proved. It should be banned!!!

Another blogger accused Scientology of being a lie that gets worse the more you progress through the levels. Someone else thought it was an elaborate money-making scheme. One Christian respondent challenged the Scientology concept of ultimate reality as "a pantheistic counterfeit for God". Another Christian complained that Scientology denied the need for a Saviour, thereby consigning its followers to eternal separation from God. Finally, a blog follower who simply signed with an 'x' quoted a supposedly official Scientology source to the effect that Scientology had no official position on life after death.

There was much in this that Matt didn't understand. Claims and counter-claims. It was so hard to know but, in any case, if the last respondent was correct, Scientology had little or nothing to say about death and dying. Therefore, it wasn't going to get a point.

Thursday 2nd April

Since the first week of his death-and-dying blog, Matt had included a permanent disclaimer directly beneath his photo.

Please do not direct me to websites, dvds or books that you may have found helpful. I could never cope with all that information. And please don't cut and paste large chunks from online resources. This blog is about YOU telling ME in YOUR own words what YOU think would help ME and WHY.

One blogger strenuously challenged his stance on this, complaining that he was effectively ruling out all the sacred writings from the different religions, and that it was these sacred writings, in and of themselves, that would be most helpful. An obviously Muslim respondent argued that the Quran was holy and perfect, and that reading it aloud, preferably in the original Arabic, was necessary for eternal life.

Matt added a few questions to the blog. *So what does the Quran teach about life after death? Is it a special heaven that only Muslims can attain to? How would the Quran help me prepare for death and dying?*

One writer from a Buddhist perspective tried a different tack to get around Matt's prime directive.

Hey don't rule out the great wisdom of past masters just 'cause you don't want to get buried in endless research. Buddhist scriptures are not about study or feeding the mind. Buddha himself never wrote anything but his sayings and discourses were passed on because his followers found them to be essential for a proper understanding of life and death.

If I quoted hundreds of his sayings, you wouldn't bother

to read them but if you listened to an audio version, you would see what I mean. Reading Buddhist poetry, prayers and meditations would be the number one thing that would prepare you for the coming transition. If you decide to follow this path, I hope you will have plenty of time to read or listen to these things. They are specifically handed down to us for the purpose of awareness of death.

There are lots of religions that try to tell you how to live but they come to nothing because they don't prepare people for death. Buddhist teachings are the exact opposite. They teach us how to live by first teaching us about death.

Matt wrestled with this. It was hard to argue, one way or the other. But another contributor went into some detail describing the "joy and extreme contentment" that her friend had experienced in the last weeks of her life. Listening over and over to Buddhist texts, according to this blogger, brought her "intense happiness", even despite her physical pain and discomfort.

Religious texts as a kind of soothing balm. Whether it was true or not, this was indeed an original, potentially helpful comment. It had to be worth a point.

Progress score: Buddhism 2 points, Atheism, Christianity – 1 point each.

Friday 3rd April

There were many things to resent about having cancer but even Matt was surprised how quickly he had begun to resent the various appointments with people who claimed to be there for him. So many people wanted to help but the pressure to see this one or that one left Matt wrestling with the feeling that he was no longer in control of his life. Doctors anticipating questions that he wasn't even asking. Nurses giving advice about crossing bridges that still seemed a long way off. Friends and family members boring him with predictable opinions and recommendations. Appointments that always had to be at a certain time on a certain day because, after all, these people were so busy and important.

This time, it was a counselling service. Julie had been very persistent. "Please son, do this for me. Just this one appointment. If you don't think it will help, I won't hassle you again. But this fellow is very good. He already helped me get things in better perspective."

So here he was. The counselling service was situated in an old stone-block residence with high ceilings and wood-panelled walls. Matt felt like a schoolboy again as he followed his mother through the sturdy entrance door with stained glass representations of various native birds. It didn't help Matt's mood when, having announced their arrival to the receptionist, his mother gestured to a couple of seats in the waiting room and said: "Come. Sit here with me."

It had already been a long working day for Matt so he was tired and hungry, and the ten minute wait only intensified his grumpy mood.

John Vickers was a tall, elegant man whose greying beard contradicted his otherwise dark hair. Matt judged his ears to be larger than normal and wondered if that made him a good listener.

Julie jumped in, nervously spurting out her hopes for the session. Vickers had to gently raise his hand to stop her. Swivelling in his chair so that he was directly facing Matt, not Julie, he offered his congratulations on the blog and said that he would be following it with interest.

"I'm curious," he said. "What did you think of the idea that Buddhist texts teach us how to live by first teaching us about death?"

"Wow! That was just last night. Why do you ask? Are you a Buddhist?"

Vickers smiled generously as he shook his head. "No, no. I don't follow any religion myself. I just thought it was a fascinating comment."

Matt was impressed but he wasn't letting down his guard that easily. Vickers continued. "Do you think your blog about dying is helping you to live better?"

78

Matt didn't want to answer the question so he just shrugged his shoulders. "I don't know. It's probably too soon to say."

Vickers nodded and tried again. "Have you made any changes in your life because of anything anyone has written?"

"No. Not yet."

Vickers studied Matt for a second, then glanced at Julie. Matt chided himself for making his reluctance to be there so obvious. The counsellor was not stupid. And Julie's agenda for the session was equally unmistakable. So Matt was not surprised when Vickers changed tack and began asking more pragmatic questions. How were the wedding plans coming along? What was he expecting from marriage? Were there any doubts or reservations? Would his new wife have enduring power of attorney? Medical power of attorney? Did he understand these things? Did he need any help?

But Matt was a closed book. "Look, it's OK. My Palliative Care people will get me through all that stuff. They seem to know all the legal mumbo-jumbo of dying."

Vickers smiled. "Good to see you're so upbeat about it all."

"Ha! I wouldn't say that. It's tough … but I'm trying to take things one day at a time."

Julie tried again to prompt the discussion. "But Matt, that's just what I've been trying to say. Live each day to the full without worrying so much about dying."

Matt curled his bottom lip and closed his eyes, as if to shut out a comment that would only infuriate him. "Mum! Why can't you understand?" He appealed to Vickers for help but the counsellor was not about to take sides.

"You both have to work through this in your own way," he declared. To Julie: "You have to trust Matt that he knows what he's doing. That he will do what's right for him." To Matt: "And you might need to be a bit more sensitive to what other people around you are going through. It's hard on them too. You're going to need to be patient with people. Especially with your Mum."

Taking things one day at a time. What exactly did that mean? Trying to find meaning in each day? Making decisions only when they were absolutely necessary? Or maybe just trying to find some fun in each day? Life was coming at him one day at a time, whether he wanted it that way or not. Some days were better than others. Some days now were abysmal. Pain, sickness, depression. Those days just had to be survived.

Matt sat alone on a bench seat near the local football ground. Men were arriving for practice. Some were already doing fitness drills along the boundary. A group of females were leaning on the fence, chatting loudly and egging on their men.

Health and fitness messages were everywhere and Matt was noticing them more than ever. Eat the right foods, avoid excessive alcohol, exercise wisely. All for the goal of a body that would feel great and look great. But what was the point? Living longer? Living better?

He watched the men train for half an hour. Running, twisting, locking against one another in strength exercises. But this was only making him jealous. And what was the point of that? He stood and turned for home. As always, there was a blog to check.

The Quran is very definite that life goes on after death, wrote someone called Sami. *But how can mere man be expected to understand such things? Paradise is described as a place of sensual delight, a beautiful garden with low-hanging fruit to enjoy, an eternal river of life flowing below luxurious carpets, beautiful virgins attending to your every need, and the fruits of religion growing and increasing forever and ever. Hell is depicted in many ways but often as judgement of fire.*

Matt made a mental note to ask Sophie how she would feel about the beautiful virgins attending to her every need. Maybe it wasn't meant to be taken literally but, even so, it sounded terribly sexist.

Another reader boldly declared that there was nothing to fear in death. He or she knew this because someone had recorded a series of conversations from the other side through a medium who operated out of Los Angeles. Matt winced when he read the blogger's apparently serious request that he watch out for this medium after his demise. *Even if it's not for years to come,* he/she wrote, *I'd love to hear your final discoveries on these things.*

Some comments could be deleted without a second thought. Others, like this last one, begged to be mocked. *So you're asking me to come back with a message for you after I'm dead?* he asked. *I don't think so. You insult my intelligence!*

Other comments were much more practical. One follower, calling herself Jenny, made the point that Matt should get all the practical, legal things out of the way as quickly as possible.

Talk to people. Work out your will, if you haven't already done so. Plan some special things that people can remember you by. Make videos and tapes for all your favourite nephews and nieces. Find out what stuff people might like you to leave them. Plan your funeral service how you'd like it. Make the medical decisions now, while you're still mentally sharp and alert. Get all that stuff out of the way and then you'll be able to cope with whatever comes without worrying about things you think you should be doing.

This sounded like good advice. Was it different from other advice that had received a point? Yes, probably. Would he follow this advice? Yes, mostly. It all seemed a bit random but the decisions were his and his alone. He awarded a point to a new category, Practical Stuff.

Progress score: Buddhism 2 points, Atheism, Christianity, Practical Stuff – 1 point each.

Monday 6th April
"I've bought you some books, son. Please take some

81

time to read them."

It was the usual Monday night family get together, and Matt's Dad handed him a plastic bag. Matt inspected the contents. The first book was called "Cancer, We're Still Dying to Know the Truth", the second was "Foods to Fight Cancer", and the last one was "Anticancer: a New Way of Life".

"Uh … thanks Dad," said Matt. "Just so you know, I'm still not prepared to believe in some miracle cure."

"No, no, I understand that," hastened Terry. "But, like I promised, I've been researching this. I've spent hours and hours reading all the books I just gave you. And on the internet. Yes, you're right. There's no simple cure. But there are some natural foods that can help fight the cancer if you're willing to commit to some positive changes."

"Wow. Sounds serious."

"Well, yes," said Terry, his frown rebuking his son's offhandedness. "I do think cancer is serious. Just about as serious as you can get."

"What else have you got in here?" asked Matt, fishing in the bottom of the bag.

"Apricot kernels, son. Ordered them in from Sydney but I think I found out where to get them locally. Apricot kernels are rich in B17, a natural cancer-fighting vitamin."

Matt's sister-in-law, Leslie had witnessed this conversation. When she saw the apricot kernels, she jumped in. "Now hang on a minute! If these things are the bitter variety, as I expect they are, you need to know that they've got large amounts of cyanide in them." Sophie pricked up her ears on hearing that and came over to join the conversation.

But Terry was not retreating. "Yes, Leslie, but tests have proved that the cyanide in apricot kernels has no effect on healthy cells. It's there as part of a chemical compound called amygdalin. You can have ten or twelve kernels per day, and it won't do you any harm. It might even do you a lot of good."

Sophie looked at the hard, crusty kernels. "Ha! They might not be too good for your teeth!"

Terry rolled his eyes. "Uhh, yeah … you have to break

open the shells to get to the part you can eat. And then most people grind them up and sprinkle them on other foods."

"But I read somewhere that they were banned in New York or something," persisted Leslie.

"I don't know about that," admitted Terry. "But ..." He paused to emphasise his point. "There are whole civilisations where they don't get cancer at all. And all these places have high intake of B17." He turned to face Matt and Sophie. "Read it for yourself. Don't take my word for it." His last comment sounded just a little sarcastic.

Matt inspected the packet again and flicked absently through the first book. But Terry wasn't finished. "The guy who wrote this book has heaps of videos on the internet. All that online stuff that you're into. If reading a book doesn't interest you, why not look him up online?"

"You make it sound so easy," commented Sophie.

"I don't mean to," said Terry. "None of these books say it's simple or easy. But, like I say, just read the stories. One man had terminal cancer, all through his bones and digestive system. The doctors said there was no hope for him but he did everything this book said and his cancer slowly disappeared."

Matt sighed. "I've been trying to accept the fact that I'm dying. And you're asking me to rethink everything!"

Terry nodded. "You've been talking with people about the best way to die. How about taking some time to think about how you might live?"

Sophie grinned at Matt. "What do you think, honey? Will apricot kernels get a point on your blog?"

Tuesday 7th April

The atmosphere at the Little Bird Marketing Agency was unusually tense. Greg was pacing back and forth in the hallway outside Matt's office, muttering something about a tax problem. There were deadline issues as well but Matt felt he was doing as well as he possibly could. So, when Greg barged in accusing him of messing up the radio campaign for an important client, Matt was stunned. He honestly didn't think he was at fault in this case. But you didn't answer back to Greg when he was in this kind of mood.

Another client called to change a campaign that she had signed off on. It was too late to make any changes but Greg overruled his own company policy and Matt's day was further thrown into chaos.

The traffic blockage on the way home would not have irritated Matt so much if he hadn't been feeling stressed and unwell by then. He had only been home for five minutes when Terry called.

"Hi Dad."

"Hi son, have you got a few minutes?"

"I just got home from work."

"I'll be quick."

Matt didn't care if his grumpy mood showed through. "Yeah, right!"

"Matt, I found someone right here in Mona Shores who does a cancer reduction diet program."

Matt just groaned.

"I called the woman and she says she's willing to take you on as a client."

Silence.

"Matt, did you hear me?"

"Yeah, Dad, I heard you. But we were going to talk about this next week or something."

"Sure, but …"

"Oh come on, Dad! Give me a break! I've had a hard day and you just expect me to make important lifestyle decisions at the drop of a hat."

"I only wanted to talk with you about it."

"Yeah well, I don't want to talk about it right now!"

"Son …"

"Some other time, Dad. Some other time."

Matt grimaced in pain as he ended the call and switched his phone off.

Deeply frustrated, Matt booted up his computer and checked the blog. The first comment infuriated him even more.

God told me last night that he is going to heal you in the next three days. Don't worry about dying. You will live to a ripe old age and you will win many souls for Jesus.

Signed: Just Have Faith.

Matt quickly hit the 'delete' button on the blog. The next comment was no better.

Ten years ago, on my birthday, I saw a spirit in a powerful vision. The spirit said her name was Astarte and she gave me a special anointing to heal cancer with holy water. If you text me your address (a mobile phone number followed), I'll be happy to come to your home.

Signed: Desirae Q.

Matt shuddered and deleted that one as well.

The Church has saints that you can pray to for just about every ache and pain known to man. Saint Luke is the patron saint for doctors, Camillus de Lellis is the patron saint of nurses, and of course you can pray to Raphael the archangel. His name means 'God has healed'. Even if these saints can't actually heal you, they will help you prepare your heart for Heaven.

Signed: Francis of the Flowers.

"Nothing helpful tonight," moaned Matt. "The perfect ending for a generally lousy day! And it's all getting weird. Who needs cancer? Life is hard enough anyway."

8 - WHAT IF IT'S A SIN?

Thursday 9th April

Cancerous tumours can affect people in ways that defy accurate medical prognosis. Matt hated the emotional ups and downs that seemed to taunt him. He worried that the downs were getting deeper and more painful. The lines between the physical, the mental and the emotional were blurring. He caught himself daydreaming, not about the future but about the past.

It had been another difficult day at Little Bird and Matt would have preferred a simple dinner, just on his own. But Sophie had prepared a full meal of roast lamb and vegetables, with a self-saucing lemon pudding for dessert. She was not the greatest cook in the world but she possessed a determined spirit and an honest desire to improve.

"Let's just eat in the lounge room," suggested Matt. "I wouldn't mind watching the news." He didn't see her snuff out the candles on the dining table because he was already in the next room.

They ate in silence and, after they had finished, Sophie cleared the empty plates to the kitchen. From the clatter of crockery and cutlery, Matt could tell she was not happy.

She came and stood directly in front of the TV. "What are we going to do about the seating for the reception?" she demanded.

"I don't care," he muttered, trying to look around her at the TV.

"Come on Matt. Seriously. Don't you have any preferences?"

"Not really. Look, Soph, whatever you organise will be OK with me. Honestly."

He closed his eyes, partly from exasperation at having his TV viewing interrupted and partly to avoid that all too familiar glare. Whether the tactic worked or not, Sophie softened her tone. "Matt, come on. Please. Are you looking forward to this or not?"

"I don't know."

"You don't know? How can you say that?" She hesitated. "You do love me, don't you?"

"Of course I do."

Something about the way he snapped his answer brought a tear to Sophie's eyes. "Look, I understand that you've got a lot on your mind. But I would really appreciate your help here. We're checking out the reception centre tomorrow. I can't make all these decisions by myself."

"Yes you can. I don't need to be there."

"What? Why … why are you doing this?"

"I'm sorry. I guess I'm finding it all a bit overwhelming." He refused to make eye contact. "You can handle things."

Sophie turned away, breathing erratically. From the kitchen door, she turned to face Matt again. "Your Mum and I can pretty much pull it all together … if we have to. But hey, this is important. And it's your wedding too. You have to have some input."

"Why?" mumbled Matt. "I don't really give a damn."

Sophie winced. "How can you say that?"

"Easy. I don't give a damn! See. I said it again."

"Matt, you're not being reasonable."

"Look, I'm feeling really crap today. Maybe you should leave me alone for a while."

Sophie stormed out of the room but returned almost immediately. "Matt, whatever happens in the future, our wedding day has to be right. For both of us."

Matt shook his head in growing contempt for the whole conversation. "I really don't want to talk about this tonight!" The last few words were uncommonly loud and aggressive.

"You're hurting me Matt! Why are you being so mean?"

"Well maybe you shouldn't have pressured me into this in the first place!"

Sophie brushed some loose hair away from her face. "What? Now you think I pressured you into marrying me?"

"Well, yeah. It wasn't just you but you should have known I wasn't ready."

Sophie burst into tears and turned away from Matt's glare. "Yeah, that's right!" he snapped. "Put on the waterworks. See if that helps anything."

Rage has a madness all its own. Rather than apologise, then and there, Matt got up from the armchair and staggered to Sophie's back door. Slamming the door behind him, he jumped in his car and drove.

For two hours, Matt drove on, propelled by self-justifying emotion, ignoring the incessant waves of pain in his side and the all too familiar nausea. When his phone rang, he hastily shut it down, knowing from the ringtone that it was Sophie. He drove on, muttering out loud: "No! No! No! No! NO!" Daylight was long gone and the darkness inside was complete. How easy would it be to just swing suddenly into the path of one of these trucks?

His eyes were blurred and sweaty. It was getting harder to concentrate on driving. So, when he came into a town with a decent looking roadhouse, he decided he'd better stop for a drink. He managed to park and found his way inside to a small corner table. By pushing the seat back against the wall, he was able to cradle his messed up head in the fold of his arms. It felt good just to close his eyes for a while.

It might have been five minutes before Matt raised his head enough to look around him. Two older women in blue waitress uniforms were watching him from behind the counter, wondering how and when to approach this obviously troubled customer. A forty-something man was in a world of his own drinking a coffee or something three tables over. And then there were two attractive young women, maybe nineteen or twenty years old, a sandy-haired girl in a plain white blouse, and a blonde sporting a floral purple and black t-shirt with a neckline that revealed the greater part of two curvy breasts. Once again Matt lowered his head to the table.

A few moments later. "Having some girl trouble, eh?"

Matt looked up, surprised to see the blonde girl standing at his table. He grunted an answer that sounded like a 'yes'.

"Can I join you?"

Matt gestured for her to take a seat and, half interested, sat up and pulled his chair back closer to the table.

"I'm Brenda." She held out her hand and he responded.

"I'm Matt." She continued to hold his hand. It felt nice, somehow reassuring. "Um, you should know I'm not very good company."

She smiled. "That's OK. I don't mind sitting with you for a while."

Brenda signalled to the waitresses behind the counter. "Two espressos please!"

"No, don't bother," Matt groaned. This was insane. How was this happening?

"It's alright. You look like you need it." She tightened her grip. "Come on, what is it? Tell me."

Matt thought of Sophie. Their argument, his personal demons. None of it was any business of this beautiful young woman. But there she was, right across from him at an intimate corner table, watching him, waiting for an answer.

"I … I'm not well."

She nodded, obviously expecting more.

"I've got cancer … and I've just had a big argument with my fiancée." There. He said it. That should drive this gorgeous creature away. But alas, it only made her more interested.

"How is she?"

Matt took a deep breath. How could this girl look so cheerful and so concerned at the same time?

"Oh, she's OK. But I don't want to talk about her."

The waitress arrived with the coffees. Brenda put some sugar in hers and offered the same to Matt. "I understand," she purred.

Normally, Matt would have challenged a line like that. How could she possibly understand? But then again, how could you argue with such a pretty smile?

"Don't feel bad, Matt. She'll be all right."

"You think so?"

"Of course."

Matt began to weep. Sniffing back a tear, he whined about what a lousy person he was. Brenda responded by bringing her chair around beside him and placing her arm around his shoulder. She squeezed him like they were best friends. And Matt's need to just be close to another human being silenced his guilt. How could he turn away?

"I like you," she whispered. "Let it all out. I'm here for you."

As Matt turned to look into her eyes, he brushed against her breast, but she only grinned at his embarrassment. "Why are you being so nice?" he stammered. "I don't even know you."

"So what?" she said, teasingly tilting her head to one side and brushing her hair back with her free hand. "Do you want me to go?"

"No. No, I don't think so."

That was enough. She gently wiped a tear from Matt's cheek.

And then they kissed.

Friday 10th April

Sophie called in sick the next morning. With her head spinning painfully, breakfast was a chore too hard but staying in bed was even more unthinkable. So, for the whole morning, she muddled around her apartment in her scruffy pink slippers and her full-length pussycat motif dressing gown. Was she sick or just angry? Did it even matter? She played a mindless game on her computer, tried to read a magazine and tended some pot plants in the covered area outside her laundry. Finally, standing under a shower that was probably too hot, she dragged herself out of her self-loathing fog and began speaking encouragement to herself.

"Sophie Gardner! This is not your fault. Matt will come through this. And so will you. Worry is only making you sick. But think now. Think! What can you do that will help you right now? It doesn't have to be the best thing. Just something different to get your mind off all the crap!" She shouted the last few words but immediately collected herself. "No, don't lose it Sophie. Think. Who is the best person to help you shake off this misery?"

She rang her sister Donna and, lunch arrangements made, dressed and headed downtown to a fast-food restaurant she would normally avoid.

The two sisters met outside the restaurant and hugged with an intensity that had Donna raising surprised eyebrows. The whole faith-in-God thing had been something of a barrier between them in recent years but today Sophie needed her sister. No past conflicts were going to stand in the way.

"Are you OK, Soph?"

"Not really." She flashed an unconvincing smile. "Thanks for meeting me. I do have some things I'd like to ask you."

As they waited in line to order their meals, the sisters chatted awkwardly about the unusual amount of traffic on the streets of Mona Shores lately. But when they were seated, Sophie wasted no time. She couldn't remember the last time she had asked Donna for anything but this was no time for holding back. No time for silly pride.

"Matt and I had a fight. Last night. About the wedding. At least I think that's what it was about. I don't really know. But he was really angry and … well, he slammed the door and walked out. I don't know where he went but he didn't go home because I went around there when he didn't answer his mobile. I was so worried. He wasn't well."

Donna leaned a little closer and nodded. Sophie measured her words.

"I've heard about people being sick with worry. But I didn't understand that until today. I think I've literally made myself sick. What if he's injured himself or something? What if he breaks up with me? Donna, I don't know how to deal with this. I don't know how to deal with the whole cancer thing. I don't have your kind of faith to fall back on."

This time the desperate, bewildered look on Sophie's face called for a comment. "Hey Sophie, it's OK. We all have our struggles."

Sophie managed a smile. "Are you sure? You never seem to have any."

Donna almost choked on her hamburger. "Wow! You really think that? Hey, listen Sophie … having God in my life is a fantastic thing. More important than anything. But it doesn't mean I always get things right." Another awkward, searching silence. "Sorry, I'm not good with words."

"It's OK, Donna. I know you love me. And Matt. You're a good person. A good sister." She hesitated and stared for a moment at her still untouched lunch.

"I suppose what I wanted to know is …" Sophie hated feeling so vulnerable but she had to press on. "What I wanted to know is … how do you pray? If you were in this mess, how would you pray? And do you think it would help?"

"I'm more than happy to pray for you," offered Donna.

"I know," said Sophie. "But I thought perhaps if you could teach me to pray, it would, you know, help me to cope. If … if I knew how to pray myself."

Donna set her hamburger down on the plastic tray, wiped

her hands and the corners of her mouth with a serviette, and then reached out across the table with both hands. "The best way to teach someone to pray is to demonstrate. Would you pray with me?"

"What? Right now?"

"Sure. No-one worries about people praying in public places these days."

Sophie glanced around the restaurant with a nervous smile. Donna studied her sister for a few more seconds, then she closed her eyes and proceeded, slowly and thoughtfully.

"Heavenly Father, please help my sister Sophie. She's pretty confused right now. Please help her to trust you. Help her to find your peace that passes understanding. And Father, we bring Matt before you now, wherever he is. Whatever he's doing. Please look after him and bring him back safely to Sophie. Keep him safe, Lord. He's searching for truth. He's confused too. Please help both Matt and Sophie to see the truth and come to know you. They need to be strong at the moment. Please help them to find strength. And peace … and hope … in you."

When Donna looked up from her prayer, Sophie's eyes were glistening with tears. She brushed them away with her sleeve, embarrassed by a reaction she could not explain. It couldn't have been the religious stuff. Maybe it was the sisterly affection flowing across the little table. Whatever it was, she felt calmer, stronger, less alone.

Donna seemed to understand this. She smiled and simply said "Amen!"

It had been a long night. Matt had finally made it back home, and to bed, about 1.30 am. Even then, he couldn't sleep, except for a few hours between four and six when total exhaustion finally set in. But, as the lightness of morning filtered into his bedroom, Matt was far from refreshed. For the hundredth time, he revisited the events of last night. He knew he shouldn't have behaved the way he had. But Sophie shouldn't have pushed him. Didn't she know that he needed space sometimes?

A train of thought can travel faster than light. On some points, some stations, it can touch down fleetingly, a millisecond or two, and then roar off in some random direction. On other points, other stops, it can get bogged down for hours, perhaps days.

As Matt finished his cereal and fruit breakfast, and then slowly got dressed for work, a flashback of (what was her name? Brenda?) led Matt to briefly wonder how Sophie was this morning. Feelings of anger resurfaced but not for long. The problem was him, not her.

The train of thought could have stopped at concern for Sophie. But no, it raced away again, finally stopping, and remaining, at a dark place of self-loathing. How could he have allowed himself to be so weak? So stupid? How could he be so driven by rage? It wasn't the first time, so how could he break the pattern?

Reality check. He was too gutless, too spineless, to change anything. Perhaps Uncle Gavin was right.

By the time Matt arrived at work, he was already forty minutes late. He grunted a 'hello' to Lauren and plonked himself down at his desk. But Lauren went to Greg, concerned that maybe he wasn't well enough for work. Greg came to Matt and quickly agreed.

"Geez Matt! You look absolutely terrible. Are you sure you're OK for work?"

Matt nodded and tried to disguise his distress. But his pained face betrayed him. "No, I guess I'm not OK. But so what? I can't just stay home every time I'm not feeling great."

Greg studied him for a moment. "Listen mate, there are days when you really need to be home. And I think today's one of those days. We'll manage. You go home and rest up. Your accounts can wait a day or two."

Matt wanted to resist but his willpower failed. He went home and tried to sleep. But a knock at the door roused him. A woman from two streets away looking for her lost dog. Then a phone call from a salesman for a solar energy company, He decided to give up and check his blog instead.

The first comment roused his interest.

I saw you on tv and, when I looked up your blog, I knew I had to write. Religion is comforting for some but confusing for others. I think my work as a hospital counsellor gives me a good perspective on death and dying and I was worried for you, that you were just confusing things with your contest. Everyone has their own way of approaching these things. And yeah I respect your approach. I confess I haven't heard of anything quite like it before. But I feel compelled to warn you that you're complicating things too much.

No single religion is going to get you through this. In the end, it's not about what's right and what's wrong. And it's definitely not a game. It's about coming to a place where you're at peace with yourself and with those who love you. Matt, please hear me. I've seen hundreds of people go through this with their families and loved ones. And every single time it comes down to relationships. Life itself comes down to relationships. Dying well is all about relationships. Peace and love. That's absolutely the best way to go.

And, when you really think about it, it's the ultimate goal of all spirituality and faith. Peace and contentment. My advice is to open up with your family and close friends, as far as they can handle. Don't talk about religion. Just talk about your feelings, your fears, your regrets. Get them all out of your system.

I suspect there will be some people who will love you enough to listen and just be there for you. And that, my friend, will be your key to peace. Then, if you get through this, it will enrich your life. If you die, you will die well.

Signed Eleanor Johnson.

Matt got up from his computer desk, walked over to his kitchen and poured a glass of water from the refrigerator. This comment was a correction, a chastisement, a challenge. Returning to his seat, he brought up his scorecard file and added a point to a new category: 'Dying Well'.

Then he called Sophie. "Please can I come over? I'm so

terribly sorry for the way I've been behaving. I need to get some things off my chest. I need to make it right with you."

Progress score: Buddhism 2, Atheism, Christianity, Dying Well, Practical Stuff 1 point each.

"Did you have sex with her?"

"No … no I didn't."

Sophie was standing at her sink, looking out the window. Matt was seated behind her at the kitchen table. "How close did you come?" She turned to face him, eyes flashing with sad but fierce indignation.

Matt squirmed. "We just sort of made out, kissing and stuff, in the corner for … I don't know … a minute or so."

"Then what?"

Matt sighed. "Umm … her friend called her. Said they had to go. She gave me one last kiss and then just got off my lap and went. That was it. I think they were both laughing at me. I didn't even watch them go. I just covered my head in my hands. I was so ashamed. I am so ashamed."

"Do you know her name?"

"Ohh, Sophie, does it really matter?" pleaded Matt. "You're the only one I want to be with."

But Sophie's glare told him that it did matter. Very much in fact. "You said 'we'! We! You and I are supposed to be 'we'. So what was her damn name?"

Matt lowered his eyes. "I think she said her name was Brenda."

"You think?"

"OK … it was. Her name was Brenda. Sophie, I'm so sorry."

Sophie took a few steps toward Matt, then turned away again. Matt could see her fists clenched by her side. Nothing else to say. The ball was in her court. Slowly, the angry fists relaxed and Matt waited. When she turned to face him again, her hands went to her hips. Her face was red but calmer.

"One more question."

Matt nodded meekly. "Yeah, what is it?"

The rage drained from her eyes and her voice lowered.

"Did you enjoy her? Will you still think of her?"

"No … I don't care about her in the slightest."

"Did you enjoy her?"

Matt sighed. "Look, I suppose in the heat of the moment, I did enjoy the attention. I'll even admit that she was a very pretty young girl. But you have to know that I was in a really dark place. I was all messed up after yelling at you. I didn't want it to happen. It just did. And I'm so, so sorry. It will never happen again."

Sophie turned back toward the window. Matt watched her in silence, knowing that he had no right to disrespect her emotions. He was guilty, she was innocent. Finally, she came over to Matt and placed her arms across his shoulders. Blinking back a tear, she simply said: "I believe you. And I forgive you."

"Thank you," said Matt, surprised but relieved. "I'm just not sure I can forgive myself."

Sophie initiated a long, gentle kiss. "I'm trying to understand how it is for you, Matt. I really am." Then: "I've got an idea. My uncle Bill has a cottage up in the hills. Absolutely perfect for camping and fishing. What say I give him a call? See if we can go away for the weekend?"

"Hi Matt, it's Uncle Gavin."

"Hello Uncle Gav," said Matt, wondering how his uncle always managed to time his calls when he was alone. "What's up?"

"Nothing. Just checking up on my favourite nephew. How've you been?"

"Could be better," he admitted.

"The cancer giving you hell, is it?"

"No, not just that. I'm not a good person, Uncle Gav."

"Nonsense! You're a fine young man going through some stuff that no-one should ever have to go through."

Warning bells sounded in Matt's head but he brushed

them aside and owned up about the fight with Sophie. And about Brenda. He admitted that, right now, he hated himself and what he was becoming. Then he added: "Please don't tell any of this to Mum. She won't understand."

"Matt, you're an intelligent man. I think you're perfectly capable of working things out. You'll know what you have to do to protect Sophie. And don't worry, I don't talk with my sister much. She won't find out about our little phone calls."

"Thanks Uncle Gav. It's good to talk to someone who really gets me."

"No worries Matt. I'll keep in touch."

Late that night, Matt checked his blog again.

Heaven and hell are cruel fictions designed to play on our guilt and fear, wrote another reader. Christians and muslims are always prattling on about sin and hell because that's how they try to control people. If you want to get free from the ridiculous charade, you have to denounce all religion and admit there is no god. This world keeps spinning through the universe and it has nothing to do with any so-called god who wants to make everyone misserable. Everyone dies eventually but we all need comfort and encouragement when our time comes. Why should we spend our last days on thw planet wondering if we're going to spend thousands of years burning in agony. No one should die with that sort of threat over their heads.

Signed: Angry Atheist.

The thought of rejecting guilt on principle resonated with Matt. Especially now. The comment was badly written but perhaps this was an approach he could try. He added another point to Atheism.

By coincidence, the next blogger took a similar, although milder, position.

Millions of people have died since the first cave-man. No-one ever came back to tell us what happens. It's a mystery that will never be solved while we're alive. So my advice is to stop thinking about this life-after-death nonsense and concentrate on making the best of every day. Think about what you know and understand, not the things you can't! Focus on understanding your life, what it's been and what it is. Focus on what it means just to be you.

Signed: take it easy.

"OK," thought Matt. "I suppose that counts as a different point. But what should I give it to?"

How would you describe yourself? he replied. *Are you an agnostic?*

The reply came back eventually.

Some would call me agnostic because I insist that no-one knows for sure. But I'm more of an atheist. I just don't believe that any kind of god exists.

Another point for atheism, but this time somewhat reluctantly.

There was one other standout among the blog comments that night.

The most important thing is that you die in peace. If there are people you need to forgive, do it now. If there are people you need to ask for forgiveness, do that too. If you have people in your life that your awkward around, or you've lied to, or you've been avoiding, I urge you to sort all these things out. You don't want to die with anything on your conscience. You're an eternal soul but, like all of us eternal souls, the thing we're searching for is peace with the universe. If you're at peace with the universe when your life is over that peace will carry into eternity.

Matt thought long and hard about this last one. It sounded like some sort of Buddhist philosophy mixed with a touch of this and that. But the blogger's name told Matt where the next point could go. New Age Nellie.

Progress score: Atheism 3, Buddhism 2, Christianity, Dying Well, New Age, and Practical Stuff 1 point each.

Saturday 11th April
Sophie and Matt set up their tent some thirty metres from

her uncle's cottage, on a level piece of ground near the track that led down to the creek. They sat together on a rusty old bench seat that overlooked a lavishly forested valley. Sophie nestled wordlessly into his shoulder. For Matt, this was a "who-knows-if-I-can-ever-do-this-again" weekend. He tried to understand what it meant to Sophie. Obviously, for her, it was all about intimacy. To that end, she was trying to be as lovable and accommodating as a girl could possibly be.

They walked and laughed and fished through the afternoon. Sophie even stripped off and went for a brief swim in the creek after they packed up their fishing gear. But the water was cold and the creek wasn't deep enough to swim properly so she emerged immediately, her embarrassed smirk giving Matt his best laugh in years.

The evening air was chilly but they made a small fire, over which they cooked their one and only catch for the afternoon, a small brown trout, supplemented by some potato salad and a tin of baked beans. The eggs would keep for breakfast. There was a telephone in the cottage if necessary but mobile phones were useless out here. So far as they knew, they were the only two human beings for miles around.

No arguments. No tense words. Just a fun time shared by two people whose good times were on notice. When it was time to hit the sleeping bags, Sophie started to unzip the single sleeping bags in order to zip them together as a double. But Matt stopped her. She stared at him suspiciously. "Why? What's going on?"

Matt weighed his words carefully. "I … was thinking maybe we should wait until we're married."

Sophie almost choked. "What did you say? I don't think I heard you right."

"I … I thought we might wait. It's only six weeks or so."

Her mouth was wide open now, in shock. Then a bewildered frown. "But Matt, we've been doing it for years already! Why would you want to stop now?" Then another thought. "Is it that Brenda chick?"

"God, no! Absolutely not! Nothing to do with her!"

"Then ..."

Matt reached out to grab both Sophie's hands in his own. "Look at me Soph. Please. What if it's a sin? I mean, what if this cancer is some kind of warning sign ... that I ... we ... have to start doing things different?"

"It's not a sin!" protested Sophie. "Not if we love each other."

Matt just shrugged his shoulders as if to say: "I don't know; that's just how I'm feeling right now."

Sophie sighed and shook her head in exasperation. "I love you Matt ... but it feels like you're rejecting me. Like I'm not pretty enough or something. Don't you ... want me?"

"I do want you! And I'm certainly not rejecting you."

"Well ..." Her voice trailed off into the next question. "What about my feelings? Don't they count for anything?"

"Of course. It's not all about me. I know that. But listen. What if there are other ways for two people to show love to each other? What if we're supposed to learn how to relate spiritually? What if we're missing out on something important because it just keeps coming back to the sex?"

Sophie threw her arms in the air, a gesture of frustration mixed with resignation. "OK, OK! I really don't get what you're saying but I suppose I can play along." She glared at him, the faintest twinkle in her eyes betraying respect rather than anger. "But you have to tell me what you want me to do, 'cause I sure as hell don't know anymore!"

They were awakened in the early hours of the morning by the sound of heavy rain. Sophie offered Matt the option of retreating to the house but he refused. He was warm and dry and it was quite pleasant listening to the rain in the nearby trees and on the tent. There was no wind to speak of, just the rain. They lay there listening for a long time, side by side in their separate sleeping bags.

"Do I think too much?" asked Matt, sensing from Sophie's breathing that she was still awake.

It took a few moments for Sophie to answer. "I think you have to. I don't know Matt. I often wonder how I could cope in your situation." Long, thoughtful pause as the rain continued pounding the tent. "I saw a movie once where this guy was supposed to be dying and he decided he was going to do all the mad things on his bucket list. Only, in the end, crossing a lot of silly experiences off a stupid list didn't do it for him. It didn't help him get ready for what was coming."

"Mmm."

"I don't know, Matt. It's all so confusing. I wish I knew."

Silence. Listening to the rain.

"I want to be there for you," continued Sophie. "I would love nothing better than to have a long, happy life with you. But if that's not to be … I guess I just want to be as close to you as I can for as long as I can."

More silence. More rain. Sophie looked across and saw that Matt had drifted off to sleep.

9 - THOUSANDS OF YEARS

Sunday 12th April

Matt originally intended to update his blog once a week, on Sunday mornings. Editing the comments that came in was a daily task but he needed to keep up some serious input of his own for followers. So, when he and Sophie returned from their overnight camping adventure, he planned to write something that would pick up on New Age Nellie's "peace with the universe" comment. But when he checked the blog, he noticed that a few readers had already posted replies. One comment especially stood out.

You cannot make peace with something that is not a person. I can make peace with my friend if I have offended her, or she can make peace with me. Making peace implies that there's been some sort of broken relationship. New Age Nellie says you should "make peace with the universe" but the universe is not a person. You have never offended the universe and it has never offended you. How can it? It's a thing not a person.

God on the other hand is personal. Not a person like you or me but still someone that we can have relationship with. Or we can mess up our relationship with Him. I think people like New Age Nellie understand that something is not right, like when you've offended a friend and you have that horrible feeling that things are not cool between the two of you. But what they're really feeling is the feeling that they are not right with God.

For anyone facing death, therefore, it is all about making peace with God, not the universe. God is personal, the universe is not. God made the rules that we break, so the problem is with him, not with the universe that he made. The great thing about the Christian message is that, because of Jesus, we can have forgiveness. By receiving him, we make peace with God.

Signed Shelley.

Matt uttered a little grunting noise, part surprise and part amusement. He didn't know he was having an argument with God. But he certainly had to concede that he wasn't having a relationship issue with the universe either. Yes, there were relationship issues with Sophie. Perhaps his decision to stop having sex with her until after the wedding was not helping. But maybe it was. And, if God turned out to be real, perhaps his decision would help with that as well.

For a moment, he stared out the window into the night blackness of his back yard garden. Gathering thoughts. Contemplating how to start, and what to say. Then, opening his laptop, he began to write.

Lots of my readers have highlighted the importance of relationships, and the fact that we don't know how much time we have left with the people closest to us. This has been brought home most powerfully to me in the past few days. Some people talk about making our peace with the universe. And, despite the fact that I gave a point to New Age theory recently, I don't really understand how this can be. The universe is made up of stars and galaxies, trees and mountains, rivers and cities, atoms and molecules. So wouldn't all those different things have to somehow be one living organism that we could relate to before making peace with it would make sense? I don't feel like I'm one with the universe. I just feel like the universe is the environment that we all live in. Whatever "relationship" I have with my environment is not a personal one. So I'm not going to take away the point I already gave to New Age but I think Shelley's comment warrants a point for Christianity. I'll be interested to see if any of my readers want to follow up on this.

Progress score: Atheism 3, Buddhism and Christianity 2, Dying Well, New Age and Practical Stuff 1 point each.

Monday 13th April

Matt was ten minutes late for his lunch date with Sophie the next day. She had already ordered and the sandwiches and orange juice were waiting with her at the two-person table beside the window. "You'd never believe it," puffed Matt, squeezing into his seat. "I've just signed up a new client and I used a line from last night's blogging!"

Sophie blinked at him. "What? How is that possible?"

Matt laughed. "Tuffet and Gidenski Solicitors. They loved the tag line I wrote for them."

Sophie gestured with her hand for Matt to elaborate but he wanted her to ask, which she did with a sigh. "And what was that?"

Matt paused for dramatic effect. "You might be at peace with the universe but come see us for everything else."

Sophie winced. "That's horrible!"

"I know," grinned Matt, "but they went for it. We're using it in a new TV campaign starting next month. Sure, it's a bit tongue-in-cheek but they didn't want to come over too serious. They thought it was perfect."

Sophie shook her head in disbelief. "What can I say?"

"Congratulations maybe?"

"Ahh, no way. You'll just get a big head. Bigger head."

Then: "Just hurry up and eat your lunch. I haven't got all day."

They ate in silence for a few seconds but Matt had weightier matters on his mind. "I'm getting the message that life is all about relationships. People say things like that all the time. They seem to think that nothing else really matters in the end. But … well …" He caught Sophie's eye. "Well, I'm worried that I'm getting more and more grumpy as the cancer does its thing in me. I'm worried that I'm going to end up stuffing up all my relationships. Like the other night. I don't know what came over me. But it scares me. How could I do that to you? And how can I be sure I won't do it again?"

"You won't do that again," insisted Sophie. No hesitation or qualification; it was an absolute statement. No correspondence would be entered into.

"Did your Mum say she can take you over to Dr Barlow this afternoon?" Matt nodded with a mixture of relief and wonder. Nothing more would ever need to be said about the pretty young blonde at the roadhouse.

For the second time in three weeks, the Monday night family dinner had to be take-away. Terry and Julie had to get their refrigerator serviced after it developed an ominous leak. So Chinese it was. Terry voiced his concern that this might not be the best food for Matt but he was overruled. Josh and Leslie collected the order on their way to Terry and Julie's home.

Matt's appointments were, by now, common knowledge within the family. Last week, he had to report on the counselling session with John Vickers. This week, it was all about his latest appointment with Dr Barlow.

Julie and Leslie shared out the food from the various tubs, paying special attention to the children. Terry wanted to know what the oncologist had said.

"Well," said Matt. "Like everyone else, he was glad to hear that I gave up smoking a year or so back." Josh immediately took on a sheepish grin. As the only smoker in the immediate family, he had often declared his intention to quit.

"And?" pressed Terry.

"And he wants to book me in for a mild course of chemotherapy." Worried looks around the table prompted Matt to continue. "He thinks my age might work in my favour. Less side-effects than an older person. Maybe. He just wants me to give it a go."

"When do you think that will happen?" asked Julie.

"No dates as yet," said Matt. "But probably starting in the next few weeks."

Sophie broke in. "They'll keep him in hospital for two, maybe three days, just to keep an eye on things."

Julie shook her head anxiously. "I've heard so many horror stories about chemo."

"So have I," admitted Matt. "But I do believe they understand a lot more about the various chemicals they use these days. Dr Barlow doesn't work out the doses himself. He'll refer me to a chemo specialist."

"Wow," said Terry. "Anything else we should know about?"

"As a matter of fact …" Matt spoke guardedly. "Yeah, one other thing. I … um … asked him about your apricot kernels suggestion."

"And?"

Matt helped himself to some fried rice. "Well, we had quite a long talk about so-called alternative therapies."

"And?"

Matt smiled at his Dad's eagerness. This was going to be a mixture of good and bad news. "He doesn't really believe that there's any solid evidence for dietary things like that. But he has read up on it and he admits there are some impressive stories out there."

Julie finally sat down, satisfied that everyone had sufficient share of the food. "Go on," she urged. "Does he think you could benefit from some of these alternative treatments?"

Matt could see that he wasn't going to be doing much eating tonight. There was so much to try to explain.

"Dr Barlow doesn't want me to do anything without

107

talking with Dr Tan. But he went on and on about cancer sufferers having the right to choose whatever treatments they feel comfortable with. He said they preferred to call them complementary treatments these days because they could often be used alongside regular treatments. He described all sorts of things, from vegetarian diets, to acupuncture, to some sort of strange microwave machine that they have in New Zealand. He gave me heaps of pamphlets and booklets. We even talked about hypnosis. And visualisation techniques. I didn't realise there were so many people trying to find ways to cure cancer."

Terry nodded. "And so many people who think they already have found cures."

Leslie frowned. "Sounds complex. Did he recommend anything in particular?"

"Not really. Like I said, he just wanted me to run my choices past Dr Tan. He wants to see what effect a course of chemotherapy might have. His main role will be to monitor the progress, or lack of progress, of the cancer. And he said that, if I wanted to try an alternative … uh … complementary therapy as well, I should make up my mind what I wanted to try, and then stick to it. He said he's had some patients that changed their minds every few weeks and nothing worked because nothing had any reasonable chance."

"So is there anything in these brochures that appeals to you?" pressed Terry.

"Well that's the thing," said Matt. "I can see that there are some important decisions to be made but I've got so much on my mind." He focused especially on his Dad. "I want to work as long as possible. And, of course, I'm getting married." Sophie grinned. "And I still need time for the blog."

He looked around at the family. Only the children were eating. Everyone else was waiting for what Matt would say next.

"Dad, I guess I was hoping that you would sort through all the various options and I'll make a time later this week … or next week … to listen to your suggestions."

Terry nodded sternly. But Matt wasn't finished. "Please

understand that I'm not holding out any hope of a full recovery. But what have I got to lose? If something, somehow, works some kind of miracle, I'll be the happiest person in the world. But I won't want to do anything that will make my life a misery in the meantime. It has to be about balancing any possible improvement with the quality of life that I have in the meantime. Understood?"

Terry nodded again. "Understood! Thanks, Matt."

Tuesday 14th April

Dr Barlow's secretary called Matt at work. The chemotherapy could start on the following Tuesday but Dr Barlow wanted Matt admitted to the hospital on Monday morning. When Matt explained about the birthday party planned for that night and how much it meant for his family, the secretary checked with the doctor and came back to the phone confirming a Tuesday morning admission instead. Matt asked if he would be able to bring his laptop and the answer was yes. They would not even expect him to be confined to bed during his treatment.

Matt spoke with Greg and offered to continue working on some accounts during his hospitalisation but Greg refused the offer. "See what we can get through by Monday and we'll take it from there. Your health issues have to take priority over your work."

Later in the afternoon, a quick call from Dr Tan's surgery revealed that the doctor was running late with his appointments. Matt was glad to fit in an extra hour at work before his appointment. He always dreaded these appointments but, driving to the medical centre, he realised this was a good chance to get some added perspective on the chemo option. He quickly rehearsed what he planned to say.

"I'm not coping well with my life at the moment." Yes, that was it. That's what he would say. And one question. "How am I supposed to cope with chemotherapy?"

Definitive answers about cancer, however, like answers about life and death in general, would prove elusive. The conversation with Dr Tan was littered with 'if's, 'but's and 'maybe's. Options were multiplying, both physically and spiritually, but Matt was only becoming more and more confused. Decisions would have to be made, but how could he know what was right?

Wednesday 15th April.

Matt had been working on an advertising campaign for a local plumber who was expanding his business. The plumber's wife, who knew the business thoroughly after handling accounts and enquiries for many years, took on the job of organising the publicity. She was especially interested to meet Matt, having seen his video and followed his blog. This was now her third consultation. Greg, Matt's boss, was concerned that things were getting somewhat off track, but he also realised that, in this case at least, Matt's blog was guaranteeing a worthwhile account.

"So tell me, Matt," she ventured. "How come you haven't given any points so far to Catholics? Don't you think our views are …" she searched for the right phrase, "… meaningful enough?"

Matt looked up from his computer. "Nah, it's not that. I don't think I've had many comments from Catholic people." He tried to recall any definite examples but ended up shrugging his shoulders. "I don't know. I suppose I thought that Catholic and Christian were pretty much the same thing. Why? Is there something unique about a Catholic approach to death and dying?"

"Well, yeah. Very much so. You see, Catholics believe in a place called Purgatory where you have to go after you die."

"Yeah. Tell me more."

"Um, I don't really understand it properly … but I think you go to a place of darkness where you sort of pay for all the sins you've done, at least the ones that outweigh all the good you've done. Does that make sense?"

Matt smiled self-consciously. This woman was a valued client, not someone to argue with. "So if you knew you were

dying ... like I do, for instance ... how would that help you?"
He thought about adding another question but decided to leave
it at that for now.

"You can call a priest to come and do last rites. I'm not
sure but I think that covers a lot of your sins, so you have less
time in Purgatory."

"Yeah, but I'm not a Catholic. The priest wouldn't
come."

"Well, I suppose you could go to a church and do
confession. That would get you started."

"What, confess all my sins to a priest that I can't see in
some sort of box?" Matt smiled, not mockingly, but sceptically.
"That will help?"

"It might." She thought of something else. "You can also
get your friends to pray for you. You know, after you've gone.
Sorry. That wasn't too sensitive of me. But ... um, I think it
cuts down your time in Purgatory if there are lots of people
praying for your soul. I mean, you wouldn't want to be there
for, like, thousands of years, would you?"

She noticed the incredulity on Matt's face. "Yes, well,
back to the matter at hand!" she announced sheepishly. "You're
saying you think we should go with the morning time slot for
our TV ads?"

Was it coincidence or just increased awareness? That
night, Matt thought he picked up on a few blog comments that
seemed to be from Catholics. Perhaps he just hadn't identified
them before. He decided to pose some questions.

*Can someone tell me about Purgatory? Is it real or just a
thing made up to scare people into religion? If I go to
Purgatory when I die, how long will I stay there? What if I'm
not a Catholic? How is it supposed to work?*

In the following days, there were a number of replies to
these questions. One respondent claimed to be a Catholic
theologian, which Matt found a bit intimidating. His answers,
sadly, went straight over Matt's head. Something to do with
different types of sins, a technical distinction between pardon
and satisfaction for sins, and "heroic acts" of people who

111

somehow dedicated their own "meritorious" works to the credit of relatives, or even people they didn't know, in Purgatory. To Matt, all this was neither convincing nor helpful. It was not going to get a point.

Other correspondents took the line that only properly qualified Catholic priests could absolve sins but the Pope could approve certain acts of contrition or service that would effectively remove any further need for payment for sins, thus removing the threat of Purgatory entirely. Matt considered these posts but concluded that they were more about one church claiming to be right where all the others were wrong.

One correspondent quoted a verse from the gospels where Jesus apparently said, "Whosoever speaketh against the Holy Ghost, it shall not be forgiven him, neither in this world, neither in the world to come." This, insisted the commentator, who called himself Logical Joe (where did they get these names?), proved that some sins could be forgiven in the afterlife. Therefore Purgatory was real and should be taken seriously.

All the same, Matt remained unconvinced.

Even Robert Smith chimed in briefly on this debate.

Purgatory is a Catholic doctrine that rests on a very shaky scriptural basis, mainly a single passage in the book of 2nd Maccabees, a book that Catholics have in their Bible but the Protestant churches have always rejected.

Don't be too concerned about that. The point is that lots of people have thought about the doctrine of Purgatory and rejected it. For good reason. It was part of Martin Luther's motivation for starting the reformation. He was disgusted that Pope Leo X was offering indulgences for people who contributed to the rebuilding of St Peter's basilica in Rome, especially when he heard one of the Pope's revenue collectors saying: "As soon as a coin in the coffer rings, a soul from Purgatory springs."

In other words, they were telling people that their donations would immediately get their loved ones out of Purgatory. Martin Luther was furious that people's religious sensitivities were being exploited for money.

Purgatory is not in the Bible, Matt. I don't believe for one minute that there is such a place. When Jesus died for our sins, He died for all our sins. The whole idea of Purgatory is very, very wrong!

Robert S.

Still no point for Catholicism, Matt's Little Bird client notwithstanding.

Thursday 16th April

The next day, Matt left for home as soon as Greg arrived back from his lunch appointment. He had already eaten a sandwich and an apple but his stomach wasn't feeling right and he thought some chocolate might help. He could also stock up on some soft drinks or flavoured tea drinks. Who knows? he thought. Depending on what my Dad comes up with, these things might be off the menu for good. May as well enjoy them now.

At the end of the confectionery aisle, a commotion was brewing. A highly flustered woman was trying to separate a boy and a girl, perhaps eight or nine years old, and a male store manager was trying unsuccessfully to calm everyone down. The children were shouting at each other.

"I did not try to steal anything, you bitch!"

The girl snapped back, a smug grin on her face. "Yes you did! I saw you!"

"Bitch, bitch! I hate you!"

"Jayden, stop using that word!" hissed the mother. The manager tried to make the point that nothing was missing. Everyone should just settle down. But the young boy was determined to convince his mother, and the whole world if necessary, that he was innocent. His sister, on the other hand, was equally determined to convince everyone that he was lying and she was telling the truth. "I saw him, Mum," she persisted.

The commotion continued as Matt moved on. From the fruit and vegetable aisle, the shouting didn't sound as loud. A couple of other shoppers caught his eye with a look that said:

"I'm so glad those kids are not mine."

Matt picked out some bananas and headed for the drink aisle. He fantasised about having some sort of truth spray that would make it easy to tell who was telling the truth and who was lying. Just a short spray into the air and everyone within ten metres would be forced to tell the truth. Ha! Wouldn't that be cool? But then again, what if both kids really believed that they were telling the truth? Perhaps his magical spray wouldn't work if the lies weren't deliberate.

When Matt arrived home, he opened his blog and posed a question.

So many different opinions and I respect all the contributions that my readers are making but how does anyone know that what they're saying is true? I'm sure you're all very sincere but, in the end, when it comes to life after death, aren't they all just unproven theories?

Friday 17th April
The next evening, a comment appeared from Robert Smith that brought up a third point for Christianity.

You've heard from all sorts of people and all sorts of religions since you've been doing this blog. And you're right to ask how we can know what is true and what is false. There is always an element of faith in these things. In one sense, we believe what we choose to believe. It doesn't matter if it lines up with reality or not. We just believe what we want to believe. But here's the thing. The Bible actually does line up with reality. It talks about the souls of people leaving their bodies when they die and I think everyone who's ever seen a dead body can admit that the person they knew was no longer there. The whole personality and soul has gone. What's left is just an empty shell. Death doesn't mean that anything suddenly ceases to exist. The body is still there when a person has died and the soul still exists too. It can't just disappear or cease to exist.

Then again, I've been reading up on near death experiences, where people stop breathing or something, and they're clinically dead for a few minutes. They often go through a long dark tunnel and then they face this being of light who takes them through a process of judging their lives. Matt, all this lines up perfectly with what the Bible says. The soul of the person continues on and they're still the same person. They can still remember things from their life. And it's just one life. They don't remember hundreds of former lives. Just one!

Matt, I know you don't want to do a lot of extra-curricular reading and I understand your reasons. But I also have to add that the Bible comes across as totally believable. There's a lot of historical detail that has been proved true. Other religious books, when you read them, come across as theories. But the Bible truly does come across as God's Word, accurately describing reality as it is. These are just some of the reasons why I am now totally convinced that the Christian faith is true in a way that none of the other faiths are. And that the Bible is exactly what it claims to be, the Word of God.

Robert S.

"Nice try Robert," thought Matt. "I'm pretty sure everyone thinks their own particular religious books are more believable than the others!"

But, cynicism aside, he had to concede it was worth a point.

Progress score: Atheism and Christianity 3, Buddhism 2, Dying Well, New Age and Practical Stuff 1 point each.

Surprisingly, this latest comment from Robert stirred up more controversy than anything else on Matt's blog. Over the next few days, several blog readers took offence at the thought that the Bible was believable. One woman called it a *"hangover from the days of myth and superstition"*. Someone else ranted that the miracle stories made the Bible *"a literary joke"* for intelligent modern people. And one simply insisted that the Bible had been disproved *"zillions of times"*.

But the most scathing comment came from someone calling himself Mick.

How can you say that the Bible is believable? It's all b … nonsense! THAT'S WHAT IT IS! B … NONSENSE! What! All the animals in the world on one boat? People walking on water? Walking on dry land through the middle of an ocean? Seriously??? It's all RUBBISH. Absolute RUBBISH! What! People living for 100s of years! Talking snakes! Water turned into wine! The Bible is AN INSULT TO MY INTELLIGENCE! It's just a bunch of cute old CHILDREN'S STORIES! Not that I would ever read it to MY grandkids! It was never even meant to be taken seriously. What! Jesus rising from the dead? Well, where is he NOW? If he's still alive, why hasn't anyone SEEN him lately? He's coming back? Really? Christians have been believing that one for thousands of years. But it still hasn't happened! Come on, mate! You've got an interesting blog but you're spoiling it when you give points to IDIOTS! I'm not going to follow it any more. Sorry.

This was perilously close to falling foul of Matt's obscenity criteria. He cleaned up a few words using dots. But, other than that, he left it up as it was. Mick's rant would, in turn, go on to draw out several new commentators, including some that Matt couldn't delete quickly enough.

One comment, though, cut across the general tone of the night's conversation.

Evolution is the really big story in the universe. There is no god. All this amazing variety of life that we see around us is the result of billions of years of evolution. It's a proven fact. I know it's not much consolation for someone in your position but nothing is wasted in this universe. Your life is part of the great meta-story of life. The constant struggle of life and death is what moves us forward and we can't change that reality. But there's nothing to fear in death. You won't know about it when it happens. There won't be any regrets or punishments. You just have to trust that you're part of a really big, wonderful story, the story of evolution.

Signed "resigned to it".

Matt didn't appreciate the sentiment but it stayed with him as he tried to sleep that night. Evolution must be true:

116

everyone said so, didn't they? And if it was true, then "resigned to it" probably had a realistic approach to dying. Matt didn't like it but he felt he had no choice but to award another point for atheism. There was meaning to life but that meaning would only be apparent after thousands of years.

Progress score: Atheism 4, Christianity 3, Buddhism 2, Dying Well, New Age and Practical Stuff 1 point each.

10 - MAKE IT WORK

Monday 20th April

The invitations for Matt's thirty-third birthday party barely went out three weeks before the event but the RSVP list was impressive. Since the birthday fell on a Monday, Julie had insisted that the party be held on the Monday evening, thus fitting in nicely with the new tradition of Monday evening family dinners. The overwhelmingly positive response to the invitations was in no small part due to the heart-felt wording that Julie included. "We cannot know how Matt will fare in the next twelve months. Please help us make this a special occasion for him."

Terry hired the local greyhound club hall for the occasion and arranged the drinks. Julie ordered in a spit-roast lamb and several trays of hors d'oevres. Then she set about preparing five varieties of salad. She baked a mammoth birthday cake, made sandwiches and baked dozens of butterfly cakes. With Sophie's help, they decorated the hall on the Sunday afternoon.

Sophie had already organised a live band that she knew Matt would enjoy.

But one aspect of the planning was beyond anyone's control. Matt woke up feeling groggy and extremely nauseous, with an intense pain in his left side. He phoned Sophie at her work and said that he didn't know how he would cope with a birthday party. Perhaps they should call it off. Sophie rang Julie, who, in turn, called Trish Owens, the charge nurse at Palliative Care, and begged for help. But Trish was unable to get anyone there until two in the afternoon. Julie fretted that their birthday preparations would all be for nothing. She called Sophie again to see if she had contacted Dr Barlow about the chemotherapy that was due the next day. Yes, she had, and he had advised that the hospital admission should go ahead as planned. They would assess things from there.

Annie caught a train from the airport to Mona Shores and a taxi brought her straight to the Greyhound Club. She bustled in with her suitcase and a dress bag, scanning for her Mum and hoping she might be able to help with something. Julie came rushing out of the kitchen, smiled and hugged her daughter fervently. Yes, there was still much to do but it would all be a waste of time if Matt couldn't make it. Perhaps Annie could visit her brother.

Annie took her mother's car for the ten minute drive to Matt's house. There was no answer when she knocked, so she opened the door a little and called out. Still no answer. For one dreadful moment, she wondered if her little brother was gone. But then a weak answer. "Annie?"

She quickly stifled her relief and followed Matt's voice to his bedroom. "Hi little brother. Happy birthday!"

Matt was lying shirtless in his bed, awkwardly propped up on three pillows. His face was jaundiced and pale, his eyes heavy and disconsolate. The curtains were closed, except for a slight gap at the top. Annie thought she could literally smell the dreariness in the room. A television was on but the sound was very low. Without taking his eyes off the TV, Matt struggled to sit up straighter. Annie took the hint and came over to fix the pillows.

"Tough day?"

Matt nodded, a frustrated glimmer in his eyes. "Some days … you know."

Annie flashed a sympathetic smile. "How do you cope?"

Matt continued watching his TV movie and Annie wondered if he had heard her question. But he admitted that he wasn't coping all that well. "I've just been lying here hoping the day would hurry up and be over."

Annie moved a food tray and sat on the corner of Matt's bed. "You know everyone's desperately hoping you can make it to the party. They've put a lot of work into this."

Matt rubbed his eyes and yawned. "Yeah, I know. I'm sorry."

Annie had mentally prepared a little speech on the drive over but wisely held it back. Now she watched as her brother, in rapid succession, shifted from weary annoyance through miserable anger and self-pity, arriving surprisingly at a moment of thoughtful resignation. "Yeah, I probably should make an effort. But I hope people will understand if I can't stick around for long."

"You worried about the chemo?"

Matt nodded. "It's pretty scary."

"Can you have visitors in hospital during the treatment?"

"Yeah, I think so."

"Good. I don't have to be home for a few days. I'll be able to visit you there."

More silence.

"Have you checked your blog today?"

"No." Several more seconds of silence, then: "Some days I don't bother."

"Is it normal to have days like this?"

Matt shrugged half-heartedly. "I don't know, Sis. If I thought every day was going to be like this, I suppose I'd have to find some way to get motivated. But so far, these days usually only come one at a time. So I just put up with it."

"Are you still finding this blog thing interesting? Is it

helping in some way?"

"Yeah, but man there's some wacky stuff out there. Sometimes it all gets a bit … I don't know … surreal?" The last word came out as a question. Matt wasn't sure it was the right word for what he meant.

"I've been following it all pretty closely. Some fascinating stuff. This guy Robert seems to write in quite a bit."

"Yeah, he's one of my regulars. One of the Christians. It'd be nice in a way if he turned out to be right. You know, Heaven, living forever, all that stuff."

"I sense a 'but' coming," prodded Annie.

"Well, it's just that … well, some days I feel like I'm losing it. Like today. If Heaven is real, I don't think I've got enough time to balance the scales. The cancer messes with my head and I end up lashing out at people. I can be pretty horrible. So I don't think I would deserve to go to Heaven anyway."

"Wow." Annie couldn't think of anything else to say. Finally, she decided to brighten things up. "Listen to me, little brother. I'll pick you up around eight if you can get showered and dressed by then. Or Sophie can come. One of us anyway. Then I'll make sure you're home by nine. Think of it as a good chance to be un-grumpy and nice, you know, to balance that scale a bit better."

Matt smiled weakly. "I'll try."

Several of Matt's friends attended the birthday party, joining family members and the entire staff of Little Bird. Some of these friends, however, were noticeably uncomfortable. What do you talk about when your friendship has been built around cricket and surfing and a social life that was rapidly disappearing? With Sophie and Matt's family claiming the prime positions in his life, and cancer forcing more and more alone time, there was less and less time for anyone else.

Nevertheless, when Matt entered the reception hall, arm

in arm with Sophie, and with Annie close behind, the cheering was warm and genuine. The band stopped mid-song out of respect for the guest of honour but no one would have been listening to them anyway.

People gathered around Matt to shake his hand or kiss him on the cheek. A comfortable seat was provided, drinks and food offered. Friends and relatives took up places in nearby seats, waiting their turn to talk. Matt cursed the timing of his bad day. He should have been enjoying this opportunity but instead it was rapidly wearing him out. And tomorrow threatened to be even worse. Would people judge him to be further down the slippery slope to death than he actually was? Would this make them more awkward around him, and maybe even drive some of them away for good? He wasn't feeling "nice" and he felt he couldn't trust himself to say the right things. The little sandwich triangles on the plate on his lap were sadly unappealing; this was just one of those zero appetite days that Dr Barlow had warned him about.

After half an hour of this, Matt excused himself and made his way to the bar where Sophie was catching up with Annie. He apologised for interrupting but, if there were any formalities to be carried out, it would have to be soon. He was not coping well. Sophie asked what was wrong but knew instantly that the question was pointless. She found Julie and asked if the birthday cake could be brought out. Annie, meanwhile, sought out her Dad and asked him to get the formalities under way. He looked at his watch but Annie nodded discretely in Matt's direction and Terry understood. Even so, it was another ten minutes before the guests were gathered in front of the little display table that bore the birthday cake.

Terry's voice boomed out over the roar of conversation. "Excuse me, everyone. Can I have your attention please!" As the chattering voices faded to a hush, he looked around at some eighty men and women, plus a smattering of much younger guests. "Thank you for coming tonight. I hope you're all having a great time. Um … I'm sure Matt will want to respond, and personally thank you for being here tonight. But before we sing Happy Birthday and do all those traditional things, I would just like to say … Matt … I think you're amazing. Your courage, thoughtfulness, intelligence and positive outlook are nothing short of inspiring. I don't think I could do what you are doing. Mum and I are barely getting by, but you …" his voice began to crack, "…you seem to find purpose in everything, even this enemy, this cancer!" The last, dreaded word was spat out with a vehemence that surprised everyone who knew him. "Matt, we all want you to fight this enemy to the last breath. We want you to fight, but …", he sighed, "… but it's your fight, Son, not mine, not ours. And that's the frustrating thing. We feel so helpless. We feel so …" no, there was no better word, "… helpless." But then: "Hey … tonight is not about cancer, or sickness, or pain. Tonight is a celebration of life." Terry closed his little speech in a crescendo of mustered determination. People responded with generous applause and Sophie stepped up to the microphone.

"Hi," she began with a nervous smile. She pointed to the birthday cake and the candles that Julie was in the process of lighting. "There are thirty-three candles on this cake. And, yeah, I know it looks a bit childish. We'll probably have the fire brigade here in a minute or two." Muffled giggles. "But I think these candles symbolise life. All our candles will be extinguished eventually. We shine for a while but …" she spoke slowly, "… we will all die one day. The doctors say that Matt is dying but, you know, he's not the only one. It might be soon, or it might be another seventy years from now. But we're all just passing through this life. The thing is to make the best of the time we have, to enjoy the friends we have, and to love someone special while we have the chance."

Sophie's musings ended suddenly and she had already moved away from the microphone before a polite round of applause broke out. Annie stepped up to lead in the singing of Happy Birthday. Matt took three attempts to blow out all his candles.

After Matt's faltering thank-you speech, Terry returned

to propose a toast. In doing so, he announced a birthday gift that he and several other family members had jointly funded. "You can think of it as a birthday present but it's also our way of helping you to have a memorable honeymoon." He handed Matt an envelope as guests cheered.

The envelope contained two tickets for a ten day cruise out of Brisbane, visiting places like New Caledonia and Vanuatu.

"We've already checked with your doctors and the cruise company. They have fantastic medical facilities on board and Dr Barlow will forward some instructions. He'll also make sure that all your scripts are up to date."

Sophie gasped and put her hand to her mouth in excitement. Matt's first instinct was to protest that it should be up to the bride and groom to plan their honeymoon. But he remembered the inconclusive discussions that he'd been having with Sophie and the doubts about just what he would be capable of enjoying. This option did indeed sound perfect. "Thank you, Dad," he admitted. "Thanks everyone. This will be much better than anything we could have afforded. Thanks!"

Tuesday 21st April

Matt woke several times through the night. Thoughts about chemo, about hospital, about Greg, Walter and Kerry covering for him at work. They had been so good, so understanding. Thoughts about Sophie and the uncertain life he was bringing her into. A life devoid of any realistic hope. Each time he woke, he tossed and turned, then rolled over and drifted back to a restive sleep. Conversations and faces from the party played out in his mind. By the time he showered and came out for breakfast, it was already 9.20. Forty minutes to get ready for hospital.

He smiled when he noticed the various trinkets, boxes of chocolates and birthday cards from the party neatly arranged on his dining table. Annie would have done that, he thought. He closed his eyes for a moment, seeking to unearth some strength for the day. Then He selected a box of cereal, some milk, a bowl and a spoon and sat down to read through his cards.

"Love to you and Sophie. Anything you need, just call. We're always there for you."

"Cancer sucks. Be strong."

"Never forget the good times."

"Wishing you more good days than bad days."

"Wish we could do more to help you."

"Constantly in our thoughts."

And there were many others.

Matt carefully placed the cards along the top of a bookshelf in his living room. Thinking back on some of the good times made him feel alive. But, on the other hand, he wondered about some of these friends. They were busy people with active lives. Would they have time for him as the cancer progressed? Would he even want them around? Would he ever see them again?

Matt's anti-cancer chemicals were administered intravenously while he sat in an arm-chair beside his hospital bed. Julie came in and sat with him for a while but left when he declared that he needed a nap. The hospital staff woke him to check his pulse, temperature and blood pressure but he fell asleep again after reading a few pages from one of Terry's books.

Trish, from Palliative Care, took the opportunity to visit, following up on the anxious calls from the day before. She told Matt that she thought he was handling his treatment remarkably well so far. But Matt didn't agree. This was just her way of doing her job; trying to make him feel better.

Sophie called in after dinner and stayed for two hours. She was exhausted and ultimately decided that the visit was senseless because they were both having trouble just staying awake. She would check in again tomorrow night.

Wednesday 22nd April

The chemotherapy drip was not required in the hours immediately after breakfast and Matt was feeling a lot brighter. He decided to take his laptop to the lounge area, where he could work on his blog in relative peace. When he tried to walk, however, he discovered that he was ridiculously unsteady on his feet. He had to have some help from one of the nurses. She helped him to the toilet, made him a cup of coffee and found some cushions to settle him in to an armchair.

By this stage, Matt had set up a filing system on his computer to catalogue the blog replies that were coming through. The biggest and fastest growing file was the one marked "Christian". He would probably need to subdivide that one but couldn't, as yet, decide on the best way to do so. One file, simply titled 'Stupid', contained a collection of comments that were too ridiculous to take seriously. Some of them were probably only intended as jokes and, had they arrived in hard copy rather than digital text, they would have immediately been screwed up and "stored" in the trash.

One entry in Matt's 'Stupid' file warned him not to die on a Wednesday because that was when the gatekeepers to the other side had their day off. Someone else claimed to have a magical pack of playing cards that contained hidden directions for the afterlife. This person offered to loan these cards to Matt on provision that they be returned no less than one week after his demise. One person claimed to be a ghost-whisperer who used a spiritual version of e-mail to communicate with departed souls. And, of course, there were occasional comments where the spelling and grammar were so bad that they were quite unintelligible. Such comments were culled on an almost daily basis from the blog or blog archives.

But there was another category of borderline responses that Matt designated as 'Weird'. Comments ended up here when Matt sensed that people sincerely believed the strange theories that they were positing. These comments were so diverse that, no matter how original or clever they might appear, there was no way any of them could qualify for a point.

Matt smiled to himself as he re-read some of the entries in his 'Weird' file.

Death is a journey. Some natives of Vanuatu believe that this journey starts with the departed soul walking along a beach until its path is blocked by a terrifying, cannibalistic ghost-goddess who draws an intricate design in the sand. If the deceased person has done his or her homework, and learned to draw this design, he or she can complete the ghost-goddess' drawing and be allowed to pass.

That particular scenario probably only applies to that particular tribe but, if we are spiritually aware, we can all take some special insight with us into the afterlife that will enable us to pass obstacles on our afterlife journey.

Matt wondered briefly if he had already been given some such spiritual insight. But nothing came to mind. The whole life after death contest was still inconclusive. Besides, what sort of afterlife spirits would devise such a diabolical thing as a secret password for some obscure afterlife journey? If different tribes or cultures had different passwords, how could you possibly be sure that you had memorised the right one? Matt wondered if astrologers, or maybe psychics, would have any answers to these questions.

Another blog comment that found its way into the 'Weird' file came from a woman who identified herself as Alice Muskogee.

The soul that seeks to live on after death must find its kindred spirit in the animal kingdom. This might be a deer or a coyote or a wild cat. Maybe a dog but not one that's been domesticated. It must be a free spirit animal. Some types of birds will work. If you link your spirit with theirs, the chains of death will not be able to hold you.

Wow!

Death and life are two sides of the same coin, wrote yet another of Matt's readers. *Each is a mirror image of the other. We can know some things about death simply by thinking about life and imagining the direct opposite.*

Hmm. Neat theory but not very helpful. Matt thought

about sickness and health, rich and poor, male and female, young and old, awake and asleep, use-ful and use-less. Life was already full of opposites. If death was the opposite of everything in life, wouldn't it end up exactly the same? No, that was way too weird to be right. Matt congratulated himself for this devastating piece of logic that wouldn't have been possible yesterday. Maybe Uncle Gav was right. Good logic would be the best way to sort out the true from the false.

Some blogs referred to the Tibetan Book of the Dead or its Egyptian counterpart. The journey theme cropped up frequently, especially in comments that harked back to ancient Greek or Roman mythology. Matt was surprised to read more than once that he would have to pay the ferryman to carry him across the river Styx. Did people still believe that?

The thought of death being a journey was intriguing. Some entries along this theme could almost qualify for a point. But none of these mythological journeys had any ring of truth. They were vague about the final destination and they contained no helpful advice. They were just weird.

At that moment, a frail gentleman shuffled into the lounge area, dressed in striped pyjamas and laboriously pushing a walking frame. He appeared to be struggling to even breathe. He acknowledged Matt with a brief smile but his eyes were set on the coffee machine in the corner. Here was a man for whom just getting a cup of coffee was a strenuous and difficult journey. It was a wake-up call. Death might be a journey but there was another road that must be travelled first. The road, or journey, of dying.

Thursday 23rd April

The chemo doctor called in at 7.30 the next morning with two young interns and a woman who was apparently the charge nurse for the ward. No time to waste, he asked Matt a barrage of questions. How was he feeling, generally? What was his appetite like? Was there any nausea? Had there been any difficulty sleeping?

Without looking at Matt, the doctor gave the clearance

for Matt to go home. The charge sister went off to make the arrangements and the doctor turned to Matt.

"OK, we'll get you back next week, and then a month later and one more week after that," he said. "Then we'll do blood tests and a follow-up MRI and we'll see how you're coping."

Matt quickly made some calculations in his mind. "Umm ... there might be a problem. I'm supposed to be getting married on 30th May and we have a honeymoon cruise booked for the following week."

The doctor nodded. "Well, OK. A six or seven week gap is not ideal but we can make it work. Either way, it should be enough to determine whether or not it's worth pursuing cytotoxic treatment."

Matt sighed. He was glad to be going home but there was so much he didn't understand about the cancer in his body. Everything seemed so random, so impossible to control. If this was all a journey, it was an exasperating one. Who would ever want to set out on a journey that promised nothing but pain, sickness, confusion and fear? Where would it end? How would it end?

The Dying Aussie blog had unearthed dozens of potential answers about death and dying but none of them could work until, somehow, he could cut through this fog of confusion. Would there be any answers? If so, would there even be time to apply them properly? Would the blog work out? Or would it prove, in the end, to be a glorious waste of precious time?

In a strange way, the doctor's words from a different context made more sense. We can make it work. "There's no choice," thought Matt. "I have to make it work."

11 - OLD HOLY BOOKS

Friday 24th April

At the birthday party, Donna had asked Matt if her pastor could visit him but, of course, he said no. As far as he was concerned, her religion was too judgemental and Matt had no desire to meet a preacher of such things. But Angie Sparrow, his boss' wife, took a somewhat different approach. She recommended a Baptist minister friend who, she said, would offer prayer for healing. "What have you got to lose?" she asked. Matt protested but without conviction. Who knows? The minister might turn out to be a worthwhile friend. If he turned out to be a jerk, he would not be invited back. No problem. Angie promised to set up a visit.

So Lachlan O'Farrell arrived at Matt's door late Friday afternoon, a wiry, athletic man in his late forties. His receding hairline was flanked by almost comical tufts of black but his sharp brown eyes sported a certain twinkle of compassion. Matt quickly decided that this man was not going to be a threat.

"What do I call you?" he asked, somewhat awkwardly, once the pastor had made himself comfortable in Matt's second favourite chair. "Father? Reverend?"

O'Farrell laughed. "I don't really care what you call me. Most people call me Pastor O'Farrell but you can call me whatever you like. Lachlan, Lachie ..." He shrugged his shoulders. "Whatever!"

"Angie did explain which church you were from but I forget."

"That's OK. I'm the senior pastor at the local Baptist Church. And you? Are you a church-goer?"

Matt shook his head. "No, that's the thing. I'm trying to work out what I believe. Have you checked out my blog?"

Now O'Farrell shook his head gently. "I'm sorry. Should I have done a bit more homework?"

"No ... not necessary. It's just that ... well, everyone I meet these days seems to know about my ..." he paused, "... my little contest."

But not Pastor O'Farrell. He honestly had not heard anything about Matt's blog, or the video, or the media interest. He listened patiently as Matt brought him up to speed but took his first opportunity to change the subject.

"Do you believe that God can heal you?"

Matt was stunned. He knew this pastor would want to pray for him but it had never occurred to him that anyone would honestly believe that God could heal someone of cancer. It was a question he'd never considered. If any sort of healing was possible, he had assumed it would be through his Dad's cancer therapy books. And he was deeply sceptical of them. But the pastor was waiting for an answer. Could God heal him? He wasn't even sure if he believed in God. But then, if God was real, and if he created people in the first place, it would make sense that he could heal them. In theory, it was possible.

Matt surprised himself with his answer. "I suppose so."

O'Farrell smiled. "I'm sorry. I threw you a bit with that question."

131

"No, that's OK," apologised Matt. "I … I don't really know what I believe."

"Have you ever known anyone who was healed in answer to prayer?"

"Uh … no, I don't think so." Matt frowned as he spoke. "Have you?"

"Sure!" answered the pastor with enthusiasm. "Lots of people." He allowed a moment for that to sink in, then continued. "I've seen people healed from asthma, migraines, blood disorders, arthritis, all sorts of different things. Ahh, yes, and even cancer."

Matt was suspicious. "You've seen people healed of cancer?"

"Yeah. There was a lady in our church a few years ago. The tests came back that she had breast cancer. But we prayed with her and she really believed that God did something inside her. The next time she went to the doctor, the lump was smaller. They did some more tests and changed their diagnosis. It wasn't cancer after all." O'Farrell shrugged his shoulders. What else but prayer could explain such things?

"Well, if she didn't have cancer in the first place, she obviously wasn't healed of cancer." It was more a question than a challenge.

"I suppose you could say that. All I know is that we had this terrified woman, and we prayed for her, and she believed. And it all worked out for her. She's moved away since then but I happen to know she's still going strong."

Matt shook his head. "I've never heard anything like that before."

"Hey, listen. I don't mean to say that everyone I ever prayed for got healed. I'm just saying that some people have. I guess I'm just trying to open your mind to the possibility."

"But isn't that a bit cruel? Suppose I believe you. Suppose I start to get my hopes up. And then it doesn't happen. What then? Wouldn't that be the worst kind of cruelty?"

It was a good question but O'Farrell was ready for it. "You've heard the saying: 'Where there's life, there's hope.' I

132

notice that you're not dead, so I reckon there's still some kind of hope. Isn't it better to live with hope for as long as possible?"

"I suppose so," said Matt, still unconvinced.

O'Farrell continued making his case. "Jesus healed everyone who came to him in faith and he told his disciples to go out preaching the gospel and healing people. As a Christian, and a preacher of the gospel, I'm just doing what I believe the Bible tells me to do. And I've seen it work time and time again."

Matt didn't know what else to say. O'Farrell pressed him gently. "I would be honoured to pray for you."

"What? Right now?"

O'Farrell nodded solemnly. "Sure. Why not?"

There was one more obstacle for Matt to overcome. "But I'm not sure if I believe in God. Or Jesus. If I do get healed, does that mean I have to believe? Will I have to become a Christian? I still have so many questions."

The pastor smiled. He had never heard that sort of logic before. "Matt, if God heals you, I promise you that a lot of your questions will just drop away."

So much to take in. But it seemed there was nothing to lose. "OK," he said. "I guess I'm ready."

O'Farrell moved closer to where Matt was seated and placed a hand on his shoulder. For a few moments, he said nothing. Then, after a deep sigh, he began to pray.

"Father God, I know you love this young man. I know you have a purpose for him. And for his life. I know you hate this terrible thing called cancer. Lord, you're the author of life, not death. You're full of compassion and goodness but this thing called cancer is all about rottenness and evil. Lord, I can't believe that this is your will for anyone. So Father, I bring Matt before you now. Heal him Lord! Touch his body! Let your healing power flow now through every part of Matt's body. Seek out every trace of the cancer and stop it in its tracks. Turn it back Lord! Turn it back! You turned water into wine. Now Lord, please hear us. Turn these cancerous cells

133

into normal healthy cells."

O'Farrell was getting worked up. "Father God, you gave me the commission to minister healing in your name. There's so much that I don't understand but Lord I just have to obey. You said that your followers would lay hands on the sick and they would recover. Lord this young man doesn't know whether he believes or not, but that's nothing to you. Heal him Lord! May he see that you are real. May he know it in his flesh, Lord. Heal him Lord … in Jesus' name!"

The prayer seemed to be over but the pastor was still deep in prayer, one hand on Matt's shoulder and the other on his head. This O'Farrell was the real deal. He believed in this stuff and Matt had to admit that he felt something.

The pastor eventually resumed his seat, with the look about him of a man who had just gone fifteen rounds with a professional boxer. Matt's head was spinning. "Wow!" was his only comment.

What would be the outcome from this? Only time would tell. O'Farrell left his business card and promised to check up on Matt, as his schedule allowed. Then he was gone.

Matt called Sophie. "Let's go out for dinner tonight. It's been a strange day and I'd love to bounce some things off you."

As Matt showered in preparation for a night out, he thought about his body. Apart from some unusually persistent bruising on his legs, there were still no outward indications that anything was wrong. There was pain and there was a general weakness but nothing constant. Some days were better than others. If God had healed him – ridiculous notion – how would he know? What would it feel like? Would it be sudden or gradual? Would God, if he existed, maybe think it was cool to string him along until he was bed-ridden in some advanced stage of the disease and then, hey presto! Miracle of miracles! Cancer gone!

"Stupid thinking," he muttered to himself as he dressed. More to the point, if he was going to have regular visits from a Christian pastor, would that compromise the integrity of his blog? Would it still be a fair contest? Would he have to invite leading atheists, Jewish rabbis and Muslim imams, just to be fair? Good question to ask Sophie tonight.

He thought about the Palliative Care nurses he had met. Trish Owens had neatly deflected any questions that touched on religious or spiritual themes. She had offered to arrange counselling but Matt remembered her words. "Our counsellors won't try to influence what you believe in any way. They respect all kinds of religious belief."

The shirt Matt wanted to wear was in the ironing basket so he fetched the ironing board and iron from the cupboard in his laundry. He understood that Palliative Care counsellors had to deal with people from different faiths but why did they have to take the line that spiritual matters weren't relevant to the process of dying? Maybe that was a bit harsh but, in Matt's thinking, that was how Trish came across.

Matt thought about his friends, his cousins, the range of people in his life. Not many of them had any kind of noticeable faith. He thought about the various conversations at his birthday party. Donna hadn't bothered to speak about her faith and neither had anyone else. No-one gave any indication that they were thinking beyond this present existence. Did that mean they didn't believe in God? Or any kind of life after death?

By the time Matt had finished ironing his shirt, and two others for good measure, he had coined a new phrase in his mind. New to him at least. Most of the people he knew were 'practical atheists'. They may or may not believe in some kind of god but they lived as though they were atheists. Practical atheists.

Sunday 26th April

Sunday morning. Josh and Leslie called to ask if Matt and Sophie would join them for a barbecue lunch in the local park. Matt looked out his bedroom window and not too subtly pointed out that the skies were grey and stormy. Josh assured his older brother that whatever rain was coming would "quickly blow over". Indeed, thought Matt, it is rather windy out there. But he called Sophie and they met as arranged. True to their word, Josh and Leslie had provided everything. Two different kinds of sausage were already sizzling on the electric barbecue, with onions and capsicum rings. Some lean rump steaks "for the adults" formed a juicy border around everything else, Josh insisting that the edge of the hot-plate was the ideal spot for cooking steak. Sophie joked that the aroma was so good that she wouldn't actually need to eat anything.

Matt was glad that he'd rugged up with a coat and beanie. The barbecue was under cover but there were not enough walls to shut out the wind. And then it started to rain. Leslie called Chelsea and Shirelle, the youngest two, to come under the shelter but they were too busy playing on the slides and had to be told three times. Ryan, the oldest of the three, was happily playing a game on his iPod, only looking up occasionally to see if the food was ready.

Josh tried his best to engage Matt in serious conversation. How did he feel? Really. Was he angry? Confused? Frightened? Matt understood that Josh needed to empathise somehow and the barbecue was a convenient opportunity. Eye contact was not a problem because the two men could simply stare at the food that Josh was cooking.

But Matt was not in such a serious mood. "How do I feel? I feel cold … and hungry! Hurry up with that food before we all freeze to death."

The rain did not blow over. To the contrary, it set in for the afternoon. If anyone else had been in the park, they might have enjoyed a good laugh at the expense of this foolish-looking family group huddled together eating their barbecue lunch on such a miserable afternoon. The gentle walk that Josh had planned was abandoned and, when everything was packed up, they scurried back to their cars and headed for their respective homes.

Sophie went with Matt and, while he napped in his favourite chair, she did his laundry. She also prepared some soup for his evening meal. It was still raining, so she took the washing with her when she left. She could use her clothes dryer and bring the clothes back later. When Matt woke, he felt cold and physically weak. He grabbed a warm jumper and stumbled out to his sunroom.

He checked the blog and one new entry, in particular, caught his attention. It was signed by a Richard D and Matt wondered for a moment if perhaps this was the well-known anti-religion professor from England.

All the main religions contradict each other in thousands of ways. One says Jesus was a prophet. Another one says he was an inspired teacher. And yet another says he was the son of god, whatever that means. Their books were all written in times when people believed in angels and spirits and fairies. They had no concept of science in those times. People were superstitious, so they believed that the universe was formed in a ridiculously short amount of time. I'm not saying that science can prove that God exists or doesn't exist, just that, if God was real, we would see some sort of evidence in the world around us. But, as it is, the evidence all points to a godless universe. All religions, therefore, are based on blind faith in superstitious fiction.

Science is the only thing we can rely on because the scientific method guarantees that it accurately describes the reality we observe. Every new discovery is peer-reviewed and tested over and over until it is proved beyond doubt. There's no such thing as peer-review and scientific method in religion. What can I say? I'm not trying to convert the world to atheism but seriously, it is the only logical and scientifically defensible position.

My advice? Weed out all the superstition. Get back to reality. That's where you will find whatever peace is possible.

Matt wasn't sure that he liked where his blog was heading. Atheists like Richard D were good at dismantling other people's faith but, in the end, their outlook on things left him with a sad, empty feeling. But this competition wasn't about feelings or wish-lists. From a strictly logical point of view, Richard D probably deserved a point.

Progress Score: Atheism 5, Christianity 3, Buddhism 2, Dying Well, New Age, Practical Stuff 1.

Monday 27th April

Matt knew that awarding another point to atheism would spark some interesting responses. He checked the blog the next morning while eating his corn flakes and yoghurt. One comment from Robert Smith vigorously challenged the statement that there is no evidence in the natural world pointing to a Creator God. He gave a few examples of complex design in living things and made reference to the "anthropic principle", which highlighted the almost uncanny suitability of Planet Earth for the sustaining of life. Robert's comments were always interesting and well-reasoned but Matt concluded that this one was not directly relevant to the discussion about life after death, and therefore could not be given a point.

Other blog respondents brought up examples of scientific theories that had been sincerely believed for years but then discarded. *If new evidence is continually surfacing,* wrote one, *how can we ever be sure that the latest conclusion is the correct one?* That's true, thought Matt, but I can't give points to comments that are simply reacting to other comments, without contributing anything new.

One comment picked up on Richard D's remark about "superstitious fiction".

The Christain idea of jugment at the time of death is ridiculus. You line up at the perly gates and, when your tern comes, you have to convinse Saint Peter that ur good enough for heaven. Angles floating on clouds with harps, devels with pichforks in flames of hell. It's all dumb superstition.

Matt smiled at the spelling and wondered if Christians really believed that pearly gates stuff. Was it really that simple, that black and white? He posted a question to that effect and then left for work. He was not surprised to find another comment from Robert Smith that evening.

Hello again Matt. The idea that people have to line up at pearly gates for judgment when they die is a silly caricature of what Christians believe. For one thing, Jesus is the judge, not Peter. And the silly pictures that cartoonists draw of angels and demons doesn't make them any less real. Satire can make anything seem ridiculous. Such pictures come from the imagination of man and have little or no basis in reality. I hope you won't take them seriously.

But on a more positive note, I've been looking things up in my Bible and I've found 28 places where God clearly promises eternal life. I can give you my list if you're interested. The promise of eternal life is not just in one or two verses. The New Testament is absolutely full of such promises. You simply cannot get around it. One of the verses on my list is probably the most well-known verse in the whole Bible. 'For God so loved the world that He gave His only begotten Son, that whoever believes in Him should not perish but have everlasting life.' The promise of eternal life is at the very heart of the Bible and Christian faith. It's the whole reason why Jesus came into the world.

Robert S.

Matt ran this past his family at the Monday night dinner. If the Bible really stresses something, does that make it true? Terry dismissed the whole idea, preferring to believe that no-one could really know what was true or otherwise. Julie didn't understand the issue. If the Bible said something, wouldn't that be true, whether it was said many times or only once? Leslie took a more considered approach.

"I guess, if God was real, and if he wanted to communicate with people, he would probably repeat the things that were most important." She laughed. "I know I have to repeat a lot of things with my kids!"

"Sometimes you have to say the same things over and over in different ways if you want to avoid misunderstanding," admitted Terry.

"So it's not just what God says," said Matt, "but what he makes a big deal out of."

"I guess so," agreed Leslie. "I'm not sure I believe it myself, but I think your Robert friend makes a good point. If a

139

promise of eternal life is such a central aspect of the Bible, and I say 'if' because I really don't know, it would mean that Christianity directly answers your big question in a very positive way."

Josh and Leslie bedded their children down in the spare room so they could stay longer with the rest of the family. Julie cleared the table and Terry produced a folder full of internet printouts and miscellaneous notes and brochures. The expression on his face showed that the research had been done; the verdict was in. And Matt was genuinely interested at last. Perhaps his Dad could cut through all the confusion that he'd been experiencing lately.

"As we all know by now," began Terry, "cancer is not just one disease. There are hundreds of different types of cancer and the medical profession tends to treat them on a case by case basis. But more and more people, doctors included, are realising that cancer is more than just a physical thing. There are very real emotional and even spiritual aspects to it. People who have positive attitudes, maybe through relaxation and meditation techniques, have significantly higher chances of complete recovery. Partly, I think this is because they feel they have some sort of control over what's happening in their bodies. Either way, people who approach the disease with positive attitudes definitely seem to cope much better."

Terry paused, scanning the faces around the table. Matt muffled a cough in his sleeve. No-one else moved. Everyone was listening.

"More and more cancer patients are abandoning conventional treatments for what is often called 'non-orthodox' or 'complementary' treatments. But there is also an increasing tendency to take the best of both worlds. Some health journals call this 'adjuvant therapy'. It means alternative cancer remedies operating alongside regular medical cancer treatment. And um … Matt … this is what I'm recommending for you."

"Out of all the hundreds of theories and possible treatments, the approach that makes the most sense to me is one that restores natural balance and health to the body so that the body itself can fight the cancer. It's not some miracle drug or chemical. The body itself fights back against the toxins that allow the cancer cells to grow."

"There's a cancer-reducing diet called the Bevington Detox Diet. It's not exactly the same as the one recommended by the local cancer detox place that I told you about. But it's close enough that they would still be willing to work with you."

"OK,' interrupted Sophie. "What are we allowed to eat on this diet?" She looked around at five wondering faces. "Well, if Matt goes on this diet, I reckon I'll have to do it as well. Especially after we're married."

Terry smiled, despite himself. "It's pretty radical but nowhere near as bad as some of the popular plans. Basically, it means cutting out meat and dairy products, and eating only whole-grain, non-processed foods."

Leslie jumped in. "Organic foods, in other words."

"Pretty much," said Terry. "The theory is that our modern food has too many contaminants. You know, stuff that's added to make things look better for longer. The exact relationship between these things and cancer is strongly debated but I'm personally convinced that there's something to it."

Matt hadn't said much until now. "I thought this was going to be all about apricot kernels," he laughed.

Terry winced in frustration. "I never, at any point, imagined that apricot kernels, by themselves, could cure cancer." Pause. "But I do believe they would be a useful addition to a clean vegetarian diet, with as much raw, uncooked food as possible. And I recommend some concentrated juices as well. They can be expensive but I'll get some for you. If you want to keep using them, I'll keep paying for them."

"What about protein?" asked Leslie. "Won't Matt need protein to keep his strength up?"

"There's enough protein in vegetables like ..." Terry checked his notes. "... asparagus, broccoli, carrots, cauliflower, garlic, onion and sweet potato. Um ... I'm not saying this diet won't leave you feeling a bit weak, Matt, but this is all about keeping you healthier for longer. Who knows? It might send the cancer into remission, or get rid of it altogether. It might make the chemo easier to take if your doctors want you to keep going with that. But even if it doesn't do any of these things, I honestly believe you'll be stronger and fitter for longer."

Matt ruffled through some of the papers on the table but Terry pointed out the dot-point summary sheet that he had prepared. He handed copies to everyone at the table. "Take whatever information you want," he suggested. "There's plenty more where that came from. But Matt, this sheet condenses it down to just the main things that I hope you'll be willing to take on board."

Julie looked on hopefully as her son mulled over the list. Sophie was thinking ahead. "Can we buy everything we need locally?" she asked.

"No problem," answered Terry quickly. "Well, like I said, I'm happy to order in the things that you can't buy locally. But there's no problem getting a good variety of raw, organic food and fruit juices around here."

Pause. Everyone except Terry and Julie were studying the list.

"Well," said Julie. "What do you think, Matt?"

Matt rubbed his eyes, then cradled his chin in his folded hands. Long pause. Then he nodded. "OK, I'll do it. Not sure that it's going to be easy but I'll do it."

Julie had one more question. "Then … will you all be OK if I follow recipes that fit with this plan for our Monday night dinners? I'll cook up other stuff for the kids."

Leslie nodded first, then Sophie and Josh. It was settled.

Matt arrived home after eleven, seriously tired but, checking his blog, he remembered the discussion about the Bible emphasis on eternal life and added another point to Christianity on the scorecard.

Progress Score: Atheism 5, Christianity 4, Buddhism 2,

Dying Well, New Age and Practical Stuff 1

Tuesday 28th April

At least with the second round of chemotherapy, Matt knew what to expect. The nursing staff in the so-called 'cancer ward' at City Central Hospital discussed the change of diet with the duty doctor, who, in turn, contacted Dr Barlow. This time, Matt decided on some light reading for his drip time, something that required little or no thinking. One of the nurses knew about the blog and offered to share her thoughts but Matt politely declined. Perhaps he would feel like checking the blog, or discussing it, when this round of treatment was done.

Time passed slowly. That evening, the hospital meal looked and tasted terrible. Maybe the kitchen messed up somehow in their attempts to follow instructions, or maybe it was the chemo. Then again, maybe it was just Matt struggling to adjust to his Dad's harsh anti-cancer diet.

Josh called in and apologised that no-one else could make it tonight. He fidgeted through twenty minutes of small talk and then excused himself. Matt wasn't disappointed. He was too fatigued for meaningful conversation. He tried watching a TV sitcom to take his mind off the sickening poison rampaging through his body. When that didn't help, he tried doing a crossword puzzle but the answers eluded his chemo-whacked mind.

Finally, exhausted, he fell into an uneasy sleep.

Wednesday 29th April

After another long day of chemotherapy and associated recovery time, it was a delight to watch a movie with Sophie in the visitors' lounge. The movie, titled 'Old Books', followed the hilarious efforts of a remote community on the shores of a mystical mountain lake to obey a series of old religious texts that came their way one at a time. The idea was that, when an older text came to light, it superseded the more recent ones. This led to some crazy upheavals in relationships between the people and modifications to the way they did things, especially

143

because the responsibility to interpret the sometimes cryptic commandments fell to a somewhat unhinged hermit who lived in a hut at the end of a rickety old jetty.

The whole thing was a not too subtle spoof on the idea of modern people basing their lives on old religious texts but Matt and Sophie didn't care. They sat closely together and thoroughly enjoyed a good laugh. But when Sophie tentatively ventured a question about the wedding, Matt pulled away from her arms.

"Let's not spoil a nice evening. We'll talk about that some other time."

Thursday 30th April

Matt managed three hours of work on the Thursday afternoon following his second round of chemotherapy. The flesh was weak but the spirit was willing. It was important to make the effort.

After his brief return to work, however, Matt decided to chase down a line of thinking inspired by the previous night's movie. He wanted to check out what spiritual theme books were popular. What sort of ideas were appealing to readers these days? Were people still turning to the old classics like the Bible or the Bhagavad Gita? Not that he knew exactly what the different classics were. And not that he expected the local Mona Shores bookshop to know about worldwide trends in spirituality. It was just a whim.

The middle-aged woman behind the counter seemed very knowledgeable. She was, in fact, the proprietor. Matt asked her where he could find the 'religious' books and she took him to a section about two metres wide and four shelves high.

"Do you have a particular area of interest?" she enquired.

"Umm … I guess I'm just interested to see what sort of religious ideas are selling these days."

The woman immediately picked up on the word 'religious'. "Would you be interested in my thoughts on that?"

"Sure. Why not?"

She took a deep breath, as if to choose the right words

for her young customer. "It's not so much about religion these days. It's much broader. People are talking and writing about spirituality more than about religion."

Matt was puzzled. "What do you mean?"

"Well, I think a lot of people, and especially the important new writers, have moved away from the main religions. They're more into exploring all aspects of the spiritual life without the … um … constraints? of established religion."

"OK. So what sort of things are these new writers coming up with?"

The woman smiled and shook her head as if wondering where to start. "I don't know. It can be anything these days. Absolutely anything. Crystals, angels, unicorns, ancient incantations, special spiritual diets, ritual sex, psychological retraining of the brain …" She shrugged her shoulders. "Anything. The old markers are gone. Now it's whatever you want it to be."

Matt thought about this for a moment. "Well, what about the old classic religious texts. The Bible, the Quran, the Bagava … whatever. Are people still reading them?"

"Maybe. I can't answer for what people are reading. But I think maybe they read them differently these days. I don't think people read them as absolute truth any more. They read them more for ideas that they can adapt for themselves." She paused and watched for Matt's reaction. "Well, for what it's worth, that's how I see it."

Matt nodded. "Thanks. Appreciate that. But hey, I might just browse for a while if that's OK."

"Of course. Let me know if you have any more questions."

Matt still had more questions than he could handle. But that night, he updated the blog.

Do any of my readers still base their life on the old holy books? Do you still read them? And do you try to do what they tell you to do? I'm guessing there are still plenty of people who try to live by the Bible. But I don't know. Are there other books that you live by? Or do you read holy books for some other reason? I'd love to know.

12 - FAITH IN YOURSELF

Friday 1st May

Sophie drove Matt to his afternoon appointment with Dr Tan. It was close to her work so she asked Matt to call her when he needed a lift back to work. The dental clinic was busy and they were already short-staffed so, after the appointment, she needed to get back as quickly as possible. Matt, however, was in no hurry to go anywhere. Sophie had to gently prod him toward the car.

As they pulled out from the little car-park behind the medical suite, Matt told Sophie about one recommendation that Dr Tan had made. A Cancer Support Group that met every Thursday evening at a nearby community centre. Carers were welcome to attend but it was mostly just the cancer sufferers themselves, sharing their experiences, all under the watchful eye of one of the nurses from the cancer ward.

"Are you thinking of attending?" asked Sophie.

"Yeah, it might be worthwhile."

"Would you like me to come with you?"

"Well I guess that would mean I wouldn't have to drive."

Sophie managed a quick glance at Matt while concentrating on her driving. "OK then. Next Thursday?"

Because of the appointment with Dr Tan, Matt failed to finish the work he had promised one of his clients. Greg asked if he could finish the work at home and e-mail it through to the office. He was planning to work back anyway, so he could review Matt's work and forward the necessary proofs to the client.

Sophie organised some vegetarian take-away, which Matt managed to enjoy, despite working on his laptop at the same time. When the job was finished, Sophie suggested going out to a movie; there was still time to make the late showing. But Matt was tired and opted for a quiet night in front of the TV. Several new blog comments also caught his attention, including three from people who claimed to base their life on the Bible. Other people mentioned the Quran and the Book of Mormon. And, yet again, Matt found a comment from Robert Smith .

Hello again Matt. Yes I regard the Bible as true. Surprise, surprise. But here's why. If you follow a recipe and the cake turns out like it's supposed to, you know that the recipe was right. Likewise if a builder follows an architect's plan and the building turns out right, you wouldn't doubt that the plans were good. If a mechanic tunes a car engine according to the specs in his workshop manual, and the car runs perfectly, he will trust that same manual for the next job. So my experience with the Bible is that the better I follow what it says, the better my life turns out. And hundreds of generations of Christians before me have discovered the same thing. This is one way I know it's true.

Robert S.

But two comments particularly interested Matt. The first was from someone who signed simply as Hope.

Death is not to be feared at all. It's just a doorway into a better life where love and acceptance are universal. This parallel reality is so beautiful that you will want to thank someone for the death that you go through. But it's not that anyone needs to be thanked. It's just the way things are. You might call it New Age thinking but, for me, it's always been obvious that the selfishness and harshness of this world cannot represent true reality. There's always been an alternate reality running parallel with this one. From time to time, we all get little glimpses of this alternate world. It's not future and it's not past. It runs alongside and above our reality. Everyone is loved for who they are. There is no abuse or pain in that reality. All destinies are fulfilled. We know this is true because there is a seed of that reality in each of us, a desire for that better world.

That was certainly original, thought Matt. The next one was equally so. Since his visit to the bookstore, he had been more aware of the exploding parameters of modern spirituality. But Paganism?

Dear Matt. I have enjoyed reading your blog for some time but I notice that Paganism has not been given serious consideration. I would like to correct that.

Paganism is a diverse form of spirituality that allows for many different gods and goddesses, as well as many different rituals. The ancient Greeks and Romans built amazing civilizations based on the recognition that the realm of the gods is just as diverse and wonderful as the world of humans, or the world of animals, or the world of plants. I think we can all agree that life is too complicated to be explained in terms of a single god.

The idea that many gods interact with humans in different ways at different times makes a great deal of sense. Wars occur when the gods of different tribes or nations become jealous or angry with each other. Some gods and goddesses spitefully inflict storms and violence on their enemies. Some minor gods and goddesses play tricks on humankind in order to be noticed and approved by higher, more powerful gods and goddesses.

The ancients actually had it right and more and more people these days are turning to Paganism because it offers meaningful connections with life and nature. In classic Paganism, there are ritual sacrifices that you can make to prepare for dying. You can choose your eternal destiny and, as long as you are tolerant of others, you will progress to a new life in the world of the gods.

This raised more questions than it answered for Matt. But the argument was original and added something significant to the debate. Both New Age and Paganism would be awarded points.

Progress Score: Atheism 5, Christianity 4, Buddhism and New Age 2, Dying Well, Paganism and Practical Stuff 1.

Saturday 2nd May

Matt was under his car in the carport of his home when Pastor O'Farrell visited for the second time. The Saturday Special oil change that he thought would be easy was turning out to be anything but. Exhausted and winded, he lay there, breathing heavily and trying to find the strength to roll over far enough to reach the spanner that had dropped away from his hand.

O'Farrell called his name. "Matt, is that you?"

"Yeah." It was a barely audible groan.

"What can I do to help?" The pastor's voice was urgent, concerned. He got down on hands and knees and looked under the car. "If I can get you out, I think I can finish the job." With that, he proceeded, inch by inch, to manoeuvre Matt out to a point where he could finally be helped to a sitting position. Then, with Matt suitably resting against the rear of the car, he slid back under and tightened the bolt that Matt had left partially undone.

Matt was deeply embarrassed when the pastor emerged, covered in dust and oil. "I don't understand," he moaned. "I felt good. I thought I could do it!"

The pastor helped Matt to his feet and gathered the tools.

Inside the apartment, he asked if it would be alright to make coffees for them both. Matt nodded weakly as he settled into his customary armchair.

"You're still young," said O'Farrell. "This is a cruel thing that's happening to you."

"Ha! Tell me about it!"

The pastor found some coffee mugs in the sink and began washing them. "Have there been any signs of improvement since I prayed with you the other day?"

Matt stared absently at the minister's back. Was it bad form to hurt a minister's feelings? "I honestly thought there were. I slept better. My body wasn't aching as much." He sighed again. "But who really knows? No matter what I tell the doctor, he just says it's normal. It's like every good thing is normal, every bad thing is normal!"

O'Farrell offered no answers. He merely asked how Matt liked his coffee, and, that task completed, he took the seat nearest to Matt's.

"What have you learned from your blog conversation since I saw you last?"

Matt sighed again. "What have I learned?" He screwed his mouth to one side in an expression of thoughtfulness. "I guess I've learned that a lot of people get their faith from old books like the Bible. I … I guess I never realised that before."

"Interesting comment," said O'Farrell. "Where did you think faith came from?"

Matt smiled. He didn't know. "I guess I just thought people grew up with the faith … or non-faith … of their parents. I mean, if I grew up in India, I'd naturally be a Hindu. Don't you think?"

"I'm sure you would. But thinking people in all religions will always want to go deeper. And that desire will lead them back to their books. Otherwise they're just nominal Christians or Buddhists, or whatever." Then he added: "Don't you think?"

"You're a very clever man," conceded Matt. "Maybe a bit too clever for me."

O'Farrell laughed at that. "I doubt I'm even in your

league!" He stared into his coffee for a moment. "But I guess a cancer diagnosis would tend to get you thinking."

Matt nodded. This preacher-man wasn't as bad as he had expected.

Monday 4th May

When Sophie called to pick Matt up for the Monday night dinner, he informed her that he would not be going this time. Knowing that he'd been well enough to work, and that Julie would be very concerned, Sophie pressed him for a reason. None came, except: "I'm tired."

"Well, I'll stay here with you," she offered.

"No you won't," he replied abruptly. "You have to go to the dinner. They'll be expecting you."

Sophie laughed, more derisively than she would have wanted. "Are you mad? They're your family and they're expecting you more than me."

"Yeah, well, I'm not going. Not tonight."

Sophie's eyes narrowed into a frown as she studied her fiancée. "What's going on, Matt?"

"Nothing. I'm just tired and I don't feel like socialising."

"What am I supposed to tell the others?"

"Whatever you want! Tell them I'm too sick to go out if it makes you feel better."

Sophie turned to go but stopped when her hand reached the doorknob. She whirled around to face him again.

"I know what it is," she announced. "You're embarrassed to face your Dad."

No response.

"You're embarrassed because you haven't been sticking to the diet you agreed to."

Still no response so Sophie came back to where Matt was seated and stood over him, hands on hips. "I'm right, aren't I?"

Matt squirmed awkwardly. "No, not really … well … maybe. Just a little."

The triumph of Sophie's guess quickly gave way to a feeling of "what do I do now?" She decided to kneel beside his

152

chair, from which position she could give him a reassuring kiss. But what to say? She didn't know. Fortunately for her, Matt started to open up.

"I had some chocolate before work this morning," he admitted. "And I really pigged out at lunch. Two cheeseburgers, fries, cake, the whole works. I even had a chocolate-coated ice cream later this afternoon."

Sophie groaned inwardly, not for Matt's dietary lapse but for his emotional self-flagellation. She hung her head in despair as Matt continued.

"I told myself it was just a little break from the diet. I deserved it. It wouldn't hurt. But after a while, I was telling myself: 'It's OK. Enjoy it now. You can start taking the whole no-meat, no-dairy thing more seriously tomorrow.'"

"I'm so sorry," she whispered.

"Don't patronise me," said Matt. "I'll be all right. I just have to try a bit harder."

Sophie seethed inwardly but there was no point arguing. Finally, after sitting silently for a minute or so, she tried again. "Come with me to the dinner?"

Matt shook his head. "No. Not tonight. But you have to go. Go cover for me … Please."

Tuesday 5th May

The regular team meeting at the Little Bird Marketing Agency was postponed until Tuesday morning because Greg had been interstate at a conference. He reviewed several accounts and introduced a new staff member who would start the following week. Matt understood, of course. Greg was not so much preparing for growth in his business as for the inevitable increase in Matt's absences.

But Greg also had some exciting news. The Goolawar Centre for Aboriginal Culture had retained Little Bird for their major new campaign. Greg had arranged to meet the Management Committee and some of the elders at Goolawar on Saturday afternoon. He asked Matt and Jim, his uncle, to accompany him on the trip. Lauren, the receptionist, wondered aloud if Matt had learned anything about indigenous concepts of death and dying. Maybe this would be a great opportunity.

Thursday 7th May

Matt and Sophie were among the first to arrive for the Cancer Support Group. The nurse, who introduced herself as Alison, greeted them both with effusive hugs. A young, buxom woman with short, neatly styled dark hair and an "I'm-here-to-make-a-difference" attitude, Matt remembered her from his first chemo treatment. She introduced them to all the regular group members as they arrived. Nothing was said about Matt's blog.

Fifteen people sat in a big circle, facing each other. Conversation was brisk and Alison obviously knew the others very well, their names and relevant information flowing freely from her crimson lipstick lips. He guessed, from the body language of the other group members, that only one was a carer, a middle-aged woman who was sitting with a much older man and watching his reactions whenever anyone said anything. One very slender woman (Matt thought she may have been in her forties) wore a delicate scarf on what was obviously a chemically-stricken bald head. Apart from Matt, only two of the fifteen were men.

Sophie smiled and nodded her way through the meeting but only spoke when directly addressed. One of the older women asked her if she was a full-time carer and seemed surprised to hear that, no, she was still working full-time.

So many different cancer stories. Matt knew, of course, that every case was different but here they all were. In one big room. The terrified older woman facing radical mastectomy, the forty-something lady with the bubbly personality and hopeful reports of remission, the fifty-something man who had learned much about winning the battle with prostate cancer, the female "survivor" whose new mission in life was to share the secrets of her victory, and the early twenties girl with leukaemia. All of them at different stages of the disease, all of them, in one way or another, feeding off the palpable optimism in the group.

Alison had one strategy for drawing people into the conversation – asking direct questions.

"So Lydia, how did you feel when the lump you were worried about turned out to be benign?"

"Sally, you said last week that you were worried about your daughter's reaction to your decision not to have any more chemo. Did you talk with her? How did she take it?"

"Tom, you've been quiet tonight. How about you tell the group how your new medication is working out?"

"And Matt, our new friend. What is your cancer story so far?"

Matt wished he had chosen a seat closer to the door but, alas, he was trapped. He mumbled something about a melanoma that had metastasised (these people would surely know what that meant). He briefly mentioned Terry's dietary plan and inadvertently sparked an argument that could have become heated if Alison hadn't intervened. Finally, he mentioned his desire to find some kind of faith that would help him through his last days.

Alison smiled knowingly. "Yes, Matt, faith is certainly an important part of coping with cancer." She gestured around the group with an open hand. "Most cancer patients find they have to look deep within themselves to find the faith that's right for them. Good on you, Matt. I'm sure your faith will get you through this, even if it's just faith in yourself."

13 - GUARDED OPTIMISM

Saturday 9th May

To get to the Goolawar Centre, Greg, Matt and Jim drove eighty kilometres north-east, to the town of Cunnington. Then they followed the main highway for a further twelve kilometres and turned down a gravel road that wound its way through a forest of old growth mountain ash and blackwood trees. Light rain spotted on the windscreen as Greg's Mitsubishi Outlander emerged from the forest into a small community of homes scattered along a ridge above a meandering stream. A little further and they arrived at an expansive car park, broken into sections by gardens of native shrubs. Greg's Uncle Jim noticed a stylised bird symbol painted on the top of a pole and explained that this was an ancestral symbol for the indigenous population of this area.

The actual Centre was a surprisingly modern building, partially built into an impressive outcrop of limestone rock. An enormous goanna dominated the dot-painting mural behind the reception area, which was, however, unattended. The Little Bird marketing delegation followed the sound of voices down a brightly decorated hallway to a small kitchen, where two women were preparing percolated coffee and arranging plates of lemon slice and chocolate cake. One of the women – Matt guessed she was in her mid-twenties – smiled a shy smile and turned her face away. The older lady held out her hand and gave each of her visitors a firm handshake.

"Welcome to Goolawar." Her tone was gruff and business-like but moderated by a kind of sing-song accent. She took orders for coffees and wordlessly instructed her young helper to see to it. Then, without bothering with introductions, she led the men down another hallway to a lounge room where a dozen men and women sat around, some in old lounge chairs and some on modern dining chairs that had been set up around the room for the meeting. A large aerial photograph of the area, beautifully mounted in a lavishly carved timber frame, dominated one wall. A well-stocked bookshelf in one corner of the room sported an array of old photographs on its top shelf. The wall opposite the door was floor to ceiling window and afforded a striking view of a well maintained garden created around a spectacular orange-red banksia. Matt was impressed.

A wiry forty-something gentleman with receding black hair jumped up to greet the visitors. He introduced himself as Clarrie and proceeded to introduce everyone else in turn, taking special care to point out the elders and the members of the Management Committee. Clarrie was, in fact, the Chairman. Greg, Jim and Matt acknowledged each one with a nod and, directed by Clarrie, took seats in front of the large garden window.

What followed was the most unusual client meeting Matt could ever remember. Everyone in the room seemed to have a different opinion about their proposed marketing campaign and they all stated their views forcefully. Almost belligerently. Some were keen to show the world that they had moved beyond the old "dreamtime" mindset and that their Centre was all about an ancient culture taking its place in the twenty-first century. Others wanted their advertising to point back to the days before European civilisation, the spiritual connection with the land and the richness of aboriginal family life. But even there, Matt sensed a certain polarisation. Some were keen to fit in with the "white men ways" while others saw their Centre as reclaiming what the white men had taken from them. The latter wanted a more political agenda for their centre, and hence for the marketing campaign.

Greg finally managed to break in on the conversation but Matt and Jim were content merely to observe. They knew that the campaign was not going to be decided at this meeting. There would be opportunity for creative input later, perhaps even on the trip home.

Greg thanked everyone for their opinions and complimented everyone on their magnificent cultural centre. He praised the elders and the committee members for their achievements and honoured them for their vision. He asked about any future developments that may have been approved and, finishing his coffee, requested a more complete tour of the facility. The elders nodded assent to this and looked to Clarrie to do the honours.

The Goolawar Centre was a complex building with diverse functions. It obviously served as a Community Centre, with two main function rooms and a small nursing clinic. But a more tourist-oriented section branched off from the main reception area. This section housed a small museum, an art gallery and a movie theatre with a small stage for cultural performances. Linking back between this part of the building and the community part was a studio where young aboriginal people could learn and practice their art and music.

Everywhere Matt looked in this centre, he observed profound links between spirituality and everyday living. He was impressed with the respect that was afforded the elders in the community but puzzled by the seemingly aggressive way that people spoke to each other.

After the tour, the team took some time to talk one on one with some of the people. Matt saw an opportunity to combine his work with his quest for answers about death and dying. Although it was a strain on his weakened body, he sat on the floor in front of an old man and an old woman. Their names were Auntie Joan and Uncle Alf.

"I wonder could you tell me what your people believe happens to a person's spirit when they die?"

The old woman was surprised at the question. "Now why would you ask a thing like that, young fella?"

Matt smiled at the friendly crustiness of her tone. He decided to be honest. "Well, you see, I've got cancer. I might not have long to live. So I've been thinking a lot about these things. I … I even have a blog on the internet about it."

"Ha!" snorted Auntie Joan. "I might not have long to live either! I'll be eighty-nine this year. But I don't know nothing 'bout what happens to you white folk."

"It's all the same for everyone," offered a young boy who had wandered in. "It can't be different for black people and white people." But he wasn't so sure, so he added: "Can it?"

"Course it can!" snapped Auntie Joan. "We have connections to the land and our spirits live on where our ancestors lived."

"But how do you know that?" pressed Matt, hoping he wasn't crossing some unseen line of protocol.

"They know it from the old stories," explained the young boy. "They believe it but they just can't prove it."

"We don't need to prove anything," snarled Auntie Joan. "Our people don't need to prove what we know inside."

"That's OK. I understand that," said Matt. "But you've asked for our help in promoting the cultural centre so I know you want your spirituality to be accurately represented for future generations. All I'm saying is that, if you could post a few things on my blog, it might help people to understand. It's not about proving anything."

Old Uncle Alf stroked his stubbled chin. He was about to speak and everyone knew it would be worth their while to listen.

"Us old-timers don't know nothing 'bout blogs and computers. But tell y' what. I'll speak to some o' the young blokes at the school. They know plenty 'bout these things. Smart fellas. Mebbe they can do sump'in for ya."

Sunday 10th May

Sophie's parents, Joe and Gwen, lived at Wooripini, a small town in a sheep-farming region some two hours north of Mona Shores. Matt was supposed to come with her on this visit but Sophie didn't want to expose Matt to the heavy cold she was battling.

Joe and Gwen had been married for thirty-one years. Sophie, now twenty-nine, and Donna, four years younger, were their only children. As Sophie drove, sniffling and coughing, wiping her eyes with tissues from a box on the passenger seat, she wondered how she had drifted so far from her parents. Was it their obsessive involvement in the local football/netball club? The long hours they both worked in low-paying, menial jobs? Or was it their nominal Catholic background, which, by assuring them that there were answers for everything, made it unnecessary to delve into spiritual themes at all. The two sisters, in different ways, had sought for something more, something deeper, something Joe and Gwen could not give them.

Now, of course, they wanted to talk about the wedding. After all, they were paying for the reception. Sophie knew they were disappointed that she had taken so long to get around to getting married. On the other hand, they were pleased that she had never lived with Matt in a de-facto relationship. Gwen disparagingly referred to such arrangements as "de-farce-o marriage".

Sophie's thoughts drifted as she drove. By the time she pulled into her parents' driveway, her mood was one of sadness, piqued with frustration. The visit would, as usual, be all about practical matters. Work, finances, wedding details, the back yard vegetable garden. They would ask about Matt's health but not about his emotional, spiritual struggles. Visiting with them would not provide the wisdom she really needed.

But they were her parents. What else could she do?

Monday 11th May

The Goolawar campaign dominated the team meeting at Little Bird on Monday morning. Matt was grateful for an interesting challenge. Work could be a panacea and creative brainstorming made the time pass quickly. A marketing plan for Goolawar was taking shape but Greg wanted a tag-line and threw the challenge to Matt.

Back at his own desk, Matt reflected on the Goolawar experience. Did Auntie Joan really believe that an indigenous afterlife could be different from a "white-folks" afterlife? If that was true, nothing they could say could ever qualify for any points on the blog. How could it? He was just a visitor on their land, not a member of their tribe. Outsiders were welcome to observe and respect this ancient way of life but it was not something you could convert into.

Four-thirty in the afternoon, Matt waltzed in to Greg's office. "See, Learn, Cherish," he announced.

Greg reasoned it through. "'See' is the initial invitation. Says that Goolawar has plenty for people to see. 'Learn' speaks to its educational relevance. A visit there isn't just about a few hours amusement. There's something there that's important to understand. 'Cherish' says that the culture is like a gift, something valuable enough to preserve forever." He nodded. "Yeah, I like it. It has emotional pull. See where you can take it and we'll build a proposal around it. Well done, Matt."

Josh and Leslie had a school commitment so, this time, they were missing from the Monday night family dinner. Sophie brought a fruit platter as her contribution to the meal. Julie had a lentil and vegetable casserole simmering on the stove. Outside, a wintry wind swirled in from the Southern Ocean, making the warm meal more tantalising than it might otherwise have been.

With less than three weeks to go, the wedding was

uppermost in the conversation. Matt was grateful that Sophie got on so well with his Mum. It took the pressure off him. He remembered the gut-wrenching family fights that, some years ago, had ruined a wedding for one of his friends. So far as he knew, that issue had never been resolved. Yet here was Sophie, laughing happily in the kitchen with Julie while they served the meal together.

A moment to see, learn and cherish.

Tuesday 12th May

Old Uncle Alf from Goolawar had been true to his word. When Matt checked his blog on Tuesday afternoon, there were several comments from the "young blokes" in the community. Some were irrelevant to the death and dying theme but Matt still read them with interest. It was hardly surprising that young people, with so much life ahead of them, had grappled only superficially with the idea of death. One young girl – the bloggers weren't all "blokes" – had written a clever poem where Australian animals discussed, in beautiful rhyming verse, the things that they each considered most important in life. Matt loved it so much that he copied and texted it to Sophie.

But there were also two comments which, to Matt's surprise, seemed worthy of points. The first was signed by a young man named Neville.

Dying is where you say goodbye to the family you've always known. Death is where you meet the family you've never known. We're all related and connected. We see many things now but our eyes don't see the spirits that we're connected to until we die. Then we will understand who we are and where we belong. Then we will understand why we were born in family and how that family has always surrounded us, even when we tried to ignore it. You're from a different family so your family connection to me is not strong. You're a white brother but I wish I could meet you. Then my spirit and yours can be linked up. Don't be afraid of dying. It won't hurt. The family you see will be there to say goodbye and the family you've never seen will be there to welcome you to the world of the spirits.

Matt thought Neville's comment rambled on a bit. And there wasn't much by way of advice that he could take from it. But there was a simplicity on one hand, and a maturity on the other, that appealed to him. And it didn't exclude "white folks".

The second comment was from a girl who signed as Serena.

The elders talk about the dreamtime, when all the things in nature were formed. I don't know if they really believe these stories or if they just love the way the stories keep their ancestors alive. I don't understand what exactly happens when we die but if part of us goes back into the ground where it came from, I think the other part of us, the part we call spirit, must do the same thing. It must go back where it came from. Earth to earth, spirit to spirit. I think that lines up pretty well with the traditional teachings and probably with Christian teaching as well. Lots of our people are Christians. Either way, the land is important and so are our ancestors. The spirit world would be too hard for us to imagine so we have the stories. They are our only clues to the spirit world that we go back to so whether they're true or not doesn't matter. The Christians have a different set of stories but it doesn't matter because they all point to a spirit world that goes on after we die.

Matt appreciated that Serena's thoughts were not necessarily typical of her culture. In this ever-changing world, spiritual beliefs were changing all the time. Would Serena still see things this way in ten or twenty years? If she had to face death personally, would her faith be so simple? Impossible questions to answer but it was encouraging to hear from such thoughtful young people. Matt added two points to a new category with a not-so-satisfactory title: Aboriginal Religion.

Progress Score: Atheism 5, Christianity 4, Buddhism, New Age, Aboriginal Religion 2, Dying Well, Paganism and

Practical Stuff 1.

When Uncle Gavin called that night, he commended Matt for his thought-provoking blog, especially the comments from the Goolawar young people.

"Thanks," said Matt. "But hey, what do you believe Uncle Gav?"

"Ouch! Straight to the point, eh?"

"Sorry, I didn't mean to put you on the spot."

"No, it's OK. It's just that it's not that easy to explain. I sort of take a middle path between the various religions. Nothing extreme. For instance, I can't stomach fundamentalist Christians who say Jesus is the only way to eternal life. If that was true, every other religion would be false … and well, that definitely cannot be right. I believe no-one should be dogmatic about what they believe. It's far more honest to admit that we never know for sure, in this life at least."

"Are you sure about that?"

"Yeah, absolutely!" Then: "Ohh, Matt, you got me there. I fell for that one, didn't I?" He laughed. "You're a very clever man, Matt. I'll be following your blog with great interest."

Wednesday 13th May

So many questions. So many opinions. Doctor's appointments. Wedding preparations. Matt couldn't sleep so he staggered out to the kitchen for a midnight snack. Or, more precisely, a 1.30 am snack. For five days, Goolawar and the aboriginal people had focused his thoughts. But now, as he stood at his kitchen bench, his body was shouting a sick reminder that he still had cancer. Points for this, points for that. Family, spirits, poetry about talking animals. Here in the dead of night, none of it seemed real. He found some vegetables left over from Monday night's family dinner, and reheated them in his microwave. Then, slumping into his favourite chair, under a warm blanket, he scrolled through some boring options on TV, flicked aimlessly through a copy of New Scientist magazine, and then just sat back and closed his eyes. Life was so confronting, so confusing.

Half asleep, he remembered that he'd forgotten his nightly tablets – again. But he was comfortable at last so the tablets would have to wait.

In dreams, Matt was on a cold beach. Alone. It was eerily dark but he was conscious of a terrifying, roaring noise. He asked a group of people, who suddenly happened to be there, about the noise and they discussed the problem passionately without reaching any conclusion. Everyone had a different theory. Then they all disappeared and, out of the darkness, Matt suddenly saw the ocean rise into an unthinkable wave, countless storeys high. There was no escape.

The next thing he knew, he was clinging to a large wooden crate that was surging through bright yellow rooms, surprised faces watching from the side as he smashed silently through walls, windows and doors on his watery rocket. Then he crashed through a ceiling and the buildings receded far beneath the raging ocean that he was somehow riding. Strange fish leapt around his head for a moment but, when he tried to catch one, they disappeared, only to be replaced by a doctor figure shooting along beside him somehow. "Don't worry," said the doctor in a clinical monotone. "This is normal. Don't worry." Other disembodied voices joined in the chorus. "This is normal, don't worry. This is normal, don't worry."

But it wasn't normal. He was going to die. The terrifying wave dipped and Matt found himself on the floor of a cave – a carpeted floor! But, as he lay there recovering, he realised that his hands were gone. Then he saw that his clothes were also gone. A leg came apart and rolled away. Then another leg. His body was disintegrating. It was flying apart. Parts of him were metres away, already turning to dust. In the last moment before he woke, the curse lunged to consume the last of him. Nothing was left.

He awoke in a cold sweat. Took a swig from the water flask on the coffee table and drifted back to sleep. Over and over, he slept and dreamed, slept and dreamed. Elusive, psychotic nightmares. But the only one that he would remember was the mighty, unstoppable wave.

"Matt, are you OK?" It was Sophie, checking up on him before she went to work. He looked around and saw that he was back in bed. He couldn't remember getting there.

"I … no … I don't think so."

"Matt, you've been bleeding!" She had spotted some blood on his pillow.

"Have I? Umm … I didn't realise."

"I think you've had a blood nose. Here let me fix you up." She went to the kitchen to get a cloth. Matt sat up and groaned. His stomach heaved monstrously and he knew he had to get to the bathroom. He didn't quite make it to the shower, however, and vomited all over the bathroom floor. Sophie found him kneeling on the floor, spitting out vileness and wondering what in the world had happened. He was fine just yesterday.

Sophie called the dentist surgery to apologise that she would be late. Then she tended to her fiancée. She also called Julie.

Doctor Tan made time for Matt later that afternoon. Sophie went to work for a few hours, while Julie watched over her son, but Sophie returned to take him to his appointment. It was apparent that Matt's medication was out of balance. Not only was he experiencing extreme nausea and cramping, but his usually sharp mind was fuzzy. He was saying strange things and Sophie could barely contain her panic. Could it be a tumour on Matt's brain?

Doctor Tan finally ordered Matt to hospital. He e-mailed his report to the Palliative Care team and phoned them to ensure that they had a bed available.

Thus began five days of drifting in and out of sleep. Pain and restless throbbing in his chest.

Pastor O'Farrell visited twice, staying each time for just over half an hour, concerned to minister hope but realistic about what he could do for Matt in his confused mental state.

Julie spent whole mornings at Matt's bedside, sometimes

relaying his needs to the staff at the nurses' desk, sometimes arranging get-well cards or picking up the day's newspaper from the cafeteria downstairs. Whenever Matt was asleep, she took time to read a book about cancer and what patients and their families could expect.

Sophie called in after work every day and stayed long into the evening. Anxious phone calls to and from her future mother-in-law punctuated the time. Unspoken questions finally were spoken.

"Is this it?"

"Is he going to die?"

"Now? So soon?"

Dr Barlow and the nursing staff were restrained in their assessment of Matt's condition but their overall message was one of guarded optimism. They would keep him in hospital and work on adjusting his medications until his condition stabilised. There would be better times.

14 - ARE YOU SURE ABOUT THIS?

Monday 18th May

Finally, on Monday morning, Matt awoke in peace. The wild dreams that had tormented him for the past five nights were gone. The pain in his chest was refreshingly mild. When a nurse opened the blinds and called out a cheery "good morning", Matt blinked back a tear of relief and nodded his response. The worst was over. For now.

As the day progressed, his clarity of mind improved. Drained and empty but restful, he was able to enjoy some mid-morning coffee and carob cake (that was supposed to taste like chocolate) with Julie. He also revisited the blog for the first time in almost a week. It felt oddly unfamiliar, like meeting an adult that you had only ever known as a child. It wasn't how he remembered it. Were readers still following? Or had the whole thing turned into a joke? Seventy new comments dragged him back to a world of conversation that now flickered at him from his computer screen.

I must apologise, he wrote, *that I've been offline for a while. The cancer has been messing with me pretty bad, or maybe it's my medications. Either way, reality has been very, very blurry. It might be a few more days before I can respond to comments or award points. Please be patient. This is very confusing for me.*

Wednesday 20th May

The hospital discharged Matt just before lunch on Wednesday. Sophie drove him home and stayed with him until he announced that he needed an afternoon nap. She promised to return later with some food. Matt slept for two hours and awoke to late afternoon sunshine filtering through his bedroom window. Getting dressed was an unnecessary hassle so he decided to fetch his laptop from the living room and prop himself up in bed.

As usual, most comments were quickly passed over, either because they were merely restating things that had previously been fully discussed, or because they were too vague. Some comments had to be deleted because of bad language or sheer weirdness. But there were a few that captured Matt's attention.

Dear Matt, you need to open your mind. You're still thinking in terms of right or wrong, true or not true. The fact is, there are spirit guides to guide us across from this life. They are not angels but departed spirits who understand the process of dying and the final destination of souls. They are wise and comforting. You will feel safe when you find your own spirit guide. It won't be a he or a she, just a spirit, and you will feel the presence whenever you need it most.

Matt groaned out loud. Spirit guides! If such a thing were true, how would you find this so-called spirit guide? He scrolled down and saw there was another paragraph.

You get in touch with your spirit guide by being open-minded and aware. You might come into a room and the light dims for a few seconds. Or it might get brighter. You might smell a sweet but unusual fragrance. Or the spirit might speak to you in a dream. Don't be afraid of these things but welcome them. Embrace them. They are preparing you, reassuring you that the heart will go on.

Matt smiled at the Titanic reference, although it seemed strangely out of place in a blog about spirit guides. He had to admit that this was a different approach to his blog theme. Spirit guides. He knew enough by now to identify this with his New Age category and he decided to add another point.

Progress Score: Atheism 5, Christianity 4, New Age 3, Buddhism, Aboriginal Religion 2, Dying Well, Paganism and Practical Stuff 1.

Thursday 21st May

Dr Barlow had requested yet another MRI scan and Julie took Matt to the hospital for the all too familiar routine. This time, however, the staff were running to schedule and he was able to go straight through. He was back home by 10.30, sipping herbal tea with his mother. Julie was all smiles, grateful to have her son back from, as she described it, "the edge of eternity". The smiles quickly turned to anxious frowns, however, when Matt suddenly declared that he wanted to go to work. And would she drive him? He was so confident about his spontaneous decision, and so determined, that her protests were overwhelmed. If she didn't drive him to Little Bird, he would only drive himself. And that might have been a worse option after the recent crisis.

Lauren screamed when Matt walked through the door and, by the time everyone else rushed out to reception, she was hugging him passionately. It had been so long and they had been so worried. But here he was, weakened in body but bright in spirit. Wanting to work.

Greg looked in on him frequently through the rest of the day, always with a breezy: "You doin' OK?" Matt appreciated the concern and lapped up the excitement he had caused but he knew the day was coming when he would have to leave Little Bird for good.

Sophie was keen to avoid the embarrassment of walking in late to the Cancer Support Group but she overcompensated and they arrived too early. Apart from Alison, the convener, there was only one woman there. Matt and Sophie both recognised her from the previous meeting, two weeks ago, but they would not have remembered her name if Alison hadn't reminded them. "Matt, Sophie, do you remember Lydia?"

While Alison was busy setting up for the meeting, Lydia seized her opportunity to harangue the two 'newbies' with information about a neighbour whose tumours had shrunk in response to radiotherapy. She raved about two books she'd been reading recently. One was about a famous female athlete who had apparently been cancer-free for three years. The other was a book about a new anti-cancer meditation technique. "I only read things that keep my spirits up," she confided, as though it was a special insight graciously offered for free.

When the rest of the group arrived and took their customary seats, Alison opened the meeting with reports on two group members who were currently in hospital. "Our thoughts are with them tonight," she said. "And a special welcome-back to Matt and Sophie. We understand it's been a tough couple of weeks for you, Matt. We're all so pleased you could join us tonight."

General nodding and mutterings of affirmation. Alison began listing some apologies but was interrupted by Carey, the girl with leukaemia who Matt and Sophie remembered from the previous meeting. She slid from her chair onto her knees, whimpering hysterically in a fearful state of anxiety. Alison asked the group to gather round her. "Come on everyone!" she barked. "Let's come around Carey and give her some love." As group members began responding, she repeated the exhortation. "Come on! Come on! Surround her with some good vibes, good positive vibes."

Matt cringed and, from that point, switched off completely. Alison was probably a lovely person. She obviously had a big heart for all these people. But Matt found her intensely annoying. The thought of enduring another two hours of this brand of support terrified him. So, ten minutes into the meeting, while a particularly chirpy woman was holding forth about an obscure brand of seaweed oil that was apparently improving her white blood cell count, Matt began to grasp his stomach, bending over with an expression of "I'm-trying-to-control-the-pain" on his face. Alison immediately offered to call for medical assistance but Matt stoically declined the offer. "I'll be OK," he puffed. But as soon as Alison turned away, he repeated the ruse, glaring for just a moment at Sophie, who was looking amused when she was supposed to be concerned.

"Matt, are you sure you don't need some help?" frowned Alison. "You men can be so stubborn!"

"Well …" Matt sighed deeply, then winced again in mock pain. "I'm terribly sorry but I think I might need Sophie to drive me home."

"Maybe you should check in at Casualty," warned Alison.

"Nah, I've got some medication at home. Oww! Um … thanks everyone but, no, I'm sure this will settle OK."

Terry happened to call Matt's mobile while Sophie was driving him home. He couldn't understand a word his son was saying. The two of them were laughing too much. Exasperated, Terry promised to call back later.

"I love you so much," said Sophie, her eyes twinkling with playful admiration. At Matt's home, shortly to be hers as well, she nestled close to him on his two-seater sofa.

"Tonight?" she enquired hopefully, kissing him on the neck. "How about it?"

Matt responded gladly to the kiss but shook his head. "One more week. Nine or ten days maybe. We can wait that long can't we?"

Later, after Sophie left, Matt checked the blog and found a comment that grated against the joviality of his evening with Sophie.

If you decide to follow the path of Buddha, you will learn about four noble truths that will help you to make sense of what you're going through. Your search for truth is good if you really are seeking enlightenment. This world is all illusion and we suffer pain because we don't see things as they really are. I will not use the technical words but there is an eight-fold path that leads to the end of suffering. Right view, right resolve, right speech, right action, right living, right effort, right mindfulness and right meditation. If that sounds too complicated, there's a simpler version. The avoidance of evil, the undertaking of good, and the cleansing of one's mind, this is the teaching of the awakened ones.

Signed Contented Now.

On one level, Matt could accept this explanation. This was a credible outline of the Buddhist faith but he could see it would take a great deal of study and countless hours of spiritual exercises to truly penetrate its meaning. On one hand, he understood how the teachings of Buddha could lead to a life of contentment. After all, if you could eliminate all desire from your life, you would be contented, wouldn't you? But how would any of this help him deal with his cancer? Or an imminent death? He decided to write a challenge to his Buddhist readers.

What will I achieve if I follow this path? Will I get to meet Buddha? What do I do once I get enlightened? Does reincarnation happen straight away when I die? And how is any of this going to help me with the cancer in my body?

By Friday evening, Matt had several attempted answers to these questions. One was a correction of Contented Now's comment. *The fifth part of the eight-fold path is usually described as 'right livelihood', not 'right living'.* Someone else insisted that Buddhists don't believe in reincarnation; they believe in birth and rebirth. Matt failed to grasp the distinction.

Another comment came from a person who went by the name of Sutaya. Matt had no idea if this was a male or a female but, then again, why would that matter?

Brother Matt, I can see that it's hard for you to let go of the religious thinking that you've picked up through your life so far. Buddhism is not religious in the way that Christianity is. Buddha is not our God and we are not seeking some sort of salvation. We don't pray to Buddha and we don't expect any special blessings in life. Our greatest desire is to be free from all greed, hatred and delusion. There is no way to adequately explain this in words. Nirvana is a word we use for the state of ultimate release from all self, hence all suffering.

Yes, but how could any of this help someone with a terminal disease? Matt was amazed at the forthrightness of the next part of Sutaya's comment.

Contact your nearest monastery and ask if there is a monk who can prepare a mandala for you. A mandala is a ritual circle with multiple layers of intricate detail. Meditate on this for two or three hours a day and you will definitely understand the reality of death. The monk should be able to guide you in this meditation.

Signed Sutaya.

Matt shook his head, partly from a natural reluctance to follow that sort of advice and partly from the irony in the statement that, by meditating on one of these circle drawings for two or three hours each day, he would "definitely understand the reality of death." The phrase 'bored to death' came to mind.

He deleted a few incoherent blog comments and one that used offensive language to mock the whole project. Going back to the Sutaya comment, he questioned his own state of mind. Am I crazy? Spirit guides? Buddhist monks? Is my whole life turning into one of those psychotic nightmares? Were Mum and Dad on the money when they tried to get me to abandon the Dying Aussie project? Or is it just the cancer and the meds still playing with my head?

He shook his head in frustration but added another point for Buddhism. There was one more comment to consider.

Why do you still assume that the afterlife is the same for everyone? The universe is far more creative than that. There are many, many paths to enlightenment, not just one. All your correspondents are right EXCEPT the ones that speak of

174

judgment and hell.

No one has the right to condemn another soul. No one has the right to tell you that your path is wrong. There are lots of open-minded, tolerant religions that you could follow. Baha'i, Buddhism, the tribal religions of Africa or Asia, the aboriginal people who wrote in last week. Anything that allows unique individual souls to find their own unique individual path to God, however they conceive him or her.

For my part, as what you would call a New Ager, I've found that certain crystals, potions and incense can awaken me to new cosmic realities. The variety is infinite and wonderful. I don't like the term New Age myself, because these methods are not new, but the good thing about it is that it points to a new era in human consciousness where we have evolved beyond the old religions of doom and gloom. The truth is much richer and more fantastic. Every soul is precious and has its own unique place in the scheme of things.

Surely you can see this! I looked up a shop in your area. New Light Cavern, on Church St. They do group readings that I think you would find helpful. Please take some time to check them out.

Matt was physically and mentally exhausted. But the idea that people could find spiritual pathways suited to their individual needs had a certain appeal. He added another point for New Age, promising himself that, if he felt up to it, he would think some more about this in the morning. Maybe he would even look up the shop. Then, desperately hopeful for a good night's sleep, he closed his computer for the night.

Progress Score: Atheism 5, Christianity, New Age 4, Buddhism 3, Aboriginal Religion 2, Dying Well, Paganism, Practical Stuff 1.

Saturday 23rd May
Saturday dragged fearfully for Matt. The persistent ache in his chest and side, combined with the all too familiar sickly heaviness, thwarted every attempt at productive activity. He

watched some old movies on TV and moderately enjoyed the escapism they provided. But as the credits rolled for the third movie, resentment and self-loathing took hold. He threw the TV remote onto a chair so hard that it bounced off onto the floor. So much for living life to the full, what was left of it. Even thinking was becoming too hard, a strange pathetic agony. He tried three times to do something with his blog but hovering over his computer keyboard with shaky fingers was as close as he got to any work.

Sophie arrived late in the afternoon, having worked overtime on special request from her boss. She was in action mode, with questions on her mind about the menu for the wedding reception and some second thoughts about the bride's floral bouquet. But she quickly realised that Matt was not in a good mood so she tactfully shelved her questions. She would ask Donna instead.

"I have to get out of here," moaned Matt. "I'm going crazy here."

"Would you like to go out for dinner? Maybe a movie?"

Matt laughed, a little grimly. "No, I'm up to here with movies!" A flat hand in front of his neck indicated the level. "I don't know what I want."

Sophie winced. The wedding was in less than a week. A stressful time for any young woman. But most young women weren't marrying a cancer sufferer. In her case, compassion had to win out over agendas. If the wedding wasn't perfect, people would understand.

"Umm … how about a nice long drive?" she suggested. "I've got a full tank. We can get drive-through … if you feel up to it. You won't even have to get out of the car."

Matt thought for a moment. The default answer in his current state would have been a 'no' but something in Sophie's gentle smile prevented the easy out. He nodded. "Sure. That sounds like a good idea."

They drove around the bay and stopped at a small lookout area where they could watch the waves crashing against the rocks. With Sophie's window wound down, the

176

salty spray sprinkled their faces. Then they drove down the Mona Shores main street, commenting on some shops that had closed down and other new ones that had opened. Coffee shops getting ready to close for the day, restaurants gearing up for a busy Saturday night. Shoppers still looking for the ideal parking spot for some last minute purchases. Sophie drove and Matt took it all in.

Further out, several cars were leaving a football ground after the day's match. They had to wait as Matt and Sophie passed. Further on again, some concreters were laying a foundation for some sort of building on a corner block where a service station used to be. Some young people, ignoring the safety of the footpath, were walking together along the edge of the road, laughing and chatting. Sophie passed them cautiously, fearing they might suddenly veer out in front of the car.

Then it was out into the country. They passed a billboard warning about the dangers of swimming alone in the surf, a vintage campervan motoring way too slowly and a section of roadworks where the workers were packing their tools into the back of a truck. Their Saturday afternoon's work was over. But Sophie just kept driving.

She updated Matt on her arrangements for moving in with him after the wedding. She had arranged for some of her furniture to go into storage, hopefully for sale at some later date. She was keeping her whitegoods and some friends were helping her to move these, along with some dressers and coffee tables, on Thursday after work. The lease on her apartment would officially run out on Friday so she would stay with Donna on the night before the wedding. In some ways it would have been easier for Matt to move in with her but Matt was buying, Sophie was only renting. Besides, Matt's house was in a better location, it had an extra room that would come in handy, and most importantly, Matt was more comfortable there.

The sunset glowed ahead of them with dazzling hues of orange and red, contrasted against a deep blue sky that gradually sapped all the colours and reduced them to darkness.

Sophie asked Matt if he thought they should be heading back but the disappointment in his eyes caused her to sigh lightly and keep driving. He was really enjoying this.

"You know I love you," whispered Matt. "I don't know what I would do without you."

Sophie flashed a generous smile. "I love you too."

They drove for more than an hour, way out into the countryside, following the national highway through towns with general stores and little antique shops. Matt had his smart phone tuned to an American station that played an easy listening blend of country rock. Occasionally, when he knew the words to a song, he would quietly sing along.

Arriving at a somewhat larger town, they found a little pizza place. Sophie objected on the basis of Matt's cancer diet but her protest fell flat. Matt was in a bizarre, edgy mood. Nervously, she went in and ordered pizza while Matt waited in the car. Fifteen minutes can seem like an eternity. She wandered back and forth from the bench provided for take-away customers to the window which allowed her a view of Matt. He seemed OK.

Matt could only eat three small pieces of the pizza so, between them, they failed to finish their purchase. Sophie asked Matt what he wanted to do.

"We passed a hotel just now," he suggested. "How about we get a room?"

"What? You're kidding! Why would you want to waste money on a hotel room when we've got two perfectly good places back home?"

"I don't know," he replied, weakly. "I've really enjoyed tonight … but I don't think I'm going to handle the return trip too well."

"Matt," she scolded, "you're the one who's been trying to keep respectable boundaries before the wedding. And now you want to get a room in a hotel?"

If Matt wasn't feeling so melancholy, he might have resented her tone and started another argument. But he simply looked at her and said: "Can I just hold you? I really need you tonight."

"But Matt! We can't afford to waste any money at the moment."

Sophie was right, of course, but she knew Matt didn't care about the wedding budget. The cancer had changed his attitude to money. Time, for him, was more limited than money.

"Do you have to be somewhere in the morning?" he asked. "Like … early?"

Sophie screeched in frustration, her hands contorting into claws as she pretended to rip out her hair. But then, furiously, she started the engine and drove the half kilometre back to the hotel that Matt had mentioned.

There were several upstairs rooms available and they chose one with a window that looked out over the highway. A supermarket sign was visible over the roofs of the houses. Some patrons at the bar below were coming and going but, otherwise, the town was sleepy and quiet.

"Neither of us has any nightwear," complained Sophie. "Or fresh clothes for tomorrow."

Matt switched on the TV. "We can wash anything we need in the shower and hang it over the rail. Stuff will be dry by morning."

"Arrgh!" wailed Sophie. "I love you Matt but I don't get you. Why are we doing this?"

Matt was already getting undressed for bed. "Doing what?"

Sophie waved her arms around, taking in the unexpected surroundings. "This!" she repeated. "You expect me to come to bed with you. I'm not sure what you have in mind but I'm pretty sure you'll be upset with me in the morning. Or else you'll be upset with yourself."

Matt removed the last of his clothes. "It's OK. I'm just going to have a quick shower myself. You can join me if you like." She declined the offer and sat on the bed quietly weeping while Matt had his shower. When Matt emerged, still drying himself with a towel, she brushed past him, undressed in the bathroom, away from his sight, and took her much-needed shower. By the time she was finished, Matt was in bed, using the remote to flick through the various channels on the TV. As Matt had suggested, she had washed most of her clothes in the shower and now appeared wearing nothing but her long, woolly jumper. Doing her best to conceal her wildly mixed emotions, she calmly asked one more time. "Are you sure about this?"

Matt didn't seem to understand her problem. "Of course," he nodded. "Like I said, I just need to be with you, to hold you. We can watch some TV together."

She removed the jumper and slipped self-consciously into bed. Awkwardly, she maneuvered her body next to his and he wrapped an arm around her. They snuggled together through an episode of a murder mystery and a short news bulletin but it was never going to be enough. When the kissing started, passions were aroused that could not be stopped. The constraints that Matt had imposed on the relationship just six weeks earlier were now swept aside as if they had never existed.

15 - WAYS NOT TO HURT PEOPLE

Sunday 24th May

Sophie awoke the next morning to sunlight streaming through the hotel window. She instantly realised that Matt was not there with her. His clothes were missing from where he had left them last night. But where was he? She checked the bathroom but he wasn't there. She quickly dressed and headed downstairs. Finding no-one, she called out, hesitantly at first, but then louder. "Matt! Matt, where are you? MATT!"

She opened the door and ran outside to where her car was parked. Still no sign of Matt. She began to panic. What was going on? Collecting her thoughts, she decided that he must have gone for some breakfast, or maybe a coffee. Checking back in the hotel foyer, she found a woman who had come down to see about the commotion. She asked the woman about possible places in town where Matt might have gone. The woman listed three possibilities; a service station, a café and the supermarket that they had seen from their window.

Checking all three would take Sophie in three different directions. She jumped in her car and started for the café, the closest of the three options. She drove slowly, scanning both sides of every street she passed. Still no sign of Matt. She found the café but it wasn't even open until nine. She checked her watch. It was still only 7.15. Next stop was the service station, about a kilometre further along the main road. She stopped and asked if anyone had seen Matt. The answer was no.

To get to the supermarket, she would have to go past the hotel so she decided to check there again. Perhaps Matt had simply gone for a walk and was now safely back in the room. The tightening knot in her stomach said otherwise. She pulled up at the hotel and rushed inside, taking the stairs two at a time. "Matt, are you there?" she called out. But there was no answer.

"OK Sophie," she muttered out loud. "Calm down. He's just gone for a walk. He won't be far away. He's not a little child. He's a fully grown adult. He'll be OK."

She continued scanning every driveway as she made her way to the supermarket, doubtful that they would even be open at this time of the morning. As it turned out, they didn't need to be. Two middle-aged male cleaners were in the process of locking up.

"Have you seen anyone walking around here this morning?" she asked.

The cleaners looked at each other. "As a matter of fact," one ventured, "there was a fella came past here about an hour ago." Sophie obviously wanted more information. "Uhh ... he was early thirties, I suppose, average height. I think he was wearing a navy blue jacket. Does that sound like him?"

Sophie nodded urgently. "Where did he go?"

The men shrugged their shoulders. "We've been busy polishing floors in here. How would we know where he went?"

But the second cleaner offered some information that Sophie definitely didn't want to hear. "Umm ... perhaps you should know. He was ... um ... hitting himself. He was hitting himself in the chest while he was walking … and sometimes in the head. He was pretty freaked out about something."

"So you've got no idea where he could have gone?"

The men both shook their heads. "There's a park a few blocks away. By the river. You might try there."

Sophie thanked the men and raced back to her car. What if Matt had hurt himself somehow? What if he'd fallen in the river? In his weakened state, he might not be able to get out.

She found the reserve that the cleaners had suggested and quickly parked her car. In her haste to find Matt, she left the car door wide open but she had already ran a considerable distance by the time she realised it. No point going back to close a door. She ran toward the river, desperately fighting back her fears. Still nothing. She stared at the river and walked along the near-side bank. The river was neither wide nor deep. It was more a creek than a river. But the banks were steep and overgrown, rendering whole sections inaccessible. She found a little bridge and crossed over to explore the opposite bank. Still nothing.

She paused to catch her breath. "Matt!" she called out. "Matt! Can you hear me?" But all she heard in reply was a chorus of birds enjoying the early morning sunshine in the trees above.

"Matt!" she called again.

She ran back to her car. Who could she phone for help? Who should she phone? She drove around the block, then down a dirt road that ended abruptly at a farm fence. She found her way back to the highway, looking for ideas. Then she drove back to the park, this time coming at it from a different direction. Several young gum trees were growing randomly in what appeared to be a kind of unofficial park extension, well away from the river. She jumped out and called again. "Matt! Matt!"

This time, she thought she heard a muffled groan. She followed the sound to a small gully cut away behind a majestic old gum tree, impossible to see from the road.

"Matt! Can you hear me?"

Then she saw him. He was lying face down in the hidden gully, in a thicket of long grass. She ran to him and fell on him with tears. "Matt! Are you OK?" She rolled him over and saw with horror that there was a great deal of blood on his face, and down across his chest. "Ohh Matt, what happened to you?"

But Matt just whimpered miserably. Sophie persisted. "Matt, look at me! Look at me! What is going on? What has happened to you?" She tried to wipe away the blood and realised that at least some of it had come from his nose. The whole area around his nose was bruised. There was some swelling under his right eye.

"I'm hopeless, Soph," he growled bitterly.

Sophie burst into a loud emotional wail, distressed out of her mind but relieved to hear him speak.

"No! No, you're not!"

"Yes!" he insisted loudly. "I'm hopeless. Damned and hopeless!"

Sophie's phone was in her handbag, which was in her car. She tried to find Matt's phone in his pocket. Failing that, she sprinted anxiously back to her car, almost tripping in her haste. She fumbled in her bag for her phone and called for an ambulance. She didn't know exactly where she was but she noticed a street sign and the ambulance people were able to deduce the location from that. "We'll be there in five."

Sophie ran back to where Matt was struggling to sit up. Seething with self-pity he kept repeating: "Hopeless, damned and hopeless."

She knelt down and hugged him, tears flowing freely. "I don't understand. What happened?" Matt was shaking. And surprisingly cold. She told him that an ambulance was on its way but he made no response. She got to her feet and paced fretfully back and forth, thinking, reacting. Then, suddenly, she turned back and glared at Matt. "Is this about last night? You know, 'cause I warned you!"

"Yeah, I know." His answer was barely audible. "And you were right."

"Are you serious?" screamed Sophie. "Are you telling

184

me that you've literally been beating yourself up because we had sex?" Matt made no attempt to answer. Sophie threw her hands in the air and shook her head in disbelief. "You're crazy! Since when do normal people harm themselves for having sex with someone they love?" Her eyes blazed with angry compassion as she waited for an answer.

"You're right," mumbled Matt feebly, submissively. "You're absolutely right. I'm crazy. And I'm pathetic."

When Sophie saw that her rage was only feeding Matt's self-loathing, she melted. "Matt, it's OK," she pleaded. "We love each other. We're getting married next Saturday."

Matt shook his head. "You don't want to marry me. I'm nothing but trouble."

Sophie brushed away a tear. "You're trouble alright. Can't argue with you there." Then she nailed him with her trademark glower. "But I do want to marry you." Pause. Then: "I love you Matt. No matter what. I love you. Are you hearing me?"

Matt nodded and, speaking slowly, began muddling out an explanation.

"Every part of me hurts. I've been lying here 'cause I couldn't get up. Can you imagine that? I couldn't even get up. I can't stand what's happening to me, Soph." Talking was obviously painful and he stopped to catch his breath. Wisely, Sophie waited for him to continue. "I promised my Dad I'd follow his diet but I keep messing that up. I try to do right by you and I just keep hurting you."

"You didn't hurt me last night."

Matt grimaced as he tried to sit up straighter. "I was the one who said we should hold off 'til we got married. I thought that would be the right thing to do. I know you didn't understand but I thought, well, I might not have long to live. I kind of just needed to get something right. I thought I could do that right at least! But I say one thing and do the opposite. I might be facing God soon. I don't even know if I believe that but I'm scared. You tried to do the right thing, 'cause you're a better person than I am. You tried to stop me but I still did the wrong thing."

An ambulance pulled up at the edge of the reserve. A man began unloading a stretcher-bed from the back while a woman with a large medical bag started walking over to the injured man and his frenzied fiancée.

"Matt," whispered Sophie. "I'm not so sure that we did the wrong thing."

Matt sighed. "I know you love me but I'm not worth loving. I'm a pathetic loser. All this blogging about how I should live the rest of my life. It won't make any difference what I choose 'cause I can't stick with anything."

The paramedic's arrival prevented any further conversation. "Hi. I'm Jenny. Now what have we got here?"

Sophie made the long drive home alone as Matt was transferred by ambulance to City Central. His injuries weren't life threatening so it made sense for him to be in a hospital where his regular medical and palliative care could be accessed.

His nose and cheek bone were severely bruised but not broken. Likewise, the massive bruising on his chest revealed no deeper injury, although further tests would still be arranged. Dr Tan reviewed Matt's medication, adding a higher dose of anti-depressant tablets that would, he assured, help him cope with his pain.

Matt's mood, however, did not improve. The raging self-hatred that had led to his early morning collapse now morphed into a grumpy listlessness. The nurses and catering staff tried gallantly to bring some cheer into his room but their efforts only resulted in bored monosyllable grunts.

Monday 25th May

Annie had arranged a week off to help with preparations for the wedding. And also to see if she could help her brother somehow. She came with Sophie to the hospital on Monday afternoon. Matt was seated beside the bed in an armchair, vaguely watching TV.

"Look out," he said when he saw the two women. "Here comes trouble."

Sophie waited her turn while Annie bent down to give Matt a very cautious hug. The normal kiss on the cheek was prevented by the obvious bruising. "What are we going to do with you, little brother?" she chided. "This is no way to get ready for a wedding!"

Matt just shrugged his shoulders. "Yeah, well …" That was it. He left the sentence hanging.

"Hi Darling," chirped Sophie. "Are you feeling any better since last night?"

"Not really."

Disappointed at Matt's abruptness, Sophie tried to break the ice. "So whatcha watching?" She came around to see what was on the TV but Matt quickly switched it off with his remote.

"Nothing."

Annie winced at her brother's attitude but she was up for the challenge. "For a while there I thought Ivan was actually going to come to the wedding but now he says he has to work." She shook her head at the thought. "Funny thing. Mum wasn't surprised at all."

No reaction.

Just then, Pastor O'Farrell poked his head around the door. "Can I come in?" he enquired. Sophie recognised the minister and nodded for him to join their awkward moment. He greeted Sophie with a two-handed handshake and introduced himself to Annie, before locking eyes on Matt. He smiled.

"You been trying to do those car repairs again?"

Matt rolled his eyes. "Very funny!"

"What happened to you, Matt?"

Sophie wanted to answer on Matt's behalf but Annie was too quick. "Long story," she said simply. Dismissively. "It doesn't really matter. He's going to be OK."

The pastor studied Matt for a moment. He had seen injuries like this before and knew they were not consistent with injuries that would come from an accident. He moved on, asking if there were any broken bones. Sophie stood quietly at the corner of Matt's bed, listening to the conversation but lost in her own thoughts. Finally, she interrupted the pastor in mid-sentence. "Excuse me, Reverend. Can I ask you a question?"

"He's a pastor, not a reverend," corrected Matt.

"Whatever …" said Sophie. She didn't care what he called himself.

"Go ahead, Sophie. Ask away."

She cleared her throat and wondered for a moment if there was a proper way to ask her question. If there was, she didn't know what it was, so she just blurted it out. "Is it wrong for two people to have sex before they're married?"

Three different reactions. Matt groaned as if to say: "No, not this again." Annie winced in embarrassment at the sheer audacity of the question. But Pastor O'Farrell smiled knowingly.

"Wow, I can see that you two have had some interesting conversations."

"Please Reverend … I mean Pastor … just answer the question. Is it wrong for two people who love each other but aren't married yet to have sex?" In her mind, the only possible answer was "No, of course not." The pastor's hesitation genuinely surprised her.

"Um … the Bible speaks very highly of marriage. Marriage is one of God's most wonderful …"

"Yeah, yeah, I get it," interrupted Sophie. "But that doesn't answer my question."

"Well I'm just trying to explain …" The pastor was noticeably uncomfortable. "God's perfect plan was always for a man and a woman to be married."

"OK, I see where you're going." spluttered Sophie. "You don't have to spell it out. You think it's wrong."

"It doesn't matter what he thinks," said Annie, breaking in. "The two of you have to decide for yourselves what's right or wrong for you. No-one else can tell you what's right or wrong."

"Well apparently God can, Annie," snapped Sophie.

"Ohh Soph," groaned Matt. "Leave it alone, will you?"

But Sophie turned on him. "It's OK, Matt. You were right. We're horrible sinners."

"Now wait just a minute," said the pastor. "I didn't say that."

Sophie was undeterred. "Will you please stop beating about the bush! Yes or no? Do you think sex is wrong before the wedding?"

"I ... uh ..."

"Yes or no?" Sophie was really agitated.

The pastor glared at her, waved goodbye to Matt, and walked to the door, where he stopped for dramatic effect.

"Yes, Sophie." Then he turned and left the room.

Tuesday 26th May

Despite Matt's gloomy mood, he had three options for convalescence after this latest hospital stay. He could return to his own place, with Sophie or Annie staying over. He could go to Sophie's place. Or he could stay with his parents for a few nights. No doubting what Julie wanted. She pointed out that Sophie's place was largely packed up in preparation for moving out. She thought Matt might feel obliged to help pack or move furniture. "Let me look after you just for a few days," she pleaded.

Matt gave in.

Terry set Matt up with a network connection so that he could attend to the blog. Maybe he could even finish some work for Little Bird. Sophie drove him home and helped him pack a few essentials into his car, which he then drove – very cautiously – to his parents' home.

The blog contest had been running for ten weeks now and Matt was losing interest. Same old clichés, same old arguments. Every time he logged in, he looked for something original that was not also idiotic. Something that could inspire him with fresh zeal for life and maybe get him out of this depression. He found a few well-reasoned and well-written comments but deleted them without bothering to read them properly.

Yet another blog reader had written in about spending quality time with loved ones. From where Matt was seated, he could see his Mum and Dad in the next room. Doing their usual after dinner stuff. But so what? How was more talking supposed to help?

On the subject of relationships, why, after so many years of imagining himself getting married, wasn't he more excited about it? Sophie was a beautiful person. He loved spending time with her. But did he really want her moving in with him? Was it really necessary? And why was she so particular about every little detail for the wedding? Would her intensely driven attitude carry over from the wedding into the marriage? Would she become possessive and controlling if there was a wedding ring on her finger?

Just occasionally, a comment would appear on the blog that bypassed the intellect and spoke to the emotion of what he happened to be going through at the time. One such comment, early on Tuesday evening, resonated with the harshness of his current emotional state.

Dear Matt. I've been following your fascinating blog for some time now. Hey mate! You sure get some b… confusing stuff sent to you! And you know what? It's all pretty much the same thing. Everyone seems to think that there's a right and a wrong way to live. Well let me tell what I think! There's NO SUCH THING as god. There's NO SUCH THING as right and wrong. If you really are dying, you should just do whatever the hell you feel like doing. God isn't real. There's not going to be some eternal judgment about how you lived your life. So you may as well LIVE IT UP. Seriously! Who's going to tell you off for making the most of your time? My advice? Experiment with new sensations. Experiment with sex. INDULGE YOURSELF. And another thing. If you have relatives or friends that don't approve of what you do, tell 'em straight that you don't want to see 'em anymore. Only accept visits from friends & relatives that affirm your choices. Mate! I know it's rough that you've got this death sentence called cancer. But it can also be a licence. You don't have to deal with stupid CONSEQUENCES any more!

Signed: Go For It.

Wow! No doubting where that blog reader stood! Matt wondered what Sophie would say. Their sexual relationship had never been a moral issue for her. Maybe she would agree! Live it up while we can! But then again, cancer or no cancer, she had always expected him to behave decently and responsibly. Right or wrong, Matt decided to award another point to Atheism, which now had a clear lead.

Matt was not surprised, that evening, to see that Robert Smith had posted a reply.

Dear Matt. I was appalled by the comment from Go For It. And, frankly, even more appalled that you gave it a point. What an incredibly selfish and dangerous attitude! I don't know if you've been tempted in any way by this "no consequences/ licence to sin" nonsense but I must point out that this correspondent is basing his (or her?) attitude to life on some seriously flawed assumptions. First, how does he know there is no God? What if he's totally wrong on that count? Where does that leave him? Secondly, there are always consequences for our actions, whether or not they are sinful isn't the issue. And thirdly, what right does he have to advise you to stop friends and family from visiting you if they don't approve of everything you do?

Christians are often accused of promoting guilt and shame but that's a misunderstanding. Yes, it's true that Christians have a clear sense of right and wrong but that's not where it ends. In Jesus, we have the ultimate answer to guilt and shame. When He was crucified, Jesus took all our guilt and shame on Himself. Can you imagine how shameful it must have been for Him to be crucified, probably naked, in such a public place? He was mocked and ridiculed, not to mention the incredible pain He went through. The word 'excruciating' actually comes from an old word for the cross!

Matt, please hear me. Guilt and shame are real because

we all sin and do wrong things. But if you ask Jesus into your life, the guilt and shame that He suffered means that you don't have to carry it any more. If you don't have long to live, indulge is NOT good advice. Much better to admit your sin and bring it to the One who can truly forgive and cleanse. Sin has consequences that reach beyond the grave but Matt, you do not have to die in your sin.

Robert S.

Things were hotting up. As usual, Robert made a lot of sense. Right or wrong? Robert was a voice speaking up for the existence of both. Guilt and shame were no strangers to Matt either. Logic was failing but, if he gave a point to Go For It, it was probably only fair to give another point to Christianity. Fair?

Progress Score: Atheism 6, Christianity 5, New Age 4, Buddhism 3, Aboriginal Religion 2, Dying Well, Paganism, Practical Stuff 1.

Wednesday 27th May

Greg called. "Any idea when you might be coming back to work?"

"Sorry, Greg. Not today."

"That's OK. Come in when you can and we'll talk about things."

Terry was at work but Julie had to go out for groceries. She promised Matt she wouldn't be away more than twenty minutes. Right on cue, when Julie drove away, Uncle Gavin phoned. The conversation quickly came around to the wedding.

"So Matt, how's things with you and Sophie? Do you still reckon you're ready for married life?"

Two hours later, Matt sat in his car at Featherwind Point, a good vantage point for watching the waves on the ocean. He wondered about right and wrong, good and bad, wise and foolish. According to Go For It, none of these categories counted for anything. At least not now. Like a good marketing campaign, weren't the so-called "good" moral decisions of life designed to ensure a bright, positive future? Weren't they about reputation, keeping a network of friends and colleagues who trust and respect you, getting people to love you because you've always done the "right thing" by them?

But Matt had no bright future to prepare for. The rottenness of cancer, growing relentlessly in his body, robbed him of that. So what was right? What was wrong? What was good or bad?

He opened the door and felt the sea breeze on his face and in his hair. So many seemingly unanswerable questions. How could he presume to give points on the blog when he had no idea what was right and what was wrong? Some things got points because they sounded logical. But then something completely opposite came along, sounding just as logical. Right or wrong, on the blog at least, was a decision that depended on nothing more than how generous he was feeling at the time.

If something felt right, was it therefore right? If something was logical, was it therefore right? Feelings or logic? Which would be the best guide to right and wrong, to life and faith?

Was sex before marriage wrong? If so, why? Maybe it was only wrong because it put the cart before the horse, so to speak. Maybe there was wisdom in abstaining before marriage because it somehow set things up for a longer, better married life. But then again, was sex before marriage worse than leading someone on when you had so many doubts? Everyone seemed to think that love was the main thing, but what if love really meant finding ways not to hurt people?

Six o'clock that evening. On urgent invitation, Sophie arrived at Matt's house. He asked her to sit with him in the lounge. Sitting on the edge of his seat, nervous as hell, he told her that he couldn't go through with the wedding. She objected. She cried. Then she objected some more and begged for a reason. She waved her arms and pulled at her hair. She howled and screeched and pleaded again for a reason. But she left with nothing. Only one empty rationalisation from Matt, ringing in her ears.

"I'm just not ready for marriage."

16 - WONDERFUL ETERNAL CHAIN

"I'm sitting here in my sunroom, surrounded by all my usual stuff. It's eerily quiet. This is the proverbial calm before the storm. I have lobbed a hand grenade at my family and my fiancée. Any minute now, it will explode, and who knows how much damage it will do?

"So what else can I do in this brief interlude but start the journal that I promised I would write? My chronicle of dying from cancer. The personal reflections that I would never go public with. The Dying Aussie blog is personal enough.

"God, if you exist, please help me to write my thoughts boldly and honestly.

"It's not that I don't love Sophie. She is an amazing woman and I have been so lucky to have her in my life. I wouldn't blame her now if she left me. But somehow I don't think she has it in her to do that. She told me so once. Ah, but it might be different now. I don't know. I think I know this, that she will never understand me. I frustrate her. Her life is one long ordeal, thanks to me. If she leaves me, she will be better off. If, by some miracle of forgiveness, she stays with me, I will end up hurting her time and time again.

"I wonder who will call first. Will I get a phone call or a knock on the door? What will they say to try and make me change my mind? They'll probably argue that it's too late, that I can't back out now. The reception is all paid for, everything is booked and ready to go. I'll be wasting thousands of dollars. And what about the cruise that people dug so deep to pay for?

"I've probably done the wrong thing. But it felt like the right thing. Mum and Dad will ..."

And there it was, a knock on the door.

Annie spoke first. "What's going on, Matt?" He retreated to his dining room where he took a seat at the table. Annie followed with Terry and Julie close behind. Matt expected anger and condemnation but his sister was too savvy to launch a frontal attack.

"What did you say to Sophie?"

Matt glared at her, and beyond her to his parents. "Well, she must have told you. I'm pretty sure that's why you're here."

Julie was not so savvy about confrontation. "How could you do this Matt ?" The veins in her forehead were at bursting point, her voice was shrieky.

Annie had to work quickly. "You told her that the wedding was off?"

Matt wavered for a moment between the inclination to apologise and the instinct that attack was the best form of defence. He went with the latter.

"That's right. I'm not going through with the wedding."

Julie collapsed into furious sobbing but Annie tried to calm her by clutching her in a forceful embrace. Terry stood back, looking at the floor, shaking his head from side to side. Annie chose her words carefully.

"What reason did you give?"

"I ..."

"There's no reason," cried Julie, interrupting. "How

could you ..."

"Shhh, Mum," whispered Annie in her ear. "Let Matt answer the question. Please."

Three pairs of eyes now focused on Matt. There was no escape now except anger but Annie's gentle stare disarmed him.

"I forget," he answered coldly.

Terry placed a comforting hand on Julie's shoulder. For a moment, Matt thought he saw disgust in his sister's eyes. He turned away.

"Matt, look at me please." Annie spoke with an authority that confused him. He desperately wanted to ignore her, or lash out at her, but instead he complied. Meekly. When he turned back, Annie spoke softly, affectionately.

"Matt, you're my brother. I love you, OK? I can see that something very deep has been going on here. Probably for a long time. Yeah, we've all been worried for you but I guess we all underestimated what you've been going through. I'm so sorry for that."

Matt nodded in mild surprise. But backing down was out of the question.

"I'm not changing my mind."

Terry spoke up for the first time. "Are you sure about this, Son?"

"Yes Dad," said Matt, annoyed at the question. "I can't go through with it."

"But why? It doesn't make sense." Terry was out of his depth.

Matt turned to Annie. "Look, I've made my decision. Right or wrong, that's it. I'm not changing my mind. There's nothing more to say except ..." He paused. The question he needed to ask forced him to soften his attitude. "Except ... um ... well, how is she?"

Annie smiled at last, but only for an instant. "Matt, Sophie is outside right now. In Dad's car. And there's no point denying it. She taking it hard."

"What am I supposed to do?"

"Wake up to yourself!" exclaimed Julie. "And stop this foolishness! You know you need Sophie. I'll tell you what you're supposed to do. Go out to the car right now and apologise. Tell Sophie you were wrong to say what you said. Beg her for another chance."

Annie saw things differently. "Mum, I know you're upset. We all are. But Matt needs to work this out for himself. You can't tell him what to do. Please try to understand."

Julie glared at Annie and, suddenly lifting her arms, broke free from her daughter's embrace. Still shaking, she moved away a few steps. Matt closed his eyes, despising the confrontation but searching for a way forward. No-one spoke. Whatever he said or did now, the consequences would be heavy. Robert Smith was right. There were always consequences. Even if he said nothing at all now, there would be consequences. Something had to break. So he struggled to his feet and swallowed his pride.

"Could someone please go out to the car and tell Sophie I need to see her."

Annie and Julie looked at each other in suspicious wonder. Was this wise? Annie nodded tentatively at first, but then with more conviction. Julie took the hint and offered to go. Matt understood that Annie didn't want to leave him alone with his parents. But that was OK. He wasn't keen to face their simmering hostility without his sister to act as mediatrix.

Time stalled as Matt waited. Would Sophie come in as requested or would she refuse? Had she already refused? Is that why it was taking so long? Matt wondered if he should start making his way out to the car. But then, Julie and Sophie entered the room, arms around each other, as if to prevent either of them from collapsing on the floor. Through puffy, weepy eyes, Sophie looked around. Terry stood statue-like, staring down at his feet. Matt stood blankly, supporting himself with one hand on the edge of the table and wondering what drama was about to unfold.

Annie manipulated the scene with her eyes. She looked at Sophie in a way that communicated two things; firstly, the wedding was still off, but secondly, Matt was hurting too. Then, catching Matt's eye, she gently tilted her head towards Sophie. The message was clear: "Go on, give the girl a cuddle."

Matt opened his arms wide but the tear in his eye would have been enough. Sophie came to him, tentatively at first, but then warming to his embrace.

"I still love you Sophie."

She nodded but her eyes were not smiling.

Annie had successfully overseen the initial reconciliation. But that was only the beginning of her work. She asked Julie to organise some hot drinks and bring them to the lounge room, where the three of them would wait until Matt and Sophie were ready to join them. Even as she sought to comfort her parents, she began hatching a proposal.

When Matt and Sophie finally joined them, Annie asked the obvious question. "Is the wedding on or off?"

"It's off," they said, in unison. Sophie's answer smouldered with sad, confused emotion. Matt's answer gave nothing away. He had won the argument but it was a cold victory.

Annie proposed a solution. Even without the wedding, there was no reason Matt and Sophie couldn't go on the cruise as planned. The time away would be beneficial, provided that Sophie could forgive Matt and allow him the space he might need. And provided that Matt could commit to opening up more to Sophie. Annie sought and obtained these commitments. Then she suggested that the wedding could be rescheduled if, at some future point, it was what they both wanted. It was never planned to be a huge wedding anyway so there was no need for shame or recriminations. The relationship was strong. It could survive this setback, if in fact, that's what it was. Maybe it was an opportunity.

Sophie absorbed every word that Annie spoke. After Terry initiated some practical discussion, mainly about who would make which cancellation phone calls, she posed a question for Matt. Since she had already given final notice on her apartment, would she still be able to move in with him? She could use his spare room if he didn't want her to share his bed. Matt hesitated. He had completely forgotten about this.

With Matt's parents and sister as witnesses, Sophie then promised that she would no longer disrespect Matt's reservations about their relationship. She would try her best to make him feel comfortable in all aspects of their relationship. She would try to be the soulmate he needed as he battled his disease, his demons and his doubts. Matt could find no reason to disagree. So he nodded.

As the tension lifted, Julie started breathing again. She attempted a summation, addressed at no-one in particular. "So Matt and Sophie are just back to where they've always been."

"No Mum," replied Annie. "I think a lot of things will be different from now on."

Friday 29th May

Sophie drove Matt to work on the following Friday morning and then returned to her unit to pack the last of her things and do some cleaning. Despite his frequent absences – this was only Matt's second appearance at work for the week – he managed to make some useful contributions in a team meeting and some follow-up calls to customers. But the cruise started next week. His clients were all being taken up by Walter or Kerry, or Greg himself. And then there was Robyn. Or was it Ruby? The newest member of the team.

Four thirty in the afternoon, as Matt walked out the door of the Little Bird Marketing Agency, he glanced over his shoulder, wondering if he would ever work here again. Would this, in fact, be an important chapter in his life quietly slipping away? He stopped just outside the door. Had he forgotten that magazine that Greg wanted him to read? No. He distinctly remembered slipping it into his briefcase.

Matt looked around for Sophie but his brother was there instead. Josh had called Sophie and said he wanted to shout Matt to a coffee . The two brothers rarely had time together without the rest of the family so this was a good opportunity.

Josh quickly took the opportunity to ask Matt about the cancellation of the wedding.

"I think I did the right thing," said Matt. "Sophie is an amazing person but I'm too mixed up in my head. I'm not good enough for her. I get angry at her. And she doesn't deserve it."

"So you're trying to keep her at arm's length?"

"Maybe … but for her own protection."

"And you couldn't do that just the same with a wedding ring on your finger?"

Matt studied Josh for a moment. Where was this going? Was he accusing him of making a big mistake? But the innocently curious look on Josh's face gave no hint of malice. Matt searched for an intelligent answer.

"There are so many kinds of relationship in this world but marriage is different. It's a full-on legal commitment. And it's so incredibly personal. It's … it's an incredibly special thing between a man and a woman that I don't fully understand. I guess I'm not ready to make the sort of vows that you make in marriage."

Josh nodded. "Marriage brings plenty of challenges. I totally agree. But I can't even imagine life without Leslie and the kids. Marriage is a part of my life I've never regretted."

Matt smiled wistfully. "I wish I had your assuredness about these things. I still feel like a hopeless sinner trying hard to be somebody worth loving … worth getting married to."

Saturday 30th May

What do you do on your wedding day when the wedding is cancelled? Sophie opted to spend the day with her parents. When Matt queried her decision, she simply said: "Matt, I can't just hang out with you on the day we were supposed to be getting married."

Annie spent much of the day with her brother. With his permission, she organised some of his cupboard space so that Sophie would be able to unpack more of her things. She also helped him pack for the cruise. Matt knew, however, that this was just part of a family decision that he should not be left alone. Not today. Julie called in twice during the afternoon and Josh and Leslie had him around for an early dinner. Nothing was said about the cancellation and, when Sophie returned mid evening, Matt was checking his blog. No awkwardness, everything was perfectly normal.

Without a word, Sophie went back and forth, packing medicines, toiletries, passports, travel vouchers, phone chargers and a few books. All this with cold, mechanical efficiency. When she had finished loading the car, she brought Matt a coffee and sat quietly beside him. Waiting. Then, when he was ready, she helped him to his seat in her car and made sure he was comfortable. Then she drove an hour and ten minutes to the hotel that would shuttle them to the airport in the morning. From there, they would fly to Brisbane, where they would board their cruise ship. At the hotel, Matt settled gratefully into a soft armchair. He told Sophie that he needed to rest a while and, while she watched some TV, the exertion of the day caught up with him and he drifted off to sleep.

Monday 1st to Sunday 7th June

Walking around the various decks of the cruise ship was not easy for Matt. Sophie laughed at his attempts to cope with the gentle rocking but he didn't mind. She could spend time out in the sun, checking out the games and competitions. He was glad to retreat to the relative coolness and darkness of the internet café. Except for an occasional group of youths using the room for internet games, it was also very quiet in there, perfect for calm reflection on blog comments.

The cruise company took special care of Matt and Sophie. Every evening, at dinner, the activities co-ordinator personally delivered their copy of the next day's printed entertainment guide to their specially arranged private table in a quiet corner of the main dining area. Every evening, he asked how Matt was coping and offered his suggestions for the following day. He also arranged for one of the chefs to consult regularly with Matt about his dietary requirements and any unexpected physical reactions to anything he ate.

When their meal was finished each evening, they retired to their third deck, ocean view cabin. Matt would lie back on the bed while Sophie would tentatively plan their program for the next day. Since everything they did was dependent on Matt's health, they generally opted for less excitement and crowds, and more relaxation and privacy. Sophie enjoyed swimming in the pool that overlooked the stern of the ship and Matt often lay in the shade on a deck chair, just watching her. He had forgotten how beautiful she was; how well-formed and supple, how perfect the skin on her shoulders, arms and legs, her delicate mouth and nose, the twinkle in her eyes when she shook her long auburn hair, flinging splashes of water in his direction.

Matt allowed himself some dietary latitude at lunch times and Sophie readily agreed. He could follow the cancer diet for breakfast and dinner, but it didn't seem fair to just ignore all that magnificent food, especially since most of it was included in the price of the cruise.

Lunch times were also their most social times. There were always new people who would ask where they were from and whether or not they had taken such cruises before. Sophie confused one elderly couple by responding to the question: "Do you think you two will ever go on another cruise?" with: "No, definitely not!" Shocked, they asked if she and Matt were not enjoying themselves, to which Sophie responded that they were having a wonderful time. Just for fun, she decided to leave it at that and the bewildered couple moved tactfully away to another table.

One of the events that they did attend was a quiz afternoon, held in a quiet corner of one of the ship's bars. The Director of On-Board Entertainment, as part of his getting-everyone-to-know-everyone-else chit-chat, pointed to the table where Matt and Sophie were seated. "And we're delighted to welcome Matt Sherwin and Sophie Gardner this afternoon. Some of you might have seen Matt on TV or on the internet, talking about his blogspot competition to find the best religion." He hesitated. "Maybe I didn't explain that right but we're absolutely chuffed that you're both here with us this afternoon. I'm sure Matt would love to talk with you later."

Matt wasn't so sure about that but a few people did come up after the quiz to introduce themselves. One woman, who had been following the blog almost from the beginning, offered some opinions. But when it was all over, Matt used the hour of free time before dinner to scan several new comments. Nothing startlingly new this time, except that one reader theorised that each person, when they died, carried their last emotion into eternity. If you died happily and peacefully, you would be happy forever. But if, for instance, you died in terrible fear, that emotion would also last forever.

"Wow!" said Sophie when Matt explained this to her over dinner. "That sure brings up some interesting possibilities," she laughed. "I suppose you'd like me to kiss you at the very last moment. A kiss to last all through eternity."

"No way!" he exclaimed. "The way you kiss always makes me want more. I don't want to spend eternity desperately wanting to make love but never able to."

People at the next table looked up as Sophie shrieked with laughter. She and Matt both responded by looking at the ceiling in mock innocence before settling back to their respective meals with mischievous smirks on their faces. Matt was glad that he could joke about such things.

There were, however, more serious moments. One morning, at breakfast, Matt ate some pineapple fritters that somehow triggered a painful reaction in his stomach. His legs collapsed under him and Sophie had to call for paramedics to get him downstairs to the medical centre, where he remained for the best part of twenty-four hours. Tests proved that the food was not the problem. The ship's doctor finally concluded that Matt's liver was barely functioning and that this would be a developing problem in the weeks and months to come.

No healing miracle as yet but at least the cruise was working something of a miracle for the relationship and for Matt's frame of mind. The island stopovers were fascinating but hot. They spent time shopping in colourful markets, sitting in shady restaurants, sipping exotic wines and juices, sampling delicious fruit and watching the local children at play. But the on-shore visits had to be brief. The heat quickly exhausted Matt and he needed rest in the comfort of their cabin. Sophie understood. She could read while Matt slept.

It was the last full day of Matt and Sophie's cruise. They attended a "Couples Conflab" in the lavishly appointed main theatre area. At first they were disappointed that they were not selected to go on stage and participate. But, as the "conflab" unfolded, the discussion became more and more risqué. The audience clapped and laughed, while Matt and Sophie blushed and shared a look that said: "Phew, we dodged a bullet there!"

After lunch, as on other days, Sophie went up on deck to the main swimming pool, while Matt retreated to the coolness of the internet café.

The Dying Aussie blog had now been going for eleven weeks and many thousands of people had viewed it at least once. Several hundred were avid readers. But Matt wondered if it was reaching a wide enough audience to draw out the best responses to his questions. Hinduism, for instance, was a major world religion that still had not registered a single point on the scorecard. Same with Judaism. Was the whole thing becoming too random? Too arbitrary? Indeed, more and more critics were writing in, challenging Matt to justify his decisions. Why had he given points to crazy things and denied points to comments that were better reasoned and more articulate? There were even a few attempts to override his safety protocols and compromise the whole project. Some readers were fanatics for some particular viewpoint and others were just fascinated by the variety of ideas that were coming through.

A Muslim writer named Saheed described Islam as "*a holistic way of life that promoted good discipline and decency*", especially when compared with Christianity, which "*allowed all kinds of wanton debauchery*". Matt decided that Saheed's remarks were not relevant to the big question about dying and preparation for death, so it could not get a point.

Finally, that Sunday afternoon, Matt found a comment that brought up the first point for Hinduism. It wasn't a classic argument, and there had already been any number of reincarnation theories, but Matt thought this one was better. Could he justify giving it a point? Maybe not, but then, he didn't have to justify his decisions. This was his journey, his blog and his life.

Have you ever wondered what it would be like to live as an animal or a bird or a fish? Have you thought about what it would have been like to live a century ago or a thousand years ago? You are a man but have you ever wondered what it would be like to live as a woman? You live in a well-to-do economy. Have you ever thought about what life would be like in a poverty stricken village in times of drought? You see, in each of our lives, we experience a tiny part of the world. We see everything through this one narrow set of eyes. But there is so much more to the world.

People say that you only get one shot at life. But that's not how the universe works. Imagine if you only had one shot at learning to walk? Or one shot at cooking a nice meal? It doesn't make sense. Why would this world be so rich in its diversity if we weren't meant to experience it through different eyes? Many, many different eyes and many, many different lives. As a Hindu, my worldview is much more liberating than so much that I have read on your blog. We have many different gods and each one adds richness and colour to the culture we enjoy.

Don't be afraid of dying, Matt. All those things you never thought you could do, you will still do them. You will be a star athlete, a Bollywood star, a hunting dog, an astronaut at a space station, a poor woman scraping together a bowl of rice for your hungry children. You will yet see and experience all the richness of life. Sure, make the most of your time in this life but don't worry if some things elude you now. There will always be another chance. This life is just another link in a wonderful eternal chain.

Progress Score: Atheism 6, Christianity 5, New Age 4, Buddhism 3, Aboriginal Religion 2, Dying Well, Hinduism, Paganism, Practical Stuff 1.

17 - AN UNEXPECTED FRIENDSHIP

Monday 8th to Thursday 11th June

By Monday night, Matt and Sophie were back in Mona Shores, seated once again at the family dinner table and answering awkward questions. Had the cruise been good for their relationship? How was the anti-cancer diet going? Josh wanted to know about the islands they visited and Leslie was more concerned with getting young Chelsea to eat the vegetable lasagna that Julie had prepared.

But cancer is relentless. It allows an occasional reprieve, when other things take centre stage, like relationship issues, a holiday, a cruise. But cancer craves the limelight and will not tolerate being upstaged by anything.

Tuesday morning, it was time for the next round of chemotherapy. Another two days in hospital, at least. Dr Barlow was overseas but two other oncologists called in, one of them responsible for choosing which chemicals would be administered this time.

Sophie was grateful to have another week of holidays, plus one extra rostered day off. She was able to sit with Matt for the first few hours each day. Then, while he slept in the afternoon, she returned to the house to unpack more of her things and catch up on some housework. She called Greg at Little Bird to update him on what was happening. Then it was back to the hospital.

For some reason, Matt coped better with the second day of this third round of chemo than any of his previous sessions. The hospital staff could not explain why it should feel any different. They simply said: "That's good." Matt wondered aloud to Sophie if there might be some benefit in continuing the treatment after the two days already booked in for next week. If it was helping, that is. But surely, he reasoned, something that powerful must be doing something to the cancer.

Sophie picked Matt up from City Central on Thursday afternoon. Then, while he rested, she prepared a pumpkin and broad bean curry for dinner, a recipe that Donna had suggested. But, less than an hour after dinner, Matt became agitated and Sophie barely managed to get him to the bathroom before he spewed up a paste of thick grey bile. "Nice comment on my cooking," she mumbled wearily. Perhaps it was a side-effect of the chemo. She would have to make a note about this for the nurses at the hospital.

A cheery voice called out from the front door. "Hello Matt, Sophie." As Donna entered the room, Sophie gestured anxiously toward Matt, who waved a greeting but couldn't speak. With one hand around his throat and pushing down with his chin, he was obviously in pain. Later, he said that it felt like a blowtorch was searing away the lining of his throat. Sophie wanted to rush him back to hospital but he objected fiercely, his free hand shooing her away.

The pain eased and Matt rested in the lounge room while the two sisters chatted in the kitchen. "Tough way to live," said Donna. "I don't know how you keep going."

Sophie smiled philosophically. "What else can I do?"

Friday 12th June

Sophie answered the telephone when Uncle Gavin called on Friday evening. After the usual pleasantries, she took the handset to Matt at his sunroom chair. He reassured Matt that he had done the right thing by cancelling the wedding, that this was not the time to change the "relationship dynamics". He went on to talk about Matt's blog. He had only recently taken an interest and he was going to send in his first comment.

True to his word, ten minutes later there was this comment.

Christianity is a dangerous religion. It promises light and goodness but it's actually all about control. Other religions are much simpler to follow. You go through a few rituals from time to time and you're in. No one hassles you, not that I believe in any of them. But Christians think they have to control their deepest thoughts and desires, even when they're perfectly natural. There's a whole organisation telling them how to behave, what to say, what to do with their money, their bodies, and everything. And they're never happy. It's always more, more, more. There's no such thing as a 'good' Christian because they judge by impossible standards. If there really is life after death, I can't imagine any of the Christians I've known making it to Heaven.

I appreciate what you're doing. I know it must be hard. But seriously, Matt. There's an easier way. I strongly recommend that you go with an atheistic outlook.

Signed: Uncle Gav.

Sophie brought Matt a coffee and asked if he was reading anything interesting.

"Uncle Gavin sent in a comment. Looks like it might be another point for atheism."

Sophie asked if she could read the comment but Matt decided to read it aloud.

"Why would that be worth a point?" she wondered. "Seems like he's just bagging Christians, not giving you anything positive about atheism."

Matt considered that for a moment. "You know what?

You're absolutely right. It doesn't deserve a point. Uncle Gav always has something to say and I guess I just assumed it would be relevant." He looked up from the computer and smiled. "Thanks."

Over the next few days, Matt was well enough to work on his blog with renewed vigour. There were more weird comments to file or delete, including one that mentioned a "spiritual telegraph moment" that occurred a few minutes after death. The theory was that the universe allowed a brief window of time for some sort of sensory message to be transmitted back to loved ones left behind. Something like the quick message you might send when you were about to board a plane. This correspondent was urging Matt to have his message ready, when the time came, because the opportunity would not last.

Another comment, from someone calling himself Jeremy C, characterised death as The Dark Lord, with the suggestion that he (or it) could be bribed by dying folk who demanded a face-to-face meeting. If the Dark Lord would not accept a bribe, the correspondent said he might be open to bargaining. Unfortunately, Jeremy C failed to mention what the dying person could possibly possess that the mysterious Dark Lord could desire.

Several comments were easily aligned with comments that had already gained a point. Others were little more than advertisements for some particular church or movement. But Matt noticed a raft of comments coming through, adding to some that had been up for months, that attempted to demolish anything to do with religion. These negative, sometimes nasty comments, attacked such ideas as a loving God, a perfect Heaven, the survival of the soul and, especially, the idea that there must be justice and order in the universe. When Matt read some of these comments to Sophie and asked her suggestion for a good name to file them under, she immediately picked up on the word 'nasty'. Thus thirty-five supercritical, hope-destroying comments were collected, without points, in a new folder titled Nasty Stuff.

Monday 15th June

On Matt's request, Sophie, Terry and Julie joined him for a late afternoon meeting with a counsellor from Palliative Care. The counsellor, a grey-haired woman with a motherly, no-nonsense disposition explained that there were different Power of Attorney arrangements that people could make. An Enduring Power of Attorney Financial would give the designated person authority to act on Matt's behalf for legal or financial decisions such as selling property, paying bills or managing bank accounts. She said that such authority would greatly simplify matters if and when Matt reached a point where he was no longer competent to make such decisions himself.

Matt looked immediately to Sophie, whose hand he was holding. She frowned her astonishment that such a question would even have to be asked. "Of course!" she spluttered impatiently. "I may not be your wife but I do know all our financial stuff. Why wouldn't I do that?"

The counsellor explained that some people have much more complicated finances, with properties and investments that may require professional management. Sophie shrugged that off as irrelevant. Matt was no high roller. His financial affairs were easy.

But then the counsellor went on to explain about Enduring Power of Attorney Medical. This was about appointing someone to make medical decisions on Matt's behalf, maybe agreeing to surgery or other medical procedures or treatments. Or refusing. The counsellor stressed that this authority only kicked in if and when Matt became unable to make those decisions himself. And it had to be someone Matt would trust to know and follow through his wishes.

Julie and Terry looked instinctively to Sophie but she was not so sure about this. The counsellor smiled and nodded in obvious relief when Sophie simply said: "Don't look at me. This is Matt's decision. But, for what it's worth, I think he

212

should appoint his Dad."

Julie started to protest but one glance at her husband, with that stern but compassionate look on his face, melted her objections away. Sophie knew no-one could argue. She was right. But, it was still up to Matt, who simply nodded. "Will you be my medical attorney thingy, Dad?"

He answered hesitantly. "I'd be happy to, Son. Of course. But are you sure?" He looked at Sophie who instantly threw the question to Matt with a respectful, over-to-you look. But the words didn't come for Matt so it fell to Sophie to explain her reasoning.

"I love Matt dearly," she said, looking into his eyes. "But I'm not sure I won't be too emotional when the time comes. This has to be all about what you want, Matt, and I just don't know if I can keep my own ..." What was the right word? "... my own wants ... out of it. I'm basically a selfish person. I might be tempted to go against what you want." She smiled weakly. Did they understand? She looked across at her father-in-law. "Terry, you're the best person for this. Matt can trust you to listen to what he wants and then follow it through. You're strong enough to hold the line on what's right. I think we can all trust you to make the right decisions when the time comes."

Speech over. Everyone, including the counsellor, looked to Terry. A small tear appeared in the corner of his eye. He couldn't speak but a barely perceptible nod showed that he understood. Julie hugged her husband and Sophie kissed Matt.

The counsellor repeated several admonitions and even found some new ones. Sophie wondered if she thought Matt was being forced into a decision he didn't want. But Matt listened patiently, nodding and smiling as appropriate, until it was obvious that the counsellor had said everything she felt she had to say. Then: "I'm happy for Soph to be my financial Power of Attorney and for Dad to be my medical Power of Attorney."

"Enduring," corrected the counsellor. "You're not specifying a particular time frame ..."

"Yeah, yeah, I understand. Do you have the forms in that satchel of yours?"

Matt used the spare time before the Monday night family dinner to post a simple request.

Congratulate me! I now have enduring medical and financial power of attorney worked out. But there are so many things to think about. Give me some more practical stuff that I might not have considered.

Because Matt needed to prepare for chemo the next morning, he and Sophie returned home earlier than usual from the family dinner. It had already been a long day. Sophie folded some washing and packed a hospital bag while Matt checked the blog again. There were two noteworthy responses.

Hi Matt. This is my first time commenting on a blog. A friend suggested I look you up. I survived breast cancer three years ago but I had a sister who died of the same thing nearly ten years ago. The big thing for us as we looked after her was to make her comfortable in every way. We wanted her to be as pain-free and worry-free as possible. We gathered around her and just looked after everything. She absolutely hated the chemo and, in the end, the prospects weren't good for continuing so, like I said, it just came back to being comfortable.

We reassured her that her two kids would be loved and cared for. We respected her wishes in every way. And I won't say it wasn't incredibly sad when she finally went but there were no regrets. We knew we had done everything humanly possible. And she died peacefully, knowing that she was loved and that she would be missed.

Dying is such a hard journey but I strongly recommend that you focus on what makes you as comfortable as possible for as long as possible. Keep your family and friends close. Let them help. It will be good for them and good for you. This kind of approach may even help you to beat the cancer. But if it doesn't, it's still the most compassionate and most thoughtful approach to a terminal disease.

Signed: Peaceful.

Okay. Another point for Dying Well. That was a nice, compassionate answer but the next comment left Matt profoundly shocked.

My advice? Let the end come on your own terms. When your good days are over and the only future prospect is pain and suffering, I recommend you gather your family and friends, say your goodbyes while you can, have some prayers if that's what you want, say whatever you want to say, and then end your life with an injection. You can find help with this on the Internet. Some call it assisted suicide but it's really just like going to sleep.

Signed: Zane.

Matt thought long and hard about this last point. Sure, thoughts of suicide had entered his mind from time to time, sometimes even on his better days. So far, these thoughts had never been about ending pain; they were more about preventing pain for Sophie, his family and so on. But such thoughts never lasted long. Suicide would only make things worse for the people left behind. Way, way worse.

But, on the other hand, who could really know how this was going to end? There had already been so many horrible, dismal days. Perhaps the day would come when he literally couldn't stand it anymore, when life was no longer worth living. How would he make that call? Until he got to that point, how would he know? It wasn't something that could realistically be covered by the Medical Power of Attorney thing. Who could know? Maybe there would come a time when Zane's advice would be the best option.

Zane's comment was surely too controversial, too radical to earn a point. But then again, it was original, and it was getting harder and harder to find original comments. Was it helpful? Maybe. Certainly not now but maybe in the weeks or months to come. Would he be painting himself into a corner that he would regret if this came out on top with the most points? Scary thought!

"OK," said Matt under his breath. "It's worth a point but

it won't affect the final result of the contest." He paused as he typed the update. "I won't let it."

Progress Score: Atheism 6, Christianity 5, New Age 4, Buddhism 3, Dying Well, Aboriginal Religion 2, Hinduism, Paganism, Practical Stuff, Assisted Suicide 1.

Tuesday 16th June

The fourth round of chemo, one week after the third, proved to be Matt's most difficult. A severe, throbbing headache oppressed him, robbing him both of sleep and ability to concentrate. The nurses dosed him up with paracetamol but they were short-staffed and the needs of other patients limited the amount of follow-up care they could give. Long into the night, he lay watching shadows from the corridor and from the LED display on his clock radio. Who would have thought that digital numbers on a clock could be so bright and so tormenting?

Closing his eyes only served to loose his thoughts to wild ramblings. Voices from the blog haunted him. There is no God. No little 'g' gods either. There's nothing out there, nothing to look forward to. Choice means nothing. Memories are nothing. Love is nothing because all knowledge of loved ones must one day cease.

In the darkness, Zane's morbid advice began to make sense. But assisted suicide? Surely he could manage suicide without assistance. There must be hundreds of easy ways to do it yourself. Obviously not now, not tonight, but what would be the harm in thinking about it?

When Sophie called in before work the next morning and asked how he had slept, Matt said he had slept "like a baby". When she asked if he experienced any side-effects from the chemo this time, he said: "No, all good."

Thursday 18th June

Sophie collected Matt from hospital at 11.30 on Thursday morning. Early lunch break for her but neither of them were hungry. Nor could either of them manage a smile. Matt was reeling from this last round of chemo and Sophie was just exhausted.

For Matt, it was one of those annoying, fidgety days. The pain was strong but not intense. His mind was clear but restless. While Sophie was at work he alternated between watching TV and sleeping. Pastor O'Farrell had left some DVDs but they were sitting on some books on the little table next to the bed, serving no purpose other than preventing the books from collecting dust.

Approaching their normal dinner time, Sophie was not yet home. Matt had already checked the blog twice, through hazy afternoon eyes, but now he checked again and found a few things that seemed to deserve points.

Hi Matt. I'd like to share an idea from Buddhism that I think is very practical. It's called divesting. And what that means is that you seek to divest yourself from everything that ties you to this life. You think about things that you could never imagine living without, and then you just let go of all dependence on those things. You have to let go of everything when you die so divesting is the ideal preparation.

I'm not good at describing this but it's all about letting go of the stuff you have in your home, your bank account, your job if you still have one, your family, your friends, lovers if you have them, feelings, things you enjoy eating, sensations you enjoy. None of these things will go with you into death and rebirth. None of these things are part of the essential you.

Finally, if you do this, the day will come when you are ready even to divest yourself of your cancer-riddled body and the breath that only prolongs the illusion. In the end, if you learn how to do this, death will be nothing less than a relief. You will cross over in peace.

Signed Phil W.

Divesting himself of Sophie would have been inconceivable even a week ago. But now, horrendous thought, it almost made sense. Divesting himself of things that could bring comfort in the face of advancing death seemed like strange advice but, on another level, if death was going to take everything anyway … if death really is all about letting go … if … if …

But this was too painful. How could any human being let go of everything? Everything!

He read some more comments, stunned yet again by the overwhelming diversity of spiritual thinking, let alone spiritual practice, that he had drawn out with his blog. The next comment was from one of his earlier correspondents, New Age Nellie.

The problem, Matt, lies with your mind. Your overthinking this, as most people do. I don't know what physical ordeals your going through but it would be a dreadful shame if you went through mental torture as well. I've been learning some cool mind-control tricks. I know you don't like following up links but this one is very down to earth, easy to read. Please look it up. (She included a link.) *It will show you how to focus your mind on the good things that you can still do. They have simple exercises that you can do. If your in control of your thoughts, you will be able to control the whole process of dying so much better.*

Signed: New Age Nellie.

Matt sighed and clicked on the link. He found a variety of tricks about mind control, some of which described things like focused breathing, spirit-channelling or the use of charms and incense. He was too tired and unmotivated to follow these things up properly, although he did quickly experiment with a deep-breathing experiment. Did it help at all? Good question. How could it? But, for now, Matt added two more points, one to Buddhism and one to New Age.

Progress Score: Atheism 6, New Age, Christianity 5, Buddhism 4, Dying Well, Aboriginal Religion 2, Hinduism, Paganism, Practical Stuff, Assisted Suicide 1.

Friday 19th June

Sophie woke Matt with a gentle kiss. "I'm off to work," she whispered. "But, before I go, can I talk with you about something?"

Without a word, Matt struggled to a sitting position in his bed. He rubbed the sleep from his eyes. "OK but I'm really dry. Do you think you could get me a glass of water first?"

Sophie did as he asked and, while he was drinking, she adjusted his pillows. One of them had slipped away to the side.

"I'm sorry I can't help you with your shower this morning. Or getting dressed. I really have to be on time today."

"No worries. What did you want to talk about?"

She reached for his hand and made eye contact for a second. Then she had to look away before she could speak what was on her mind.

"Yesterday, when I got to work … late again … I asked about the possibility of going on compassionate leave. As I was going out the door to come home last night, our office manager stopped me and said it had been approved. They're willing to give me compassionate leave for as long as it takes."

Sophie hoped that Matt would be pleased but feared the opposite. Nervously, she watched for his reaction. At first, all she saw was a blank, hollow stare. But that soon gave way to anger and frustration. He slowly shook his head as if he had been offered a plate of tasteless, unpalatable raw vegetables by an irresponsible adolescent who should have known better.

Sophie fired up. "Why? What's the problem? I was only trying to help!"

"Were you just? Then why didn't you discuss it with me before you made the enquiry?"

"Well, duh, that's what I'm trying to do now!" She turned her back, more than ready to slam doors on her way out. But, instead, she hesitated long enough to remember that the gentle approach was the only thing that worked with Matt when he got into one of his moods. She swallowed what little pride was left and came back to sit on the bed.

"OK, Matt. Tell me what you're thinking. If you don't want me to take leave, please explain your reasons. Don't treat me like some stupid kid. I can't read your mind. I honestly don't know what you think about this, so … please … tell me." The last words were spoken softly, pleadingly.

Matt fumbled over his answer, unaware that Sophie was inwardly chafing about the likelihood that she was going to be late for work. Again.

It wasn't about the money. Matt's superannuation had a generous terminal illness component that would pay out in due time. It was more about a sense of independence, managing on his own for as long as possible. He hadn't even ruled out going back to work. Things would be OK. If and when his health deteriorated to a point where he could no longer cope, that would be the time for Sophie to take indefinite leave. Just not yet. In the meantime, he didn't want to be a burden on her. No, Sophie should keep working for as long as possible.

Sophie desperately wanted to challenge the line about being a burden. And she doubted that he would ever work again. To her, Matt's answers made no sense. But she thanked him for being honest, kissed him like she meant it, and left for work.

Two hours later, Matt's old cricket buddy, Shaun, arrived with a young friend, whom he introduced as Craig. No surname, just Craig.

Craig, a stocky man in his mid-twenties, with dense black hair, surprised Matt by acting like an old friend, right from the first "Hi, how y'doin?" He took a seat without being asked but immediately jumped up, asking if he could get coffees for everyone. Shaun got up to assist. "Craig and I have been hanging out a bit at the Regal," he explained. "He said he'd like to meet you. Hope you don't mind."

Matt shrugged his shoulders, wincing a little from some unexpected pain. The two friends, thus approved, stayed and chatted for almost two hours. Shaun explained that he had a rostered day off but Craig, apparently, was unemployed. On first impressions, Matt wondered if Craig was, in fact, unemployable for some reason. Maybe some subtle mental disorder. And yet, he didn't seem unintelligent. If anything, he was unusually outgoing, almost effusive. He talked about the saxophone lessons he was taking on Thursday evenings, a newspaper article he'd read about alleged criminal activities of an American spy agency in Nigeria, and a rabbit hutch that his Dad was helping him to make. Shaun jumped in from time to time, supplying just enough banter to balance Craig's enthusiastic ramblings. No talk about cancer, or death and dying. No talk about doctors or palliative care. Craig oozed friendliness and Matt was in no mood to object. But he had been checking his watch regularly and, finally, he announced the end of the visit.

"Sorry guys. I have a doctor's appointment in twenty minutes. I have to go."

Craig quickly offered to help. "I'll drive you. It's probably on my way."

"Oh … um … OK. I'll just see if Sophie is still at work. She was going to pick me up." He quickly called Sophie and, hearing that she was still busy with some accounts, he accepted Craig's offer.

Craig's car was a mess. Empty soft drink bottles, bent up magazines, soiled papers and clothes, and some woodworking tools littered the back seat and all floor space except that in front of the driver. A musty smell permeated the car which caused Matt to sneeze a couple of times. But he was grateful for the lift.

Thus began an unexpected friendship. So many old friends had dropped off the radar since the cancer but, with Craig, there was not the slightest hint of awkwardness. When Matt thanked him for the lift, Craig offered to wait for him, an offer that Matt quickly declined. When Matt thanked him again, Craig said: "No worries, mate. I think you're going to be my new best friend!"

18 - NO PLEASANT SURPRISES

Monday 22nd June

Craig arrived at 9.30 on Monday morning. Matt had not yet showered but answered the door in his boxer shorts. Craig busied himself with some newspapers that were sitting on Matt's coffee table while Matt took his shower. When Matt emerged wearing only his towel, Craig asked if he needed any help. Matt said no, he was just going through to the bedroom to get his clothes. And, having done so, he retreated to the bathroom to shave and dress. Craig called out some comments about the day's news and asked Matt how often he had visits from carers. When Matt came back to the lounge room, he was surprised to see Craig eating chocolate biscuits. "I brought you some chokky bikkies," he declared. "They're good. I've already had three."

Matt poured some cereal and took a seat at the dining table, inviting Craig to join him, not that Craig needed an invitation.

"So, what do you want to do today?" he asked.

Matt was a little stunned. "What do you mean?"

Craig smiled a "don't be silly" smile. "What do you want to do? I can drive you around, help you get groceries, take you to appointments … whatever."

"I hadn't really thought about it. Except that I'm meeting Sophie for lunch at Ritchies."

Craig thought a moment. "Have you checked out that new antiques and memorabilia shop out at the Star Plaza?"

"No, I haven't," replied Matt indifferently.

"Tell you what," grinned Craig. "I'll take you out there when you're ready. I reckon you'll enjoy it. They have lots of stuff. Old movie posters, replicas of swords and guns from famous movies … you name it."

"I don't know. I'm not feeling good for a lot of walking."

"No problem. I've got a disabled sticker on the car 'cause of my Mum. I can park right outside the main door to the centre. Won't be much walking at all. And I'll have you back in plenty of time for your lunch with Sophie."

"OK, but give me some time. I can't rush things these days."

"No problem," said Craig again. "Take your time. Oh, would you mind if I checked out the news on TV?"

"Who is this guy?" asked Julie at the regular Monday night dinner.

"Just a friend of a friend," answered Matt. "He drove me around a few places today."

"He's not … like … some sort of official carer?"

"No Mum, just a friend. He's OK."

All the usual crowd were there; Matt's parents, Josh and Leslie with their children, and, of course, Matt and Sophie. Julie had prepared a vegetarian quiche with extra mushrooms, lightly cooked carrots and beans, with a selection of herb breads on the side. Josh brought a bottle of Cabernet Sauvignon, for no special reason. Leslie brought a maple syrup pudding on request from her children.

223

Cancer had ceased to be the focal point of these gatherings. It was even OK to make jokes and laugh. But not so for Terry. He wanted to know every detail of Matt's latest visit to the oncologist or the palliative care people. As Matt wearily explained the latest changes to his medication regime, Terry listened with deliberate intensity, as if his reputation as a father depended on knowing and understanding all the minutiae of his son's medical journey. The rest of the family absorbed these details with nonchalant ease, except that the children were usually finished their dinner and onto their computer games or videos by that stage.

Returning from a visit to the toilet, Matt stood unnoticed in the doorway. Josh was showing his Dad a video clip on his tablet computer. Chelsea was chatting merrily with her grandmother as they cleared away the dishes together. Sophie and Leslie were sitting around the corner of the dining table, engrossed in conversation about one of the recent themes in Matt's blog. Something about the idea of divesting from material things. Leslie seemed to be arguing that such things, far from being a problem, could add comfort and meaning to each and every stage of life. Leslie had a knack for bringing practical wisdom to thorny philosophical problems. Matt couldn't see the other two children but he could hear them chasing each other in the next room.

He marvelled at how well Sophie fitted in with his family. That was a good thing because she rarely contacted her own parents, and they rarely contacted her. Only last week, on the way home from the family dinner, she had mentioned that she couldn't remember a single conversation with her parents that was half as interesting as the regular conversations around the Sherwin dinner table.

Julie was the first to notice Matt standing there. "Good, you're back." She dried her hands on a hand towel and called out to her family: "Excuse me. Can I have your attention for just a minute?" She retrieved a manilla folder from the drawer in the crockery cupboard. "I've written a little something and made copies." She handed everyone a neatly folded sheet of parchment paper marked on the outside with the words: "Thank You to my Family". Then she watched as each one unfolded the paper and silently read the note.

"Dear family. When I first heard about Matt's cancer, I was terrified. I didn't believe that I could cope. I didn't think that we, as a family, could cope. It was a nightmare with absolutely no upside. But I'm learning, slowly and painfully, to allow these times to be about life rather than fear. I'm learning the meaning of the word 'cherish'. You all need to know how much I cherish you. Cancer is a terrible thing but it hasn't broken this family. I know now that it never can. You are all so wonderful. Thank you. Thank you. Thank you."

Thursday 25th June

Craig certainly had some weird ideas. He talked about séances and strange paranormal goings-on in his grandmother's old house. Sharing a coffee with Matt in a busy coffee shop, he admitted to wondering if the Christian view of things was not, in fact, a distortion of the true reality. "How do we know," he speculated eagerly, "that the devil wasn't really the good one and the Christian god the evil one?" Matt gave him a bored, half-worried look but Craig was undeterred.

"You know they say it's only the winners that write history. How do we know the devil wasn't raising some legitimate concern with God way back when? Maybe he was only asking for a fair deal, but instead, he gets kicked out of Heaven and, from that moment on, he gets blamed for everything bad in the world. Maybe the devil was telling the truth and God was the one telling lies."

"Oh, come on," groaned Matt. "That's ridiculous!"

"Ah, but how do we know? Have you heard both sides of the story, or just one?"

"I ... uh ..."

"See!" Craig's whole face beamed a vigorous challenge. He was ready for a debate that Matt would rather have avoided. "Put it this way. Why are maps always drawn with the northern hemisphere up and the southern hemisphere down?

Think about it, Matt. It could have been the opposite. There's no up or down in space. But the first maps were drawn by people in the northern hemisphere so that's how we always think of it. Australia is "down under" but it didn't have to be that way."

Matt shook his head in disbelief. "You're mad."

It could have been taken as an insult but Craig accepted it as a compliment. "I know," he grinned. "But I just might be right."

"OK, tell you what," said Matt. "Write up all this God-is-bad, Satan-is-good stuff and send it to my blog. Let's see if you can make a case that warrants a point … for … um … I don't know. What would it be a point for?"

Craig squinted his eyes. A funny habit whenever he needed to think. "I dunno. Satanism, I guess. But OK. Challenge accepted. I'll see what I can come up with."

Friday 26th June

Julie stepped in once again to take Matt for a scan at the local hospital's radiology department. Dr Barlow wanted more information about the precise locations of Matt's tumours in order to determine if the chemotherapy had achieved anything.

Lying in the machine, listening to music that took him back to his childhood, Matt's thoughts wandered. What was it about the word 'lying'? Why the two meanings? For one thing, it described what he had to do in this horrible machine but it also meant speaking things that were not true. Why was that? Was there some connection, apart from the fact that he was doing a lot of both lately?

He thought back to times when he had lied to his parents. The pornographic magazines and websites that were so carefully concealed. The various little 'incidents' at school that he was too embarrassed to admit. The many, many nights he had told his mother that, yes, he'd finished his homework when, in reality, he was just listening to music or dreaming about sports.

He thought about the countless summer hours he'd spent

hitting a tennis ball against the brick chimney at the back of his childhood home. The bounce was never predictable because the mortar between the bricks was uneven, as was the grass in front of him, so he would have to react quickly to the changing trajectories of the ball. But the aim was always to keep the ball in control for as long as possible. He thought that was a bit like trying to deal with the unpredictable bounce-back of the cancer in his body. The goal was the same, to maintain some sort of control for as long as possible. But not forever. That could never be possible.

He thought about some of the girls he'd fallen for in his teenage years. The ones he'd kissed. The ones he'd written little love-notes for. The ones who totally spurned his awkward advances. Would any of those girls have been better partners than Sophie?

He remembered his first meeting with Sophie. She had attended some cricket matches with a friend whose brother occasionally got a game in Matt's team. He had noticed her. Really noticed her. But the opportunity to meet her didn't come until some five or six weeks later. Their team had won a semi-final and everyone had gathered at the Regal Bar and Bistro to celebrate. Sophie and her friend were sitting together at a small table under a wall-mounted TV on which a soccer match was being telecast. Matt saw his chance.

"Good game, eh?" Those were his first words to Sophie and he had confused her from the start. He remembered her screwing her neck to look up at the TV on the wall. "Dunno. Haven't really been watching." Her first words to him.

"No, no, I meant the cricket. Our match. Today."

Matt thought about the one big lie he had told to Sophie after they had been seeing each other for a few weeks. The question had come up about sexual partners. "Just once," he'd said. "It was nothing. Just some girl I met at a party and never saw again."

What Matt neglected to mention was Michelle, the love of his life in his late teens and very early twenties. Michelle, who had drifted in and out of his life over a period of four or five years. Michelle! Controlling, unreliable, painful Michelle. The flighty young girl who had schooled him in love but also schooled him in emotional disaster. The wreckage from Michelle had veered him away from romance and into media studies, from where she faded into such obscurity that she didn't warrant even the slightest mention when a new love finally arrived on the scene.

But now, here he was. Lying motionless as he passed, section by section, through a big ugly machine. So much to regret. So much unfulfilled potential. Yet somehow, if the blog could only lead to something that would make sense of it all. If something could somehow connect up all the dots. Maybe it could still work out the way it was always meant to.

Saturday 27th June

"You've got that comment from Craig on your blog this morning," called Sophie from the lounge room, where she was trying to sort out a box of tangled computer leads. Matt was in the dining room, grappling with his fruity muesli and yoghurt.

"Well how do you know that?" grumbled Matt.

"Pardon?"

"How do you know that?" replied Matt, much louder this time.

"He phoned while you were in the shower."

"Oh … Thanks."

Five minutes later, armed with a strong coffee, Matt settled down with his laptop, Sophie kneeling on the floor on the opposite side of the room. A few clicks on some familiar keys, and there it was, Craig's answer to God.

The Christian God is opposed to freedom and self-actualisation.

Matt wondered how Craig came up with that.

The Devil wanted to give people more choices in life but God was too mean to give the Devil his request. God made things even tougher for people as a result like Phairo in Egypt when Moses asked him to let the people go, and he made them work harder instead.

Again, Matt marvelled that Craig would know about such things.

The Devil was thrown out but not destroyed. He's still out and about to this day, keeping busy and waiting for his chance to overthrow God. So Matt, you see it's all a great big gamble. When we die, we might find out that the Devil was telling the truth and God was lying. I wouldn't be surprised if Christianity was a big cosmic trap for our souls. This so-called god wants to make us all little cloans but we should be exploring our full potentual. Forget the stereotipes. Choose Satan. Choose life and real liberty.

For the first time, Matt felt pressured to allocate a point against his better judgement. Craig appeared on the doorstep later that morning, his sheer enthusiasm putting Matt on the back foot. Strangely enough, Craig stopped short of claiming that what he had written was true. It was an option, a plausible explanation of things that deserved a point. Was it original? Yes, there had been nothing quite like it on the blog before. Craig argued that he had fully researched Satanism on the internet and it was, in fact, a serious religion. He went into some detail describing the worship rituals that he'd read about on one site. He pointed out that Satanists had their own Bible, a fact Matt already knew.

But was any of this helpful to Matt? Craig waxed eloquent about the need to be open-minded, to face one's "dark side", and to explore all possibilities. Matt had to take some prescriptions to his chemist so Craig drove him there, and from there to a shopping centre, where he shouted Matt to a sushi bar lunch. Three times, they were in and out of Craig's car; and three times Craig held forth about the merits of his blog post. Finally, more from exasperation than genuine conviction, Matt agreed to award a point to Satanism. What harm was there? Satanism was never going to win the contest anyway.

What Matt didn't foresee was the backlash that this would cause. Several blog followers wrote to say that this was the last straw. The contest had become a farce and the blog was no longer worth reading. Worse than that, Craig's post inspired a mini-flood of bizarre concepts. Sifting through them became something of a nightmare. More and more comments blurred the line between reality and fantasy. More and more comments found their way into the 'delete' bin, sometimes without due consideration. A few key words popping up on the first line was all it took.

But one new comment intrigued him.

I believe there is a way to know what happens after death. Since the mid nineteenth century, people have been recording the words of mediums who contacted spirits of the dead. For example, a Frenchman called Allan Kardec wrote a book that he called 'Le Livre de Spirits', published in English as 'The Spirit's Book'. It had more than a thousand questions that he asked mediums when they were in contact with disembodied spirits. The answers were not freaky and ridiculous but calm and reasonable. The stories that the mediums told him led Kardec to conclude that each individual soul is evolving through a limited series of reincarnations and that the universe itself helps in this process. So the physical universe is a stage for every individual consciousness. It means we don't have to worry too much about dying because it's all part of a good, positive process. Some disembodied spirits are assigned to help dying souls through the reassignment of their consciousness. Modern mediums who communicate with the dead can help you understand. Signed: Jonas Free.

Matt wrote back, asking Jonas what religion this was. A reply came, almost instantly.

Lots of religions believe and use mediums for one thing or another. I would say most people who sincerely explore these teachings would call themselves spiritualists.

Two new categories thus made their debut on Matt's chart.

Progress Score: Atheism 6, Christianity & New Age 5, Buddhism 4, Dying Well & Aboriginal Religion 2, Hinduism, Paganism, Satanism, Spiritualism, Practical

Stuff, Assisted Suicide 1.

Wednesday 1st July

The backlash continued. Matt was shocked to hear that he had been mentioned by an American news network.

"Popular Australian blogger, Dying Aussie, has turned out to be a fraud. Matt Sherwin has attracted worldwide curiosity by launching a contest between the different religions. He says he's dying of cancer and, after July 31st, if he's still alive, he will convert to the religion or philosophy that has the most points according to his own highly-contrived points system. But now it appears he's just a fake. He doesn't even have cancer and the whole thing is a not-so-subtle attempt to promote his own religious views. Professor Selwyn Hobbs, of University of Southern California, has analysed all the posts. The professor pointed out today that comments published on the blog were obviously written by one person trying to feign different writing styles. "

The announcer shook his head. "Apparently you can't trust anyone these days."

The whole news item took just twenty-five seconds. But people somehow believed the unsubstantiated accusations. A British newspaper published a piece that assumed the fraud and went on to discuss the "psychology of internet notoriety". An Australian radio station joked about it in a talk show. Funny thing, though. No-one called Matt, let alone his doctors, to find out if the accusations were true or not.

Of all Matt's family and friends, Julie was the only one genuinely distressed by the whole affair. "They think my son is a liar!" she fumed at Terry. Donna offered to post her name and address for anyone who might want to verify Matt's story. That way, she could protect him from unwanted media glare and, hopefully, put an end to the false accusations. Matt called Greg Sparrow to ask his opinion. Should he respond to the accusations? "No", counselled Greg. "This sort of thing is quickly forgotten. All you could achieve by responding would be to perpetuate the foolishness." Sophie thought the whole thing was funny.

For two days, Matt was engulfed in the craziness, huffing and spluttering about the ignorance and sensationalism of the media. But a Friday afternoon appointment with Dr Barlow brought him back to more pressing issues. His white blood cell count had dropped. The chemo hadn't slowed the cancer at all. New tumours were appearing, especially in the stomach region. Dr Barlow's nurse gave Matt an injection to help compensate for his dropping immune level but the prognosis was grim. The cancer was moving dangerously fast.

The mood in the car hovered somewhere between shock, anger and despair as Sophie drove home from the doctor's rooms. "Won't this ever end?" thought Matt, but then again, that was the problem. Life was hurtling to an ending. An awful ending. Matt closed his eyes and swallowed hard.

"Can I ask a favour, Soph?"

Sophie heard but drove on in silence for a few moments. Then she nodded gravely. "Yeah, of course. What do you want?"

"Can you drop me off at the beach? I just want to watch the ocean for a while."

She looked across as if to see if Matt was serious. "It's pretty cold today. Are you sure?"

Matt nodded.

"Well, I can park at Featherwind Point if you like. We can watch the ocean together from there without even getting out in the cold."

"No, just drop me off at the main beach. Please. I … just need some time alone." That wasn't exactly right because, with Sophie working, he had plenty of alone time. "I'd just really like some time on the beach," he added. "I'll text you when I need you to pick me up."

Sophie had been right. The stiff southerly breeze chilled his bones as he leaned against the railing of the platform above the beach. From a medical point of view, this was a bad idea. But this wasn't about a diseased body. The wind couldn't blow away the cancer but maybe it could blow away some of the confusion and despair in his soul.

I'm letting everybody down. Everything I do gets messed up in some way. I'm not a good person. I've even managed to make enemies on the other side of the world. People who've never even met me reckon I'm a fraud. And maybe I am.

Tears rolled down his cheeks and he didn't even care, not out here, not in this biting, face-chilling weather.

Monday 6th July

"How do you guys handle depression?" asked Matt at the family dinner. "I mean, what do you do when things are getting you down?"

No-one answered for a moment. Leslie was the first to jump in with an answer.

"I think about my kids."

Julie nodded. But somehow, Leslie's answer failed to resonate. Children could be wonderful to have around. But they grew up. They got themselves in trouble. And sometimes … well … sometimes they got cancer.

Sophie smiled a cheeky smile. "Sometimes, when I'm starting to get depressed, I ask my little sister to pray with me."

Matt was shocked. He hadn't known about Sophie's occasional lunches with Donna. "Does that help?"

Sophie shrugged her shoulders. "Not sure. It doesn't hurt."

"I've always wondered why people pray," ventured Terry, ever the logical realist. "If God knows what we need, why do we need to tell him? And if I'm praying at the same time as … I don't know … fifty million other people, how can God sort my prayer out from all those others? It never seems to change anything anyway."

"Do you speak from experience?" asked Julie, staring down her husband as only a wife can.

"Not really," said Terry, glaring back.

"Do you pray, Mum?" asked Matt, interrupting.

Embarrassment flashed on Julie's face. "Not as often as I probably should," she admitted.

233

"See!" Terry pointed a finger at his wife. "You only pray when you think you should. You don't actually get anything out of it. Otherwise you would pray a whole lot more often. That tells me that you don't really think it makes any difference."

Josh jumped in. "I don't think I've prayed since I was a little kid."

Julie was horrified. "What, you haven't even prayed for your brother?"

"No, not really," said Josh. "Hey, it's not that I don't care. I just don't see how it can help."

"Honestly, Julie," said Terry. "If prayer would get rid of Matt's cancer, I'd be on my knees every waking moment. I don't know how many people are praying for Matt … and I don't mean to be cruel … but it's not working!"

Julie shook her head in obvious indignation. "You should be ashamed of yourselves. What have we got to lose? We should all be praying for Matt every day."

Through the week, the comments on Matt's blog decreased significantly in numbers. Was this due to the "fake" allegations? Surely not. That wouldn't make sense. A little bit of unwanted publicity should generate more interest, not less. Some days now, even with the deadline approaching, Matt ignored the blog. It was all getting a bit predictable. Like the cancer. Everything had an air of inevitability. There were no pleasant surprises anymore.

19 - A GOOD LEGACY

Wednesday 8th July

Another rough day, medication not working well. Matt had always been capable of enduring a fair amount of pain when he knew it was only temporary. But this pain, this weakness, was different. There were no confident assurances any more. Matt was wrestling demons of rage and self-pity, desperately wanting to protect Sophie from the worst of his moods but failing. He tried to will himself to work on his blog but frustration was starting to show through.

Come on! ranted Matt on the blog. *Give me something fresh. Where are the Mormons, or the Witnesses, or the Kaluthumpians? I don't even know if Kaluthumpians are real. If they are, I probably didn't spell it right. But I've only got a few more weeks. Give me something fresh!*

Thursday 9th July

This latest challenge was quickly answered.

Dear Matt. I have been following your blog but I wasn't sure how to make my case. I'm a member of the Church of Jesus Christ of Latter Day Saints, otherwise known as the Mormons. You have awarded points for some very strange views and it's made me think about why we believe what we believe. For my part, I believe the teachings of our church for several reasons that I think are valid and relevant to your situation.

First, we believe the Bible but so, it seems, do most other people. The problem is that the Bible, in itself, is incomplete, and therefore open to interpretation. More divine inspiration was needed and that's exactly what we have in the Latter Day Saints. The Book of Mormon is actually another Testament to go with the Old and the New. Then we have Doctrines & Covenants and The Pearl of Great Price. Altogether, this makes for a complete understanding about how God wants us to live.

Secondly, none of the other main religions properly explain where our souls come from. Latter Day Saints can speak with authority about where our souls go when we die because they explain where our souls were before we were born. We were with God before we were born and God gives us this life so that we can experience good and bad and therefore choose the good. And I think that makes a lot of sense.

Thirdly, and lastly, although I could go on, the Latter Day Saints far exceed all other churches in their moral outlook. We promote healthy marriages and families and it's not just talk.

At the point of death your soul leaves your body and enters eternity. The Church of LDS gives the clearest picture of eternal life and therefore the greatest assurance to the saints. I don't think we will win your contest but that doesn't mean what I say is not true. Please consider what I have written.

Signed: Joseph Emmanuel Caruzzo.

OK, thought Matt. One point for the Mormons. Let's see where this goes.

Progress Score: Atheism 6, Christianity & New Age 5, Buddhism 4, Dying Well & Aboriginal Religion 2, Hinduism, Mormonism, Paganism, Satanism, Spiritualism, Practical Stuff & Assisted Suicide 1.

A blogger from Brisbane, unknown to Matt, picked up on his comment: "I've only got a few more weeks," and, assuming that Matt was talking about his life rather than the contest, the blogger claimed this was evidence that the whole thing was a fraud. *These are not the concerns of someone in the last stages of cancer!* One of Matt's regular readers alerted him to the post but, having read the offending comments, Matt decided not to respond. It was not possible to control what readers might think.

A first-time blogger contributed an analogy from nature.

When a seed is buried in the soil, it effectively dies so that new life can come. All through nature, we see a pattern of death and resurrection. Night gives way to morning. Winter gives way to spring. Check out a forest six months after a wildfire and you'll see new growth happening everywhere.

The apostle Paul used this to describe how resurrection works. Life comes out of death. Jesus rose from the dead and we believe because of him that we will also be resurrected in the last days.

The promise is not for some airy-fairy, surreal, floating on clouds heaven. I don't know how this can be but God has promised that, when Jesus returns, there will be a resurrection. We will have perfect new bodies, like Jesus had after his resurrection, and we will live forever in a perfect new world.

The Christian faith offers more than just the survival of the soul. It offers resurrection to eternal life through Jesus our Lord and Saviour.

Signed John.

In the following days, this "resurrection in nature" argument was savaged by one blog reader as *illogical and ignorant*. The new in nature was always different from the old that disappeared. Individual things disappeared but new

237

individual things appeared. New life was a theme in nature but resurrection was nonsense. Matt wasn't impressed with the refutation. After an especially difficult few days of life-sapping pain, he was not about to discard a message of hope so easily. Besides, he had already awarded another point for Christianity, which now moved ahead of New Age and level with Atheism.

Progress Score: Atheism & Christianity 6, New Age 5, Buddhism 4, Dying Well & Aboriginal Religion 2, Hinduism, Mormonism, Paganism, Satanism, Spiritualism, Practical Stuff & Assisted Suicide 1.

Friday 10th July

Yet another slow, painful morning. Sophie was at work, everything on television was exceptionally boring, and even Matt's best rock music compilation left him feeling listless and jaded. Craig arrived just before midday, bearing fried chicken and an idea. "Let me shout you to a movie," he enthused.

"I'm not supposed to eat fried chicken," groaned Matt. "But what's the movie?"

"World Pursuit," grinned Craig. "This guy's girlfriend gets murdered and the woman who killed her walks free. So he vows to chase her down and get his revenge. But, in the meantime, he's made himself some powerful enemies. So he's chasing this woman killer all around the world and a hit-man is chasing him. It sounds great! The afternoon session starts at two."

The movie was twenty minutes in and the action had moved to Buenos Aires. Craig was obviously loving every suspenseful moment but Matt was labouring under increasingly intense pain. The hero was climbing a tower, scanning for some cryptic landmark when Matt decided he could take it no longer.

"Please Craig. I need to get home."

Craig was stunned. He glanced back at the action. "But …"

"I'm sorry, mate. I'm really not feeling well enough."

Craig didn't say a word on the way home. Matt watched him drive and concluded that the unusual silence wasn't anger. Craig was just doing the right thing and inwardly weighing the cost.

Matt had to look some things up in his dictionary before awarding his next point.

I urge you to consider Feng Shui. Not only does it offer comfort and peace to the dying but it can be a key to healing and longevity. There are real forces around us that must be kept in harmony for optimal living. For instance, if your bed faces the sunrise, even if blinds are closed, or walls cover the rising sun, wellness is enhanced. I contacted a Feng Shui consultant recently and the results were outstanding. My husband and kids have stopped arguing, I'm not stressed out any more. I sleep better at night. Things are correctly balanced at last.

People think Feng Shui is just about the way you arrange furniture in your house but it can be applied outside the house as well. The same principles can help with your garden, or any other environmental factors that you can control. I hope, even yet, that you will go on to enjoy a long, happy life but if I was dying, I would want my environment to be as conducive to peace and harmony as possible. Let me know where you live and I'll arrange a consultant to visit you.

Signed Linda Z.

A little exploration on the internet revealed that Feng Shui was an ancient Chinese philosophy, that the name meant wind and water, and that its link with New Age thinking in recent decades had earned it a whole new popularity, especially in Western countries. Was it worth a point? He had to admit that his life had been unbalanced and out of whack lately. The advice seemed reasonable enough. But Feng Shui could not have a category of its own. Matt decided to award the point and, if New Age came out on top on 31st July, he would take up Linda's offer to arrange a visit.

Progress Score: Atheism, Christianity & New Age 6, Buddhism 4, Dying Well & Aboriginal Religion 2, Hinduism, Mormonism, Paganism, Satanism, Spiritualism, Practical Stuff & Assisted Suicide 1.

Into all this confusion and pain, Robert Smith once again chimed a note of hope. What was it about this guy? Faith was meant to be something outside of logic. How come he could write about faith and make it sound so logical and real?

Dear Matt, I want to make this very clear. God help me to find the right words. Some people think Heaven is a kind of reward for people who do a lot of religious stuff all through their lives. They think good people "go to God" when they die. But that's not what the Bible teaches. Eternal life doesn't start when we die. It starts the moment God's unique kind of life fills our soul. And THAT happens when we are born again by repenting of our sins and asking Jesus into our lives. When that happens, a whole new life starts. That's what "born again" means. We come alive in a way that you would never believe unless you experience it yourself.

Life is not a complicated web of mantras and spiritual rituals. Life is a person, Jesus Christ. In him, we pass from death to life while still in the body. Because he has already won the victory over death, the life we have in him is eternal. It surpasses physical death. So the best way to prepare for dying is to receive Christ.

Robert S.

Another point for Christianity. Matt wondered if the critics were right after all. Christianity was popping up more than any of the other religions. Largely due to Robert of course. So was it all just moving toward an inevitable conclusion? Was the competition collapsing into boring predictability? Was Christianity somehow getting an inside track run at the ultimate prize?

But no, that couldn't be right. He still had too many questions. Too many baffling doubts. A few bloggers insisting that Jesus came alive after he was dead didn't mean it was really true.

No. In his own mind, he was still honestly keeping all options open. And there were still two more weeks.

Progress Score: Christianity 7, Atheism & New Age 6, Buddhism 4, Dying Well & Aboriginal Religion 2, Hinduism, Mormonism, Paganism, Satanism, Spiritualism, Practical Stuff & Assisted Suicide 1.

Sunday 12th July

Sunday afternoon. It had been raining all weekend but the sun was shining through at last. Sophie decided that it was a good chance to deal with some of the weeds that had flourished in the back garden. Matt thought she looked a treat in her daggy shorts, gumboots and Texas windcheater. She enjoyed his mild mockery but, undeterred, clipped the cordless telephone to the top of her shorts and headed out the back door.

Five minutes later, she had barely commenced her work when the phone rang. She slipped her right hand out of its already muddy glove and pressed the 'talk' button. Matt was watching a football match on TV but happened to look out the window in time to see Sophie's reaction to the call. Something was obviously wrong. Sophie was holding her left hand up to her other ear, as if to be sure that she was hearing the news clearly. She walked in tight circles, asking occasional questions with an evident urgency, although Matt couldn't hear a word. Finally, she ended the call and turned towards the house, locking eyes with Matt through the sunroom window. Matt braced himself.

She slipped off her boots at the door. "I'm so sorry!" she said, with a despairing shake of her head.

"What is it?"

She came inside, took Matt's hands in hers and said: "It's Craig. They found him this morning, washing against the rocks at the bottom of Kennedy's Bluff."

Monday 13th July

The mood at the Monday night dinner was more sombre than usual. Matt's latest appointment with Dr Barlow had confirmed, yet again, that cancerous tumours were steadily growing in Matt's duodenum. Smaller tumours were detected on his large intestine and his liver was now only functioning at fourteen percent. On Julie's urging, Matt had asked, again about the possibility of a transplant but, again, the oncologist could only shake his head sadly. He had done his homework and discussed Matt's case with a surgical oncologist friend. Surgery was an "unrealistic" option. Matt was entitled to a second opinion but there was little hope that another oncologist would recommend surgery at this late stage. Surgery had, for all intents and purposes, been ruled out from the beginning. What would make it a more acceptable option now?

Was it the tumours or the news about Craig? Matt barely touched his meal. The mouthfuls that he did take produced a new, unnerving distress in the bowel region.

But Dr Barlow had not given up completely. He had arranged some further chemotherapy sessions. Although chemotherapy normally could not target any particular area of the body, the chemo specialist at Mona Shores hospital wanted to try a new combination of chemicals which had been shown to target cancers in the stomach and bowel areas.

Friday 17th July

It was odd to realise that Craig had a family. But of course he did. Both parents, both sets of grandparents, two older sisters and several other relatives attended his funeral, all of them with reddened eyes from incessant grief, all perplexed at the obscene waste of such a young life. A large gathering of other friends and acquaintances, many of them quite elderly, filled the large Catholic sanctuary.

None of Matt's many conversations with Craig had fleshed out his family as real people. But here they were and Matt felt like an intruder. His grief was different from theirs and it piqued his conscience. He had only known Craig for a few weeks but, during that time, the friendship had been both profound and one-sided. Matt was the one with a terminal disease and Craig was the one doing all the giving. Matt had no clue about the demons that must have been tormenting his strange friend.

The two sisters read eulogies from bits of paper held in violently shaking hands. One of Craig's uncles read a heart-wrenching message from the bereaved parents, neither of whom were anywhere near composed enough to read it themselves.

What sort of friendship had this been anyway? The funeral revealed Craig in all his many dimensions; the playful, mischievous child, the ever-curious reader of unusual books, the larrikin practical joker, the overly generous son. All of these things were new to Matt, who now wondered how he could have been so selfish.

That night, after dinner, Matt logged on to his blog and tried to express what he was feeling.

I attended a funeral today for a friend. I didn't know him for long and I never really made any effort to understand him. He gave freely of his time but I took him for granted. It was like I thought I deserved the things he did for me. But now I feel bad, not for me but for him. Cancer is a horrible thing but it shouldn't be an excuse to treat people badly. I don't know how to deal with this. I don't think I'm a bad person but dying seems to be making me intolerably selfish. I'm so scared for what I'm becoming.

Saturday 18th July

Matt awoke early the next morning. It was Saturday, time for a sleep-in. But his head ached and he was too uncomfortable to continue in bed. He stumbled into the spare room, where Sophie lay, wrapped under her doona and sleeping deeply.

"Are you awake?" He said it again. "Soph? You awake?"

She groaned. "No! I'm asleep! Go away!"

"Could you get me a coffee?"

She rolled over and half opened her eyes. "What?"

"Could you get me a coffee … please?"

Sophie rolled out of bed and stumbled to the kitchen. When she eventually returned and placed a steaming hot coffee on the little table next to Matt's bed, he ventured another request.

"Could you get my laptop … please?" As she turned wordlessly to get it, he called out: "Love you."

"Love you too," she nodded on her way out the bedroom door.

Concentrating was not easy. Propped up in bed with pillows, coffee and laptop, Matt was surprised to find some seemingly intelligent comments.

My friend, I hear you. What you're going through is bringing you face to face with a reality that offends your inner being. It's not how you want it to be. So you struggle with who you are. But there is hope where you would least expect to find it. Death is not the enemy here. Your real problem is the same problem we all face. We hold so tightly to the concept of self and we're terrified of letting it go. Self is the problem. Letting it go is the way to life. Death can be a friend that brings enlightenment because death breaks down the illusion of self.

If you meditate on death, you will see that I'm right. It will become your most cherished friend and you will be able to look outside of your self. Your individual self will fade away and you will die a better person.

You've given points to Buddhism before. I hope you see the relevance of what I'm saying.

Signed: Sun Yat.

Matt freely acknowledged that 'self' was a big concern. He closed his eyes and tried to imagine the demise of 'self'. It was an impossible exercise. But the contest had another ten days or so to run. He didn't need to put any of the blog suggestions into practice just yet. If Buddhism came out on top, he had some good starting points lined up to help him with that.

244

Progress Score: Christianity 7, Atheism & New Age 6, Buddhism 5, Dying Well & Aboriginal Religion 2, Hinduism, Mormonism, Paganism, Satanism, Spiritualism, Practical Stuff & Assisted Suicide 1.

Monday 20th July

The previous chemotherapy therapy sessions had involved two nights in hospital. This time, it took three nights because preparations were more complex. Matt was not allowed to eat anything on the Monday night but he didn't care. He wasn't even hungry. The rest of the family met together as usual, except for Sophie, who stayed with Matt until almost midnight.

The chemo was administered on Wednesday and Thursday. Matt noticed a steep increase in the amount of nursing attention he was getting. Only one of the nursing staff was male but, male or female, it didn't matter. He made an effort to strike up conversation with each one. It was important that, somehow, this latest hospital stay was not going to be miserable and self-centred.

Thursday 23rd July

Computer time was not just about the blog. There were games to play with intriguing challenges and levels to attain. There were no routines any more. Sometimes, he checked the blog in the evening, sometimes in the afternoon or morning, sometimes not at all.

Thursday morning, 7.30. Matt was already sitting up in his hospital bed, working the blog, when Sophie called in before work. She came and sat on the chair next to his bed.

"Anything interesting?" she enquired.

"Another point for Atheism," he answered. "I've had comments along this line before but I think this one pulls things together a bit better. Let me read it to you."

OK, let me say up front, I think the whole Believe in God thing is a blatant denial of common-sense. I am absolutely convinced that no such god exists. But that doesn't mean your life, or mine, has to be pointless. Human beings have evolved far beyond anything else in the animal kingdom so now we have an enormous capacity for both good and evil. The thing is, we can appreciate the difference. Anywhere we look, we can find value and meaning. So ...

My advice is that you leave a kind of roadmap. Write down all the signposts that you're seeing and feeling on this cancer journey. Lots of people before you have done this sort of thing but you will have unique insights that others will benefit from. Your path leads you to discover things about yourself. Other people go down different paths that show up different things in them. It's not just leaving a legacy of your life, though that's part of it. I guess what I'm saying is that "God" is not real but you are. Leave a roadmap of your discoveries about yourself.

Signed Smithy.

"Wow, looks like a close finish!" She grinned cheerily and Matt found strength, as always, in her enthusiasm.

"True. I still don't know which way it will go. But I've got a new project. After I make my decision, I want to make a video about my life from that point on. It's not just about what I choose to believe; it's about who I really am. And it's about leaving a good legacy."

Progress Score: Atheism & Christianity 7, New Age 6, Buddhism 5, Dying Well & Aboriginal Religion 2, Hinduism, Mormonism, Paganism, Satanism, Spiritualism, Practical Stuff & Assisted Suicide 1.

20 - WRESTLING

Friday 24th July

Sophie had long ago tried to create a special, comfortable spot for Matt. But which room in the house would suit best? At the time, he wanted to set himself up in the sunroom. Not that there would be much sunshine in the Australian winter, but it meant he could take full advantage of whatever sunlight there was. And he didn't mind watching the occasional rain or hail storm drenching the back yard.

A little table suitable for his laptop – and regular coffees – was one of the first modifications. Then came a small cabinet (for storing rice crackers and fruit bars) a magazine rack, a smartphone dock and a DVD rack. He could watch movies on his computer, or on the TV hooked up to the computer, but sometimes he opted to watch one of the many DVDs from their combined collections.

But when the cancer struck hard, and the crippling sickness lasted for several days, the sunroom proved to be too far away from his bed. Sophie suggested setting up a bed in the sunroom but there was hardly space for that. Eventually, Sophie replicated most of Matt's sunroom space in his bedroom. There, he could sit or lie in bed as long as he needed but, whenever he felt a little better, he could move to the chair beside the bed. Both spots, sunroom and bedroom, soon became cluttered with newspapers, books, medications, coffee mugs and assorted mail, most of it totally unimportant.

The next question was what to do when visitors arrived. There would have been room for another chair or two in the sunroom but the clutter around Matt made that difficult. Sophie tried to tidy things up when she came home from work but then Matt couldn't find things when he wanted them. He became grouchy and Sophie backed off. If Matt was really sick, visiting him in the bedroom was the only alternative. On the worst days, Sophie would stay home and sometimes she would ask the visitors to come back on a better day. But, on his better days, he was embarrassed to host visitors in his messy bedroom, so a third spot was set up in the lounge room, this time, hopefully, with much less clutter. Now, if Sophie was at work when the doorbell rang, Matt would come out, either from the sunroom or the bedroom, to the lounge, where there was room to host visitors in comfort. The kitchen was close by as well, so that Matt could offer tea, coffee and other refreshments.

He was in the bedroom early Friday afternoon when his sister Annie arrived, along with his niece Jennifer. Annie had convinced her daughter to accompany her on this quick visit. She hadn't seen Matt since she was a child. Annie didn't want her to miss her uncle altogether.

Jennifer waited in the lounge room while Annie helped Matt on with his pyjama top and then held his arm as he made the move to his lounge chair. Matt had seen photos of his niece but he hadn't expected the movie star good looks. Long dark brown hair brushed back from the hairline to frame a softly rounded face and perfect smile. Her larger than expected eyes revealed an elegant self-confidence tinged with the timidity of a young adult in a somewhat uncomfortable situation. She greeted her uncle with a warm hug and Annie set about making coffee.

"I looked up your blog on the trip down," admitted Jennifer while Matt settled into his chair. "I really admire you for what you're doing."

Matt asked her about her latest auditions. She had been cast for an appearance in a TV drama that, for one episode, featured a Jewish family living on the Gold Coast. Matt asked her how much she understood about Jewish culture and religion. Not very much, she admitted. She would get some coaching before the episode was filmed.

Annie pointed out that there had been no points for Judaism on Matt's blog. He replied that there had been very few posts about Jewish religion. He did know that there was an elaborate set of requirements for funerals and mourning. He vaguely recalled one Jewish respondent explaining that Judaism focuses more on this life than the afterlife. All in all, there simply hadn't been anything about Judaism that was new and helpful, or that hadn't already been said. Maybe, if there was still time, he would post a question to tease out more Jewish responses.

Annie called the rest of the family and invited them over to Matt's for a simple dinner. She arranged everything. Sophie would pick up some drinks on the way home from work. Annie and Jennifer would have to leave the next day. This was an important family opportunity, not to be missed.

It had been a long, tiring day for Matt but he found the energy to check his blog before retiring to bed. With just a few days to go, his contest was really hotting up.

There's another aspect of the Buddha's teachings that you might want to know about. Nirvana is not an impossible goal that can only be obtained after millions of lives. At least, that's how I read it. By seeking to overcome the human suffering you see around you, and then, to whatever extent you can, trying to relieve worldwide suffering, you can find a kind of shortcut. Now Matt, your blog has worldwide exposure, so that means you may have a chance to speak up for compassion and brotherly kindness in a way that could make a real difference. If you spoke up as a Christian, you would not get much of a hearing because people are tired of the violence and oppression that has been associated with Christianity. Buddhism is a more acceptable platform these days. Therefore, I urge you, please, when you add up your points on Friday, please make sure that Christianity doesn't get across the line first. Even living as an atheist would be better. I have friends who call themselves atheists but in practice they follow almost all the principles of Buddhism.

Signed: Gautaman

"Wow!" thought Matt. "This guy doesn't think much of Christianity." But again, he didn't have to prove that Gautaman was right on all counts. All that mattered for now was whether or not the comment warranted a point. Matt decided that it did.

Progress Score: Atheism & Christianity 7, New Age & Buddhism 6, Dying Well & Aboriginal Religion 2, Hinduism, Mormonism, Paganism, Satanism, Spiritualism, Practical Stuff & Assisted Suicide 1.

Saturday 25th July

Of all the regulars on Matt's blog, Robert Smith was by far the most prolific. Of course, if the Christian God was not real, Robert's frequent comments would amount to nothing more than an elaborate, well-intentioned mistake. But the same thing could be said for Buddhism, Hinduism, Mormonism, Islam or any other 'ism. Even atheism, with its insistence that science was the only reliable source of information, would be an unspeakably tragic error if it turned out to be wrong.

Having slept in until almost eleven, Sophie tried to get Matt to agree to a walk in the botanical gardens. But he just shook his head. That level of activity was out of the question today. He was staying in bed. Sophie positioned his pillows, arranged some nibbles and cold drinks on the bedside table, and then left to do some shopping.

As Matt checked his blog, he found himself wishing he had never started this mad project. So many people with persuasive arguments about death and dying. So many different approaches but so many contradictions. And all the while, under his skin and throughout his body, more and more healthy cells were turning cancerous. Time was ticking away, not just a minute, or a day, but a whole life. Life itself was ticking away. Despite all the wonderful assurances of a peaceful afterlife, this was truly frightening.

Matt sighed deeply. (Sophie said he was doing that a lot lately.) What he really needed right now was someone who could just carry him. Someone who wouldn't burden him with more to-do lists, but someone who could cut through the confusion and just ... well ... carry him. He was tired. His body was aching and weary but that was nothing. The real problem was that his mind was showing signs of terminal exhaustion.

Robert Smith had posted again. Somehow, amazingly, he had anticipated the way Matt was feeling.

Hi Matt. Me again. I've been reading back through some of your blog conversations, even some of my own comments. And you know what strikes me now? So much of what has been said assumes that you're going to be strong, with it, and in control, right up to the end. But I'm not so sure that a disease like cancer is so accommodating. What if the medication they give you for the pain makes it harder to think or focus? How will you be able to do any of that stuff if you're struggling just to get through each new day?

And here's the thing. When someone is actually dying, I mean, taking their last few breaths, I don't think at that point they're really in control of anything. They might be so determined to survive that they cling to life a little bit longer. But they succumb in the end.

I reckon it's like when we're born. Being born is not something that we do ourselves. It's something that our mother does for us. We don't know what's going on when we're born.

It just happens. And I reckon it's probably a bit like that when we die. We're not in control any more. So here's my final argument for Christianity that I hope you will consider.

Jesus is not only the greatest teacher about life after death, and life before death. He's not only the one who has gone before us into resurrection life. He's not only the way, the truth and the life, as if that wasn't enough! But Jesus, my Lord and Saviour, will carry you through your dying days, hours and moments. He will personally take your hand to get you through where no-one else can go. He will carry you!

I even found a Bible verse that says so. Isaiah 46:4. "I will be your God throughout your lifetime – until your hair is white with age. I made you, and I will care for you. I will carry you along and save you."

Robert S.

"Ohh Robert," groaned Matt out loud. "I would so love to think that you're right on this one."

Progress Score: Christianity 8, Atheism 7, New Age & Buddhism 6, Dying Well & Aboriginal Religion 2, Hinduism, Mormonism, Paganism, Satanism, Spiritualism, Practical Stuff, Assisted Suicide 1.

Wednesday 29th July

"Any mail?" asked Matt, knowing that Sophie had just checked.

"A few bits and pieces," she replied. Nothing all that important."

"I was hoping to hear some news about my superannuation payout. The money would come in handy about now."

"Sorry," she said with a sigh. "Nothing from them today." She came over to Matt's chair, bent down and kissed him. "Will you be OK for a while? I may as well go and get those scripts filled. And I can get you something nice from the chocolate shop next to the chemist." She winked at him. A naughty treat might lift his mood.

Matt almost forgot that it was a question but Sophie's eyebrows were raised in that unique "well-I'm-waiting-for-an-answer" kind of way. He nodded. "I'll be fine." Then "thanks."

While Sophie was out, Matt fired up his computer to check the blog. Time was running out. Just two more days. He was disappointed about the delay in the super payout but perhaps there would be some last-minute surprises on the blog.

There was one comment that picked up on Matt's mood of disappointment.

Let me tell you what the problem is, here. People lead you to expect a better life after this one. It's always false hopes and expectations that lead to frustration and disappointment. Now I admit that I don't see how you could be disappointed when you die and the afterlife turns out to be a false hope. I mean, if you're dead, you're not going to be disappointed, are you? But living with false hope is a lie. God is not real so surely it's better to face death honestly, without the pretence of some kind of eternal afterlife.

The false hope might make you feel better but I honestly think you'll feel better if you go the grave knowing that you weren't kidding yourself. There's a certain integrity in facing death that way.

Signed: Atheist Al.

Matt thought long and hard before allocating a point to atheism, knowing that, with such a short time to go, atheism and Christianity would be level on eight points. The following morning, however, several bloggers had responded to Atheist Al. It seemed they all wanted to point out a fallacy in his logic. One comment that summed up many others came from someone called Lee.

Atheist Al is missing the point. If God is not real and His promise of eternal life is false but you believe in Him anyway, you've lost nothing. But if He is real, and His promise is true, and you don't believe Him, then you've lost everything. If there's no life after this one, you won't be disappointed, because it will all be over. But if there is life after this, and I absolutely believe that there is, and you turn your back on

God's offer. Well let's just say 'disappointment' wouldn't even begin to describe how you would feel.

Signed: Lee

Matt threw his head back and gazed thoughtfully at the ceiling. Yeah, that made sense too. If Atheist Al gained a point, it was only reasonable to give one to Lee, on behalf of the many others who made the same point.

But correspondent Lee was not content to present the issue of life after death as some sort of intelligent gamble. He had one more point to make.

Why am I convinced that life goes on after our physical death? Because the God I worship is not just some old deity who left behind a book of instructions. He is Father, Son and Holy Spirit. He promised that the Holy Spirit would come to us as Comforter and Counselor. It happened just like he said in the Book of Acts and it happened in my life too. In one place, the Bible calls the Holy Spirit "the guarantee of our inheritance" (Ephesians 1:14).

So many religions are all about what you have to do. They have a god or gods that just sit back and watch to see if we can make it. Christianity is different because God knows we can't do it in our own power. Life is tough and there are all sorts of obstacles. So, when we put our faith in Jesus, God has something else to help us. He gives us his Holy Spirit to guide and help us through our lives. He fills us with amazing power. And by doing that, he literally proves that all his promises will turn out exactly as he said.

That put Christianity out in front once more. Two days to go.

Friday 31st July

Nine o'clock in the morning. This was it, the last day in July, the pre-arranged time for Matt's final decision. Sophie, having taken a day off for the occasion, hovered near the bathroom, ready to assist Matt if he needed help with his shower,. But Matt was enjoying a burst of energy today. The suffocating anxiety about his big decision had given way to a surprising flush of relief. This was exciting! For the first time in weeks, it all made sense.

It was the same with cancer treatments. You had to make a choice. Chopping and changing from one treatment to another only guaranteed that nothing would help. In the same way, no-one could live sensibly in a religious hotch-potch. Bits and pieces of everything would never satisfy. There had to be a choice. Living an authentic life of faith demanded it. And, for Matt, the choice would be definite. Very, very definite! One option would rise to full and total acceptance, everything else would be forever rejected. From this day forward, there would be no more confusion. Hence this unexpected euphoria of relief.

In the last few days, the blogosphere had gone crazy and the number of visitors to Matt's blog had passed sixty thousand. Several media outlets, including one television station, had contacted Matt to see if the "contest" was still going to finish on the agreed date. "Yes, it will," he replied. Had he found a winner? "No", he told them. "Not yet."

Sophie prepared a bowl of hot porridge but Matt only ate half of it. He also drank half of a protein shake and took the rest with him to the sunroom where his laptop was already waiting. Lowering into his armchair, he placed his drink in the cup-holder and swung the adjustable table to a comfortable position just above his lap.

This time, as Matt checked the blog, he wondered how much he would miss this routine. Sophie watched him from the doorway, smiling with surprise at his fresh enthusiasm. "You're looking forward to your decision?" she observed with a laugh. Matt glanced at her but he was already refocused on his computer when he nodded.

There were still some surprises.

One man who claimed to be a lecturer in philosophy wrote a stinging criticism of Matt's point system. He ranted that the whole contest had become a farce because points were awarded on such a subjective basis. *I hope that your inane judgments will not influence any of your readers*, he

255

concluded.

Another blogger criticised Matt equally harshly, but for virtually the opposite reason.

It's been fascinating to follow your blog but I can't believe that you're apparently going to become a Christian on the basis of all these tired old arguments. Come on Matt! It's the twenty-first century! How come you can't see through all the clichés? Spirituality is not so narrow these days. You asked some brilliant questions. Please don't go back to the narrow-minded, institutionalised dogma of such an outdated religion!

There were more criticisms of the Christian faith and, indeed, the Bible. More comments about the "angry genocidal god" of the Old Testament. And one comment that challenged the whole Christian view of an afterlife.

Hi Matt. I've enjoyed reading your blog. Although I'm a Hindu myself, I've studied the Christian worldview at doctoral level and I must warn you that the Christian scriptures present a number of contradictions about what happens after death.

Some passages seem to indicate that the soul migrates immediately to heaven, others suggest that the soul has to wait for the Parousia, the alleged second coming of Jesus the Christ. Some passages portray heaven as somewhere up above the clouds and some passages talk about people going down to a place called Hades. There are other passages that talk about a renewed paradise here on earth.

Taken as a whole, the Christian picture of life after death just doesn't add up.

Signed Mareesh.

Matt didn't know what to make of that. On one hand, he couldn't argue the point; he just didn't know the Bible well enough. But, on the other hand, wouldn't you just have to trust? Somewhere, somehow, wouldn't you just have to admit that death is a mystery and that, if life after death is real, that you would only find out for sure when it happened to you?

But there was one final comment from Robert Smith.

Dearest Matt. You have been a big part of my life for the past four months. I have so enjoyed our back and forth conversation. I have tried to be faithful to what I sincerely believe and to present the gospel message as accurately and honestly as possible. I have tried to focus on the positive aspects of knowing God, and Jesus, rather than the negative and scary descriptions of hell that other Christians often resort to. Please understand that I will be praying for you, that you will make the right decision, which for me, of course, means that you will choose Jesus.

The point score on his blog showed Christianity leading with nine points, Atheism next with eight points, followed by Buddhism and New Age with six points each. Nothing else was close enough to be taken seriously, although one Mormon respondent mounted a concerted last-minute effort, listing nine reasons to join the Latter Day Saints. Obviously, he was hoping that Matt would award one point for each of these reasons, and subsequently convert to Mormonism. Some Muslim bloggers checked in, admitting defeat but warning Matt, somewhat sarcastically, that he would pay an eternal price for rejecting the knowledge of Allah.

The broad "Dying Well" category had two points, as did "Aboriginal Religion".

But now, all that was over. The time had come for Matt to block his blog from all further comments. Enough had been said. It was time for the final evaluation. The rules of the contest, as initially laid out, were simple enough. Whatever religion or belief system had the most points at the end of July would win. On that basis, Matt would become a Christian by the end of this day.

But could he live with that decision? Could he, finally and forever, disregard all the arguments against the Christian faith and leave behind all the other arguments that had impressed him at one time or another?

The point system and its ultimate results began to seem fluid. Even now, if his instincts took him in some alternative direction, it would not be hard to award the necessary points on this last day of opportunity.

Sophie sensed his hesitation. Why else would he be

staring at his computer like that? "Still a hard decision?" she asked.

Matt nodded. "I thought I had it sorted … but … well, I really don't want to get this wrong."

"Some people seem to think it doesn't matter in the final wash-up."

"Yeah, I know … but it matters to me."

Sophie stood behind Matt and gently draped her arms around his neck. "Out of all these things that people have been talking about, what would you most like to be true?"

That was a good question. Matt thought about the materialist, atheist viewpoint, that there was, in fact, no afterlife at all. He didn't want that to be true. He thought about the myriad religions and cults that believed in some sort of rebirth or reincarnation. If any of these were true, he would inevitably be caught up in it, but would he remember this life? Would today's decision mean anything at all in the great cosmic cycle of life? He didn't want that to be true either. The psychic musings about various spooky, surreal afterlife scenarios were no more appealing. That left the religions that promised Heaven. Christianity in its various forms, Mormonism, JW-ism, Islam and maybe Judaism. He thought about the bloggers who promised that the universe itself was moving toward an overwhelming final enlightenment that shared some characteristics with the idea of Heaven. Everyone, it seemed, wanted to take the sting out of death.

The idea of resurrection, as compared with reincarnation, was certainly attractive. But that depended on whether you made it with God or not. Some of the religions that promised Heaven also warned of Hell.

"I guess what I really want to believe," said Matt, slowly and deliberately, "is that there is a Heaven that makes sense of the life I'm living now, a heaven that I can get to without having to do lots of hard spiritual stuff."

Sophie resisted the impulse to say something. She could see that Matt was not finished.

"Classic Christianity! That has to be it! It has the most

points and it's what I most want to be true." He turned to face Sophie and they shared a jubilant kiss. "Thank you! Thank you!"

Later that night, Matt crafted his results summary.

Dear blog readers. First, let me thank you for the wonderful contributions that I have received from so many of you. Although this has been a difficult journey for me, both physically and mentally, I have no regrets. The popularity of my competition has both humbled and astonished me. I am continually amazed that so many people have taken an interest in my life and my search for meaning. It has been truly remarkable.

In the end, I awarded a total of forty points and Christianity came out on top with nine points, followed by atheism on eight points, then New Age and Buddhism on six points each. Some people were offended when I gave points for comments that they felt were outrageous or ill-informed, and I sincerely apologise to those people. In some cases, I must admit, when I awarded points, I did so in the knowledge that the worldview in question was never going to win overall. In some cases, there were overlaps and some readers may have been confused by that as well. But I have tried to stick with my original criteria, namely that I would award a point for comments that were both original and helpful. Many excellent comments did not warrant a point because either their points had been made before or I could not find anything specifically helpful in them.

Despite some rumours to the contrary, I am suffering with terminal cancer and the blog competition has been a genuine thing. I emphatically deny that it was rigged in any way.

As a result, I am now a Christian, a follower of Christ. I hope to be with him in Heaven someday. In some ways, my journey starts now.

Thank you for coming with me through this life-changing experience. May God be with you!

Saturday 1st August

Two American TV networks and a popular internet news service phoned Matt the following morning but he was not feeling well. Sophie took the calls and brought the phone to his bed. She also brought him a protein shake and one of those extra 'discretional' tablets that he was allowed to take on days like this.

One of the television networks wanted to set up a three-way conversation between an expert on comparative religion, their regular hostess and Matt. Sophie objected at first, knowing she would have to work out how this could fit in with Matt's doctor's appointment and, at the same time, perform some sort of miracle to get Matt ready, not to mention cleaning the house to make it presentable. But Matt insisted that he wanted to do it.

Because it was a live hook-up to an evening talk show on the American east coast, a crew of three men and one woman arrived at Matt and Sophie's home early in the afternoon. Make-up, backgrounds and technical preparations were hastily accomplished. Then, suddenly, Matt was on air, acknowledging the welcome from the American TV hostess, who then went on to read from Matt's concluding blog statement.

The first question was directed to the comparative religion expert. "Doctor Warner, you've written a book about the different ways people choose to convert from one religion, or no religion. I know you've been following Matt Sherwin's online journey. So what would you like to say to him?"

The expert, a middle aged man sporting a bushy ginger beard and a multi-coloured striped sweater, grinned widely and nodded acknowledgement of the question. "Well, Matt, may I say it's great to have this chance to talk with you. Your blog has been fascinating."

"Thank you." For one brief moment, Matt wondered if he was expected to elaborate but Dr Warner quickly jumped in.

"First of all, Matt, how you're feeling today? How are you going with the cancer?"

"Uhh, I'm managing."

That formality out of the way, the religion expert made his first point.

"You know, Matt, most people tend to fall into their faith, either through their upbringing or through the people they come to associate with. Your approach has been so refreshing. Seems to me that you came to this exercise with a genuinely blank slate. Is that a reasonable assessment?"

"Um, yeah. Of course. I meant what I said at the start. I would take up whatever faith would have the most points by the end of July. And that happened to be classic Christianity."

"Did that surprise you?" asked the hostess.

"Yeah, a bit," admitted Matt. "I guess there were a lot of things about the Christian faith that I never realised."

Dr Warner quickly moved to his next question. "Matt, in allocating your points, do you think you were more guided by reason or by intuition?" He tried to explain what he meant. "Was it more about what made more sense ... in a strictly logical way ... or more about what felt right?"

"Wow, tough question. Umm ... I think I took a more logical approach through the whole process. I tried to think honestly about the comments I received and I certainly didn't give any points to things that didn't make sense to me." He remembered Craig. "Well, there might have been one or two exceptions. But your question is interesting because, when I had to make the final decision, I knew it had to feel right as well."

The hostess had a question. "Some folks might say that, at the end of the day, you simply chose what you wanted from the beginning. Isn't it true that we all end up believing what we want to believe?"

Matt laughed, a nervous little laugh. "I don't know about everyone. But I certainly didn't start out wanting to be a Christian. If anything, I was pretty turned-off with Christians I knew." He thought of something else that he needed to say. "But, as I thought about what the various religions were offering me, I guess it's true that part of me wanted Christianity to win."

"You gave a lot of points to atheism," observed Dr Warner. "But atheism is hardly a religion. How do you explain that?"

"Oh, that's not hard," answered Matt. "It was never just about religions. I was looking at belief systems and philosophies in the broadest possible way. Sometimes the challenge was to categorise things properly. I think atheism got a lot of points because people who don't believe in God have lots of different ways to explain … you know … what they see as true and what they see as wrong."

The expert smiled. "Good answer," he admitted, but then the clincher. "So Matt, do you now believe that everyone should become Christian?"

Matt's last answer had left him feeling confident but this shook him a little. Dr Warner sensed this and rephrased his question.

"It goes to whether truth is always subjective or whether it can also be objective. What I mean is, do you now believe that the Christian explanation for things, including its explanation of the afterlife, is literally and factually true? Do you believe that the other religions and, yes, the other philosophies as well, are all wrong and that Christianity has the only truth?"

Matt wanted to wipe the sweat from his forehead. He was still feeling very ill. But he was painfully aware of the camera in front of him, and somehow an answer came. "I believe it must be true. But I can't say that I know it's true. This is only my first day as a Christian. Maybe I'll see it differently when I've lived it for a while. But I've been wrestling with this and I honestly can't see how all the religions … or philosophies … can be true. They might all be wrong, including Christianity for all I know at this point of time, but they definitely can't all be right."

When the interview was over, Sophie congratulated Matt with a kiss. "You did well," she said. The visitors agreed and, thanking Sophie for her hospitality, they started the process of packing up. Matt had a doctor's appointment to get to.

21 - SOMETHING GOOD FOR SOPHIE

Sunday 2nd August

Sophie came up behind Matt as he stood before his bathroom mirror and tried to adjust the tie that he had found in a bag of old shirts. "Does that look right?" he asked. "I think so," she muttered, straightening it anyway. She was conservatively dressed in a knee-length black skirt, cream undershirt and a crimson top with sleeves that draped loosely to just below her elbows. She really didn't know what you were supposed to wear to church.

"I know you told me before," she laughed, "but what church are we going to?"

Matt shook his head in mock frustration at her forgetfulness. "You know, the Anglican Church on West St, just near the shops where you get your hair done. We've been past there lots of times. I'm sure you'll know it."

"I guess I never paid much attention. Do they know you're coming?"

Matt went through to the bedroom and grabbed his jacket from where it was laying on his bed. "No, I didn't tell anyone." He sighed. "OK, let's roll."

They made their way out to the car. Sophie locked the front door and helped Matt into the passenger seat. His walking stick was already laying across the back seat.

"Why this church? What was so special about this one?"

"I really don't know," admitted Matt as Sophie fired up the engine and began reversing out of the driveway. "I suppose I wanted classic Christianity. And I guess I thought that you couldn't get more classic than a church that's more than a hundred years old."

"I suppose that makes sense," conceded Sophie with a grin. "I hope it meets expectations."

It did and it didn't.

The old gentleman who met them in the entry foyer was friendly enough. He gave them a bulletin sheet and asked if they were new to the church. Sophie wondered if it was that obvious. They introduced themselves as Matt Sherwin and Sophie and hesitantly made their way through a tall wood-panelled door into a strange, unfamiliar world. The building itself, with its soaring ceiling, age-darkened walls and dusty shafts of light emanating from stained glass windows, exuded history in a way that surpassed even the church where Craig's funeral had been held. But, if the building spoke of times long past, the congregation was very much in the present. Some thirty or forty people were settling in for their weekly service, acknowledging each other like comfortable old friends. A few ladies, picking Matt and Sophie for visitors, came up and shook their hands. Sophie realised that some of the pews had cushioning so she suggested one such pew to Matt. "Are these seats taken?" she asked the elegantly dressed forty-something woman past whom they would have to negotiate passage. The woman smiled and swayed her legs to one side so the newcomers could pass.

When the somewhat arduous process of sitting was completed, Matt took a deep breath and looked around. At the front and off to the right, was a massive pipe organ, the elderly female organist seated near the base was already pumping a slow, deliberate melody. Matt identified the pulpit and correctly guessed that the large wooden table was the altar. Three rows of pews could be seen at the back of what Matt thought of as the 'stage' but there was no choir today. A set of three stained glass windows soared high above the whole arrangement, and it was all protected by a wooden rail that seemed designed to separate the stage area from the congregation that was slowly filling most of the forward pews.

Matt and Sophie looked at each other. What happens now? Their unspoken question was answered when a gorgeously robed priest appeared through a door beside and slightly below the stage. The priest negotiated the two steps up onto the stage, passed in front of the pulpit where Matt thought he would stand, and took his place behind a simple wooden lectern. He spread his arms expansively as a gesture of welcome to his congregation. "Welcome friends. The Lord be with you."

"And with you," chorused several of the congregants.

The priest went on to give a special welcome to "Mr and Mrs Sherwin, joining with us for the first time today." Matt and Sophie exchanged surprised glances; someone had wrongly assumed that they were married. But there was no point correcting the mistake, so they nodded at the people in front who turned around to smile at them.

When it was time to sing a hymn, the lady at the end of the pew showed Matt where to find the right page in the hymnbook. But she neglected to tell the newcomers that they were expected to stand when the organist had finished her introduction and the first stanza was about to begin.

This was a steep learning curve but Matt was more interested in the sermon than in the singing. He already knew a lot about Christianity but he expected even more information. About God, about Jesus, about the Christian life. As it happened, the sermon was a mixture of current affairs commentary, quotes from presumably famous religious writers and some anecdotes from the preacher's own life. Not that it was bad. It was all about what it means to love your neighbours in difficult modern times.

After the service, Matt and Sophie were invited to a small adjacent hall for "coffee and biscuits". The people were nice and it was all very pleasant but Sophie was bored silly. On the way home, she challenged Matt.

"Well? What did you think of all that?"

"It was good," said Matt. What else could he say?

"Were you surprised that no-one realised who you were?"

"A little," Matt admitted. "I was kinda half expecting to be something of a sensation, what with all the publicity of late, and all."

"Was it what you were hoping for?"

Matt had to think for a moment. "No, not really. It was nice but … well … I don't know. There was something missing. I just don't know what."

Over the course of the following week, Matt watched a number of movies with a Christian theme. In a way, this was an escape from the intellectual argie-bargie of the previous five months.

He had seen 'The Passion of the Christ' before but this time he was deeply impressed by the resoluteness of Jesus in the face of terrible pain and suffering. The Saviour had flesh like any human but his flesh was cut and scourged until it resembled a piece of meat hanging in a butcher shop. Sophie couldn't bear to watch this one.

'The Lion, the Witch and the Wardrobe' was more to Sophie's liking and she actually sat still long enough to watch the whole movie. When she asked Matt if Aslan the lion was supposed to represent Jesus, he gave what he thought was an insightful answer. He even attempted to explain why Jesus had to die.

'Courageous' was more about a Christian commitment to marriage and family but there was enough action in the movie to keep Matt entertained. Same with 'Fireproof', a movie about a man whose work was hot but whose marriage was cold.

'Left Behind' brought Matt down to earth a bit. He watched it while Sophie was at work and tried to explain it over dinner that night. The movie's prophetic themes of rapture, Antichrist and tribulation left him bewildered. Was any of this stuff in the Bible? Perhaps he would ask someone at church on Sunday.

'Bonhoeffer' and 'Amazing Grace' were historical movies, both inspirational but both showing a dark side of humanity that had to be resisted. Evil to be confronted. Apparently, Christianity had social and political ramifications.

But the movie that hit home most of all was 'Letters to God', a movie about an 8 year old boy, dying of cancer, who coped by writing letters to God and entrusting them to the local postman. Matt found himself wishing he had more faith and less intellectual wrestling.

Thursday 6th August

Sophie was fifteen minutes late for work but, before she had the chance to collect her thoughts after a busy morning looking after Matt, she was already taking her first call. A mother was seeking an early appointment for her young son who was suffering terrible pain in his upper gums.

"I'll see what I can do," promised Sophie.

And then she started to cry.

"Ohh, Sophie, what's wrong?" Jess was a dental nurse who happened to be in the office.

Sophie barely managed to shake her head, she was sobbing so hard. "I don't know," she wailed.

Jess came over and placed a caring arm around Sophie's heaving shoulders. Then, sensing that this was serious, and not knowing what else to do, she called the wife of one of the dentists.

"Please come quickly. We need you here."

Barbara had trained as a counsellor while her husband-to-be completed his degree and, from time to time, her skills came in handy. She found Sophie in the storeroom at the rear of the complex, rocking back and forth on an old wooden chair.

"What happened Sophie? Can you talk about it."

Sophie sniffed noisily and Barbara found some tissues, which Sophie gladly received.

"I don't know," she said, trying to compose herself. "I just fell apart."

Barbara watched her carefully. Wordlessly.

"I know what triggered me off," spluttered Sophie eventually. "I was taking a phone call, a request for an appointment … and I just said … I'll see what I can do." The tears flowed again. "I'm so sorry. I feel like such a fool."

"It's OK," soothed Barbara. "Just let it out, honey. Whatever it is, just let it out."

Sophie sobbed heavily for another five minutes, Barbara waiting patiently. When Sophie spoke at last, her voice sounded shrill, anxious.

"I'm so sorry," she cried, shaking her head from side to side. "It hit me so hard. It's always, yeah, I'll see what I can do. I'll see what I can do." She looked imploringly at Barbara. "That's my life now. My whole ridiculous life."

"Looking after a seriously ill partner is a big job," nodded Barbara.

"But he's got cancer. He's dying. I can't let it be about me."

"Ohh, Sophie. Listen, I don't know much about your circumstances but I'm sure you're doing a fantastic job."

Sophie smiled through her tears. "I work so hard. Everything I do, I'm trying so hard to do everything to the best of my ability. Matt doesn't want me to give up work. He wants to be as independent as possible and he says we still need the money from my wages. So I have to find time to do the shopping, the housework, pay all the bills, cook all the meals.

Not to mention running around after him. Even the gardening. It never stops! Not for one lousy minute!"

"Go on."

"Well, he gets grumpy with me. I try so hard and he gets in these moods where nothing is ever good enough. I'm there for him like a wife would be but … but I'm not! I'm not his wife and I don't think I ever will be."

Barbara nodded. "Go on."

"Yeah, I know he's having a really tough time. But so am I! The difference is that I have to be the one who's always bright and cheery. I have to be the super-strong, all-loving woman who handles everything without ever getting tired or angry."

She settled down and wiped the last of her tears away with a tissue.

"What am I supposed to do, Barbara? How am I supposed to cope with this?"

Barbara answered thoughtfully. "OK, I know there are people who can help. Palliative care, home help, even respite care. But …"

Sophie braced herself and Barbara spoke cautiously.

"But … no-one else can take your place. You might not be his wife but you're the one he's depending on. He's going to need you more than anyone else. Does he get much support from his family? Friends?"

"Family yes, friends not so much now. He doesn't get a lot of visitors. I think his mates backed off because his blog was way over their heads. Most of them found it all a bit intimidating."

There could be no doubting Barbara's compassion. "Sophie, this is a really hard time for you, physically, emotionally, relationally. Every possible way. But it's a season in your life that's not going to get easier. I think you have to steel yourself to keep going. I suggest you talk with Matt. Ask if he would mind you organising some extra help. Talk to the people at Palliative Care. Talk with the rest of the family. And don't be embarrassed if you break down from time to time. Be assured that you're doing an absolutely brilliant job. You will get through this!"

Sophie smiled ironically. "I'll see what I can do!"

Monday 10th August

Six o'clock Monday evening, the family was gathering for the weekly dinner at Terry and Julie's home. There came a knock at the door and Julie jumped up to answer it.

"Oh, I forgot to mention. I saw Donna at the supermarket this morning and I invited her to come for dinner tonight. That's probably her."

"Wow! Didn't see that coming," said Sophie. Then: "Hi Sis," when Julie brought Donna through to the dining area.

Donna had never spent much time with Josh and Leslie but their children quickly warmed to her. Chelsea, now seven years old, enthusiastically invited her to: "Sit with me. Look, there's room here."

Matt wondered if there may have been some hidden agenda in inviting Donna. There was an agenda but it didn't stay hidden for long. When the meal was served, and everyone was ready to eat, Julie asked Donna if she would say grace. "Matt's going to be a Christian now," she said. "It only seems right that we honour that."

Donna complied, despite the awkwardness of the moment. Then Julie explained further.

"Matt, you told everyone that classic Christianity ended up winning your contest. Well, fair enough. But I didn't understand what classic Christianity meant. So, when I saw Donna today, I asked her about it." She turned to Donna. "Could you explain it again please love?"

Donna flinched. "Well … um … I'm certainly no expert. But I suppose Matt was referring to the traditional historical teachings of the church."

"As opposed to what?" asked Leslie.

Terry jumped in suddenly. "As opposed to the new-fangled, glitzy, money-grabbing version of Christianity that you see on TV."

"Woh Dad," exclaimed Josh. "I had no idea you felt so strongly about these things."

"Well, yeah, I do," conceded Terry. "It's a disgrace!" His voice assumed a mocking tone. "Send us your money and God will pour out a blessing. Send for our latest series of messages. They'll show you how to live a perfect, worry-free life. We are so wonderful and we are here to help you make all your dreams come true. Just send us some more money!"

Stunned silence. Until Matt broke the silence with a laugh. His Dad was not known for his passionate views on religion.

"Matt, I hope you know what I mean. I sincerely hope that's not the kind of Christianity you intend to follow?" It was a statement that turned into a question.

"Uh … no … I don't think so."

"Matt's way too smart to fall for any kind of manipulative religion," declared Sophie. "He analyses everything too carefully for that."

"It's not just that," continued Terry. "All this talk about God pouring out money from Heaven, answering your every prayer, meeting your every need. I mean, life just isn't like that. Look at Matt. He's got cancer, for God's sake! What sort of blessing is God going to pour out that can ever compensate for that?"

The conversation carried on for a few more minutes. Josh joined his Dad in venting against the "emotional hype" of modern religion. Leslie tried in vain to offer a balancing perspective. Matt mentioned some of the "religious nutcases" that had written in to his blog. Sophie repeated a joke about people from different religions appearing at the gates of Heaven which caused Julie to shake her head in exasperation. But Donna, having prayed grace and spoken out one short sentence, ate the rest of her meal in silence.

Tuesday 11th August

The next morning, Matt was back in hospital. Another scan. More chemotherapy. More doctors with charts and files.

So many times now Matt just wanted to be free from what he called "the system". Not that he had any specific complaints. From the top specialists to the lowliest volunteers doing their weekly hours on the ward, the conscientious attitude of the medical establishment was utterly commendable. Everyone seemed to genuinely care. But taken together, day after day, it was stifling.

This time, Matt had visits from one of his aunts and two of his cousins. He wanted to tell them "don't bother". It was awkward for him and awkward for them. And seriously, he wouldn't think any worse of them if they just left him alone.

Sophie called in each morning before work and then again in the evening. When Matt was in hospital, she indulged in quick take-away meals on her way to (and sometimes from) her visits. She would never admit it but Matt's strict diet was driving her insane and she thoroughly enjoyed the occasional hamburger with potato wedges and sour cream.

Terry made no effort to visit Matt in hospital. He said that Julie did enough hospital time for the both of them. But these were still the days of short hospital stays for Matt. Should that change, Terry would be there too. He wouldn't know what to talk about but he would be there.

Sophie called the West St Anglican Church that they had attended once, just to let them know that Matt was in hospital. To see if they would bother. When she told Matt, he shrugged a gesture of indifference. But she told him off.

"I thought you'd appreciate this a bit more. I know you want to follow through with this Christian stuff."

Uncle Gavin called in once. When Matt mentioned the church, Uncle Gavin became suddenly evasive, as though he had a secret that he was unwilling to share. Matt sensed this and pressed him for a reason.

"Look, it's none of my business Matt, but …" He hesitated.

"But what?"

"Well I've heard some things about that church, that's all."

"What sort of things?"

"No, I probably shouldn't say. Just ... well, just be aware that things are not all that they seem to be. There's ... stuff going on that you wouldn't want to get involved with."

The church did, in fact, send someone to see Matt. A young intern (Matt didn't quite figure out what that was) called in just before dinner on the second night of Matt's stay. A pleasant young man with curly black hair, he introduced himself as Farron. After hearing a little about Matt's competition and subsequent commitment to Christianity, he borrowed Matt's laptop and set up a link to a sermon website that boasted thousands of sermons arranged by topic. Matt tried to listen to some of these messages when he was too tired to read but, of course, he drifted off to sleep and missed large portions of the sermons. Still, he found it interesting. Whatever was going on in this church, they were certainly clever and well resourced.

Wednesday 12th August

Cancer still mystifies people with its capricious twists and turns. Unexpectedly, teasingly, its relentless advance calls time-out. Sometimes the advance even morphs into discernible retreat. For the cancer patient, no word is more welcome in the oncologist's room than 'remission'.

Dr Barlow was far too circumspect to speak of remission. For Matt, the damage had already been done. But, over the next two weeks, the tumours in his stomach and bowel regions decreased slightly, while Dr Barlow described the cancer in the liver as "stalled".

Was it the chemotherapy? Was it the diet? Was it something else entirely? Dr Barlow's money was on the chemo but he couldn't be sure. Matt experienced a gradual resurgence of strength and his appetite returned. The overall sickliness that had dogged him for months became intermittent. It was a time to enjoy.

In preparation for the wedding that never happened,

Sophie had sold off several items of furniture that would not be needed in Matt's house. Some of Matt's possessions also had to go but one item in particular became a point of contention, his old road-bike. Sophie could not imagine that it would ever again get used. She encouraged him to let it go but he refused.

Now, in this surprising season of relative good health, Matt decided he wanted to take the old bike out again. When the whim had not passed after a few days, Sophie borrowed a bicycle from a colleague at work. She reasoned that, if Matt was determined to ride his bike again, she would have to ride with him.

Saturday 15th August

The wind blew gently as they set off together on Saturday morning. The plan was to ride to the nearby botanical gardens and follow the designated bike tracks before returning home via a narrow strip reserve along the local creek. Matt struggled initially to find his balance and Sophie, following behind, tried to overcome her fears by joking about how awkward he looked. He was too busy pumping pedals with every ounce of determined energy to reply.

The challenge was completed in part. Sure, they turned back at the entrance to the gardens because workers were mowing lawns. And sure, they skipped the track along the creek because Matt noticed some dangerous looking potholes. But he achieved his goal and they made it home safely. Matt carefully returned his bike to the dusty back corner of his garage, never to be spoken of again.

Monday 24th August

The date would have gone unnoticed but for Julie. Six months had passed since Matt's cancer diagnosis and he was feeling better than he had for several weeks, so Julie decided that a special celebration was in order. Without telling Matt, she sent out formal invitations to the Monday night dinner. Grandma Davis (her mother), Donna, Greg and Angie Sparrow, all the other regular staff from Matt's time at Little Bird, Trish

Owens (from Palliative Care), Uncle Gavin and several other relatives. Pastor O'Farrell was on the invitation list but he sent an apology. Julie's biggest coup was persuading Annie to make the trip. She had been planning a visit anyway.

Leslie, stunningly dressed in an off-the-shoulder turquoise and white evening gown, met Matt and Sophie at the door. "Welcome to your surprise party!"

Sophie grinned, she knew what was happening, but Matt was puzzled. "Surprise party?"

Leslie nodded. "For your half anniversary. Six months since you found out you had cancer."

"Oh! Really?" Matt didn't know what to say. "Uhh, but how can it be a surprise when you just told me? Isn't everyone supposed to jump up from behind the furniture and yell 'Surprise!'"

"Don't worry," laughed Leslie. "You'll be surprised enough when you see who's here tonight. Not to mention when you see the shirt your brother is wearing!"

Chairs were crammed together in Terry and Julie's living room. Leslie and nine year old Ryan shuttled back and forth from the kitchen with plate after plate of cleverly disguised vegetable savouries and fruit trays. Grandma Davis informed Matt that his Christian faith was obviously not helping. He was getting thinner. But then, with a wink, she admitted that he was looking remarkably well. Greg, unaware of Matt's days and weeks of inner darkness, commended him for his positive attitude. One of Matt's uncles from Terry's side of the family offered him a seat in a members' box at an upcoming football semi-final, an offer he respectfully passed up. Lauren, from Little Bird, had some serious questions about Matt's faith journey since winding up his contest but Annie interrupted that conversation before it could get too serious. Terry, as usual, made a speech.

"I want to thank everyone for coming tonight. Six months ago, we were stunned and shocked to hear about Matt's disease. We couldn't believe it was happening. But here we are. Six months have come and gone and we're all celebrating, because …" he choked back a tear, "well, because we still have you here with us, son. It's been a rough time for you, and for all of us, but we appreciate every day, every week and every month that we can spend with you. You've got a beautiful, awesome girlfriend. Maybe she will be your wife someday. And … and you're looking great!" A spontaneous eruption of applause affirmed his words but Terry kept going.

"Who knows? Maybe, just maybe, we're witnessing the start of a miracle. Maybe there's hope after all." He held up a glass to toast Matt's improvement but, although Matt smiled glibly, he was not amused.

Later that night, when he walked through his front door with Sophie, Matt threw his walking stick down the hallway, in the general direction of Moggy, the cat. "What the hell!" he fumed. "Why does he damn-well have to say things like that? Now I'll have all these people expecting some sort of miracle that's never going to happen."

Sophie tried to calm him down but it wasn't working. She retreated to the bathroom while Matt plonked himself down in his favourite chair and angrily grabbed at the TV remote. Julie's good intentions had backfired.

Over the course of the next week, Matt began a video diary and sorted out some old photographs that had been lying in a forgotten drawer in the spare bedroom. Pastor O'Farrell called and left a 300-page book about different Christian understandings of the afterlife. Matt surprised himself by reading the whole thing in just three days. He even looked up the author's website and spent some time making notes about certain Bible verses. Then, late one night, after Sophie had gone exhausted to bed, he jotted down some thoughts about his own funeral. It would be a burial rather than a cremation because that was what Pastor O'Farrell's book had recommended for Christians. He would have two hymns that pointed to eternal life, if such hymns existed. He would have to ask someone. He started writing a poem that he would like someone to read out. And, realising that he could stay awake no longer, he uttered a sort of closing prayer.

"Please God, if I'm to die soon, please help me to do everything I need to do in the meantime, especially now while I'm feeling a bit better. And God, please show me how I can leave something good for Sophie."

The last part of the prayer was answered sometime through the long night. Matt lay awake for hours, brooding over his life. And Sophie's. The old doubts were still there but, this time, he knew what he had to do. When morning came and Sophie offered him breakfast in bed, he insisted on getting up and sitting with her at the kitchen bench. He held her hands while he gave thanks for the food. And longer, lingering thoughtfully. He chose his words carefully.

"I love you Sophie. I don't think I'll ever be completely ready. I have zero confidence in my ability to ever be a good husband. But I have to do the right thing. By you and by God. How soon do you think we can get something organised?"

22 - ROBERT MAKES A GOOD POINT

Monday 31st August

"Ohh, check out the waves!" Sophie dropped the first of three suitcases onto a maroon divan sofa, squashing two yellow and white floral cushions against the wall.

"Sure is windy out there," agreed Matt, stepping carefully into the room with only his walking stick for support. The entire south-west wall was a series of windows, punctuated only by a glass door, which opened onto a track that wound its way through a rugged, rocky foreshore to a point, a hundred or so metres away, where ocean waves were crashing violently against random black rocks. As they watched, a white spray catapulted into the air, hovering longer than either of them thought possible.

"Through there," said Sophie, moving on. "That's the bedroom."

Matt followed, amazed to see another whole wall of glass. Uninterrupted views of the foreshore and ocean. "Wow! Impressive."

But there was only one bed. Sophie watched for Matt's reaction. When he smiled and nodded, she cheerily headed back to the car for the groceries they had brought. She called back over her shoulder. "I hope this will be a feel-good week for you."

"I'm sure it will," he called back. By the time Sophie returned, he had already unpacked one bag into the off-white tallboy on his side of the queen-size bed. "People sure are generous."

Three night's holiday at the very private Ocean Vista Resort, complete with relaxation massages for both of them, all paid for by the staff at the Raymond Hill Dental Clinic and their collective fundraising efforts. Matt felt overwhelmed. But now that they were here, his only obligation was to have a good time.

Quality of life, said Dr Tan, was the aim of good cancer treatment. Quality of life, enjoyed for as long as possible. So this was it; a chance to enjoy life for a while.

The Monday night dinner was cancelled for only the third time since Matt's cancer diagnosis, and the first since the cruise. Terry and Julie drove out to join Matt and Sophie at the resort, hoping that a brief visit would not be seen as an intrusion. They needn't have worried. They were warmly welcomed, especially since they brought a feast from the kebabs takeaway in nearby South Point. Julie, stimulated by the elegant opulence of the resort, babbled on about a seaside holiday that she and Terry had enjoyed in England some fifteen years before. When she realised that everyone else just wanted to quietly watch the ocean while they ate, she bit her tongue and joined the silence.

The churning waves reflected all the changing colours of the setting sun. Light rain began to spray against the windows. Time bowed to the majesty of creation.

"Can I ask you some hard questions?"

Matt and Sophie were back home after their Ocean Vista mini-holiday. Trish Owens was visiting with a new palliative care nurse named Valmaira. Matt nodded. "What sort of questions?"

Trish had never been known to beat about the bush. "After the other night, you know, the party at your parents' place …" She paused, not from uncertainty about what to say, but for emphasis. "Have you been tempted to think that you might not die? That maybe you might beat the cancer after all?"

Matt shook his head gravely. "No!" he insisted. "Not at all. But, you know, my Dad …" He took a deep breath, whistling out through his teeth, and left the sentence dangling.

"That's often the hardest part," suggested Trish, partly to help educate her offsider. "When you want your family to be positive, their fear of the unknown reflects back on you. But when you want them to be realistic, they cling to false hopes that only make things worse. So many of our patients have loved ones that are totally out of sync emotionally."

Matt nodded. But then: "Yeah, I get that. But I'm so up and down myself that I don't see how anyone could ever be in sync. Yeah, I'm enjoying life at the moment. But I know it won't last. It's good and it's bad. I had a great time at Ocean Vista with Soph but the good times sort of just give me more to lose. Do you know what I mean?"

"Does the thought of dying scare you?"

Matt sighed. "I've come to believe that life goes on after death. And I think that helps." He remembered that Trish had always refused to talk about matters of faith and religion. "Why do you ask?"

Trish reached out and took both Matt's hands in her own. "I'd like to suggest something that I do for some of my guys," she said. "I take them to sit for a while with men and women in hospital who are close to death. You know, people in their very last days. Or hours. Just to watch. Nine times out of ten, death

280

in these situations comes quietly and peacefully. It can even be a beautiful thing. It's nothing to be afraid of really because, sooner or later, we all have to die."

She looked at Matt but he responded with a frown. Valmaira chipped in.

"It's true. I was in and out the other day when this old girl was breathing her last. She had two sons and a daughter with her and she just sort of slipped away. It was sad but it was precious. I felt so honoured to have been there."

"Okay, okay," said Matt. "As long as I'm not getting in anyone's way, I'll do it."

Sunday 6th September

Matt and Sophie had twice managed to attend services at the old church on West St but Sophie had encouraged Matt to check out some other places. An advertisement in the local paper for Shores Christian Centre intrigued Matt. "Come and experience the transforming power of God," it read. So off they went.

Matt was surprised that this group didn't have their own church building; they met in a community centre. An A-frame sign outside the front door confirmed that Matt and Sophie were in the right place, while two additional signs led the way from the front entrance to the actual meeting room. The sound of electric guitars being tuned and microphones being tested would have led them to the right place anyway.

The atmosphere was rushed, a dozen people working hard to get everything ready for the 10.30 start. Someone was bustling around in a kitchen at the back of the meeting room. Someone else brought some trays with tiny little cups to a table at the front, near a glass lectern. A teenage boy was adjusting a data projector and clicking away on a laptop computer. Given that it was already 10.25, Matt wondered when everyone else would arrive.

"Everyone else" drifted in over the next fifteen minutes. Two couples with young children came in after the music started, then two teenage girls and a middle-aged woman snuck in later still. Altogether, there were less than thirty people in attendance. What they lacked in numbers, however, they made up for in enthusiasm. Some of the older members waved their arms and danced their way through the song service while, curiously, the younger people remained in their seats. Sophie felt (and looked) painfully conspicuous, especially when the pastor asked everyone to welcome "our two first-time visitors". People clapped and came over to shake their hands. Big smiles all round.

When the pastor stood up to preach, the teenage boy tried to fire up a screen display from the laptop computer but something wasn't working. When all efforts to rectify the problem had obviously failed, the disappointed pastor gave up. He thanked the boy for trying but resolved to do his sermon without his pre-arranged visuals.

"Please stay for a cuppa," implored an attractive-looking woman (evidently the pastor's wife) when the meeting was over. Matt didn't want to hurt anyone's feelings but he knew Sophie was desperate to get away, so he simply said: "No thanks, we can't." These people were trying so hard. Matt understood that. They wanted the world to know about their Jesus. But he and Sophie would not be going back there.

That afternoon, at 3.15, Matt's hiatus of improved health came to an abrupt end. He collapsed on the floor of the sunroom with blood oozing from his mouth. Clutching his abdomen as he lay on the floor, he quickly passed out. A terrified Sophie grabbed her phone and called for an ambulance. She placed a pillow under his head and tried to make him comfortable. When the paramedics arrived, they rapidly assessed the situation as serious. Repeatedly shouting his name, they only managed to get a semi-conscious whine. With due precaution but utmost haste, they prepped him for the ambulance and, sirens blaring, sped to the emergency entrance at the hospital. Sophie stayed with him, holding his hand in the ambulance. She sent a text to Julie: "Rushing Matt to hospital. It's bad and I'm scared : ("

Five minutes later, in an Emergency Ward bed, Matt revived for a few minutes but vomited immediately, a foul, blood-streaked substance. Something inside had ruptured. His fearful groan sent shivers up and down Sophie's spine before he blacked out again.

"What's happening?" screamed Sophie, but the emergency ward doctors were too busy to answer. They called out for a morphine drip and a chart of Matt's medications.

After they had stabilised Matt to some extent, he revived again, complaining of severe pain and unbearable nausea. When they tried to give medication orally, he convulsed violently and brought everything back up. Terry and Julie rushed in to the ward but a nurse ushered Sophie out to meet them. "Just give us a few minutes," she urged, whipping the curtain around Matt's bed space.

"Is he going to be OK?" hissed Julie but, of course, Sophie didn't know. There were other things happening on the ward and people were rushing everywhere.

"Let me get you a coffee," offered a frazzled-looking ward clerk. "There's a spot just around the corner where you can wait, and I promise we'll bring you in as soon as we can."

For more than forty-eight hours, Matt hovered between life and death. Unable to retain any fluids or solids, he deteriorated rapidly. Drifting between a sleep state and unconsciousness, he was unable to speak except for brief periods. Julie visited the hospital chapel and prayed but Sophie stayed with Matt as much as possible. Terry visited and called frequently but otherwise took the role of a link person passing on news to the rest of the family. Trish Owen and her staff checked regularly on Matt and also spent time with Sophie and Julie.

From Sunday afternoon until Wednesday morning, every snippet of news was progressively worse. Whenever he woke, he vomited painfully. Colour drained from his skin. "Don't worry, he'll be alright" became: "We're doing everything we can" and, by Tuesday night, it was: "You have to know, this is really serious, we might not be able to save him."

The first glimmer of hope came when Matt took some fluid on Wednesday morning. After half an hour, nurses began to believe that he could hold it down. Then, later in the day, some evidence that doctors were getting control over the nausea. Matt's new medications seemed to be working. By Wednesday night, he was fully conscious and talking freely, although not yet out of danger. Seeing how utterly exhausted Sophie and Julie were, he urged them to go home and try to get a good night's sleep.

As the relative darkness and quiet descended on the hospital ward for his fourth night, he lay thinking back over his life, and especially the past nine months. Cancer diagnosis, leaving his job, the wedding that almost was, the cruise, the blog contest and subsequent conversion to Christianity, all interspersed with visits to various doctors, multiple tests and frequent times in hospital. One thing now rose as imperative. He had to contact Robert Smith. In the past five weeks, he had tried to live as a Christian and, in his zeal, he had almost forgotten about Robert. Now he decided that there may not be time to waste. He asked if Sophie could bring him his laptop.

The next morning, after bringing Matt his laptop, Sophie swung by the dental clinic. It was 7.55 and she knew it was the best time to catch everyone before the first patients arrived. "I'm so sorry," she said. "I can't keep doing this. I need to be with Matt 24/7 now. If there's a position for me when this is all over, I'll be happy to come back, but otherwise, I'm afraid this is goodbye. Goodbye and thanks for everything."

Although the competition was long settled, the original blog was still open. Not having an e-mail address for Robert, Matt decided to risk a public post.

A special thanks to those who have continued to watch my blog, even though my own entries have dried up in recent weeks. Unfortunately, I've been pretty sick lately. During my competition, someone called Robert Smith posted several helpful comments. If possible, I would love to get in contact with you Robert, whether by e-mail or by phone. If you read this, could you please supply contact details?

He didn't have to wait long. The next evening, an e-mail arrived.

Hello Matt. This is Robert Smith. Sorry to hear that you've been so unwell. I hope you're doing better spiritually and that you're growing in your new faith. I would be only too happy to help you if I can. You can contact me at this e-mail address.

Josh heard about this and cautioned his brother about taking this e-mail at face value. It would not be hard for anyone to claim to be Robert. He suggested a simple test. Delete Robert's first post and the interaction that immediately followed from the blog archives. Then ask this e-mailer to recall what was said. Hopefully this would be something that only the true Robert Smith would know.

Matt e-mailed his reply. *Just so I know it's really you*, he wrote, *can you recall my response to your first post. If you can accurately tell me that and what you said in reply, I'll know it's you.*

Within an hour, the reply appeared in Matt's inbox.

You said: 'So Robert, have you been a Christian all your life? If not, how old were you? And what's your take on life after death?' I answered and said: 'I haven't been a Christian all my life. That happened when I was 12. Long time ago now.'

So Matt, it's definitely me. Now how to meet with you. I should confess that I already know where you live. I did from the very beginning. And I don't live far from you. But, if it's OK with you, can I meet you Sunday afternoon, three o'clock at the Chelsea Corner coffee shop? Your health permitting of course. Kind regards.

Robert.

Matt printed the e-mail exchange and kept it on his beside cabinet. Over the next few days, he showed it to Sophie, his parents, Josh, Leslie and various doctors and nurses. How could Robert know where he lived? Nothing in any of the blog comments had given any indication that Robert lived in

Australia, let alone in or near Mona Shores.

He even showed the e-mail to Dr Tan and Trish Owens. Neither of them could shed any light on the mystery. He would just have to wait for Sunday. The good news was that he had improved enough to be released from hospital on Saturday morning.

Sunday 13th September

Sophie drove Matt to the Chelsea Corner coffee shop and helped him through to a quiet table in their outdoor area. It was a beautiful setting for such a highly anticipated meeting. There were three other tables scattered among dramatic monstera plants, small raised beds of exquisitely shaded pansies and hanging baskets of maidenhair, but no other customers. The sun's rays refracted through a laserlight ceiling, patterning the whole area with wide stripes of light and shade. Matt laid his walking stick on the ground and took one of the laminated menu cards from the perspex stand in the middle of the table. But his mind, sharp and clear today, was not focused on food or coffee. He was mulling over what he would say to Robert. How could he say thanks? What questions would he ask? What clever greeting could he come up with? "Hello my old friend. Pleased to finally meet you." No, that just didn't seem right.

Matt knew and trusted Robert like a brother but the off-putting truth was that the relationship had always been one-sided. So rich, so genuine, but always so one-sided. He knew absolutely nothing about Robert's personal life.

A young waitress came to the table, order pad and pen in hand. "You must be Matt Sherwin and Sophie." Matt nodded. "That's us," grinned Sophie. "Do you know about us? Do you know what's happening here today?"

The girl nodded. "Oh, yes! This is so exciting!" She beamed eagerly at Matt. "You're going to meet Robert Smith, the guy who wrote so many pieces on your famous blog." She tilted her head in the direction of the other staff, not that they were visible from there. "We're all so excited for you. I hope it goes really well."

Then, when she took their orders and scurried off, Matt and Sophie were left waiting. It was already five minutes past the agreed meeting time. Matt was seated in such a way as to directly face the doorway that Robert would have to come through and Sophie was seated at the side of the little square table.

They waited silently.

And watched.

But then the unexpected. Sophie's sister, Donna, appeared in the doorway and began making her way over to their table. Sophie reacted quickly. "Oh … uh … hi Donna. Um … this is not a good time. We're meeting some … one …" The last word trailed off in a puzzled frown as she glanced at Matt, his eyes growing wide with shock and wonder. Donna, on the other hand, was smiling sheepishly at Matt as she pulled up a seat at the table. "Donna," insisted Sophie. "Did you hear me? We're meeting someone."

But Donna didn't answer. She could see the astonished glint of realisation in Matt's eyes. She knew he was desperately processing the unthinkable. She had to give him a moment to take it all in. When she finally spoke, her voice was gentle and calm. "Are you angry?"

Sophie jumped in. "Why would Matt be angry?" She glared at Matt. "What's going on?" Then suddenly, she understood what she was witnessing. She slapped her hand over her open mouth. "Oh my God!"

"I don't believe it," said Matt with a shake of his head. "I don't know what to say."

Donna smiled graciously and repeated her question. "Are you angry?"

Matt stumbled over his words. "I … I don't know." Then: "NO! No, why should I be angry?"

Sophie leapt to her feet and, hands on hips, glared at her sister. "You're Robert Smith?"

Donna nodded. Her sister's indignation was too much for her and she started giggling. Matt likewise started chuckling. Sophie was furious but the laughing quickly escalated to a contagious level and she couldn't help herself. Matt struggled to his feet and reached across the table to give Donna a big hug.

Tears of relief appeared in Donna's eyes, even as she battled to control herself. "I thought you hated me," she stammered.

"No. No, Donna. I never hated you." Another bewildered shake of the head. "You're Robert Smith?" All three burst out laughing again.

Matt finally resumed his seat, still trying to collect his racing thoughts. "You wrote so many amazing things. All these wild and wacky ideas … from all around the world. And one person really made sense, over and over again. One person got through to me. And it was you! It was you all along. I had no idea."

"But why?" interjected Sophie. She threw her arms in the air. "How? Why? What? Arggh! I just don't get it."

"OK, sit down and I'll explain it all," offered Donna, sporting the broadest smile Sophie had ever seen.

"Yes please!" said Sophie. "This I gotta hear!"

The waitress appeared with three coffees, two large slices of strawberry shortcake and a macadamia muffin. She obviously would have loved to join in the glorious uproar but she had other tables to serve. Donna pulled her seat a little closer to the table and began her explanation.

"I never intended things to work out like they did," she recalled. "It was one anonymous comment on your blog. I didn't expect you to write back asking for a name. I had to come up with something." She shrugged her shoulders. "And I just came up with Robert Smith."

"I thought you were an older man," said Matt. "Maybe fifty or sixty."

Donna grinned. "Yeah, I guess I was happy for you to think that. I led you on a bit, I suppose. Sorry about that."

"I was way off," said Matt, as if to himself. "My imagination ..."

"But Donna," interrupted Sophie. "I thought Robert

Smith was some university professor or something. I never knew you were that ..." She struggled to find the right word but opted for the easy one. "... that smart!" Laughter erupted again.

"You have no idea," continued Donna when the laughing settled down again. "I've spent so many hours researching my answers. And then endless rewriting before I was ready to post. This has been a really big thing for me. And I was so worried that it was all going to blow up in my face somehow."

"All those questions," mused Matt, thinking aloud. "All those questions that I thought no-one in my circle of friends could answer. Ha! There was one person. All along! If only I'd known!"

"It wouldn't have helped," said Donna. "I would only have mucked up the answers you needed. I might be OK at writing but I'm pretty hopeless when it comes to face to face stuff."

"I'm not so sure about that," said Sophie, gaping at her sister with unfettered admiration.

Matt was thinking ahead. "You must have been so excited when I finally decided to become a Christian. I mean, after all the back and forth discussions and all."

Donna's grin instantly disappeared. She looked Matt in the eye, cautiously but with a steady determination that reminded Matt of Sophie in her most serious moments. "Matt, I'm still not convinced that you are a Christian. Not yet."

Matt was shocked. "What do you mean? I made my decision. I wasn't kidding. I really meant it."

Donna nodded but her eyes were fixed on her coffee until she felt she knew what to say. "I know you meant it," she agreed. "You made an intellectual decision to be a Christian. You compared all the different religions and theories and you decided that Christianity had the best answers." She looked deep into Matt's eyes, imploring him to understand. "You know all the arguments and you pretty much know all the answers I could ever come up with. But do you know Jesus? Have you experienced the peace that he gives?"

289

Matt wasn't sure how to answer this new line of questioning. "I certainly felt a kind of peace when I finally made my decision. Is that what you're talking about?"

Donna knew she would have to be gentle with her answer. "Matt, please hear me. There's a world of difference between believing some stuff about God and actually having him in your life." She bit her lip softly and momentarily averted her eyes from Matt's intense stare. Then she continued. "Christianity is not just knowing stuff, it's knowing Jesus. It's a real relationship with a real person. Jesus. God. The Holy Spirit."

Sophie was puzzled but she could tell that Matt needed to hear more. "Keep going Sis."

Donna sighed heavily. "I'm not sure you've really given your heart to God." She looked at Sophie. "Matt, it's like this. You love my sister. I know you do. You could never be content with just knowing about her. You could never be satisfied with anything less than a full on relationship with her. Well, when you really give your heart, and not just your mind, to Jesus, he actually comes into your heart. That's when you're born again. That's when you really get to know him."

"But my decision was real."

"I know, and that was fantastic. And you're right. I was excited. I danced around my living room for best part of an hour. I was so thrilled for you. But believing the right things is just the first step."

"Well, what else do I have to do?" Matt was intrigued.

"Well that's what I'm trying to explain." Donna fumbled with her thoughts. "Jesus died to pay for everyone's sins. We've covered this in the blog. But you're not really a Christian until it becomes personal. For you. It's not the same for everyone. I was twelve when I asked Jesus into my heart. So that was a bit different. There was nothing intellectual about it for me back then. I just knew that, deep inside, I was a sinner that needed forgiveness."

Matt nodded wordlessly. That was his problem too.

"I went to a youth rally and they gave an invitation for

people who wanted to ask Jesus into their lives. Sophie was there that night. She can tell you. Well, I went out the front and this lovely old woman prayed for me. Just like that, I knew I was forgiven. I cried and cried and cried. The old lady stayed with me for ages, with her arm around my shoulder, feeding me tissues." She laughed at the memory. "I was a hopeless case."

"Go on," said Matt quietly.

"Well my life changed that night. I was just a kid but Jesus met me and it was real. So, so real! And since then … I've had a relationship with him. He came into my life."

Sophie had never understood her sister's faith. It was all a big joke to her. But she was listening now. She reached out for Matt's hand. "I wonder if this explains what you were talking about last night."

Donna didn't need to ask. Matt saw the curiosity in her eyes. "I suppose I was complaining that I didn't feel any different since I made my decision. I was expecting some dramatic change, like you said. But it just hasn't happened. It's been six weeks now, I think, and I'm still messed up in the head. I'm still not sure. And … well, I nearly died this week but I didn't feel any closer to God. I guess I was wondering if I'd made a big mistake. Maybe Christianity couldn't do what I hoped it would do for me."

Donna listened very patiently. "Yeah Matt, that's exactly what I mean. You've made an intellectual decision but you don't know him yet."

Matt thought about this for what seemed an eternity. "So Donna …" He spoke very purposefully. "Or should I say Robert? Can you help me with that?"

Donna nodded joyfully. "I would love to Matt. I would love to."

Monday 14th September

Sophie worked for hours, with Matt's blessing, on a large banner that she hung across the back wall of Terry and Julie's dining room. She had already arranged, with Matt, to pick

Donna up on the way to the Monday night dinner. They entered the room a few steps ahead of Donna because, like everyone else in the family, they wanted more than anything to see the look on Donna's face.

In a heartbeat, Sophie's younger sister went from utter shock to tears of elation, then hugs from each and every member of the Sherwin family.

The banner read: "Welcome – Donna Gardner/ Robert Smith".

The extended family table was laden with roast meats, vegetables and assortments of herb breads. Plenty of options for Matt as well. Everyone was seated, ready for the feast, but Leslie stood with an announcement.

"Just before we eat," she said, glaring at two of her children who were starting to pick at the food. "I have a small presentation to make." She cleared her throat and continued. "We have all shared an incredible journey with Matt over the past six or seven months. Around this very table, we've had some of the most extraordinary discussions that I can ever remember. Theology, philosophy, medical science, you name it. But time and time again, we've talked about the latest blog comment by a certain Robert Smith. We all got into the habit of checking the blog before we came here. If there was anything new from Robert, none of us wanted to be the only one who hadn't read it. Now I pride myself on being something of a clear thinker. I don't like half-baked or emotive arguments that lack any real substance. But I remember, on maybe five or six Monday nights, admitting that … well, yes … Robert makes a good point."

Donna squirmed in her seat, embarrassment preventing her from making eye contact other than with Leslie, who continued her little speech.

"Tonight, we want to honour you, Donna, with a permanent invitation to our Monday night family dinners. You have rocked all our worlds in the most amazing way. We have underestimated you but I think that's a mistake none of us will ever make again."

She reached across and handed Donna a neatly wrapped parcel. "Just some imported chocolates," she said, "but they come with a message from us to you. The message is, first of all, thanks for everything you've done for Matt and also for Sophie. And second of all, please consider yourself from now on part of our little family group. Please come each week, if you possibly can, to our family dinners. And please give us the chance to get to know you. You're an awesome person, Donna. We love you dearly."

The applause and cheering that followed brought fresh tears to Donna's eyes. Questions about how she had managed to maintain the deception, and how that sat with her Christian values, would come up in ensuing weeks. For now, the mood was celebratory.

23 - PREACHER DUDE

Thursday 17th September

Winter was over. Temperatures were rising. Flowers were springing up in Matt and Sophie's back garden. The wattle tree hanging over the fence from next door shone resplendent with brilliant yellow blossom. Matt looked out from his sun-room and wondered if the cancer was somehow retreating in light of his new-found faith. He smiled as he realised that, in his mind, he had called it *the* cancer, not *my* cancer. And why not? It was an unwanted guest that didn't deserve to be owned.

Sophie was meeting her parents for coffee at a point halfway between their respective homes. She would not be home for at least another two hours but Matt's appetite was keen. A hamburger would hit the spot nicely, his diet not being so strictly adhered to these days. He paced back and forth between the kitchen and the sunroom, enjoying the morning sun but gradually talking himself into a risky decision. Why not drive to the local take-away? Sure, it had already been more than two months since he drove anywhere. But, then again, he really felt like he could do it. Sure, his legs were weak and that frustratingly ever-present body ache was still there. But he could shut that out. His mind was sharp enough. He grabbed his old car keys and hobbled out to the garage. Lifting the door was a challenge but he accomplished it on the third attempt.

He stared for a moment at his old Corolla, sitting neglected and dusty in the darkness. For some reason, it seemed more like a stranger than an old friend.

Two voices, in particular, pushed into his imagination. His mother was saying: "Oh Matt, don't you think you should wait until Sophie gets home?" Sophie, for her part, was yelling, almost screeching, at him. "No, Matt! Don't even think about it!" But what did they know? Who were they to tell him what he could and couldn't do?

He opened the driver's door and took his old seat. It took him several minutes to adjust the seat, mirrors and steering wheel. That was a surprise. As far as he knew, he was the last person to drive the car so it should have been perfectly adjusted for him. Somehow, it didn't register that his body might have changed since he last drove. Reaching back for the seat-belt was another challenge. He wondered for a moment if he really needed it. If he got caught driving without it, the worst that could happen would be losing his licence, something he was needing less and less. But then again, if it was the right thing to do … well, it was the right thing to do. He swivelled his body to the best of his ability and, this time, he was able to grab the belt from over his right shoulder with his left hand and bring it down to the clip by his left hip.

He turned the key in the ignition and prayed a quick prayer. "Thank you Lord for giving me this chance to do something normal one more time."

But driving proved to be much harder than Matt expected. He managed to reverse out of his driveway easily enough. Swinging back into the street, he took a moment to catch his breath. Then he continued on, turning the car into the busy street that would take him to his destination. Suddenly, the pace of the traffic exploded around him, faster than he ever remembered. Much, much faster. A food van that he hadn't noticed thundered past him in the right hand lane, causing him to swerve from his line momentarily. He battled his nerves. "Hold it together, man," he muttered to himself.

The hamburger, which he purchased at the drive-through and ate in the car park without leaving the car, tasted magnificent. He even polished off some fries and a large Coke. This was a treat, a taste of freedom to be relished. He listened to some music on the radio and sat in the car park for a further fifteen minutes, mourning his loss of independence but fantasising that it might not be over after all. But then it was time to head for home. Back into the manic traffic frenzy.

It was just a cat, running out to his right from behind a parked car. Matt was never going to hit it but he over-reacted and swung the wheel just enough to clip a late model Kia that was parallel parked by the left kerb. Horrified, he over-reacted again, this time bringing his Corolla directly into the path of a white Honda Accord. The other driver swerved at the last second but Matt slammed into the rear drivers' side, the impact spinning both cars in opposite directions. Dazed, and facing the wrong way down a busy road, Matt stared disbelievingly from behind an activated air-bag at the carnage he had caused. After what seemed an eternity, the young man who had been driving the Honda came storming over to Matt's car. "What the hell, man? What do you damn-well think you're doing?" Matt couldn't answer. He continued to stare blankly ahead. The young man finally realised that anger was not going to achieve anything. He changed his tone. "Are you OK man? Are you OK?"

Matt didn't know. He was too much in shock. "I'll get an ambulance," declared the young man. Then he was gone. People started coming out of their homes to see what had happened. Other drivers were out of their cars, talking anxiously in the middle of the street. A woman was pressing for some kind of response. "Sir, can you hear me? Nod if you can hear me. Sir?" Matt nodded. Then there were lots more voices, urgently calling out somewhere in the distance. Matt closed his eyes and passed out.

Matt awoke only spasmodically during the next several hours, briefly and vaguely. When he finally emerged from the stupor, late in the evening, he slowly became conscious that Sophie was sitting beside his bed, watching him. Was she trying to pray? He opened his eyes a little wider.

"Hi Soph." The words floated in his head.

Sophie smiled, tired but compassionate. "Hi Matt." She reached for his hand and the touch revived something inside him, breaking his sensory isolation. He remembered the guy he'd smashed into. The anger. The pointless anger because, after all, Matt couldn't help what was happening. He looked again at Sophie. Was she angry too? No, all he could read was patience. Finally, in a soft, weary voice, she spoke out what she was thinking.

"I'm not giving up on you Matt." A long pause. Then more resolutely. "I'm not giving up on you. You're a good man. I won't break. I can only take so much. But I won't give up on you. I won't. I won't. I won't."

Friday 18th September

Pastor O'Farrell called again the next day. Wedding plans to discuss. Matt managed to raise the back of his bed to a more comfortable level for talking but he was far from comfortable, either with his own physical wretchedness or with the spiritual ambiguity that was proving so hard to bring into focus. Nevertheless, he told the pastor about Donna and the whole Robert Smith thing. He asked his opinion about Donna's comment that he was not yet a Christian.

O'Farrell said that it was not his place to judge such matters, that each person must find their own connection with God. He seemed to be struggling for his words. Unusually so. Matt asked about his former boss, Greg, and Greg's wife Angie, who had first arranged for the pastor to visit Matt. It was a conversation point but O'Farrell didn't really know Greg. Angie was doing OK.

"Why is it so easy for some people to find God and so hard for others?" Matt was looking out the window.

O'Farrell shrugged his shoulders. "Maybe some people make it too complicated."

Matt thought about that. Was he one of those people? "So what should I do?"

"Just keep praying. Keep believing."

"But … but what if I never get through to God? I'm dying! I may not have much time."

The pastor weighed his words carefully. "Are you trusting God or your own ability to trust him?" Seeing Matt's puzzled, almost impatient expression, he continued. "Well, knowing God is not necessarily about you doing stuff. Even stuff that you do in your head. It's more like a surrender. Raising the white flag. Like, God I can't prove that you're there. So I'll just stop all the striving and doubting. I'll give in. Surrender. OK, God, have it your way."

"Surrender?"

"Well yeah. Surrender. Give everything over to God. Surrender."

Matt closed his eyes and clasped his hands together in an expression of thoughtfulness. "I still don't get it. I'm wondering if I ever will."

O'Farrell drew a deep breath and sighed thoughtfully. "Keep praying. Keep believing."

That evening, when Donna visited his hospital bed, Matt raised the same question with her. Surely Robert Smith would have answers. Sophie watched in semi-detached fascination as her husband-to-be and sister wrestled with questions of faith and doubt.

"Have you been praying?"

Matt nodded. "Yes but … but I feel like I'm talking into the air. I don't know if anyone has been listening."

Donna grinned. "God's been listening. He always does."

"Well maybe, but it doesn't feel like I'm getting through."

"Have you been playing those Bible CDs I brought you?"

"A little bit. And I've read a few pages of my Bible. But …"

Donna waited for Matt to gather his thoughts.

"But it's still like a foreign language to me. The way you talk, Donna. It's like you hear God when you read it …"

"I do," she nodded with a generous smile.

"But I don't!" There was no accusation in his tone. Donna couldn't be expected to understand. It was easy for her.

"Dear, dear Matt," she said, brushing her hair back from her face. "I know what I should say. I should tell you that God heard you the first time you prayed, that now you're one of God's people." She drilled him with those compelling blue eyes. "But I'm sensing that God doesn't want me to push you at all. I can't do it for you. There's a place of full and complete trust … but you have to get there yourself."

She wasn't finished. "When you're feeling well enough, can you and Sophie come to my church one Sunday? I've answered all your intellectual questions but this is not the sort of thing I can help you with. But maybe my pastor will speak with you. Maybe God will touch you through the worship and the good people that go there."

Matt looked at Sophie, who willingly agreed. Matt sighed again. "OK Donna. I expect they'll want to keep me in this weekend. But we'll try to get there next Sunday. After the wedding."

Monday 21st September

"Hi Matt," said Uncle Gavin, poking his head around the hospital room door. "How's my favourite nephew faring today?"

Matt checked the clock on the wall. It was almost four in the afternoon. "I guess I'm not going home today. Possibly tomorrow."

"I thought Sophie might have been here at this time of day."

"Nah, she left a few minutes ago," said Matt. "Things to do. And you just missed Mum as well."

Gavin nodded and pulled a chair next to Matt's bed. "I hear the wedding is back on."

"Yeah, we're having a very small celebration at Mum and Dad's place on Saturday. Pastor O'Farrell is doing the service and, if it comes to that, he'll even do it in my hospital room."

"Are you happy to be finally getting married?"

"It's now or never, Uncle Gav. I've had my wake-up call."

"Sophie is a real trooper, isn't she? Tough. Patient. Resilient."

Matt nodded. "She's all that and more." Then he added: "I'm doing this more for her than for me. I think it's the right thing to do."

Gavin shrugged his shoulders. "Well, if that's how you look at it. You always were a bit old-fashioned."

Matt frowned suspiciously. "Old fashioned? You think I'm old-fashioned."

"Well, you know. Getting married is an old-fashioned idea, don't you think? Back then, people tended to think it was more important than it really turned out to be."

Matt asked his uncle to move the hospital tray closer, so he could pour himself a glass of water. This allowed a few moment's reflection. He took a sip of his drink.

"I'm not so sure that marriage is old-fashioned, Uncle Gav."

"Well, OK, but you know what I mean," added Gavin, a little more defensively. "Marriage goes hand in hand with all that outdated Christian stuff. And you know what I think about that. These Christians should all just pull their heads in and stop trying to tell us how to live our lives."

Matt sighed. "What do you think of Donna, Sophie's sister?"

"Oh, Matt. Don't get me started."

"You don't think she's the real deal?"

"Do you really want me to answer that? They're all the same, I tell you. Yeah, Donna's a nice girl. But she's even more old-fashioned with her views on things than you are."

"Sophie and I are hoping to visit Donna's church on Sunday. If we can get there, it'll be our first outing as husband and wife."

Gavin groaned at the thought. He was about to express his concerns when Julie stormed around the corner.

"Gavin!" she snarled, ignoring normal courtesies. "You've been spreading your poison for long enough. Get out! Leave my son alone."

Gavin feigned innocence. "Whatever do you mean?"

"I've been listening outside the door for the last few minutes," she shot back at him. "And it all makes sense to me now. You were the one who put doubts in Matt's head back when they were originally getting married. And you're at it again now. Old-fashioned? You're trying to say that marriage and Christianity are old-fashioned? Really? Is that the best you can come up with?"

"Julie! Settle down, please."

"No, I won't settle down." She grabbed a magazine from Matt's hospital tray and starting bashing her brother over the head. A nurse appeared at the doorway, ready to restrain Julie if necessary. But Matt motioned with his hand that no intervention was necessary. Not yet at least. Julie turned to face Matt.

"I don't know if you've ever talked with your Grandma Davis about why she doesn't believe in God?" Matt nodded meekly, eyes wide, mouth open in shock. Where exactly was this going? Julie proceeded to explain.

"This uncle of yours ..." she pointed an accusing finger, "was never the same after all the hoo-ha about your grandfather and the church. We tried to help him move on but oh no! He refused to let go. He took all your Grandma's hurt and latched on like it was his own. He became a hateful, spiteful man and his poison was all aimed at the church. Not just our own little church from back then, mind you. Oh no! He's been fighting the whole Christian Church ever since."

"Come on, Julie, you can't seriously think …"

"Oh yes I can! But you're smart, Gavin. You're very smart. You never take the full-on frontal approach. It's always fifth column, white-anting, sowing doubts wherever you can. I thought you might have changed but now I see that you haven't."

"Julie …" he pleaded.

"No Gavin! I'm sick to death of your bitter, spiteful ways. Get out! Get out now!"

She resumed her magazine assault, all the while driving her brother toward the door.

Overwhelmed by the force of her anger, and shielding his face with his arms, he finally retreated. When he was gone, Julie came over to Matt, hugged him passionately and broke down sobbing.

"I'm sorry," she blubbered. "I'm so sorry."

Matt was too busy replaying conversations in his mind to speak. All this time, his trusted uncle had been undermining his future, sabotaging his last best chance at happiness. How was it possible? And yet, now it all made sense.

"I'm sorry," moaned Julie yet again.

"Don't be sorry, Mum," said Matt. "You were fantastic. I've never been so proud of you. Thank you. Thank you."

Saturday 26th September

Sophie wore a pearl white wedding dress with a thin golden sash around the waist. No veil to hide her face (Sophie declaring that a pointless old tradition) but a golden tiara on her stylishly arranged hair conveyed exactly what she wanted, graceful modesty. She carried a small bouquet of crimson roses. Matt was seated on a bar stool in front of the old fireplace in his parents' lounge room, Josh standing by his side. Sophie's Dad escorted her, arm in arm, from the kitchen to the lounge, where Donna was waiting to take her place. Matt was amazed how beautiful his bride looked and he thoroughly enjoyed her "I'm-glad-you-like-what-you-see" smile. The look they exchanged when she reached the appointed spot by his side was one of pure joy. Nothing to fret about now. This was a moment to treasure, a moment of intense clarity.

The service itself was remarkably brief, no more than ten minutes from beginning to end. Pastor O'Farrell gave a thoughtful three-point message about how life unfolds, faith comes and love grows. "Nothing is ever perfect or fully grown at the beginning," he said. Then he led them in their exchange of vows, traditional ones because the promise to love each other and make their home together, in sickness and in health, for better or worse, described their intentions most admirably. With only ten family members present, not counting the actual bridal party, it was far smaller than what had been planned back in June. But it was perfect. Cancer was not mentioned once. It was solemn and thrillingly comforting, all at the same time. It felt right.

Finally, the words "I now pronounce you husband and wife!" and "You may now kiss."

Matt and Sophie kissed, the tenderness of love, expressed in the softness of cool lips and cheeks, rendering them oblivious to the cheers from the little family congregation. Matt was surprised at the power of his own emotions. He wanted this moment to last forever.

Sunday 27th September

Donna's church was, indeed, different from anything Matt had experienced before. Sophie unloaded Matt's wheelchair from the back of her car and helped him to get comfortable. She had allowed plenty of time and they entered the Faith Life Fellowship some five minutes before the ten o'clock starting time. Several people of diverse ages and both genders met them in the foyer. Some of them knew who they were, Donna having mentioned they might be coming. Everyone seemed excited to see them. The welcome was infectious.

Matt scarcely had time to look around before Donna appeared and welcomed them both with an affectionate hug. She ushered them gently into a wide auditorium that sloped gently down to a busily furnished stage area. Matt could see drums, guitars, keyboards, music stands, speakers and even a grand piano. Behind the stage a deep blue curtain contrasted vividly with the brightly coloured t-shirts of the musicians who were praying in a tight circle under rich spot lighting.

The seats were nothing more than padded benches, easy to move and easy to set up. Each one could hold five or six people but Donna took them to a place near the front where she had allowed room for the wheelchair. Matt quickly saw that he wasn't the only one in a wheelchair today. He also noticed an old lady who had apparently been given her own special armchair. People were buzzing around, organising things and talking noisily. Matt and Sophie looked hopefully at each other. Whatever else might happen today, there was no doubting the atmosphere of expectation in this place.

When the singing commenced. Matt made the effort to stand with everyone else. Sophie stood with him, holding him steady as best she could. The music was loud but not unpleasantly so. The young woman who introduced the songs encouraged the congregation (Matt guessed there were around two hundred people) to focus in on God. And they did. Some were still attending to small children and some were still finding their seats but, by the third song, most were in a curious state of worship, hands raised, eyes closed, swaying in the presence of a God Matt wished he could see. Or at least feel.

It was easy to get caught up in this. Matt saw that Sophie was weeping but she smiled assurance. "Don't worry about me," she whispered in his ear. "Just find what you have to find."

Thus released, Matt allowed himself to join in the worship. He was out of his depth but it didn't seem to matter. After one of the songs, the song-leader simply said: "Let's just enjoy God for a while." Matt noticed that some people were seated now but, seated or standing, everyone was rapt in a divine presence that Matt was likewise feeling for the very first time. Gentle, melodic singing continued long after the actual song was finished. It wasn't necessary to do anything; being there was enough.

A sweet softness had descended over Matt by the time a slightly older man took a microphone and invited everyone to resume their seats. He welcomed everyone, including Matt and Sophie and some other visitors, and explained some changes to the day's program. Then he asked the congregation to watch a video presentation of coming events at the church. The lights dimmed and two bubbly young people on the large screens either side of the stage took turns at promoting the latest church happenings. Their enthusiasm chipped away at Matt's doubt so that, when the preaching began, he was ready to open his heart to God in a whole new way.

"George is not our regular preacher," explained Donna to both Matt and Sophie as the congregation settled in to hear what God might have for them this week. "We have two assistant pastors here, plus a children's pastor and a youth pastor. George is one of the assistant pastors. He only preaches once every two or three months."

George preached about the death of Jesus, drawing on some research about the unique agony of crucifixion. It made Matt squirm. Somehow, despite movies like "The Passion", he had always pictured Jesus as an other-worldly, spirit-type man, impervious to pain and human suffering. George comprehensively smashed that image. Smashed it forever.

The second half of the message was George's answer to the question "why?" Why did Jesus have to suffer so much? Why would a loving God allow His Son to experience such agony? Matt thought he knew the answer but George was easy to listen to and Matt was intrigued.

At the end of the sermon, George called for a response. "If you've never accepted Jesus as your Saviour, you can meet him today. Step out from your seat and come down here in front of the stage. We have people waiting to pray with you.

Please don't hold back. God loves you and he will wash away all your sin and guilt. He will forgive you and make you new from the inside out. Come now. Don't hold back."

Matt could tell that both Sophie and Donna were expecting him to respond. Sophie motioned her willingness to wheel him forward but he declined the offer with a definite shake of the head. He had already done this. He had asked Jesus into his life. He didn't need to do it again.

After the meeting, while people everywhere were praying for each other, or simply chatting, Donna approached a mostly bald man with a thin grey moustache and beard. Matt thought he was probably in his early sixties. As Donna spoke with him, he looked across at Matt and nodded. He had some other people to attend to but, back out in the church foyer, he caught up with Matt and the two sisters.

The man introduced himself as Pastor Bill Considine. "I'd love to catch up for a few minutes. Could I offer you a nice brewed coffee in my office?" Matt glanced at Sophie and Donna but the pastor had that covered. "The girls can get something from our main cafeteria," he suggested. "But only if it's ok with you. Do you mind? Can you give me just a couple of minutes?"

Matt, still in his wheelchair, shrugged his shoulders. The pastor was friendly in a non-threatening sort of way. What harm could it do? Donna led the way down a short corridor to the pastor's office and then left with Sophie.

"Donna told me about you," ventured Pastor Bill. "She was so excited when you decided to become a believer. But I didn't realise until yesterday that she was actually Robert Smith."

Matt smiled at the irony of the pastor's comment. Donna was the quintessential young female. There was nothing masculine about her at all. And yet she had successfully presented herself online as a man. For several months. "Yeah, I'm very lucky to have her as a sister-in-law."

"So how's it going? Your walk with God, I mean."

Matt hesitated. Did he really want to confess his doubts

and frustrations to this man? Pastor O'Farrell hadn't helped that much. Nor, for that matter, had Donna. But Bill sensed Matt's reluctance and gently prodded for an answer. "You're not sure?"

"No, I'm not sure," Matt admitted finally.

The pastor watched Matt carefully, scratching his beard and smiling a knowing smile. "Can I pray with you Matt?"

Why not? Matt nodded and the pastor came over to Matt's wheelchair and stood beside him, one hand on Matt's shoulder. He began to pray.

And then Matt's world burst open. The gruesomeness of the cross that he had heard about in the service somehow flooded and obliterated the gruesomeness of his own sin and failure. The time of self-loathing when Sophie had found him lying in the grass. The rage in his spirit. The sin. The uncleanness. The hopelessness. The emptiness. It all came together under the blood of Jesus. A commanding torrent of God's love was washing him. He felt God. More than that. The divine presence was crushing him, so that he felt he could scarcely breathe. He would later describe the sensation as an overwhelming lead blanket of love and grace. Things he had never fully grasped before. But this was real. This was Jesus. This was God.

It was only a few minutes but it seemed like an eternity to Matt. Bill rejoiced with Matt, offered some kindly encouragement and then asked a young man who was walking past if he would see Matt safely to his wife in the cafeteria. When Donna saw Matt, she immediately understood that something special had happened. She jumped up from her table and ran to give him a hug. Sophie quickly followed.

"You're positively glowing!" gushed Donna, happy tears welling in her eyes.

"I know," said Matt, reciprocating the hug from his sister-in-law, who then made way for Sophie to follow suit. "It's real to me now!' he chirped excitedly. "There's no going back now. I've met God for myself! Ohh! This is amazing!"

All three were now weeping freely. "I'm a real Christian

now," spluttered Matt through his tears. "It's real! It's real! It's so, so real!"

Some experiences fall so far outside the normal expectations of life that they are impossible to fully describe. Matt understood now why it was called being "born again". It was so new, so unprecedented. Sophie sat with him that afternoon as he scoured the bible Donna had given him. She listened gladly as he attempted to explain.

"Donna told us that Christianity is a relationship, not a religion, but I still thought it was up to me to make it work. And the way I've messed up in relationships before, that didn't leave me with a lot of hope that I could ever get it right." He searched for a response in Sophie's wondering eyes. She nodded to show she was keeping up.

"But this is a totally different kind of relationship. God is so much greater than us. His love is so incredibly unselfish and … and so complete. When the pastor at Donna's church prayed for me, it was like God suddenly decided to touch me with his little finger. Just one quick little touch. But it was like Heaven burst open over me. Unbelievable love and power. I never knew love could be like that. Any more and I think it would have killed me. But … well, God obviously wasn't trying to kill me. He was giving me a whole new start in life."

Sophie wiped a tear from her eye. "So, this God of yours … do you think He would want me too?"

Later that night, the long-tortured limits on Matt and Sophie's physical intimacy were stripped away. Slow and gentle was all Matt's body would allow but so what? What was wrong with that? In the past, as Matt recalled, it had always been about pleasure, making the most of a physical sensation. Now it was about giving, a pure, uncomplicated kind of giving. Two people entwined as one. Becoming one.

There were other differences as well. Intimacy took on a whole new meaning. Matt's desire was for Sophie, the whole package that was her, not just her body. This was unrestrained commitment, husband and wife, freely given to each other in naked love. For the first time, Matt understood the connection between sex and marriage, and why God had designed it that way.

As they lay together, quietly enjoying the closeness, Matt continued to explore the implications of having God in his life.

"I'm forgiven, Sophie. God has totally forgiven me. Do you understand what that means?"

She tilted her head thoughtfully on his shoulder. "You're a good man, Matt. I don't really know what you needed to be forgiven for."

"No Sophie," he argued. "I haven't been a good man. I've been self-centred, angry, confused …" Sophie snuggled in his arms as he searched for the right words. But she had her opinions too.

"Listen to me," she said. "You've got cancer. It's no wonder you've been battling with your emotions. I understand. I love you and I understand."

Matt kissed her on the forehead because that was easiest to reach. "I know you love me. And I love you too. But I think maybe it's too easy to make excuses for our bad behaviour. This morning, when I felt the full force of God's love, I realised that it's much better to acknowledge the sin and let God deal with it. As long as I'm trying to justify myself, I can never really be free from my feelings of guilt and shame."

"Wow!" she said with a grin. "I'm married to a full-on preacher dude."

24 - WAITING FOR A TRAIN

Monday 5th October

Matt was back in City Central Palliative Care ward but not in one of their beds. He sat quietly in the corner, watching while a woman in her seventies comforted her dying father. She spoke to him in normal conversational tones, telling him all the latest exploits of his great-grandchildren and the recent arrival of two great-great-grandchildren. But, if he heard at all, there was no response. The way the woman held his hand led Matt to think that she was memorizing the feel. The way she stared at his face told him that she was attempting to imprint every wrinkle, every blotch, every dried up piece of skin, permanently into her memory.

Life was indeed a precious thing, but even more so when the love and forgiveness of God came in. Matt wondered if this old man and his daughter knew the Lord. It was not his place to ask but he prayed silently. For an instant, he thought he saw the old man smile.

Matt and Sophie managed to attend the Faith Life Fellowship for two of the following three Sundays. Pastor Bill visited Matt twice, once in hospital and once in their home. George, the assistant pastor who preached that first Sunday, made efforts to take Matt "under his wing". The church offered resources that were appreciated but not needed. Matt found new potency and consolation in his own times of prayer. The reality of that first encounter with God persisted and even sweetened. When he slept, he was blanketed with calm gratitude although physically, he was still deteriorating.

Sophie, and sometimes Donna, would read passages from the New Living Bible. Or the popular paraphrase version, The Message. He didn't have to understand everything. He didn't have to do anything. People were willing to minister to him.

Minister. That was a word Matt had never understood. Churches had ministers but he had always understood that as a mere title. Now he saw that it was a kind of gift. Somebody needed something and someone else provided it, not in a leave-it-on-the-doorstep sort of way. More the let-me-feed-it-to-you way. Let me massage this gift into you. Personally and intimately. Let me see to it that my gift meets your need. Let me minister to you.

Sophie, Mum, Donna. They were the three who could minister. Others could care, and help, and comfort. Three people could go beyond that and minister.

Wednesday 21st October

Each step was painful. Breathing had to be timed perfectly, so that the oxygen entering his lungs would furnish strength enough for each step. But Matt was determined. Reaching his destination, the bright green, self-imposing letterbox that rose sentry-like above the fence at the start of the driveway, he paused to catch what was left of his breath. It felt strange to observe in himself what had become automatic, a brief offering of thanks to God. Not for the difficulty of this latest task but for the strength to accomplish it, perhaps for the very last time.

So many things now were potentially the last this or that. The once vigorous body that could surf the waves, wield a cricket bat and bench press a hundred and twenty kilograms was now irreparably feeble. But it was OK. Awareness of the divine presence transformed every lost hope into a means for enriching the present. Making love was a grateful memory, not a bitter regret. He had tasted love. And significance. Good food and good living. The times of foreboding and terror of darkness were easier to handle now, and far less persistent. Instead, a general feeling of well-being pervaded each new day. Life expectancy was irrelevant thanks to the "peace that passes understanding" as described in his new favourite Bible verse.

He picked a small handful of mail from the letterbox and, looking up, he noticed Sophie watching him from the kitchen window. She caught his eye and smiled. Perhaps she understood.

Tuesday 10th November

It was raining steadily. Skies were grey but backlit by sunshine seeking to break through. Matt sat alone in his bedroom watching the tree outside his window. The leaves at the tip of the branches swayed in the breeze, yet, at the same time, hung drenched and tired under the weight of the rain. Swaying, hanging. Passively soaking up what they didn't create.

Matt turned his mind to prayer, speaking the words out quietly but purposefully.

"God, thanks for hearing me. Thanks for being there. But God … you have to know, I'm running out of fight. I'm … well, I'm barely hanging on. I'm so tired!"

He rested his head back on the pillow. "So tired." But then: "God will you please look after Sophie when I'm gone. She's an awesome person. Thank you so much for giving her to me. Please help her to cope with all the stuff I leave behind. She's so brave and strong … but God, I think she'll have to be even braver and stronger in the not too distant future."

He closed his eyes. "God, you made this world, I know that now. I don't know if you made cancer. It sure doesn't seem like something you would do. What I do know … is that you also made Heaven. Cancer doesn't get the last word, God … you do. And I thank you for that … I can … I can …"

It was enough. He drifted off to sleep, yet again.

Friday 20th November

Matt was in hospital again. Late afternoon. Sophie brought some mail from home and found Julie sitting beside Matt's bed doing a crossword puzzle. "How is he today?"

Julie looked across at Matt, as if she needed to check before she answered. "Same. He woke up for a while about an hour ago."

Sophie sat on the end of Matt's bed. "I slept in pretty much all morning myself. Then I had to get my car serviced. Two hundred and seventy dollars this time."

A male nurse called in to check something on Matt's chart. Smiled politely at the two women but left without a word. Julie finally broke the silence.

"Can I ask you something?"

Sophie answered without bothering to look at her mother-in-law. "Sure, what?"

"Well, I've been thinking lately about Matt's contest. I suppose I always saw it as a contest between different religions but now I'm not so sure what it was."

"What do you mean?"

Julie hesitated. "Well … maybe the real contest was between God and Matt. Looking back now, I wonder if God wasn't somehow working through it all to break down Matt's resistance. You know what I mean?"

Sophie nodded. "Matt says he had to surrender to God. He's used that word a lot. Surrender."

"So," continued Julie, "the contest wasn't so much a media thing as a spiritual battle in Matt."

"A spiritual battle." Sophie pondered the words. "Yeah, I

313

suppose it was. But isn't there supposed to be a loser in a battle? You could say that God won the battle but it's not like Matt lost. He found what he needed. He found peace."

Silence. Then Sophie spoke again. "Maybe the loser was the darkness in Matt that scared me so much. That scared him so much. Maybe that's a battle we all need to lose."

Sunday 29th November

Long hours in bed, waking occasionally, sometimes to an empty room but sometimes to the warm presence of a caring wife, sometimes to the hovering compassion of Terry or Julie, or less frequently, to Josh, Leslie or some other relative. Other friends were no longer coming. This was something only the closest family could endure.

And Donna. She came as often as she could, each time taking one of Matt's limp hands in prayer, each time looking deeply into his eyes. The windows of the soul, so the saying went. The time for 'thank you's was long past. Matt accepted her devotion as natural and understandable. No questions any more. No need for conversation.

Some days he awoke in his own bed, and some days his first conscious thought would be: "Oh, that's right. I'm in hospital again." Nothing came as a surprise any more. Nothing was ever new. Those walls, those faces, those flowers and get well cards on the ledge. The nurses' voices that floated in and out of his dreamings.

Matt could still remember the fits of panic, the horrible, stark moments of reality when cancer gripped his soul as much as his flesh. The terror of death, the loneliness of finality. But no, that too was just a memory. Now there was peace. Not the resignation kind of peace that would say: "Oh well, what will happen will happen." No, this was a far more positive peace. Not the Buddhist "embrace your mortality" type of peace. This was the Christ-given peace of trust and rest. This was not the end but a beginning. He was waiting for a train, a train that would soon chug into the station and take him home. Quiet anticipation. It won't be long now.

Two o'clock in the morning. Matt was aware of Sophie squeezing his hand and vaguely aware of nurses coming and going. There was no pain for once. No throbbing aches or gut-heaving sickness.

"Do you love me?"

The question didn't come from Sophie. She was just there, breathing, loving, praying but silent and still.

"Do you love me?" The softness of compassion in those words was unlike anything Matt had ever experienced. No hidden accusations here; this was an invitation. And he understood.

"Do you love me?"

Somehow Matt knew, this time, that he could take a whole eternity to answer if necessary. The train would wait as long as necessary. But why wait? The conductor's hand was outstretched. Getting on board would be the easiest thing. Everything was paid up. There were no bags of sin and guilt to somehow drag on board. This was no punishment. The conductor had paid for all that long ago. Now there was nothing but a supremely loving invitation.

"Yes," said Matt. "I love you … my Lord and my God."

One step and he was lifted into the doorway of the train, and yet the train still waited. For a moment, Matt wondered at the pause but the conductor gestured with his eyes at something behind him on the platform. Matt turned to see Sophie, smiling through her tears.

By a miracle of grace, Matt's next words echoed all the way back to the hospital bed and the faithful woman watching over him there. It was little more than a whisper but Sophie heard well.

"Goodbye my love. I'll see you again."

MEET THE AUTHOR

Steve McNeilly has worked for many years as a Christian pastor but now owns and operates a bookshop in Moe, Victoria, Australia. He has been married to Sandie for 40 years. In 2008, he published a non-fiction book called "Our Culture in Christ". He wants people to think seriously about what they believe and why.